Violet

BROOKE HARPER

H.A.B. Publications LLC

Cover Design: Angela Haddon Romance Cover Design
Interior & Formatting: Jennifer Laslie
Editing & Proofreading: Deb Anderson

Trigger Warning

This book contains dark themes and highly sensitive topics.

For a full list of triggers, visit Brooke Harper's website:
https://authorbrookeharper.com/Omegas-in-bloom/

Gardener Family

Rose Finley
Ω

Heath Gardener
A

Violet Gardener
Ω

Iris Gardener
Ω

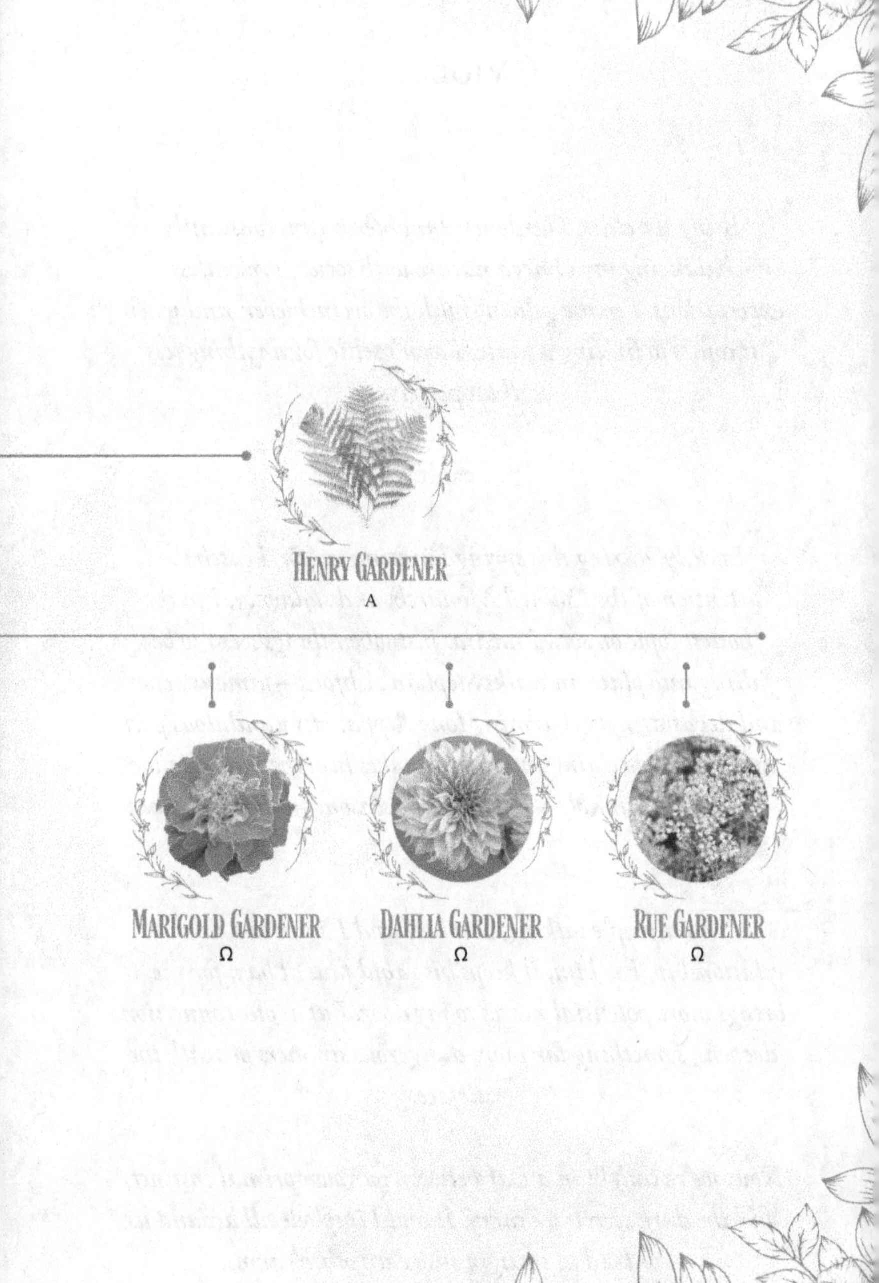

HENRY GARDENER

A

MARIGOLD GARDENER
Ω

DAHLIA GARDENER
Ω

RUE GARDENER
Ω

Violet

Being the eldest Gardener daughter means constantly balancing my Omega nature with society's relentless expectations. I'm the golden child, the overachiever, and when it comes to finding a mate, I won't settle for anything less than perfect.

I can't.

Luckily, during this spring's mating season, I catch the attention of the Council Monarch, and suddenly, I'm the hottest topic on social media. Just when things seem to be falling into place, in walks Stephan Ashford—famous actor and devastatingly charming lone Alpha. His scandalous past and refusal to claim an Omega makes him the most eligible —and unattainable—Alpha of the season, but he's just what I need.

To get people talking, Stephan and I agree to a fake relationship. For him, it keeps his rabid fans at bay; for me, it brings more potential mates to my door. But as our connection deepens, something far more dangerous simmers beneath the surface.

Now, we're caught in a war between our own primal instincts and the dark secrets we carry. It could implode all around us —or lead us straight into each other's arms.

To the readers who were pissed when Regé-Jean Page didn't come back to play Simon after Bridgerton's season one,

this one's for you.

All right, Hivemind, it's that time again.

*The Season is almost upon us, and you know what that means: The tea is steeping, the hive is buzzing, and the Monarch of the Isle is getting ready to don her satin gloves and declare the **Season officially open**.*

*Translation? The mate hunt is **ON** and the Monarch is eager to name her next Luxe Omega.*

Now, let's be real—last Season was a total flop. No Luxe was picked because, in the Monarch's words, no one had that "special sparkle". Ouch. But this year? Oh, honey, the hive is swarming. A fresh batch of Omegas is about to step into the spotlight.

Maybe even one of the Gardener daughters.

And here's the real stinger: Word in the hive is that a certain Alpha is returning. I don't want to name any names yet, but you know who he is. His last movie had everyone (and I mean everyone) swooning. Yes, even the Monarch herself was spotted sneaking into a matinee in Sabine.

Hmm, but is he looking for a mate? Will he be served up on the Season's golden platter? And more importantly, this year, will there be a lucky Omega who'll catch his eye?

So, my little bees, stay tuned to my Stitch channel because this honeyed tea isn't done steeping yet. Trust me, this Season is going to be sweeter—and messier—than ever.

Keep your wings ready, your teacups steady, and your lips a-buzzing because Queen Bee will be flying back with another tale soon.

- Queen Bee

Chapter One

Violet

"Vi! Vi! Did you see Queen Bee's latest Stitch? O.M.G!"

My fourteen-year-old sister Rue runs into the living room, long dark hair streaming behind her, waving her phone.

"Mom's going to have a cow if you run in the house." I look around anxiously, making sure our mother isn't in eyeshot, but I don't see her.

"Mom won't, Vi!" Rue slams her hands on her hips as she lies, bouncing with exuberance in the sunshine streaming through the window. Rue is light to the darkness and noise to the silence, which often drives people batty. Like Mom.

"Let me see." I take the phone and press *play*. The mysterious Queen Bee, identity and voice disguised, talks about diamonds, the Luxe, rich things, and the start of the Season.

My Season.

But I don't care about those things. Not like most Omegas in their Mating Season do. I'm just trying to survive it and hopefully end it with a mark on my neck and a respectable mate.

"The Monarch's throwing the balls this year, so, what?" I say. "It's life as usual."

"She's looking for the Season's star, Vi. And it's your first Mating Season!" Rue looks up at me, eyes wide. "It could be you. Maybe you could do one of your dances!"

She pirouettes.

"Rue, stop." I pack up my book. "You know that I'm not good enough for that. Besides, I quit a long time ago."

I had heard Mom talking about cutting costs, and dancing came up. So I dropped out.

"Do you think, when you mate, he'll have a handsome Alpha brother?" Rue asks, flopping down on the window seat where I'd been sitting. Outside, Mom's garden is in full bloom, a living masterpiece. "I think I'd like that. Then we could be together!"

Rue melts my heart. She's innocence personified and sunshine brought to life. Even though she's oblivious to the real stressors in life.

"Maybe I won't meet anyone. Maybe I won't be courted."

She looks at me in disbelief. "But...you're *Violet*. So pretty. And talented. My sister."

I almost laugh.

I'm not like Dahlia, gifted brilliant musician with an

affinity for math. I'm not like the artistic Marigold. Nor am I quick-witted and fiery like Iris, who's going to be a renowned writer, I just know it.

It should be Heath, the eldest, in this Season, but Dad's death and five Omega girls has him weighed down. He's head of the family, and I'm the eldest girl, so this year's Season falls to me. It's up to me to be perfect and make it successful.

Of course I'd rather hide away. But I have to secure our place in society, and make sure the Gardener Omegas have a smooth path in and are seen as special catches.

"C'mon, we need to get chores done," I say.

"Chores, Vi, are boring." She sighs heavily. "Are you joining Heath in being *boring*? Although his friend he was on the phone with sounded dreamy. He wouldn't turn his phone, so I couldn't see his face."

"It was probably one of Dad's friends—old, fat, and balding. Maybe that one guy who looks like he's about to drool."

She shrieks with laughter.

I worry about Heath. At twenty-five, he's changed from a dashing young man, full of life and bad jokes, to someone suddenly decades older, wearing his mantle heavily.

We both carry burdens.

I'll find a mate, ease those burdens of his, open pathways for my sisters. No matter how my stomach eats at me.

"Where is he, anyway?" I ask.

"Study," Rue says.

Of course. It's almost a rhetorical question at this point.

He's up at all hours in Dad's study, hunched over books and ledgers, instead of being out and meeting Omegas.

Rue leans forward, eyes on the Queen Bee's Stitch post as she rewatches it, then she looks up. "Maybe a prince will come!"

I laugh. "No princes."

"What are you going to wear to the first one, Vi? The Bee says the Monarch might be looking for a jewel or silk or perfume or—"

"Rue." I cut her off. "It's ages away."

She bites her lip and looks out the window, down onto the grounds of our country home. We have a townhouse, too, for when we have evenings in the city. "I know, it's just..." Rue turns back to me. "Being seen as the most precious thing is dreamy, and I know it's going to be you."

"Puh-leeze." Iris stomps up to us. She snatches the phone, presses play, and rolls her eyes as Rue takes back her precious phone.

"You should get the app, Iris. Or a cat."

"I don't want either, brat," she says. "I don't need the Council or a wannabe telling me how to be like everyone else and get excited by archaic chauvinist ways. Just because I'm an Omega doesn't mean I need to sniff a man out so I can feel complete. That's bullshit."

"Iris!" Rue gasps and melodramatically clutches her chest. "My ears!" Then she preens. "We're all beautiful and glorious Omegas. Five perfect Omegas under one roof! We're practically famous, Iris. Famous!" She holds out her left hand and gazes at it. "Destined to mate well." Rue looks at Iris. "And you try to burn my perfect Omega ears!"

"If anyone should be getting mated" —Iris makes air

quotes with her fingers as she leans against the wall— "it's Heath. But he's finally realized no one can stand his attitude and decided to skip it."

"He's running the family and Dad's business," Rue says, crossing her arms.

"And get your boot off the wall, Iris," I scold.

She's stunning, big green eyes and dark hair. She's wearing her makeup armor—thick eyeliner and dark lipstick—and a black T-shirt with some band's name that I don't recognize, and a short black pleated skirt with thick black stockings and big boots.

"What if we all mate with five handsome brothers?" Rue looks at us.

"Oh, God." I face palm.

"You're hopeless." Iris rolls her eyes at Rue.

"She's young," I say with a small smile.

"And blissfully naïve."

I shrug.

"You should get off your phone, Rue," Iris says. "It'll rot your brain, turn you into an automaton."

"And get a mate?" She sighs happily. "I can live with that."

"Can you live with this imaginary mate going to jail?" Iris raises a brow. "You're fourteen."

"Depends," Rue says cheerfully. "Is this a cushy imaginary prison?"

"I need to get some chores done," I mutter to Iris. "Can I trust you not to kill Rue?"

She deadpans. "No."

"Yes!" Rue cries. "No one would kill me." She jumps up onto the window seat and spins. "I'm too cute."

I pull her down. "You'll be dead if you break that window. We're on the second floor."

Rue suddenly sits. "I miss Daddy."

For a moment, none of us speak, and the grief of his unexpected passing grows in the space between us. It's been over a year now since that accident claimed Dad. The one Heath witnessed. The accident took Dad from us and changed our lives.

"Heath's changed," Rue adds. "I liked him before better. He was fun."

"He's still fun," I say, ignoring Iris's fake coughing fit. "He's just busy. It's a lot, running the house."

It's not lost on any of us that our staff's been pared back. But I don't comment on it, just like I don't agree with Rue out loud.

"Well," I say with as much perk in my voice as I can muster, "I'd better start preparing for the Season."

A wave of panic hits me hard. How the hell does one prepare? Which of our handbooks do I read? I try and suck air in but my lungs don't work, and someone is wheezing —*me*.

Heat floods my face and pin pricks dance along my skin.

I need to calm myself. I need—I need to lie down.

"Rue, run along," Iris says as if from a long way away as my chest tightens. I worry my heart's going to explode. "Violet and I are discussing the finer points of the Omega Feminist Movement."

Someone takes my arm and makes me walk as black dots explode in front of my eyes.

I'm shoved in a room, pushed down onto something

soft, and then warm arms come around me and Iris makes me lie down with her as she tells me a story.

It's about a plucky feminist who runs off to rule the world and turn all Alphas into slaves. It's so funny, I forget I can't breathe, forget the steel-like band around my chest and the panic that's slicing through my blood, and the world comes back into focus.

"...and then surrounded by many slave men—and women, our ruler's an equal opportunity lover—she lives happily ever after."

I smile against the soft skin of my younger sister's arm. Now we're in a guest room. I know because I recognize the green velvet of the chair in the corner by the window.

"Mom's going to lose it over us messing up the bed," I say.

"Take a chill pill, Vi. I'll fix it."

She's not wearing her perfume blocker. Iris loves the heavily spiced and sophisticated ones. But right now, she smells like her namesake. A soft, powdery sweet scent redolent with green leaves, a hint of wood, musk, and soft spice.

Her look is all angles and barriers, but her natural scent is soft roundness and an invitation in.

I bite my lip. "Dad must somehow owe money. Or rather *owed*." We have barely any staff, and old wealth is about social standing over bank accounts. I can't be the only one noticing the differences since Dad's death.

"Heath will figure it out—"

"I know." I turn and face her. "He's become obsessed with it. It's why he's skipping this Season and it's falling to me."

"Nothing's *falling* to you, Vi. You have a choice, you know. You don't *have* to find a mate this Season if you don't want to."

She doesn't understand. I *don't* have a choice—not really. Mating well will determine how the rest of my sisters mate. It could help Heath with the finances. It would make life easier for Mom, who's still living in the shadow of Dad's death. It'll make things easier for everyone.

I sigh.

"Heath's an Alpha. He gets the ability to do whatever he wants and mate when he wants. But you don't always have to say yes, either. You can push against the norms. It's your life. We could get jobs, live on our own."

I laugh. "I'm twenty-one. You're nineteen. We can't do that, just abandon Mom and the family."

Not just that but it'll bring shame on our name, and all the doors to society would slam shut. Everyone here's so...shallow.

Her mouth turns up. "You think too much."

She's not wrong, but I shake my head. "You may not want to slide into your role you were born into as Omega, but our sisters do. And it's how things are done on Sabine."

"So you're telling me that you actually *want* to get mated?" Iris asks.

"Iris..."

"You don't have to do this."

"I want to." The words are a lie and the truth. Am I ready to mate? Probably not. Am I happy to do something to help my family? Absolutely.

"Nah." She sits up. "Fuck the system."

I sit up, too. "Iris, please." As she gets to her feet, I grab her hand. "I-I need your help with this. I have no idea what I'm doing, and there's the pre-Season picnic tomorrow."

"Vi..."

"I want to do this the right way. I need to make Mom proud and make things easier for Heath. If I can figure this out, it'll be a walk in the park when it's your turns."

"I'm not prancing around for Alphas to pant at me. There's no way I'm doing that shit."

"Iris. Help me, please?"

She sighs. "If I have to."

I take that as a yes.

Because I'm going to need all the help I can get.

CHAPTER TWO

Stephan

The city of Emporia, mecca of movie magic, spreads out before me from my home in the hills.

My agent talks as I sip my bourbon, and I cut her off. "I don't want that role. I want some meat, something good. Fuck, I'll even do theater."

Clea bounces her foot as she sits cross-legged on the cream leather sofa opposite mine. Clea sighs into her seltzer. If we weren't such good friends, I'd fire her ass. But the woman is not only loyal, she's a shark.

"You know, Stephan, most actors look at theater as something to be revered."

"I'll take your word for it."

She pins me with a look. "I'm not here to talk about the role or what you want next. I'm here about your favorite co-star."

"Felicity?"

"She wants the next set of fluffy roles—"

"Felicity Fine can go—"

"She wants to. And she wants to use these films. She's ambitious, too." Clea taps a finger against her glass.

"I'm aware."

"You slept with her way back, and you both have huge fanbases. But you're getting a reputation. You drink too much. You've been arrested for driving under the influence—"

"One drink—"

"And one line too many?" She starts ticking things off on her hand. "There's the Omega you had the affair with who was meant to mate with that politician—"

"She hated him. They weren't a match." We weren't a match either, but it was dangerous fun.

"She was an Omega—"

"No one," I tell her firmly, "cares about that stupid hierarchy here like they do in high society." Like they do on fucking Sabine. "True mates happen, but it's not all by the damn book. The Council—"

"Image matters."

"Is that all?" I ask, going for bored.

"Felicity wants certain things."

My stomach plummets. "Like what?"

"You to do the final movies in the series." Clea flashes a smile. "You're Asher St. James and Felicity Fine. Money in the bank. But she really wants a career push, a change of roles."

I pour more bourbon in my glass. "So tell her to back out and take on other roles. Like I want to do."

"I'm not her agent. Felicity wants your agreement to do those films and then wants you to step back to give her limelight time," Clea says, standing.

I snatch up my drink and stand as well. "But you know her needs. She asked you for, what? Hiatus from me? I'll do *that*, but not the films. Take that back to her."

"You want meatier roles, right? She has dirt and wants things her way, so this is what we do." Clea smooths her black dress. "Postpone the movies till next summer. Announce you need some personal time, thinking time, attrition time this summer for all those bad behaviors. That's just built-in press for you. You're from Sabine, right?"

"Yeah, so?" My aunt wants me to visit and, knowing her, she has likely told the entire island I'm coming back. Which I have no plans to do.

"Go for the summer, say you're taking a break and laying low because of some things you aren't proud of."

Anger flares. "Why the fuck would I do that?"

"Because like I said, Felicity wants more limelight and she has dirt on you, Stephan. She wants you to do those films, then you step back and let her broken heart—"

"One fucking date, Clea. Nothing's broken but a nail."

She goes on as if I never spoke. "If you don't give Felicity that chance, then she'll announce you not only broke her heart, but that you did it after getting her pregnant."

"That I *what*?" I nearly choke on the word and keep away from memories that start to crowd.

"It doesn't matter. I'll get things sorted." Clea takes a breath. "I can get you out of the films later, but you have to take the summer, get the fuck out of Emporia so she owns it. No statements from you, nothing. You have some contrition time away on the lovely Sabine, she can wallow in her pain. I'll make sure your career grows as well. She'll just have first crack at all the gossip pages. I can hire a PR coach for her. Give her all the gossip pages, her way."

"Absolutely not. I won't be blackmailed." I grind my teeth, then I look up.

"Really? Because the thing is, Felicity must know someone from Sabine. Because she *knows*."

A darkness spreads through me, and I don't move. "Knows what, Clea?"

"What do you think, Stephan?"

I nod slowly. "Be very specific in what it is she knows."

I listen to what she tells me, all in hushed tones and heartbreak. She knows my past—the part of me I've been trying to forget.

Fuck. My skin starts to crawl. It's not Clea repeating it that bothers me; Clea knows. Some of it. But Felicity—fuck knows how she got her grubby fingers on any of this—is a different matter. But I shut the memories of that part of my past down.

"How do you know she hasn't said a word?"

"It would be everywhere."

Okay, okay, how bad could this be? "It'll blow over."

"This is up there, Stephan, and stuff like that doesn't blow over. Your past will be dug all the way up. Full exhumation." She goes to the bar and adds gin to her seltzer. "They'll talk to the family, to enemies, so-called friends."

"This is Emporia."

"They like scandal just as much as they do on Sabine. You know that."

I shrug.

"Pretending this is nothing might work on someone who doesn't know you, but..." She comes right up to me. "I know you."

"It's a sad fucking story, at the heart." I grip my glass. "And it's ancient history. I'll survive and get roles."

A film of filth sticks to me at that.

"Stephan, I'll be real. Others out there don't know who you are, not really. Just a really pretty face from Sabine who can act. The Monarch won't be happy."

No, she'll be pissed.

In fact, this very much is something that could kill my career dead in the water and no second coming to be seen, courtesy of one old woman.

"You know how powerful she is. Sabine may be enough to distract her during the Season, at least, but since you've been on her shit-list before, you'll be smack dab in the line of fire if you cause a stir again. *She's* the one who'll bring you down."

I take a swallow. "Only if this gets out," I clarify, but it doesn't make me feel any better. "Can we trust Felicity?"

"I've got ironclad NDAs ready," Clea says. "I've got lawyers and some sharp-clawed Alphas ready to have words with our starlet. She hasn't breathed a word of her so-called relationship or break-up yet. She wants what you do, meatier roles, and sympathy for her going through an emotional wringer will make women empathize and men want to pick up the pieces."

Her words sink in.

"She'll use you to get there." Clea's serious gaze cuts into me. "So we should control how. She'll only talk if you don't play ball and let her say all the carefully crafted things I'll coach her on. Got it?"

Oh, yeah. Got it. "Shit. So if I don't go?"

"Say goodbye to any chance of expanding your reach as an actor. Hell, say goodbye to your career altogether."

I stare at her some more. Looks like I don't fucking have a choice here. "Fine, I'll pack my bags."

It's night, late, when my helicopter touches down in the countryside at the family estate.

Fucking Sabine. The last place I want to be.

Too many memories. Too much everything.

But at some point, carefully crafted shit will hit the fan. I should have let the career go. Gone into producing, directing, something like that. The screenplay in my bag is the meaty something else I want to do.

I've got other scripts, but that one...it's my baby.

I get in the car waiting for me, and when we reach my aunt's place, I let myself in. She'll never forgive me if she's not my first port of call. I'll go to my townhouse after.

Of course Penrith's up and waiting for me.

"Stephan!" The smile on her face is one of love and devotion, the one I remember from childhood and miss. She may be up there in age, walking with a cane, but none of it seems to be slowing her down.

I sweep her up, hug her tight. "Pen," I say. "Are you happy I finally came back to this god-forsaken place?"

"Like you had a choice?" She laughs, pats my cheek, and it makes me wonder if she means that as a joke or if she knows more than she's letting on. Pen's known for seeing things others don't usually see. "How long are you here for, darling?"

"Only the summer." Then I look at her. "How's the battle-ax?"

Her smile falters. "You need to see her, you know. She won't be happy to find out you've snuck onto the island without saying hi."

As if that devious woman ever just wanted to do something as innocent as just say hi.

"No way," I say. "Not even if hell freezes and the demons become angels."

Penrith smiles again. "Oh, Stephan. You haven't changed at all."

Chapter Three

Violet

"Don't bite your nails, Violet." Mom swats my hand away from near my mouth.

"I'm not."

"Isn't it a beautiful day, girls?" Mom beams and sweeps her gaze around the park where people are wandering and kids zipping about. The warmth of the sun in the cloudless sky strokes my face and makes sweat cling.

"Perfect," I say, even though I had prayed hard for rain.

A band plays on the small open sound stage. The music is non-confrontational and about twenty years old but not even cool enough to be called retro. Since the picnic's only a guise for the Monarch—Sophine—who is head of the Council and lives on the isle during the Season to observe and pick out a "lucky" Omega to be deemed her Luxe. The most beautiful and desirable Omega of them all.

Why does she do this? Tradition? Boredom? No one really knows why she focuses so much on Sabine in the summer, but that's how it's been forever and no one dares question her authority.

It's hard not to wrinkle my nose at such strange and almost archaic customs, but I've had years of practice being the perfect daughter. Even before Dad's accident, and Heath stepping away from finding a mate, I've known that the first-born Omega daughter is a duty I have to wear like a crown.

Best behavior, perfect manners, and generally being someone an Alpha would want by his side.

"Imagine," Iris says, coming up behind me as Mrs. Hyde hijacks Mom's attention. She points at the woman's brightly colored dress that's too tight for her and pinches her body in all the wrong ways. "What do you think goes on under that over-fluffed hair of hers? I bet it's just the whistle of the wind blowing through her ears."

"Iris Anne Gardener," I say, trying not to laugh. "That's our neighbor, Mom's friend, and your best friend's mother you're talking about."

She rolls her eyes. "She's cruel to Quinn. I hear stories. And it doesn't matter how rich the Hydes are, or that her brother's an Alpha. For some reason, a once-celebrated Omega gave birth to Beta girls."

"They can still get mated. Everyone can." Not participate in the Season, though—only Omegas and Alphas can do that. But Beta, Delta, and Gamma girls can still find a match. It's just that no one watches them under a microscope like they do with us.

At least on Sabine.

But I push that out of my head and smooth my fingers down the pretty floral fabric of the summer dress Mom picked for me. I fix my gaze on my sister. "Now go, find your friend, and keep out of trouble."

"And if I want to get into trouble?"

I clutch my stomach. It's been in knots since I woke up this morning. "Don't, Iris. Please. This is the first Season we're taking part in, and Mom..." I flounder for the words, for breath.

"Don't worry, Vi, I know. Mom wants this, and she misses Dad. But you—"

"This is Mom's first real outing after Dad's passing. It's important we support her and we be the perfect family. So if you're going to act up..."

I run an eye over her outfit: a dark-blue dress ending above the knee, showing off thick black lace stockings, and her chunky boots on her feet. She's at least got her hair pinned up, but the audacious makeup is still her signature.

"Then go meet Quinn somewhere. You need to stay here for at least thirty minutes. You need to last that long."

"I'm wearing a dress. What more do you want from me?" she hisses.

"For me, Iris. Be good for me."

"Fine." And she stomps off in search of her friend.

With her on her Iris version of good behavior, which will have to do, I search the crowd. Jade's in green, her rich auburn hair dotted with sparkling green gems, her dress flowing and beautiful. We used to be friends in school. Same with Samantha Li, the pretty girl with the shining black hair shimmering with pearls. But they both look at me, lean in and cover their mouths, and giggle.

Heat shoots through every pore.

Dahlia's standing off to one side, making sure Rue's reined in. Which is an impossible task. As I get closer to them, ignoring the boys who catcall any girl passing, boys who aren't yet ready for their Season, I make my way to the big, welcoming oak. And I take a moment to bask in the shade.

"Look." Rue's suddenly beside me, thrusting her phone at me.

The animated, sexy bee—if anthropomorphized animals can be sexy—slinks across her screen, pulling a banner behind her.

On it is a picture of a monarch butterfly with a board behind it, a board with girls pinned like insects to it.

"Oh, good god," I say. "Anyone know if the Monarch's seen this?"

"We're trying to catch a glimpse of her, but she's supposedly over there, in that cabana." Rue points at the fanciest looking tent that's set up. "All the QB says is—"

"QB?"

"Queen Bee." Dahlia rushes overs, out of breath. "It's Rue's new nickname for her, one she hasn't shut up about since we got here."

"Not *my* nickname," Rue says. "I didn't come up with it. But everyone's using it on Stitch."

I look at her. "What does the QB herself say?"

Rue holds the phone closer to her face to read. "'Bee-siness not as usual. The Monarch herself is cocooned at the picnic. Is she going to emerge as something even better after her Season's trip to her dermatologist? Or just pick her chosen girls? Honey pots in a row. Stay tuned.'"

"So nothing," I say.

"*Everything*," Rue squeals. "Do you think the Queen Bee is the Monarch in disguise?"

Both Dahlia and I turn to her. "No."

"Fine." Rue turns and races off, hair flying, toward a friend in a matching pair of flowery jeans and summer tank.

I sigh and lean against the tree, gazing out. There's Heath in the distance. He's munching on a finger sandwich among a copse of trees and rose bushes that lead down a path to one of the mazes. I can't see who he's talking to. A guy, one who's at least as tall as Heath.

But though I'm drawn to find out, I make myself look away and try to center myself before having to make polite conversation with any potential mates.

"I wish Rue had put on a dress," I say.

Dahlia, who's wearing a long flowing dress with line-drawn flowers, shrugs. "She's fourteen. Jeans for fifteen and under is allowed."

I bite my lip, hating myself for being the watchdog, when all I want is for everyone to be happy, our family shining the way Mom wants it to.

"You don't look like you want to mingle, Violet. You could sneak home."

"I can't do that to Mom. Besides, it's my Season. I'm supposed to be getting a look at the eligible Alphas."

"And the competition," she says, as more Omegas pass with their families, all dressed up in their pastel colors and matching hair accessories.

"Mom—"

"Had hers."

I turn to her and shake my head. "Mom wants what's

best for us, and so do I. And this is making her more like herself. After Dad's death, I want that, don't you?"

She nods.

"Besides…" I put on my brightest smile. "It'd be nice to finally have a mate who cares for me. Maybe make a pack of my own with lots of children." It's the perfect thing to say, something I've rehearsed in my head since it was decided this summer would be my Season.

Having a family and kids of my own is what I've always wanted, but now, the stress of getting those things is weighing down on me. It's too much.

"Violet…" Dahlia's voice is calm and full of concern.

I draw in a deep breath and paste on my faux smile. "Don't worry about me. I'll be fine."

"Can I come with you, at least?"

"Of course."

We head out, arm in arm, and Marigold, who some might describe as flighty but is much sharper than others give her credit for, sees me and bounds over. "You need more backup?"

"I don't need—"

"You may want to reconsider. Mom's working the picnic for you, but these girls are all out in their catty glory, so you need backup." Mari leans in. "Besides, I want to catch a real glimpse of the Monarch herself. Do you think she'll mingle?"

"I don't think mingling is on her to-do list," Dahlia murmurs.

"But," Mari says, "she'll have spies everywhere. Not to mention the Queen Bee." She nods once. "Keep your eyes peeled." Then she dances off.

As she does so, two girls approach us, both blonde. Lara I know, the other I don't. Lara's hair is the color of ice, and she wears the palest blue with sequins, gems, and glitter. It's like an elevated summer dress pretending to be a ball gown. And the other girl is in gold to go with her gold hair. Her dress says fancy cocktail hour with the stars.

"Alicia, this," Lara says, looking me up and down, "is Violet Gardener."

"Nice to meet you," I say politely.

The other girl smiles prettily, but there's no warmth in her blue eyes. "I've heard a lot about you."

Mari suddenly appears. "Cupcakes?"

The two girls rear back.

"No," Lara hisses. "Do you know how much fat is in those?"

"And sugar?" Alicia says, the gold woven through her hair glinting. I get the sinking feeling I'm woefully underdressed. "Why not just offer us an XL on a plate."

"Along with a heart attack." Lara shudders.

Mari smiles and bites deeply into a cupcake, then closes her eyes and moans. "So buttery, so sweet, so *good*."

Alicia looks down her nose as though she's just seen something utterly disagreeable. "Just know you and your... common little family might have bred a whole lot of Omegas," Alicia says, "but that's nothing on real money, real beauty, real class. By first ball, no one will even know your name, Daisy."

"It's *Violet*," Dahlia says, voice tight and small.

"You have to admit," Lara says, "you've never stood out, and looking at you now, you still don't. But you were once nice to me, so I'll make sure to send the leftovers your way.

Rumor has it someone famous will be in the Season this year. And he's all mine."

"Mine, you mean," Alicia says. "That dreamy movie star, Asher St. James."

"Who?" I ask.

I know *of* him. His name is familiar, but I haven't seen any of his movies, unlike Mari and Rue. But why would a famous Alpha come here to our little island when he has a dazzling career in Emporia?

"This isn't a competition," I tell them. "We're looking for our mates, possibly our love matches. So I wish you both the best—"

"Did you hear that? Little Miss Boring believes in *love*." Lara smirks.

"You'll get the dregs, if you're lucky. Maybe on your fifth Season—" Alicia stops as someone barrels into her. Then she shrieks. "Oh my god. Wine? You spilled wine on me!"

"Oh no," Iris deadpans. "My bad. And it's not wine. It's extra-concentrated cranberry juice. Very hard to get out."

The two girls stare, Alicia close to tears.

"Of course you Gardener weeds would gang up," Lara says. "But it won't work."

They stomp off, and people around us murmur, gossiping.

"I need to sit," I say, staring at my sisters. I know Iris did it on purpose, and part of me thanks her, but the other part... Oh, man, what problems is this going to bring?

And like it or not, the Queen Bee will report it. Those girls will twist it. They'll—

"Come on, *Daisy*—

"Don't call me that, Iris."

"Violet." She kisses my cheek, then rubs the lipstick off. "Let's all go mingle. Now."

"What if—"

"If someone wants to report the incident, let them. I tripped, and they were being downright nasty, not becoming of Omegas ready to have their Season." Iris links arms with me and Dahlia and Mari take my other side.

Rue sees us, waves bye to her friend, and rushes off to be with us, and together we join the picnic as a united front.

CHAPTER FOUR

Stephan

"Are you going to talk to her?" Pen asks from under the cover of her cabana in the shade.

She doesn't usually like the displays of the hypocrisies of society. Then again...

"Nope." I throw myself onto the cushions, big fat ones in silk and brocade. It's quite comfortable, actually, because whatever was laid down on the ground for cover is soft and slightly bouncy.

And I'm not letting my mind explore ways I could make this floor fun. Not with my fucking aunt so close.

We're on a small hill under a huge tree, and Pen has the pale green gossamer curtains drawn back to watch everyone run around and try to impress the fucking Monarch. Who, in typical fashion, is not showing her face.

But she'll be watching. And no doubt expecting me.

"It's only proper, you know."

"Don't care, not going to happen, Pen."

She makes a sound from her chair. It's a lot like disapproval. While disapproval isn't something I've had to experience since I became famous and the darling of the screen and Stitch posts, along with the tabloids themselves, I know it well. And it sends me tumbling back into the past.

One of her staff offers me fruit and cheese on a platter. I'm fucking loaded even without the family money, but I don't have staff like servants. It's a different world here, all right.

"I didn't realize you two were on talking terms."

Pen flicks a crumb of cake off her throw that covers her legs and sips her drink. "We're not. She's—"

"A controlling battle-ax without one shred of humanity?" I say, offering her the smile that's made me millions. "I thought so."

"Don't flash that thing at me, Stephan. It won't work."

The smile vanishes, and I narrow my eyes. "What thing?"

"That award-winning idiotic smile. It belongs to the movie star, not to you."

"Hate to break it to you, Pen, but I *am* that movie star."

She lifts her chin, her gaze sweeping back out to the scene below. "What do you think of our available beauties?"

Something in my gut tightens. "I'm not interested in mating. And if I were, the Omega in question wouldn't be some boring hothouse thing with no idea of actual life."

She takes a deep breath. "This is a nice place."

I get up, after helping myself to a handful of grapes. "So's the real world, Pen."

"There are some lovely Omegas. I'm quite taken with the Gardener one. Violet? A surface pleaser, but with substance." She nods thoughtfully, watching as some kids tear past.

I go to the tent's opening and scan the park and the picnic. It's the stuff they like to make movies about—with me in them.

Overdressed girls swan around in groups, mothers crane their necks to see what other mothers are doing, or fuss over their kids. And the guys? They're just waiting for the fruit to fall and get sampled by them.

I'm sure there's some who want the real thing, a romantic match. But it's all fucking bullshit.

The only truth in this whole scenario is Pen's well-meaning ways, and how pretty much everyone out there is trying to catch a glimpse of the old self-labeled Monarch herself.

She does rule the Council everywhere, but she prefers to stay here, where society is everything.

"I'm not about to go near a Gardener girl."

"Why not? Even a dance, Stephan? But as far as matches go, you could do worse."

I turn and face Pen. "I'm not on the market, and I'm not courting."

"Stephan—"

I stop her with a hard look. "You know that Heath's my best friend. So any Gardener girl would be from his family, and therefore off my radar completely. Got it? Good."

One penciled eyebrow rises in a challenge, but she doesn't say a word. It fucking annoys me just the same.

"Anyway, I've got things to do."

With that, I leave.

The trouble with making a dramatic exit is I really have nothing to do. I don't want to go and mingle with the boring well-bred. I certainly don't want to have to sign autographs or make small talk with fans.

Scratch that. No one here is that gauche to ask for an autograph, but I don't feel like playing nice.

I don't want a fucking cupcake, and I don't want to give any mate-hungry Omegas the wrong idea.

Heath's here, but I spoke to him already, and just from that small exchange it was clear that even his burdens have burdens, this day being one of them, so he's going to be no fun.

I could go set up my town home, rearrange some things, remove dust covers, drink the booze cabinet dry.

Which is a problem. I know I shouldn't do the latter, not on my first day.

There are people I have to see, people I don't want to see who no doubt don't want to see me, but...I need to do it. So I skulk through the wild maze, one that will take a person out to the other side of the park, and then I can just go to the lower side of town, catch a show, pick up a girl, have some—

"You look like you don't want to be here," comes a young female voice with a note of accusation. I turn.

There's a girl there, long dark hair, jeans and yellow top. She's got a bedazzled phone in one hand that matches the color of her top, like it's got chips of yellow diamonds and topaz all over it.

She's pretty, on the teen cusp between grownup and child. She tilts her head and puts her hand on her hip. "Why?"

"Go away, kid." I start walking away.

She follows, skipping along. "You were talking to my brother. How do you know Heath?"

Oh, fuck. Is she his sister? That girl, Violet? Health barely spoke of his family when we were in school, but I know he has sisters. Everyone knows the Gardeners were blessed with a handful of Omegas, but their names are what I don't know.

What the fuck is wrong with this place? She's a child. She should be playing with her friends, not looking for a mate. Why would Pen even mention her as a good match for me? That's fucked up.

"We went to school together. Now go away... er...Violet."

She gasps. "O.M.G., do you know Violet? Do you think I look like her? She's so pretty." The girl grins. "I'm Rue." She glances at her phone then at me. "Do you have a younger brother? All the online info about you says you don't talk about family, but if you do have a younger brother, do you think he'll like me? I want to mate with a handsome man just like Violet does, so you're handsome and you'll mate with her, and your brother can mate with me!"

Oh, for fuck's sake. The girl might be thirteen or something, but she clearly is already mate-hungry.

"No brother, and I'm not looking for a mate."

She isn't bothered. Rue rolls her eyes, tosses her hair, starts trotting along next to me to keep up with my longer strides. "Why are you here, then? Everyone knows all the boys—except my brother because he's too busy filling in for Dad—are looking for the perfect Omega. We're all Omegas, did you know that? Of course, Heath isn't. He's an Alpha. He should be finding a mate, hopefully one with some brothers because I plan to have a group to pick from when it's my turn. I can't spend a whole summer devoted to mate hunting. But see, Heath can't do that, either. Not after Daddy died. He's head of our family now. But Violet's in the running. She's better than the other girls. They're all fake."

I don't think she took a breath *once* during all that.

Her phone pings, and I can hear the familiar voice from the speakers. A Stitch post.

"....so no use crying over spilt honeyed cranberry. Not even if it ruins a gown of gold. Accidents happen..."

Rue gasps.

Is this fucking kid going to follow me all the way to the Lower Side? I've got to ditch her. "Don't you have something to do?"

"Well...I could eat more of those cupcakes with the lavender icing, but Mom said not to. We've gotta save face for Violet. She could totally be the Monarch's next Luxe, so Mom doesn't want me to ruin her chances. It's so cool."

"Other people have Omega daughters," I mutter.

She makes a soft sound of delight. "Did you hear what the QB said? She just mentioned when Iris accidentally on purpose tripped and spilled her cranberry juice over that *bitch*." Rue drops her voice to a whisper on the last word.

"Those girls, Lara and her new friend, were being nasty to Violet. And Vi's the nicest person ever. Iris says too nice."

She pauses, and I speed up.

"Wait up!"

I stop, turn, and smile tightly. "Go back, kid. Okay? I'm just here for the summer. If you want an autograph, you can have one, or a photo. But just go back to your stupid picnic and see if you can spot the Monarch."

She looks at me like I just slapped her.

"I'm fourteen. Not a kid. And I was being nice. You're rude. I don't want a photo or your stupid autograph. You know what? Heath might like you, but sometimes he's got terrible taste. And as for Violet—"

"I'm not looking for a mate, okay?"

Rue sniffs. "She's way too good for you."

And with that, she spins and stalks off, breaking into a run.

With the kid gone, I continue on, ignoring the guilt over being mean to Heath's little sister. I'll give her a signed photo. She'll want one, when she gets over this. I'll get her tickets to my next movie. Whatever.

But one thing is for certain—I'm not taking part in any of this circus of fucking balls and dances. And I'm not courting or mating with anyone. Especially Violet fucking Gardener.

Chapter Five

Violet

Two days later, I open the door and greet Iris's best friend. A Beta, who hasn't come into her scent yet. "Come on in."

"Hey, Vi." Quinn Hyde hooks a flyaway strand of red hair behind an ear. "Did you survive the picnic?"

"You left early?"

"You stayed?" she asks as I usher her in.

I put on a bouncy smile. "Of course, to the very end. Mom left early with a migraine."

"Oh, man, I'd have been out of there as soon as she was." Quinn hugs me. "The picnic's nothing more than a gawk fest of who the chosen girls might be, who's making their debut into the Season. And gossip."

"And courtesy of Iris," I say, "and her little accident with the drink and Alicia's dress, they all got something to gossip about. Mom was worried, but I showed her the Queen Bee Stitch and other Stitchers' comments. Everyone was nice, and as Rue said, we weren't singled out by the 'QB' as monsters, so…"

"It'll blow over," Quinn says.

"I hope you're right. Anyway, I think the Season is going to be a lovely one," I say, doing my best to mask my fears.

"Violet Gardener, I never took you for a traditionalist."

"There's nothing wrong with a good match, Quinn. And I'm happy for my first Season." The lie burns on my tongue.

"And last."

"I hope so. I'll get Iris." I'm about to show her into the living room when Rue darts past.

"Iris! Your other half is here!" She grins at Quinn, eyes going to her hair, something she covets. "Why won't *my* hair turn red? I'd dye it but Mom might keel over."

"Yeah? Well, I think my mom wants to keel over every time she sees my hair. It draws eyes to me naturally…and not in a good way, according to her." Quinn rolls her eyes. "But there's no way I could ever be a Luxe, so I don't know why it matters."

"You might one day," Rue says, sliding back so she can curl a strand of Quinn's hair around her finger.

"We Hyde girls are Betas." She looks at me and gives an impish grin. "Much to Mom's Omega heart's dismay."

"You'll still have a Season." They're so rich, Quinn will be one of the few Betas with their own version of it. Not as much of a fuss the way Alphas' and Omegas' Seasons are, but still as nerve-wracking.

"Next year, Vi. Gotta be at least twenty-one."

I curse my ancient age mournfully. "I know."

"Mom said Sophine is eyeing a few ladies for the Luxe Omega this year," Quinn says, "including the newcomer, Alicia Dell."

"Love your boots, Quinn." Rue's been quiet for about half a minute. Far too long for her. "Did you see the Queen Bee's latest? What was your take? Did you like what the Bee said?"

"Nah, I don't read that nonsense. And I was barely there."

"Like Iris." Rue sighs. "I bet the Bee's *sooo* sophisticated."

Mari walks in, her bouncy bob and soft smile as welcoming as ever. "Hey, Quinn. Iris is getting ready. Dahlia's about to practice. She'll be playing at some of the events this year. Want to come hear?"

"I'll get some tea and cake. Or coffee. Or...or...soda! And cake." And with that Rue takes off toward the kitchen.

I truly envy pretty Quinn. She'll have to pick a mate eventually, being a rich Beta, but no Beta is ever made to stand in the spotlight and be fussed over, no matter how rich or well-bred. That's reserved for Omegas. Like me.

Then again, I won't be the Monarch's chosen one. When she finds an Omega she deems worthy, she picks her star.

The thought makes me want to puke.

Marigold tucks Quinn's hand in her arm. "Mom's pretending to tend to the front garden so she can catch the mailman. She's waiting for the first invitations. And Iris?

Wardrobe drama. I mean, she mostly wears black, so how much drama can she find?"

With Quinn whisked off and Dahlia playing the piano, I have no option but to follow them into the living room.

My brother's there, reading on his tablet. It'll be the newspaper. That's what he does now around this time. Like our father, except Dad always had the real thing.

He's pacing and then stops as he sees us. His dark gaze zeroes in on Quinn. "Why is the orange stray here?"

The corner of his mouth actually twitches.

"To claw up your favorite seat, *Heather*," Quinn says.

His eyes narrow at the nickname she's given him since first befriending Iris years ago. The one he *hates* and she won't let up on. "All I hear is mewling."

"All I hear is—"

"Girls! Heath!" The front door slams, and Mom comes hurrying in, cutting off the well-worn sniping of old friends. She's waving a thick cream-colored envelope so fragrant I can smell it from across the room.

It's a sweet smell. It makes me nauseated.

"From the Monarch herself!" she shrieks.

"O.M.G., Mom!" Rue rushes in holding a box of crackers and waves her phone. "Save a tree, you ancient people, use Stitch or even email."

"Hush, Rue." Mom's eyes scan the page. "It's the list of Omegas the Monarch is considering as her Luxe."

"Oh, God," Iris says, stomping in. "Not this nonsense again."

Dahlia hits a few dramatic notes on the piano.

Mom is not daunted. "To pick her Luxe, someone that

will make all the eligible Alphas vie for her, Sophine is requesting presentations from all the Omegas on this list."

Iris grunts. "It's just a list of this year's cattle to line up and bid on for the slaughter."

I let out a nervous laugh, and Heath straightens sternly but I don't miss his eye roll.

My mother suddenly starts almost hyperventilating and flapping her hands in excitement. "Violet! Oh, Violet! Your name is on here! Sophine wants a special presentation from you!"

Every eye in the room swings toward me, and I freeze on the spot. Blood rushes in my ears.

Me...? No... There's no way. *Me?*

No. No. No.

"Oh shit..." Iris breathes.

"Wait, Violet?" Rue's jumping up and down and clapping her hands. "Our sister! A Luxe!"

"She's not a Luxe yet, Rue. Shut it," Iris snaps, but their voices are starting to fade into the distance, muffled by my own raging pulse.

Mom is all fluttery. "Do you know what this means?"

"I-I—" I can't even form words. My tongue is stuck on the roof of my mouth.

Mom grabs my hand and grips it tightly. "It means we have to go shopping!"

Mom pictured grand, deep-violet satin to go with the amethyst family tiara, one from my grandmother's collection, where the majority of the Gardener properties and riches came from.

But the dress and tiara aren't me. I can't pull off high fashion, so while I don't want to bring shame to my family, I also don't want to wear something so out of my league.

We settled on a lovely pale-lavender dress in silk, simple and more *me*, and with it, pretty amethyst-studded hair combs.

Hopefully it's enough to make me stand out to the Monarch. At least that's Mom's prayer. I'm hoping it makes me forgettable enough.

Getting a good mate is one thing; being deemed this year's Luxe is another. And that's not the kind of pressure I think I can handle right now.

The world spins, and my skin's about a thousand degrees hot and hypersensitive. The smooth silk is like rough sandpaper on my skin.

The room is very grand, with paintings on all the walls, and a few sculptures on pedestals, including a Degas ballerina. I focus on that beautiful sculpture, studying the little girl in a frozen pose, and it centers me. At least enough so that I can function.

I'm meeting the Councilwoman Sophine Adams, the highest Alpha in our society. Monarch, as she likes to be called.

She's standing on a raised section of the vast room, where a dapper male Omega stands in powder-blue velvet to her right, near a rich red high-backed armchair with golden legs. There's a delicate marble coffee table near her, and on my side of the sitting area is a smaller pale-rose seat, like a rounded pouf ottoman, with no back.

In my head, I can hear Rue saying *whoa*.

All the other Omegas who'd been on the Monarch's list already came and went. I am the last in the line. Some were in here for half an hour, others over an hour. The shortest time was twenty-three minutes. I timed it.

It's only been three minutes since I walked in, and it already feels like an eternity.

Somehow, I stop myself from clenching my hands nervously.

"You should look at me, since we'll be talking," the Monarch says.

Her voice is like thick smoke, and I look up. I'm covered in blocker, which blocks my scent. Not the Councilwoman, though. She smells like rich linen and sunlight. Effortlessly cool, effortlessly luxe.

It makes sense. I didn't really get the word *Luxe* before, apart from being Sophine's catchword for the Season. But now I do. "Something you're born with."

A single penciled brow rises. "What was that?"

Startled to realize I had spoken aloud, I lift my gaze to her again. She's heart-stoppingly gorgeous. Timeless beauty.

"I...I'm sorry, Monarch." I do a small curtsy, and the male Omega snickers, only to stop when she cuts him one brief glance. "I'm Vi—"

"I know who you are." She sits. Her long frame is in a cream-colored suit, like she's off to set order to the world.

But her dark-blue eyes are on me, intensely intelligent, intensely interested. "What did you say?"

"Something you're born with. Luxe, I mean. I get it now. I just...I hadn't meant to say it out loud."

Her eyes narrow, and I know I've screwed up. I made her sound vain, simpering, and I want the floor to eat me or the ceiling to fall.

"Do you think *you're* that?" she asks, head tilting.

I gasp. "No, Monarch, not at all."

"Sit. Tell me about you."

"You're more interesting."

"I'm not here to be flattered."

Misery rocks me. "I'm not attempting to flatter." That's worse. "I just...I'm not interesting. In a house full of five Omega sisters, it's not easy to stand out." Out of desperation I lock onto the ballerina sculpture again. And I make myself breathe slowly because I refuse to have a panic attack here. Minutes, hours, seconds pass, and finally I say, "Is that an Edgar Degas—"

"What about movies?"

I blink at the sudden change in subject matter, but I answer her. "They're all right. I don't go much. I've always been the one at home helping our mother with my family... Should I go now?"

"Sit."

This time, I do.

Sophine looks me over. Slowly. Decisively. "So you're not into entertainment? Celebrities? Gossip?"

"Not really."

She nods at her Omega. "Frederick, pour her an iced tea. Bring my drink and then go."

Sophine doesn't do anything until the drinks are served and the door shuts.

When we're alone again, her attention snaps back to me. "Why do you want me to choose you?"

"I don't," I say frankly. "Being seen by you is enough."

Now she looks at me like I'm something rare. "Don't you want to shine?"

"There are other girls, talented, nice, who would love being labeled Luxe."

"But not you?"

I breathe out. "I don't need that. I'm fine with this year just being my debut, and if I catch a good Alpha's eye..."

"You don't want to impress me?"

"I'm sorry. I'm not impressive in that way. My only wish is to find a mate who makes me happy, and who will also be the best for my family. They mean the world to me. Then when—well, *if*—someone chooses me, we'll make a family of our own."

"Children?"

I can't help but smile. "Lots." Then I bite my lip. I didn't mean to say that, but it is true. As the oldest daughter, I've spent most of my time caring for my younger sisters. Sort of like a second mother to them. It's what I'm used to, what I'm good at, what I want for my future.

"So here you are, Violet, a normal girl, pretty but normal, and in your own words boring and not seeking favor or the limelight, simply the right match?"

I didn't say boring, but I won't correct her. And I can't think of what to say, so I nod.

"And do you know who the Queen Bee might be?"

"Er... My sister thought it could be you, but I can see it's not. I don't go on Stitch."

As soon as I say that, I know I've blown it. She frowns, deep lines crossing her forehead, as if she's disappointed in me or I've wasted her time. Most likely both.

The rest of the interview happens in a haze, and before I know it, I'm shooed out of the grand room to meet Mom, who is waiting just outside the doors.

She looks at me, puzzled. "You weren't in there for very long."

I know. I must've hit the record for shortest interview compared to all of the others.

"Can we go, Mom? Now? Please?"

We leave, and as we drive home to the townhouse, I'm already thinking of ways to make Mom feel better about my screw-up with the Monarch. Her silence during the entire ride tells me of her disappointment, too, and upsetting her is the one thing I'd rather die than do.

I messed up. Big time.

Mom wanted me to be the Luxe apparently more than I thought. Even if that's not what I want, I should have tried harder for her. I should have—

It doesn't matter. Now, I need to switch my focus to finding a mate, one she approves of who can lift the family up and set the tone for my sisters and their Seasons.

It's all up to me.

So I really can't mess this up too.

Hivemind! A special Stitch from the Queen Bee to my brood...

PEARL FOR THE PEARL?

Oh, yes.

*From A to V, the special gaggle of Omegas has been chosen. And as you read this, they're in the Butterfly's lair, presented like **PEARLS OF CAVIAR** on a spoon.*

Who will be the shining celestial body, the richest velvet? Who will be the falling star, the roughest cotton?

Time will tell.

Tick. Tock.

I do know the blonde Alicia D was stunning in gold. Actual gold. Jade L looked fantastic in—not green—red. Bold choice, but it worked.

And then there was a flower plucked from the garden.
Simple, natural, a beauty. Miss Violet G in pale lavender.
She was inside for the shortest time.

So...who will the Monarch choose?

Fill your honey pots because we're going to find out real soon.
You know I'll be the one to break the news!

This Season-long tale has yet to begin...

- Queen Bee

Chapter Six

Stephan

The hot blonde I met at the bar after the damn picnic had all the markings of an uptown Omega slumming it. I didn't ask if she was mated. She wasn't wearing a mark, and she seemed a little too young to already be cheating.

But it takes all sorts.

Point is, I don't care. She smelled good enough, drank enough with me to talk me into going to the hottest underground club, and then I fucked her in some low-rent back street room that charged by the hour.

Girls like her love that shit, and I just needed release.

Now, two days later, I still feel seedy. Some might call it regret; I just call it too much fun offered without much return. She wasn't a virgin, and I didn't come in her. Didn't knot, either.

Omegas make that hard because sometimes, when you're balls deep in one, the baser instincts surge and the need to knot overwhelms. It can cloud all common sense and reason.

Fuck that.

I'm more than hormones and nature.

I won't knot in anyone ever again. I'm an Alpha from a long line of extremely strong Alpha blood. We tend to only produce Alphas. But love, a mate, children... They are not for me.

Not anymore.

And here I am boring myself.

In yet another bar, baseball cap on, I watch the traffic. The chaos.

The divide between the classes is strong in Sabine. Upper side's genteel, lots of trees and foot traffic as well as sleek cars and limos. And parks. The big townhouses and properties help, too.

Then there's the countryside in Sabine. That's divided, too.

Grand fucking palatial grounds and houses for the rich, and villages where farmers work the land and many of the household staffers live.

There's a divide, but I like the grittier side. It's more real.

Fuck, someone should make a film about the poor or working class of Sabine.

It would probably flop.

As the sky darkens and the lights outside come on, a girl darts between cars, narrowly missing being squashed.

I don't know why, but she piques my interest. Maybe

it's the fluid and graceful way she runs, the gym bag bouncing on a tight ass in tracksuit pants cut off at the ankle, and thick-soled sneakers that she somehow moves in like they're heels.

She's got a hoodie on, so I can't see her face. And she disappears down an alley, one that has a mix of buildings, mostly industrial, and a highly illegal brothel for the discerning mated man who requires discretion.

Is she...?

I find myself having another drink as I wait to see if she comes out, and then a third.

Fuck. A hooker.

I don't blame a girl for making a living, but...she'd moved like she came from society.

Maybe tomorrow I'll visit and see.

Not to fuck her, obviously, but to see if she's a whore—

What the hell am I thinking?

The soon-to-be disgraced and rakish heart-breaker Asher St. James caught in a brothel?

No fucking thank you.

Of course, Clea decides to text me at that exact moment, and I read the update, which is all about Felicity's movements this week. I really don't care, as long as none of my real secrets come out.

I send Clea a thumbs up emoji, then slide my phone into my jeans pocket and grab my light overcoat. It might be entering summer on Sabine, but summer nights on the upper side are cooler—and I want to go visit the beach like I used to.

"Stephan, you ass," I mutter as I drop a twenty on the table for a tip.

I take the long way, following the boardwalk as it weaves wide around the beachfront to where it meets the parks, and then up further to where the boathouses are.

I find an empty one and sit on the bench in there and watch the water.

"Hey," I say to the dark-blue water, clearer than the murk that flows closer to the shore. "I'd say long time, but it hasn't been."

I chuckle, then stop.

Footsteps.

I breathe in deep, trying to discover who it is. My nose is hit with a void of scent, the kind only possible by a fairly strong scent-blocking perfume. Omega. Has to be. Any other type doesn't need to work so hard to mask their personal scent. And how do I know it's a female? The light, dainty footfalls give her away.

Then, I get a sudden burst of something as the footsteps come close. Faint gardens...no, a flower of some sort. Just a tinge on the breeze—

A shadow falls across the boards, courtesy of the rising moon and the setting sun. And she appears, just as the promenade lights come on.

Long dark hair in a ponytail, damp, and her cheeks are pink. She's pretty—very, very pretty. Naturally so. Without any makeup or artificial enhancements that I'm used to the women having in Emporia. I can't tell the color of her eyes, but I read the shock, and I wait for recognition of who I am to flare in her eyes.

It doesn't.

"Sorry," she says, "I thought I was alone." She looks at me uncertainly. "I'll go."

"You can stay. I don't bite."

The girl hesitates, then runs a hand over her hair, opens her bag, and pulls on a hoodie.

It's the girl from the Lower Side. I knew it the moment she stepped into the light. My heart lurches. Probably because she's unexpected.

She starts to stretch.

Anyone else and I'd think they were showing off, doing a strange mating dance, but she isn't. This is for her, and it's like I stop existing while she does it.

Stop existing because she's taking up all the space.

I'm still trying to sort out how I can make out her scent, especially when it's clear she's wearing a blocker. Maybe it's because she's been working out and sweating, but whatever it is, the floral smell is invading my senses. Especially with her being so close to me.

"Do you have a name?" I ask when she finishes her stretches.

She spins to face me, and her eyes are wide like I just gave her an electric shock. "Do you?"

"I do."

"Me too."

She leans on the seat built into the wall opposite and breathes in, closing her eyes now, and lifting her face to the soft breeze.

I was right. The girl—woman—is an Omega. Along with the regal lines of her face and where she is, I can put together that she's also upper-class, probably part of the fucking Season since she doesn't look any older than twenty-one.

The rich sable shade of her hair reminds me of

someone, but I can't put my finger on it.

"Your first Season?"

Startled, she looks at me. "You're not from here."

"I am."

"But you haven't been here in a long time." At my arched brow, she shrugs as she threads her fingers together. "I mean, you're clearly rich. Your coat, your demeanor."

And I'm famous.

But she doesn't say it.

If she wants to play coy, I'll let her. It's nice actually, not to be fawned over or have my stage name blurted at me. Like that blonde I fucked did.

"Guilty. And you..." I smile. "Does anyone know where you were tonight?"

The girl gasps. "No. I... How did you..."

"I won't tell," I say. "Just curious."

"Why would you be curious about me? I'm not interesting enough to be curious about."

Oh, Sophine will love this one. She's so polite she might choke on her manners, and I can see her being the perfect Omega, making her family proud. And yet behind it is a secret, like she's got a rebel heart beating away inside her.

"Oh, I think you might be interesting. What's your dark secret?"

She flashes me a scandalized look. "I don't have any dark secrets. Not even beige ones."

"I saw you downtown," I say, leaning in.

She goes completely still. "No, you didn't."

"Relax, I'm not after shit. I've got enough complications, so you're safe. Besides, you know who I am."

"No," she says, "I don't."

She is still pretending. Interesting, indeed.

I breathe out heavily. "As I was saying, I saw you on the Lower Side, playing chicken with the cars before racing down an alley where there's an establishment of 'ill repute'—or so I'm told. Do you turn tricks on the side? Lead a double life as an ingénue lady of the night?"

"What?" She jumps up, eyes wild. "No! Mikel Petrov was there, giving a dance class, so I had to go. Please don't tell anyone."

"Why would anyone care?"

"I snuck out." She hisses this like she committed murder. "And dressed like this!"

"I don't see the problem." She looked hot in the tight dance top before she put the hoodie on, and she still looks good. Athletic and dancer-sleek.

I'm kinda fascinated by her. Or maybe it's just the power of her Omega scent in such a small space that's making my head whirl.

"Why did you come here?" I ask. "Inside this boathouse?"

"I could ask the same of you," she says, plucking at her sleeves. "But if you must know, I like it here because it's always empty and I can be alone to... think." She glances away, as if she just revealed something about herself she'd rather keep private. "People who fish come very, very early in the morning, so it's..."

"Private."

She's using the same boathouse I used to visit when I lived here, to escape, to get away. But from what?

"You like the shadows, then? You don't want to stand

out? You don't seem to like being asked things, either, so how are you going to catch a mate?"

"I never said I wanted a mate."

I scoff. "You're an Omega."

"And you're an Alpha. Do *you* want a mate?"

Touché.

She groans. "I'm sorry. That was rude."

"I thought it was actually funny," I say with a laugh. "But you got me there. I definitely do *not* want to find myself a mate. I enjoy my solitude too much."

"And you can do that, as an Alpha. Omegas don't have the same liberties." Then she shakes her head and mumbles, "I'm starting to sound like my sister now."

"Your sister?"

"Never mind." She relaxes down into herself. "But yes, I'm one of those Omegas who's participating in the Season to *catch* a mate, I'm sorry to say. But the Season hasn't started properly yet anyway. I've got time to lay traps."

There's surface acceptance, even the sound of excitement, but it's cold behind that little façade. I know when someone else is acting—it's my profession, after all. She doesn't want to go out there and preen and be fussed over. She doesn't want to be looked at and judged.

But she will.

For...reasons.

Because she's trained to?

Has to?

I'm really fascinated now. This Omega is scared of the Season, but she's doing everything she can to pretend she isn't.

In that instant, I decide I'll be going to the first ball after all. Pen will be pleased.

And the battle-ax, the Monarch, Sophine?

Fuck what she thinks.

The Omega's bag starts to buzz, and she pulls out her phone. The light hits her face and highlights how pretty she is. Even with messy hair and her cheeks pinked from her dance workout, or maybe because of it, she might be the prettiest thing I've seen.

"Oh, damn, I'm running late." She texts fast. Then drops her phone in her bag as she scoops it up. "Nice meeting you. I have to run."

And with that she takes off.

I rush out of the boathouse after her. "Your name?" I call, but she's already disappearing into the wilder edges of the park.

She's gone.

Well, fuck.

I kick the ground and notice something. Purple.

A ribbon.

I pick it up, press it to my nose, and breathe in. It smells faintly of flowers and detergent. Of her.

I can give it back to her at the ball.

It'll be fun stalking little Miss Cinderella there.

One ball this Season.

That's it.

Just one.

Chapter Seven

Violet

As I get home, I ease the side door closed and head to the back stairs, hoping to shower before dinner.

"Violet!"

I jump at Heath's call. I'm not sure why I'm so jumpy, why my heart's a little wild and thready, but I guess it's because I haven't snuck in since...I don't even know when.

Holding my breath, I try and put the scruffy-faced, hot stranger from my head. But my mind is buzzing like it's holding a swarm of angry bees. Panic rises.

Calm down, Vi.

Calm.

I breathe.

He had a nice voice: a touch of velvet, a touch of smoke, a touch of gravel, and even a touch of something unexpectedly warm.

And his scent... Oak.

A girl could swoon over that. Alphas and Omegas tend to be on the natural side when it comes to their scents, and he smelled like his voice. Smoke on a cold day, yes, like oak. A deep, earthy, rich scent, the wood charred to release more of the essence, and a slightly sweet edge that makes it somehow more masculine, like something to bury my face into. A sweater by the fire on a winter's evening. Comfort.

To smell like that must cost a fortune. More than we can afford nowadays.

I think he's—

"There you are, Violet. Didn't you hear me?" Heath appears in the doorway, frowning as I kick my bag behind me, but he doesn't comment on that. "We need to talk."

I start to shake. "Talk?"

"The thing with mouths and sound? A form of communication? Yes." He points to the study door. "In there, now."

He marches ahead, leaving me no option but to follow. Inside, I close the door carefully behind me. "Yes?"

"What happened?" Heath asks, voice terse. For a moment, I think it's because of how I'm dressed.

I wasn't supposed to be out, and I shouldn't be going to dance classes. They're too expensive, and Dahlia's so talented that she needs the money for her piano lessons. Iris disdains lessons in the fine arts—she calls it *subjugation*—and Mari isn't really interested in art classes unless they center on real life and not theory, or something.

And Rue? She really hasn't shown much of a passion for anything apart from social apps and technology. She can paint a little, play a decent tune on her violin probably well enough to secure her a chair in an orchestra. She can also sew, cook, and do all the things a nice little Omega can do. Like all of us.

But guilt swamps me as Heath continues to stare. I not only went to a class we can't really afford, but it was in the Lower Side, and I was dressed like this.

No one saw me. Except the young, handsome man from the boathouse. But who is he going to tell?

Hopefully no one.

"I'm sorry," I whisper. "I went to a class in the Lower Side. A dance class. Mikel Petrov was teaching and was offering a free introductory lesson, so...I went. It was a once in a lifetime chance. No one saw me."

"What the hell are you on about, Vi?" He shakes his head. "I was talking about the meeting with the Monarch."

"Oh. That."

"*That.*"

I've been avoiding thinking about it, of how I embarrassed myself royally during my interview, and now it all comes tumbling back.

I blink rapidly, swallowing hard to prevent myself from bursting into tears in front of my brother. I don't even want to be part of this stupid Season. I don't belong in the limelight.

I close my eyes.

"She asked me to tell her about me, and I..." I snap open my eyes. "I asked her about herself instead."

"You deflected."

"You know me, Heath. I know this is important—"

Heath starts to pace, taking up so much room I edge

back until I'm pressed against the door. He shoots me a hard look. "So you threw it? You deliberately sabotaged the interview?"

"Of course not. I would never." I stare at him as he gouges at my heart. "Not in a million years, but Heath... I... I just didn't know what to say. Her questions were unexpected, and I was afraid to say something wrong. I overthought it like I usually do, but I did the best I could."

He stops pacing and wipes a hand over his face. Most likely in annoyance.

I ramble in my embarrassment. "I complemented her on the Degas sculpture, which I'm pretty sure was real. You know the one, the ballerina who—"

"Violet."

My name's like a crack of a whip, and I jump. "I'm not used to all this attention. But I'm working on it. I'm trying. It's just...I want to have the best Season for Mom, to make her proud."

He pauses, his gaze softening as it searches my face. "Vi, you make us all proud."

It's not true, but I smile anyway.

Heath walks over to me and touches my shoulder. His dark eyes lock on mine as if he's trying to look past my mask, past the lies. And out of everyone in the family, he may be the one to find the truth in me. Before Dad died, we were pretty close. And there's a hint of the old Heath in whom I used to confide in his expression now.

"Vi..." he starts. "Maybe we've been expecting too much from you."

"I want this. I do," I blurt out. I don't want anyone—

especially him—worrying about me. He has enough going on. "It's going to be fine. I'll figure it out."

I swallow. He's so stressed. I know he could have found a girl with a rich father or fat bank account of her own. He could have mated her out of duty to us, brought her here, because Heath would never abandon us.

But I don't want him to just settle. He's meant for big things, I know it. And if I can take some of the burden off his shoulders, I'll be happy. That's why I'm glad to have a Season. I'll make him and everyone proud. I'll take the burden away and let their Seasons be easier.

Then *they* could mate for love.

He leans in, his voice low and conspiratorial. "The others can't know—don't even tell Mom—but our finances... They're..." He sighs. "It's not good, Vi. I'm trying to fix things, but..." Another sigh. "But if you don't want this, I'll find a way. You just need to tell me."

"*How* not good, Heath?"

"Dad..." Heath rakes fingers through his hair. "Dad had massive gambling debts."

I can't breathe as panic scrabbles at me. "Mom didn't—"

"She doesn't know. She just thinks the finances were worse than Dad let on. We're okay for now. I've cut a lot. But I don't know how long we can stretch it. I don't want to start tapping into trust funds to make ends meet."

That *is* bad.

Oh, Dad. What did you do?

"Don't worry," I say, trying to inject warmth and caring into my smile. "I'm going to fix this. I'll find myself a good

Alpha, one who will help care for all of us and pave the way for our sisters."

He sighs again, and drops a kiss on the top of my head. "This isn't a burden you should be carrying."

"I could say the same for you."

He shakes his head.

"At least it's a little less heavy if we're carrying it together," I insist.

His lips twitch at the corners—another flash of the fun-loving guy he once was. It quickly vanishes when he leans against the desk and crosses his arms. "Vi, I have to ask you something."

"Sure. What is it?"

"This is just between us, okay? But I have to know."

Christ, why's he so stiff-sounding?

"Just ask, Heath, please."

He clears his throat. "Have you had your first heat yet?"

All the blood in my body rushes to my extremities. And my stomach is like ice. My face and toes feel on fire. "Why?"

"Answer."

"No." I push it out between my teeth. "But Mom says soon."

"Apparently, according to the social norms, that makes you more pristine for some reason. More desirable..."

This is going to go down as the most hideously embarrassing conversation ever. "Why are you asking?"

"Because, Violet, the Monarch just sent us this." He scoops up a thick card from his desk and holds it out for me to take.

I do and see the Council's infamous butterfly insignia

first—more specifically, the symbol of the Monarch. But before I can even read the fancy script underneath, Heath speaks again, confirming my fears.

"Congratulations, Violet. You've been named the Luxe Omega. Sophine has picked you."

Crap.

Chapter Eight

Stephan

"Kill me now," I mutter into the finest Sabine Summer Ale.

I've been here a handful of days, and apart from the pretty girl in the boathouse, the quaint beauty of Sabine is already under my fucking skin.

I'm a man who's got it all. Emporia movie star, check. Famous, check. Rich as fuck, check. Pick of the girls, check, check, and check.

Not that anyone at McNally's bar would care.

For the billionth time, I check my phone, waiting for fucking Heath Gardener to text or call me back. We had caused quiet a stir in college, over on the mainland. But that feels like ages ago. I'm a very different man than I was then. And from the little bit I saw of Heath at the picnic, so is he.

I take another swallow of my drink and listen to the music as it rolls over me. My phone lights up.

HEATH

Busy, man. But I'm at the townhouse.
Come by.

Booze?

HEATH

You know it.

I finish my drink, get up, and leave.

Sabine's big city is full of parks and old buildings. Once you get out of the lower end and the business and shopping districts, then it turns into a pretty, leafy neighborhood, close to the biggest park and the glittering Council building that's like a fucking castle.

When I reach Heath's place, I go through the high front gate and past the small, private garden, a place of memories from college when we'd occasionally have it to ourselves while his family was away visiting the mainland.

He's sitting outside, glass of whiskey, his preferred drink, in one hand.

"Gardener," I say.

"Famous asshole."

I grin. "Only my friends get to call me that."

"Dickwad?"

"Mr. Ashford to you, Gardener."

I throw myself onto the chair opposite him. The garden hasn't changed much, perhaps not as well-kept as I remember, but I prefer rougher edges to crisp manicured foliage. It gives the impression that wilderness might burst free at any moment.

There's a bottle on the green-painted ironwork table between us, and I sigh. "That bad?"

"Not great," he says. The muscle in his jaw works, and I know Heath well enough to know he'll talk when he wants and not before. He's a stubborn Alpha.

I pour myself a shot into the glass he thoughtfully provided for me. "No luck prowling the streets of Sabine for a mate?"

His eyes cut to me. "Fuck no. I don't have time for that.

"Not even sex?"

"Unfortunately, no."

Of course, he stepped up when his father died. Maybe the rumors I've heard of money issues have some merit. I'm almost afraid to ask.

"I have a family I need to take care of, Stephan." He shakes his head, then refills his drink as he brings his long legs in and leans forward. "Five sisters. Can you even fathom that? Five pretty Omegas to find proper mates for, who will look after them and not use and abuse them. I can't let Mom handle all that." He stands. "We should take this inside."

Heath picks up the bottle, and I follow him inside. The Gardener home has always had a mix of scents to it, such as beeswax and lemon and fresh flowers. What you imagine Spring to smell like. But this time, the floral scents are more overpowering than I remember, fogging my senses.

I must be too used to the blockers people wear to hide and dull their own scents in Emporia.

This is much nicer, more...evocative.

We head down the hall and into his father's meeting room, where deals were done, important business guests entertained. But I know what it is. A private gaming room. Where high stakes poker and other card games were played. The dark woods and gold and claret décor are like most gentlemen's clubs, a step back to another time.

This one's small, and the bar's well-stocked. Heath puts on some post-grunge music as I go to haunt the bar.

"This whole island is full of double standards." I pour a healthy bourbon.

"It's the same everywhere, Ashford. Don't pretend it isn't."

"But all these rules. The strict hierarchy... It's crap."

"The hierarchy is part of us. It's part of our core nature."

I glare at him and down half my drink. "It shouldn't restrict you on who you can mate with. Sure, things tend to fall into Alpha and Omega, but if a Beta falls for a Delta or an Omega or even an Alpha, then whatever. But here... Jesus."

"I don't make the rules, Stephan. Besides, if you hate it so much here, why did you come back?"

"Would you believe it if I said I missed our small talk?"

He huffs out what could be a laugh. "I'd believe it more if you said it was my liquor cabinet."

I raise my glass in a toast to that.

"It doesn't matter what I think about it. It's the way it is here. My sisters..." He stops, shakes his head.

That's the problem with this fucking microworld of Sabine. Rich and powerful and full of old money, old ways. It's the headquarters of the Council. And they make sure

Omega girls are brought up to be innocent. A whole bunch of virgins who pant for babies and the right mate as if that's their whole world. The answer to everything.

They don't have life experience. They probably don't even know what a dick is.

"You're playing into the system," I say.

He slams his glass on the bar. "Don't you think I know that? I get the double standards, the pressures on people to play the part, but my father left us broke, Stephan, and the only hope now is to play by society's rulebook. Keep my sisters sweet, pristine, and all that shit..." He shakes his head wearily. "And now Violet's not only making her debut, but the Monarch has picked her as her Luxe Omega."

"No shit, really?" Maybe I need to meet this sister...this *Violet* everyone keeps talking about. The battle-ax doesn't pick just anyone to be her Luxe. This Omega must be special.

"This can be her chance to make the perfect match. For all of us," he says.

"That's a lot of pressure to put on your sister."

He groans and rolls his eyes to the ceiling. "I know. And she knows. She's ready for the responsibility, but she doesn't like being the center of attention."

The Luxe will definitely be that. Once word gets out, Stitch is going to explode.

The door clicks and partly opens. A girl's head pops in but she gasps, surprised to see us in the room, and quickly shuts it again.

I wasn't able to get a clear look at her, but her scent wafts in, filling my nostrils with a faint clean and floral scent.

That scent. The same flowery one that haunted my memory since the boathouse.

But how…?

Heath's eyes cut to the door. "Sorry—my sister was about to barge in." Then he raises his voice. "Whose ears must be burning."

The mythical Luxe sister? Violet? Maybe that's what I smell…but a violet is an old lady flower, isn't it? Like…mothballs.

I pinch the bridge of my nose. There's no fucking way Heath's sister is my little Cinderella Omega.

"That was her?" I start to turn, not sure what I'm going to say. "Gardener—"

"My sisters are nosey."

My mouth has gone dry from the shock, and all I can think about is the beautiful dancer with the perfect manners and sharp tongue. I've been carrying her ribbon in my pocket since that night, had even visited the dancing studio she'd talked about and the boathouse where we'd met at dusk, hoping to catch another glimpse of her. But she's stayed away.

Just the thought of her being here—so close—makes my heart skip.

"Maybe we should let her in," I say. "It might be something important."

But Heath shakes his head adamantly. "If it were urgent, she wouldn't be the only one storming in here. Believe me. And besides, I'd like to keep you away from my sisters for as long as possible."

"Ouch, Gardener." I sit on one of the chairs at the gleaming black gaming table. "What's wrong with me?"

He tops up my drink, then sits. "What's right? You're Emporia elite, you drink too much, take too many drugs, fuck too many women, and make shitty movies."

"Movies that women like." I don't disagree about them being on the cheesy side, mostly rom-coms and feel-good types about finding love and being true to oneself. Soppy bullshit, really. "And stop reading social media."

"Keep away from my sisters."

"I don't want your sisters. Any of them." Then I pause. "I do owe your little sis—Rue?—an apology, though. I'll send some signed pics."

"Her favorite star isn't you, dickwad. It's Trixi Belle."

"That hack? She can't even sing."

He stares at me.

I sigh. "I'll get Rue some signed merch from her, then." Honestly, kids these days have no taste.

"Wait, why do you owe her an apology? She's *fourteen*."

I'll have to punch him if he pulls big angry brother on me, but as I eye his slowly curling fist, I say, "She followed me to bombard me with questions at the fucking picnic. I didn't know who she was, but I was...me."

"An asshole."

"Yeah." I rub the back of my neck. "So how bad are things, Heath? Do you want money?"

"For my sister?"

"No, shithead, to help with the debts your father left."

He sighs. "I can't just show up with debts magically paid."

"Why not?" I shrug. "I can afford whatever it is."

"Because you're my friend. And if and when it comes

out, my sisters will suffer. I can't even sell off land or property."

"I fucking hate this place," I grumble. "What if your sister catches the eye of one of the fat older fucks?"

Heath's jaw works hard. "I'm not letting a disgusting, abusive man touch her."

"Even if he's rich?"

He balks at that. "What do you think I'm trying to do? Prostitute her out? No, Violet deserves security. Love. Happiness. Probably more than any of us. When Dad died, Mom was a mess. Couldn't function. Vi stepped up and ran the household, kept us all together. I just..."

He stops, and I see the torment in his gaze. This has been weighing on him for some time. I may not have the close family the Gardeners have, but it's clear Heath loves his sister. He wants what's best for her and the rest of them. The stress of it all is hardening him.

"You know, if you want to keep your family out of the rumor mill, you can't go to the places these Alphas tend to haunt. But I can." He's about to protest, but I stop him. "I'll help. Listen at doors. Gather information. Make a list of the best possible mates for her."

He frowns. "I'm not asking you to do that."

"I'm offering, Gardener. And they'll talk around me, reveal themselves in a way they wouldn't during the social events. Besides, I've got nothing to do for the summer but read scripts and fuck around. Save me from more boredom by letting me help you. I'll let you know who to steer Violet away from."

"I don't know..." His gaze narrows on me. "Why are

you back on Sabine? I didn't think after what happened with CeeCee you'd ever show up here again."

The mention of Cecilia's nickname is like a punch to the gut. But I try to act unbothered.

"Co-star trouble. I'm attempting to keep my nose clean until it blows over and try not to be bored." I explain the Felicity issue. "So if you need help, I'll even come to the damn ball and mingle with the Alphas..."

His jaw tightens. Fuck, the local girls must be dropping their panties and their well-bred morals to bag him. And I'm betting he doesn't even notice. Too much in his head to see what's in front of him.

Goodlooking, stoic bastard.

We made quite the team in picking up pussy.

"You'll be busy wrangling those sisters," I say, even though I know my true motives are to get a glimpse of Violet again for myself. Maybe talk to her. Just one more time.

He stares at me a moment. "Fine. Let me know who to ban from courting my sister and who'll work best. Besides, it's not like I can stop you."

"Nope." Then I lean back in my chair and grin. "Now, let me tell you about the pussy you keep missing by not visiting me..."

PSSSST

Can you see me?

BLINK!

Here I am... Ta-da!

Let's get real, Hivemind. Ever since the Omegas from A to V were called in for a one-on-one with the Monarch, you've all been working overtime. The bees are a-buzzing with all the gossip.

At first your Queen Bee thought our blonde newcomer would bask under the light of the Monarch's touch. Then your Queen wondered about that glorious dark beauty, Bentleigh.

But no. Miss Madame Butterfly decided to go with a more... natural approach for this year's Luxe and chose...

VIOLET MAY GARDENER

Pretty, sweet, unpretentious. Worthy.

Or a fragile flower ready to be stomped out?

Let your thoughts run wild below.

...

But actually this quick note is about the first ball and the theme of this Season.

Masks are in.

A masked ball. And a Season full of secrets.

Perhaps the Monarch wants our Omegas to stand out on their own, not depending on their looks and scents.

I can't wait.

Spread that honey! See you there at the ball!

- Queen Bee

Chapter Nine

Violet

I stare down at the dress hugging my body. It used to be Mom's, but the cut...

Sharp nails gouge my stomach and throat from the inside as I swallow. "I can't wear this."

Rue sits on my bed, dressed in a rose-red gown and taking selfies like a teenage femme fatale.

"I give good face," Rue mutters, posing again.

Mom wrings her hands. "The dresses aren't new, but I thought for the first ball—"

"You have to make a splash," Rue says, weary like an ancient soul, "everyone knows that."

"Maybe you should go downstairs, Rue." I plead with my eyes. Luckily, a commotion erupts outside the room.

"Just me, Mom, and Violet at the ball, Mari," Heath's

voice thunders. "No one else. I need you and Dahlia to watch Rue."

Rue jumps up. "What? No! I need to go! I need all my potential mates to sniff me!"

Mom gasps. "Rue! You're too young for that."

But Rue's already out the door, trailing silk and lace. "We'll see about that!"

Mom picks up a dress from the ones laid out, and my heart slams hard and the guilt rises high.

"That girl, I don't know what to do with her." She doesn't look at me as she hangs one of the other gowns on a padded hanger, then zips the protective bag up. She may be able to go about the necessary steps of the day, but she's a shadow of the woman she once was when Dad was alive. It was as if his death stole a piece of her soul. "I wish they were all like you, Violet. So agreeable. So accommodating."

I swallow hard, heat rising. "They're just young, Mom. They'll grow, and learn."

"You've always been so mature for your age. I never had to worry about you." She places her hand on my cheek and looks at me with her graying blue eyes. "I hope this Season you'll find a mate to give you the love you deserve."

"Mom..."

I can see the tears swimming in her eyes, but she blinks quickly and turns around. "But first—first, we'll go to the store. Get you something prettier than my hand-me-downs—"

"No, no, it's okay. I'll wear this one. I love the idea of wearing something from your Season. It's just that this dress is...daring. I'm not sure I can pull it off."

Mom suddenly laughs. "It's what I wore when Henry and I announced our mate bond. It's perfect, trust me."

I just wish the bodice wasn't so fitted and the décolletage didn't dip quite so low.

"It's perfect, Violet, because of this." She opens a smallish box and pulls out a half mask. It's the same burnished bronze like the satin and velvet of the dress. She slips it into place. After she pins my hair in a loose knot, I look in the mirror.

A vixen who understands the world stares back. An Omega who knows what she wants. Cat-like, sly, like I know how to wrap men around my finger. I look like—

A fraud.

But the longer I look, I can see it: some makeup, heels, and I'll both blend in and be on show. Hiding under the cover of the mask. I don't even have to do a thing. The outfit with the mask does it for me.

I know the fashion for this year calls for short dresses with puffed skirts, or something asymmetrical, either at the shoulder or the hem. But everyone wears those. Of course, there are more traditional cuts, but they all have that same hemline, the same sleeves.

This dress, though... Bare shoulders, bare arms, long and touching the ground all around, clinging. When I walk, the skirt's clever pleats at the left hip allow me to move with ease. It also has a hidden slit in the pleats that ends just above the knee.

And with the mask...

"Here's a little bag you can put the mini tablet in," Mom says. "Every participant in the Season will have one so that Alphas can book a dance, ask for a date, or take you for a walk. It's so exciting, don't you think?"

All I can do is offer her a smile.

As the ruckus downstairs grows, she glances at the door. "I'd better see what's going on." She hesitates. "Are you sure about the dress—"

"Yes, trust me. I love the dress. It's perfect."

My words bring relief and joy to Mom's face.

"I'll be right back." She hurries downstairs, and when I'm alone, I give in to the shaking. Still staring at my reflection, I slide the mask off carefully until my worn and uneasy expression stares back at me, the one I hide from everyone.

This is going to be harder than I thought.

Taking a deep breath, I try to relax, but my mind drifts back to the man in the boathouse, the one with the warm smile and oak-y scent. I don't know why I'm thinking of someone I won't see again.

What I need to do is concentrate on the damn ball and getting through it without losing my sanity.

"You can do this, Violet," my reflection says. "I have confidence in you."

I'm glad someone in this room does.

The entire ballroom is a whirlwind, the amount of scent blockers painting the air with a strange void-like nothingness that feels stiff and unnatural. It presses down on me, along with the weight of tonight's lofty expectations, and I feel so exposed.

"Breathe, Vi." Iris presses a drink into my hand, and I look down.

"Is that wine?"

"You're twenty-one," she says. "You're allowed to get wasted."

Iris wears a super cool blue tartan dress she made out of an old one, and she has her combat boots on.

"I don't want to get wasted." I try to hand the drink away, but she shoves it back.

"Have a few sips for courage, and remember, you're the hottest girl here."

I take a sip to shut her up, just as Trixi Belle sings over the sound system. The tune's catchy, boppy without being too much. There's a band setting up on a dais for later, but this earlier hour is meant to be a mix and meet part of the evening.

I swallow down the wine. I don't like the taste; it's dry on the tongue, but there's a hint of oak and that makes me think of the boathouse Alpha again.

And now it's like my feverish mind's conjured his ghost because I swear I can smell him. Through all the blockers, even.

Another drink is pressed into my hand, the empty glass replaced. I drink that one, too.

"Thanks, Dahlia. I don't want to leave her," Iris says. I don't even remember Dahlia coming over. "Is Mari keeping Heath distracted?"

"Yes, and Rue's with Mom...for now," Dahlia says.

Iris cranes her neck to get a look at them across the room. "Just...keep the drinks coming. Vi's going to need it."

The conversations from other guests filter in from a

distance, and I try to stop drowning in panic. I look at the peaked ceiling, all cast in marble and draped in gold silk. The lights above us flicker, and it makes me wonder if the Monarch had her chandeliers set with real candles or if they're using some kind of artificial ones to bask the ballroom in a warm, romantic glow.

"Violet?" Iris hisses my name. "Vi, listen. Dahlia's getting you something stronger to drink. But just sip that. Don't guzzle it."

When did she learn so much about drinking?

"And where's your Season's mini tablet?" She grabs my small bag and pulls it out. "No one's reserved a dance. You need to look welcoming yet mysterious."

"Here." Dahlia's back.

I take one small sip from the fresh glass and make myself focus on the taste, the slide of the fiery liquid down my throat.

Iris says something about trying to mingle, before taking Dahlia by the arm and leading her away. They melt into the crowd.

I'm alone.

The nerves make me shake, but I force myself to get it together. I breathe, stepping back, then back until I'm concealed by a shadow, near a massive potted plant.

I almost scream as fingers touch me, feather soft, against my arm. And then I smell the earthy, slightly sweet richness of oak, and my stomach doesn't settle, exactly, but the wildness there turns from wanting to throw up to something else.

The scent's subtle, so subtle. Almost not there, and I wonder how I can smell it at all when wearing blockers is always a requirement for the Season's events. Either way, it makes me want to turn to find solace in the woodsy aroma.

"Violets."

I spin. "Excuse me?"

He's tall, broad, with dark brown hair, and the scruff of his short beard should be wrong with his wolf mask, but it isn't. It gives him a devilish, creature of the wild look.

His eyes through the mask are...hungry.

It's *him*.

"Do you know you smell faintly of a flower? I've been trying to put my finger on which one, and I finally figured it out," he says in that voice with a hint of smoke. "Violets."

I gulp in a breath. It isn't enough.

"I-I shouldn't smell like anything. My blocker—"

"Only up close." The nose of his mask whispers over my hair. "And I've got an excellent sense of smell."

His hand slides down my arm, taking hold of mine, and everything in me lights up like a flare. It blankets out everything but him.

"I *like* it," he says.

Oh my god...

"I didn't think I'd see you again," he goes on.

It takes me a while, but eventually I'm able to find my voice, as small and pathetic as it may sound. "Well, here I am."

Just then, whispers and giggles reach me.

"Look at her. She's hiding in the bushes." A group of three Omegas laugh as they stroll by arm-in-arm.

Face burning, I turn away, snatching my hand back from him. I'm coming apart.

"Calm down," he says, his tone suddenly growing in

strength and intention. I feel it down to my bones. He's using his Alpha voice on me.

I'm flooded for a moment with peace. Calm. It's an instant relief.

I glance at him.

"There. That's better," he says.

He takes my hand again, his fingers slipping mine open so he can hold it in his big, fiery hot one. It's not a fire that burns, not in the usual way. It's a fire that warms and unsettles things I didn't know existed.

The peace shatters, and my nerves jump.

"Hey, you're like ice," he says, not using the voice this time, but the memory of it envelops me. "Relax. I just wanted to ask you for a dance."

Somehow, I unstick my tongue. This is ridiculous. He's just touching me.

But we don't even know each other.

"I have my mini tablet. You can use yours to pencil one in," I reply, and curse myself for opening my mouth. That sounded so forward.

He doesn't laugh. "I don't have a...a mini tablet. But I'll get one." He looks past me, something catching his attention, and straightens. "Save a dance for me, okay? But first I have to go see the ba—the Monarch."

Shock slaps at me. "No one can do that."

"Trust me, I don't want—"

"Mr. Ashford?" The male Omega in blue appears, the one I'd seen at the interview with the Monarch. It must be who he'd seen. "The Monarch wishes to see you. Now."

That's his name? His last name at least—Ashford.

Next to me, Mr. Ashford sighs.

"She can wait," he tells the man, and I nearly choke on my next breath. No one makes the Monarch wait, not even for a second. He leans in. "I'll see you soon, Violet."

A new wave of panic washes over me full force. The world's too big, too small. And my skin's hot on my chest and face, while my hands and feet are like blocks of heavy ice.

As if sensing my distress, Iris and Dahlia join me.

"Fresh air. That's all you need," Iris says. They lead me to the courtyard door where the breeze wafts in, and I stare out, longing for the dark quiet of the huge expanse of the estate grounds. The glittery lights make it a fairy land.

I draw in huge gulps of fresh night air.

"Okay, I got you some dances." Iris scrolls through the mini tablet. "Who was that you were talking to, the big bad wolf? I said mingle, not lurk."

"Sorry."

Iris snorts. "If it was me, there's no way—"

"Iris." Dahlia's voice is both soft and hard. "Stop."

"Fine, we'll get you another glass of wine." Iris stomps off once more.

Dahlia fixes my hair. "You're going to be great. Just be you. Oh, Jenkin Bader is heading over. He asked about you at the refreshments table. Harmless from what I hear, so he'd be a good first dance."

And then she goes, too.

The panic rises tsunami high, and the guy I've never really thought about since the time he knocked my books from my arms in sophomore year heads my way.

Someone steps in front of him, a red phoenix-masked girl, and she whisks him off. I think it's Jade.

Alicia, in a dazzling white and gold dress, swoops in and gives me a withering look through the mask that covers half of her face. "I'd tell you hands off Stephan—"

"Who?"

"—since he's mine, but why bother? He's so out of your league, it's laughable." Another girl in a gown of shimmery colors like a butterfly comes to join us. "She's supposed to be the Monarch's Luxe, but look at her," Alicia tells the newcomer. "What a pathetic outfit."

"Oh, *Violet*?" She turns to Alicia with a scoff. "She's nothing to worry about."

Alicia eyes me. "You're right. She's just an ugly little weed in the Gardener family."

And with that, Alicia giggles and they move off.

The world wavers. My family is here, but to reach them I'd have to go back inside and cross the ballroom that now seems as big as an ocean and so bright I might melt and burn.

My heart hammers dangerously, and my chest is tight. Every breath is growing harder and harder to take.

I need to get away, farther from the noise and the judgmental stares. Now.

I can barely see or hear past the great thud of my heart. But knowing I can't step foot back into that crowded room, I do the only other thing I can think of at the moment.

I kick off my heels and run.

CHAPTER TEN

Stephan

I remember this fucking estate.

The four floors, the countless rooms, the attic and basement where secrets sit in trunks and boxes, none of which are mine. I spent some winters here growing up, when I was too young to understand society decorum and thought the place a maze to be explored.

Now, it's just the epitome of everything the Council stands for. And I hate it.

I follow Frederick up to the room that really should hold a throne, one so large and empty yet crammed full of invisible things.

History, honor, rules, suffocating demands.

When the golden doors open, I step in.

There's a big cream-colored leather chair, silver-edged,

curved and high-backed, in the center toward the back, situated on a black rug.

On the floor next to the chair are her discarded high heels, and an open bottle of bourbon—the fucking one I like that comes from the depths of the South—rests on a small white round side table.

There's no other furniture, just cleverly hidden lamps that bathe her starkly white hair in soft golden light. The huge picture window behind her acts like the dramatic backdrop to the evening, light that bleeds to sparkles, to black, and then the glitter of stars.

In Sophine's elegant hand is a tablet, and I'm betting she's watching the ball from her many hidden security cameras.

Was she watching me?

Must have been.

And the pretty vixen whose hand I held, the girl from the boathouse. I recognized her the moment I walked in. I could smell her, even though she had on a full blocker. I could sense the strange void tinged around the edges of her natural floral scent. For some reason, her violets slither through the blocker. At least to me.

Violet.

Heath had been hanging with his family near the refreshment table, with his mother and two other young Gardener Omegas, one of them being the youngest, Rue. Heath looked stressed beyond belief, so talking to him at that moment wasn't going to happen.

But I was drawn to Violet, the vivacious woman dressed in bronze with a sleek feline mask.

Her touch still zinged beneath my skin, the coldness

that turned hot under my hand. The way her pulse pounded in her neck, the swell of small and perfect breasts. Her smell was sweet, floral, and... Shit. I can still smell it here, as if it has branded itself inside my nostrils.

I want to get back to her. But instead, I'm here, facing down the Monarch and her Omega manservant who's hovering by her side.

Sophine doesn't look up as I approach, and I'm getting more annoyed by the second. Why summon me up here just to have me wait around? I should be downstairs with—

"You've always been impatient, Stephan," she says, her crystal-blue eyes lifting finally. "Too quick to jump without thinking about the consequences."

Knowing that she's talking about CeeCee, about how I fled Sabine to be with her, despite the Monarch's rules, I grind my teeth.

"You really *are* a battle-ax, aren't you?"

"I've never been called that before," she says. The nickname doesn't seem to faze her at all, and that only angers me more.

I'll never fucking forget what she did. And I'll *never* forgive her.

"Stephan," she begins, "why are you on my island again?"

Her island. I huff at that.

"I'm here for entertainment, Monarch, nothing more."

"How's Penrith?"

"Ask her yourself."

"Watch your tongue, Stephan. I'm your—"

"Nothing. Absolutely nothing. That's what you are."

"What the blazes are you upset about now? You've

made money, whored yourself out to the world, and now you're mad because I asked about Penrith? You came back for the summer, crashed this Season's second event, and *without* an invitation, I might add... And you're dressed like you're participating in the Season. Like you're looking for a mate. Have you finally come to your senses?"

I scoff. "I'm not looking for a mate."

Sophine hands her glass to her Omega, slides a finger across the tablet's screen, and then she starts to type on the virtual keyboard at a feverish pace.

"Oh, but you are. As of now. I've added you to the list of eligible Alphas for this Season."

She's kidding. She's got to be kidding.

As if reading my mind, she flips the screen so that I can see it. And there's my stage name right at the top of the list —Asher St. James.

Fuck.

A growl rumbles low in my throat. "I'm not on the market. Never will be."

She stands to her full imposing height, her eyes narrowed. "This isn't Emporia. You can't play a role here. So now, I expect you to take part, be a gentleman, court one of the many pretty Omegas, maybe find a mate."

"Screw you. I had a mate."

"Language!" Sophine snaps. "You need a more *fitting* mate."

Rage coils in my gut.

More fitting? I *loved* CeeCee. Even if she wasn't an Omega, she was everything to me.

"You bi—"

But her stare stops me in my tracks, spiked with a silent

threat. As much as I want to curse her, I know—from experience—it will only hurt me way more than help. She holds too much power as the Council leader, the Monarch, or whatever.

Frederick steps forward and presses a mini tablet in a sleek leather case into my hand.

I close my fingers around it, my muscles stiff.

That's when a slow, satisfied smile lifts her lips. "Welcome to the Season, Stephan."

Girls swamp me when I get back into the ballroom. One squeals, fangirling, and a blonde dressed like a bird starts pushing them all out of the way, grabbing for my mini pad.

"A dance for me, Mr. St. James?" she asks.

"Me first!" another Omega barks.

"Over my dead body."

This is worse than I thought. I'm fairly used to the attention of fans in Emporia, but even those women know I'm not looking for anything serious. Thanks to Sophine, I now have a big target painted on my chest to every mate-hungry Omega.

"This way, asshole." Heath has my arm and drags me into the men's room, an outdated lounge area thick with cigar smoke and full of older mated men and bachelors.

"Thanks, man." I slap him on the back. "I owe you one."

"You just couldn't help yourself, could you? Had to steal all the attention for yourself," he says, and I can't tell if he's joking or not from his tone.

"The battle-ax fed me to the lions."

"The Monarch?" he asks. "What happened?"

"She added me as one of the Season's available bachelors."

"Shit."

I rub a hand over my face. "Yeah."

Gaze dancing across the smoke-filled room, he leans close and whispers, "So I'm guessing you haven't had the chance to scope out the competition then?"

"Not the competition—I'm not really on the market, no matter what Sophine says. But no, I haven't had much of a chance. I'll find out more. We can go to one of the bars, see who's there." At his raised brow, I add, "Our part of town. Like a club. Then when you go, I can see what's said."

"Okay, okay."

The sister I'd seen Heath talking to earlier walks through the door and comes bouncing up to us. Her hair's light, almost golden, and cropped short at the shoulders. Freckles kiss her cheeks and across her nose, and I can't help but think about how she would glow on screen.

"You shouldn't be in here," Heath says to her.

"I don't care." She shrugs and then looks at me. "Who's your wolfy friend, Heath? He looks familiar... Oh, right! You're the one who tried to crush Rue. Can't be done. She said you thought you were famous or something, but... Got it—you're Asher St. James from *Knot a Chance*. I loved that movie."

"His name is Stephan. The other's his screen name," Heath says.

She ignores him. "But how do you know the stone formally known as Heath?"

"This is Marigold, the third-eldest sister at eighteen." Heath gestures to the girl.

"Hey," I say.

"Call me Mari."

"Better yet, don't call her at all." Heath glares.

"Are all your sisters here?" I ask.

"Yes, I lost that battle. Mom's here, too. It's a nightmare," he says as Mari elbows him. "Now, Iris is..." Heath frowns. "Actually, I don't know where Iris is. She and Dahlia were helping calm Violet down. I think she's a little overwhelmed. She's—"

"Prone to panic attacks?"

"No." Heath blinks, as if he's wondering how I came to that conclusion. "She just isn't used to the spotlight, that's all. Unlike you."

Now I'm really intrigued by Miss Violet Gardener. When I'd seen her before, she was on the verge of a full-blown breakdown. It's probably why she was hiding herself behind a plant. Yet, she's managed to keep her anxiety hidden from her own brother? From the rest of her family?

Damn. She must be a better actor than I thought. Award-worthy.

My next question is why?

What other secrets is she holding?

I want to find out.

Looks like it's time for me to find her and collect that dance I was promised.

CHAPTER ELEVEN

Violet

I run past the maze and rose garden, through the small smattering of trees, and then slow, walking by the clipped entrance to an old maze, one that's tall and thick.

Trying to shut off my mounting thoughts, I focus on making the moon and stars my only guide. The glow behind me of the house is in the near distance. The noise and the music is mostly now only background noise, and the fresh air loosens the tightness of my chest and lets me breathe.

Somewhere a frog croaks and crickets sing.

It's getting cooler now.

The grass is soft and springy under my feet, slightly damp. My shoes are... I don't even remember where they landed when I kicked them off.

I stop and carefully remove the mask, then continue, turning a corner as I find a little-used path.

Something shimmers like dancing silver, and I realize I've reached a small lake. I focus on calm to quiet down the little rivulets of panic that come at me in waves. There's a gazebo so I go to it, climbing the short steps. The path might not be used much, but this structure is kept painted and clean, and there's even a lamp on the table in the middle as if it was meant to be used by guests.

I perch on one of the built-in benches and carefully set the mask down to close my eyes a moment.

The lap of the water soothes. And the songs of the night are magic.

I could stay here forever.

I can't, though. I'm going to have to go back in eventually.

It's just...those girls. The stares. The pressure.

My thoughts waver as my senses spark.

The scent of oak drifts on the lightest of night breezes, making me start to buzz.

My breath catches fast in my throat, but this time it isn't panic. It's everything but.

Jumping to my feet, I turn—and there he is. The man from the boathouse, Mr. Ashford, looking too good in that wolf mask and scruff. The suit's made for him. It's way more stylish than anyone else's and black in this light. But it isn't pure black. I remember seeing the blue and almost purple threads that run through the material when he stood with me, holding my hand, using his Alpha voice on me so softly that the command still reverberates in me somewhere.

"I'm sorry." I reach for my mask. "I'll go—"

"You still owe me a dance, Violet."

My name on his lips shocks me, and I don't move as he approaches.

He walks with intent, and he commands my attention, all without saying anything else.

I know if we were in a crowded room, he'd draw all the eyes. He probably did earlier, but I was too on the verge of a full-blown meltdown to notice.

In the dark, the only light is the silver moon reflected on the water and the stars above, and it somehow feels more powerful than if we were somewhere brightly lit. I want to breathe in his oak and rich earthy scent, the sweeter undertones, see what he is beneath that expensive blocker.

He's so familiar. Beyond meeting him at the boathouse. Maybe I've seen him in town and just don't remember.

But a man like him a girl can't easily forget. So where is this hint of recognition coming from?

I rise slowly as he stops in front of me.

He smiles, that million-dollar smile, but it's what's beneath the surface that interests me. It whispers sensual thoughts in my head, like what it would be like if he did more than hold my hand.

If he traced a path along my spine, my throat, over my lips...

Now my chest tightens for an entirely different reason as every pulse point throbs out a rapid beat.

"You know my name?" It comes out breathless, and I cringe, stepping back, bumping into the bench.

Of course he knows my name. I'm the supposed Luxe

after all, the object of much derision from the other girls, so he must have heard someone—

Maybe those catty girls at the ball—

"Your brother," he answers.

For a moment excitement fills me. This is solid ground, something that could connect us. If Heath approves... If Heath sent him my way... "You know Heath?"

"Just like a princess," he mutters. "Pretending not to know."

I frown. There are lots of rich, pampered girls here, girls who could fit that label. But me? "I'm not spoiled."

He comes closer, takes my mask and runs a finger along its cheeks. "Not that kind of princess. You're the untouched type, the high tower sort. You're...the good princess who would never allow butter to melt near her mouth." He pauses. Turning the mask over to trace the underside, where it sat against my face, and I shiver. "But if you really don't know, I went to college with Heath."

"He never brought his college friends home. I think we went to visit him once. Maybe you were there?" I'm babbling. "What's your name? So that it's fair."

He studies me for a long moment, head tilted to the side like he can't believe I don't know him. But I don't. Should I?

"Are you sure you don't know who I am?" he asks.

"How can I when you haven't told me?"

"Hmm."

I swallow. "Somone said Ashford?"

His mouth turns up. "Feeling coy?"

"No, I..."

"Have you looked at your mini tablet lately?"

I pause. "No. Why?"

Slowly, he takes off his mask.

Like before at the boathouse, the vague familiarity is there, but I don't know anyone with a scruffy beard, especially here on Sabine. No one would dare sport one when taking part in the Season.

He raises a brow, and his dark eyes, a dark gold-brown in the lamp light, almost twinkle.

Oh god, he's good-looking. It takes my breath away.

He frowns. "Stop pretending. You recognize me. Your sisters did."

"Dahlia, too?"

"Who?"

"My sister, Dahlia. She's too focused on her studies to be interested in gossip or anything to do with the Season. So if she knew you..."

"Forget her."

"She's my sister." I want to laugh; delight bubbles in me. The more frustrated he acts, the more relaxed I get. "I couldn't do that if I tried."

"Wow, you're incorruptible. I can see now why the Monarch picked you. But I still..."

"I don't even know what that means."

"It means," he says, sighing heavily as he sets our masks down, "I think you're more of a princess than a Luxe. Innocent and unscarred."

This time I laugh. I can't help it.

"But if you truly don't know," he continues, "I'm a movie star. An actor. Played in movies like *Knot a Chance* and *Summer Heat*."

"Are those porn films?"

He steps back, eyes wide in shock, and I instantly regret my words.

Stupid, Vi. Stupid! Just insult the man. Perfect way to get a mate.

Then, to my complete surprise, he laughs, shoulders bouncing and all.

My cheeks burn.

"You know, now that I think about it, they could sound like those kinds of movies. But no. They're not. Just regular run-of-the-mill romantic comedies. Name's Asher St. James."

"So not Ashford?" I ask.

"Ashford is my real name. Stephan Ashford. Asher is my stage name," he says.

He's the famous Alpha everyone's been talking about.

God, I'm an idiot. How do I save this conversation?

"I'm sorry. I-I haven't really had time to go to the movies in a while."

"Not on Stitch at all, either?"

"No..."

"See what I mean?" He smiles. "Princess."

I move away and sit, but he comes and sits next to me, our thighs touching. It's warm, nice, unsettling in a way I could crave.

"I'm not into Stitching," I say, "unless it's with a needle and thread."

"You're only making my case for me here."

Damn, I guess I am. "So, you're Heath's friend? Nice to know he's got one."

He laughs. "I have stories."

"Does he have stories about you?"

"Your brother's turned into a gentleman. He'd never share."

The tease in his voice is like being fed something delicious.

"And you?" I ask. "Are you an actor *and* a gentleman?"

"Your eyes are a pretty hazel, green, brown, and is that gold? I bet they're spectacular in the light." My heart squeezes and my stomach flips. He comes closer, his mouth so close. "And to answer your question, I'm definitely not a gentleman."

For the first time in my life, I might faint, and it's not from a panic attack. I'm not wracked with anxiety. I'm... excited, and—

"You still owe me a dance, Violet."

"I-I don't dance."

"The princess lies?" He fakes surprise. "I know you do. Don't forget I saw you all sweaty after you raced down an alley from a dance studio. I've seen you in your workout clothes."

"I don't know what you're talking about," I say but smile. "I've never met you before tonight."

"Fall from your princess perch already?" Amusement dances in his eyes. "I get it. It wouldn't have been proper for us to be together like that, alone. At night. Kind of like we are now."

Panic suddenly grips me.

He's absolutely right. We are alone, in the dark. An Omega and Alpha participating in the Season without a chaperone. People will talk. My chances at finding a mate could be ruined.

What was I thinking!

I jump to my feet, glancing around wildly for any passersby. My stomach somersaults. I have to leave. I have to go, right now, before someone sees us.

"Wait." His hand snatches mine to stop me. His touch burns in, imprinting itself on me. "I didn't say that to scare you."

"It's true, though. We shouldn't be here. Together like this."

Even though my heart is pounding, his grip on me is soft, no pressure, the kind of thing I can fall into. It grounds me in place.

"I don't want you to go," he says, voice lowering. "Not yet."

I know he's just being nice, but still... The slight plead to his words makes tingles race along my spine.

"Can I at least have that dance, Princess?" He pulls out a mini pad.

The light hits his face, and I peek at him. So handsome, I could swoon. And his eyes are a rich brown.

My purse shakes and pings. I pull out my own tablet, and there's his name on my dance roster.

Stephan Ashford.

I glance at him again. "Really?"

"Really."

His handwriting, even digitized, is strong.

"I can change it to my stage name, if you like."

"I don't think anyone else sees the mini pads." I bite my lip. "You don't have to be kind to me because of Heath."

"Actually, I prefer to give Heath a hard time over anything else." He catches my chin again and brings me to him. My breath is shallow, uneven, and my pulse pounds hard. "If he knew I was here right now, talking to you, he'd kill me."

"What? Why?"

"He already warned me to stay away from you."

He did?

Stephan brings me right in, and I know he's going to kiss me. "Don't worry. He doesn't have to know."

His lips touch mine.

Everything in me explodes like fireworks. I'm pure cascading color and light. His lips are warm and soft, but he doesn't lift them from mine. He shifts, applies a little pressure, and then his tongue is in my mouth.

Everything implodes to that. He's sweetness and something sharp, a slight dizzying burn I want more of. There're all kinds of whispered promises that don't quite form, and I chase them like fireflies. I'm flying and...and it's over.

A barely-there kiss but momentous. For me, it's transformative, and I want more but he's already up, away from me. I try to speak, but I can't. I'm changed. I'm staring. I'm still looking at him as he holds out his hand. "Dance with me, Princess?"

I should say no. I should just go into the ballroom alone and forget this.

But I find myself putting my hand in his, and I nod.

Chapter Twelve

Stephan

Dancing with her is harmless.

And if it shuts those bullying girls up, all the better. I'm not invested; I don't really care, but she's my friend's sister, and if people see her with me, she'll land a decent enough match.

Fame's good for some things.

I fix her mask in place. It's intimate. And that kiss? Nothing at all, a little boost to a girl who's quite clearly never been kissed.

It doesn't matter that she tasted so sweet, a fresh taste that held the hint of wine. Like a thread of wicked teased from the pure.

Of course, there's no way her brother can know I kissed her. He wouldn't get it, how she needed it, like a dose of courage.

"People are going to notice we were gone," Violet says. I had scooped up her shoes earlier, so as I lead her down the steps of the gazebo, I bend and pick them up from where I dropped them and hand them to her.

She releases me and slides them back on.

"Mom, maybe Heath. Definitely Iris, if she's still here." She looks at me through her mask. Worry swims in her hazel eyes. "They're going to kill me. I shouldn't have run—"

"Hey." I put my hand on hers and tuck it around my arm. Her touch makes my skin heat. Her violet scent threads through me. The fact that I can still smell her past her blockers—who the fuck knows what that means? I've always had a good nose, but I'm not sure if it's that good. Maybe just with her.

"What? It's true," she says.

"Only if you let it." I lead her down the path and back toward the mansion. "We must have just had the same idea to come out to the gazebo at the same time."

There's a pause. "Right. It'd be silly to think you came out to check on me."

"I actually did. But that's not the lie we're going to tell." I laugh. "The 'chaperone' rule is stupid, if you ask me. We're adults. We shouldn't need a babysitter to talk."

"It's so Omegas aren't taken advantage of."

"Is it?" She's so innocent, taught well to take on her Omega role in a pack. "Don't you get sick of how rigid life is here on Sabine?"

"It's the only life I know." She shrugs. "But it doesn't matter if I like the rigidity or not. It's—it's how things are done."

"Like getting mated, popping out a whole litter of pups?"

"If that's what someone wants, then they should have it."

She's not saying the truth, not entirely, but I don't push. Violet's life isn't my problem. I'm just here for the summer and then I go back to my career. So I leave it be.

"You're with one of the best actors in Emporia, so trust me. I'll be able to get you back to the ball without anyone questioning your...integrity."

"I trust you."

She shouldn't, I know that. But then again, I have zero intentions on my friend's sister, pretty and honest and unexpected as she is.

No one saw us, no one but her sister, who'd been by the doors, eyeing the stage and musicians setting up their chairs and music stands. Dark-haired, quiet, blending in, she seemed to be in her own little world, but when she saw us, a smile bloomed for Violet and a slight frown for me.

Violet walks over to her. "Dahlia, did anyone—"

"No." Dahlia's gaze hits me with a sharp look.

The girl looks young. Maybe as young as Rue.

"Is everything okay?" she asks.

Violet glances at me. "Yes—of course it is. I—"

"Your sister was just feeling a bit too warm inside and needed fresh air," I lie with ease and pull out her delicate purple ribbon from my pocket. "I saw that she'd dropped this and went to return it to her."

Violet stares at it.

Dahlia eyes me suspiciously. "Then why is it still in your pocket?"

Ah shit. She's smarter than I thought.

"Because we knew we had to come back inside to avoid senseless rumors." I take Violet's hand, place the ribbon into her palm, and curl her fingers closed over it.

"Where did you..." But then she realizes Dahlia is still watching us intently and clears her throat. "Right. Thank you, Mr—?"

"Ashford," I reply. "Stephan Ashford."

"Violet Gardener." She dips her head in a proper introduction.

Dahlia's gaze passes over us, back and forth, like she doesn't quite buy our story, but luckily she doesn't press.

The three of us step further into the ballroom, but once I'm in the open room, a flock of Omegas rush over to me, surrounding me and shoving Violet and Dahlia out of the way. Their blockers are almost as suffocating as if they wore their natural scents.

"Asher! Asher! A dance for me?" an Omega with a peacock feathered mask and green dress asks.

She's pushed back by another one, this one wearing black. "Me first!"

My mini pad is buzzing nonstop in my pocket, but I don't dare look at it. Instead, I'm craning my neck over the swarm to find where Violet is. I spot her and Dahlia by the stage, where the musicians are taking their seats and readying their instruments. The purple ribbon is tied around her wrist.

This is Sophine's fault. She thinks she's playing chess with me, but I've never been known to play by the rules.

I start to push my way through the crowd. "I'm sorry, ladies. I've already been promised for the evening to the Luxe. I'm taking up every space on her dance list. Maybe next time."

It takes some work, but I'm able to make it out the other side in one piece. Luckily, the hungry Omegas have taken me at my word and don't pursue me as I cross the room and walk up to Violet again.

Just as the music swells—a slow, romantic song—I hold out my hand. "Are you ready for our dance?"

She pauses, and for a moment, I think she may turn me down. But then she slides her hand in mine.

I take her in my arms, one hand on her waist and the other holding out her hand. Stiffly, she lets me glide her farther onto the dance floor, where other couples have begun to circle and sway to the melody.

"Relax," I say against her ear, and then breathe in the lingering ghost of violets. "I won't step on your feet or anything."

She laughs a little but avoids meeting my eyes. We may be following all of the Season's stupid rules with how we're holding each other and moving, but our bodies are still close, her chest pressed against mine and cleavage on full display.

She had been so much more relaxed when we were alone in the gazebo and in the boathouse, but now with everyone watching, she's as rigid as a board.

"Do you think Heath would have a fit if I stop by for a visit soon?" I ask.

"Why would he?" she says.

"He's always kept his family life more...private."

Her gaze flicks up to mine. "I'm sure he'd like to see you. You are his friend, after all."

"To be frank, I'm already at my limit with him," I say and touch the ribbon on her wrist. "What I'd really like is to stop in to see you again."

Her full attention is on me now. Even as I twirl her and bring her back in, she stares at me. "You don't have to pretend you want to. It's okay."

"I want to."

Do I? I want to say *no, not really*, but the longer the song goes on, the calmer she gets until her dancing is more fluid, languid, and her body is in perfect harmony with mine and the music. Her eyes are closed and she's humming along, almost forgetting that I'm even here. Serene.

This is the true Violet. Just a taste of her. The one that intrigues me and I wouldn't mind learning more about.

So maybe I will pop by the Gardener household tomorrow, see her again after tonight. Just for the hell of it.

And pissing off her big bad older brother? Well, that's just a bonus.

My Hivemind, were you at the first masked ball?

Did you witness it all?

From A to V the Omegas came out in a variety of outfits.
Some from the runways and red carpets of Emporia.

But one stood out—our Luxe, Miss Violet Gardener. She took
a risk last night by wearing something vintage, and while
some may have ridiculed her, her borrowed bronze ensemble
was absolutely stunning on her.

She's cat-sleek, shapely, and though her dress might have been
decades out, the daring neckline and slit in the gown did their
jobs and snagged herself the dish of the eve.

ASHER ST. JAMES

But will this budding romance turn into a nothingburger?

Or the match of the Season and a mating ceremony?

Time will tick, tock, and tell.

The tale's starting to twist.

- Queen Bee

Chapter Thirteen

Violet

I hold up another dress, and Iris snatches it away.

"This is nothing but subjugation." She throws it in a pile. "Wear the jeans, heels, and the pretty flowing top. It's a good compromise."

"I can't. Mom doesn't want me in jeans—"

"The day after the ball should be casual, to show you're not a painted wonder." Then Iris pulls a face and sticks a finger in her mouth, mimicking gagging. "A new dress every day is ridiculous."

Last night, Stephan invaded my dreams, his scent and touch, his kiss... I didn't want to wake.

"We can go to a seamstress," I say. "Or I'll just repeat wear. It's fine."

"Nope. You're the Luxe. They'll crucify you for wearing something twice."

"But you just told me to wear jeans. They'll crucify me for that, too."

"Less likely, but never mind. I'll handle it." She pulls out more clothes. "We'll repurpose. I can make you new outfits, from casual to dressy. Mom has gowns I can rework, too."

"If she lets you—"

"She will." Iris pulls out a simple loose dress, throws me a pair of black leggings and a black thin cardigan. "Wear these with these shoes." She hands me a pair of slightly heeled black sandals before pointing to my bathroom. "Go. Put it on."

Iris knows more about fashion than I do, so I listen and head to change. When I'm done, I stare in the mirror. With the cardigan, the top has shape and the heels and leggings give it an edge. It's like a new outfit.

I open the door. "What do you think?"

"Fab," Iris says. Then she gathers the mound of clothes.

"For real?" I say. "And are you sure you can redo all those clothes? It's a lot."

"I'm the best with needle and thread in this house. Just call me your fairy god-sister. But I'm also expecting my bathroom cleaned for a month."

I gasp. "A *month*?"

"Hey, we had to let a lot of help go. And I refuse to scrub toilets." Iris cackles out a laugh. "So, do you want new clothes or not?"

I sigh. "Fine, deal."

"Great." With a wide grin, she pushes out of my room just as Rue bounds in, her phone held high.

"O.M.G., Vi! You're famous. Are you going to mate with him? I asked him that, but he was mean to me."

My head spins. "Stephan?"

"Yeah." She rolls her eyes and flops on my bed, crossing her legs as she starts to scroll. "But he probably thought I was a fan. Mom said Heath's received a flurry of invites from Alphas wanting to take you out on a date!"

More Alphas?

I should be thrilled. This is what I wanted, after all, to have my pick for my mate. But this feels like it is much too soon.

And Stephan...

Spots of color burst in front of my eyes, and I sit, limbs suddenly too heavy and too weak to support me. My chest tightens.

"Has anyone come to visit today?" I ask, voice small.

"Not yet!" Rue almost squeals. "But soon, you're going to have men kick down our door just to see you. How exciting!"

I can't breathe; my throat's closing.

Calm down.

Think oak.

Rich, earthy, slightly sweet.

Yes...

The stress eases a little, and I breathe in.

"QB posted about you and Asher. All of Stitch won't stop talking about you two. Want to see?" Rue thrusts the phone to my face.

I lean back a little to read the small print under the Queen Bee's symbol of a bee with a crown. "Oh, God."

And it's double oh god when I see it. "She called my dress vintage…"

"That's just the QB keeping it real. The dress was retro, but you sizzled! Asher couldn't take his eyes off you. Did you notice?"

"I-I didn't." And that spotlight's hot, even in my room. "But his name's really Stephan."

"I like Asher better. More… flashy. But Trixi is my all-time favorite star. I wish the Monarch would let pop concerts play here, or Mom would let me go to the mainland. She sells out every show, but maybe Asher can get me tickets. When you mate him…"

Rue keeps rattling on, but I tune her out.

A line of Alphas interested in me, wanting to take me out? I shudder.

But it's the only way I'm going to be able to find someone nice, someone with money who can help boost the family. Getting mated during my first Season would be the best-case scenario—most girls take three. It would mean clearer, better paths for my sisters, too.

I have to think about them first.

I can't be too picky.

Rue's stopped talking, and she poses and takes a selfie.

"Are you coming for the walk?" I ask.

Nodding, Rue jumps up. "You bet. Being seen after the ball's *sooo* important. Especially for the Luxe."

"This is…" *Horrible.* "A lot."

"No, it isn't. You've just got to play it cool. Not seem desperate. Don't jump at the first date invitation you get. Maybe wait until the next event. Oh, and you can't be all over Asher—"

"Stephan."

"—there. Mix it up, mingle. And then you can start rejecting and accepting. And I can help! It's gonna be fun. Come on, Vi! We need to go." Rue stops, draws a breath, and then plunges back in. "We'll bring Mari, she's a natural at drawing attention while seeming not to be doing that. You're perfect at making everyone at ease. And I'll do the talking. It's the perfect team. Let's go!"

It's a nice day, the perfect amount of warmth and breeze. Mari wants to go to the lake and draw. Rue wants to window shop, so we do both.

Mid-morning is spent in and out of shops, from the latest teen designer shop full of rip-offs, to an old-school arcade hall we have to drag Rue out of.

But what we don't do is join the town square crowd that's gathered to watch an oncoming parade. The buildings are old and beautiful, with residences above them and bars, restaurants, and exclusive shops on the ground level. We could have blended in if we wanted. Instead, we head out to the parks.

Mari takes us to an empty section of beach that's cool and shaded and partly hidden under the boardwalk.

As we settle, we eat lunch—some sandwiches Rue made—and sink our toes into the wet sand. She doesn't stop her bouncy conversation, even when Mari starts to draw in her sketchbook. Finally, Rue's so engrossed in some show she's watching on her phone that she stops talking.

I look over at Mari. There really isn't anyone here. It

isn't a spot to be admired and seen in, and I wish the whole Season was a metaphor for this spot. But it's not. The Season is the town square parade on steroids.

"Hey, I'm going to stretch my legs, go up to the boardwalk."

"Go. I'll join you in a bit. I want to get this seagull." She nods at the bird that's just sitting in the sand, feet tucked in and eyes closed.

I like the darker quiet of the ocean and the worn wood of the boardwalk, but my mind is on one thing and I see it in the distance.

The boathouse.

It's stupid to think Stephan would be there again, at this exact moment. But the possibility of seeing him again has me drifting toward it.

Someone's there, and my heart starts to go wild.

Oak is redolent on the breeze.

It's him.

I don't think; I just walk towards him. "Stephan?"

He turns, and my knees nearly buckle. The scruff's still there, and he looks so good. Handsome in this light. Better than the pictures I looked at last night when I'd searched him on my phone. He hadn't been lying about his filmography. Or about his reputation as a bit of a wild card in Emporia. But those things made him feel more like a dream. Here, he looks real. Tangible.

I smile, but he doesn't return it. He looks up and down the boardwalk promenade and then grabs me, hauling me into the shadows of the boathouse.

"What are you doing!" I hiss. My head spins. All I can smell is him, and his heat becomes a part of me.

"Shhh!"

He's close, way too close, and everything throbs in time with my heart.

"We're everywhere on social media." I breathe the words. "If we're seen in here alone—"

"I know." His gaze drops to my hair ribbon still wrapped around my wrist since last night, and a small smile lifts his lips. "I wasn't supposed to be part of the Season, but the fucking Monarch wants to torture me."

I swallow. I want to touch him. "You could leave."

"I can't."

"Why not?"

"It's complicated. I'm here for the summer and apparently now on the fucking market."

"It can't be that bad. You could find a mate..."

He laughs softly and misery streaks through me. "Not my style. I like my independence."

My lungs twist. "Oh..."

Stephan captures my chin with his fingers as he tips my face to his. "You sound disappointed, Princess."

Oh god, I start melting, and thinking is beyond difficult.

"I'm not," I say, trying to seem aloof. I shake off his hold on my face. "I have a line of Alphas interested in me now. All because of the ball."

His eyebrows rise. "Oh really?"

"You said it yourself, you're famous, and that elevates me," I say. "Because of our dance, I now have my pick of all of Sabine."

I'm exaggerating, but his comment about not wanting a mate wounded me and I'm not sure why. Maybe because all these secret touches and that kiss... It means it meant nothing.

"The problem for you is that the girls will hate me and want you more. You won't be able to escape the swarms of Omegas. Not to mention that if the Monarch has her way, which she almost always does, you'll be mated by the end of the summer, whether you like it or not."

His expression falls. He knows I'm right.

Silence stretches between us, and I debate about leaving. I've already been gone too long—Mari and Rue will realize I'm not on the boardwalk anymore and come looking.

"We could help each other," he says suddenly. "Team up in a way."

I look at him. "Team up? How?"

"I don't want a mate—that's obvious—and the only way for it to stay that way is for me to pretend to pursue you. Like you are the only one I have eyes for. I'll be smitten. Lovestruck. And if my heart is set on you, the other Omegas will step off."

"An act..."

He nods. "It'll make you desirable to every one of Sabine's Alphas. Even the most untouchable ones," he says.

"There's no way that's going to work," I reply.

"Men always want what they can't have. And when there's another powerful Alpha interested, it sparks competition. Believe me." There's a mischievous gleam in his eye. "Then at the end of the Season, you and I part ways —me heartbroken, blissfully single, and ready to return to Emporia, and you in the arms of your perfect mate. I get to trick the Monarch into thinking she's won, and we both get exactly what we want. It's perfect."

I frown. "It sounds too risky."

He searches my face. My heart flips and spins. "You need buzz. The title of Luxe can only do so much, so we create drama. Bend the rumors in our favor. We give Stitchers like the Queen Bee what they want."

"You're confident this will work?"

"Acting to be in love? Easy. It's sort of my specialty."

It sure is. And I had almost fallen for his charms, but it's clear now Stephan Ashford and Asher St. James are just two sides of the same coin.

Anger stirs.

How many other girls has he led on?

I'm an idiot.

But his proposal has some merit. His acting skills fooled me into thinking he was interested in me, so I have no doubt he could convince others.

Stephan steps closer to me, his earthy oak scent engulfing me and making my head whirl. "So, Princess. What do you say? Do we have a deal?"

This could lift me, help me pick the best Alpha for me and my family. And then, at the end of the Season, I'll never have to see him and his stupid handsome face ever again. I'll be happy, mated, and I'll make sure to never watch an Asher St. James movie for as long as I live.

"Deal," I say.

Chapter Fourteen

Stephan

I wanted to kiss her.

Really kiss her. Not like that small, pathetic peck I gave her at the ball.

But that's rule number one through fucking thousand: Do not kiss my friend's little sister.

She's not my type, anyway. She wants this whole thing—the mate, the pack, children.

And now, with our arrangement, it'll complicate things. So if it's not part of the show, I have to keep my hands to myself.

Even if touching her is becoming an obsession.

But despite the itch to grab her and taste her lips again, I let her walk away and return back to her sisters after promising I'd be seeing her soon.

Then last night, my dreams were plagued by her. And not innocent by any means.

She's naked, hovering over me, her sweet, perfect pussy so close to lowering onto my painfully hard cock. Even in my dreams, I want to rut, to knot, and claim my princess in every way possible.

I woke up panting, sweating, and cock stiffer than steel. Heart thrumming hard and fast like it's speeding, and the ache there, too, my balls high, my body burning.

The dreams sucker-punched me out of nowhere, but no matter how many times I tossed and turned or scolded myself to stop thinking about her, the moment I closed my eyes again, there Violet was, begging for me to fuck her senseless.

It had felt so real.

At four a.m., I gave up fighting and wrapped my hand around my hot, hard dick. Starting to stroke myself, I envisioned it was her hand around me, soft, knowing just how to squeeze, where to rub, right under the head. And then it was in her mouth, that hot mouth with the soft tongue, licking and teasing.

The things I imagined her doing... It had me coming almost instantly. I jerked into my hand, calling her name and letting the knotting swell. The exquisite pleasure of that act filled me, and I knotted and came, hard and long and wild.

It was a sea of release, and I rode it, all the waves, until I was left breathless and more confused than ever.

Today, those dreams haunt me. Even when meeting Pen for drinks and lunch at her place. I'm trying to clear my head while I'm dodging questions about the damn ball, but the dreams keep coming back.

Me. Violet. Naked. Exploring every inch of each other…

"What are you planning, Stephan?" Pen's frowning at me from across the table and the vast lunch spread she's set up for us.

Shaking my head to cleanse it of its dirty thoughts, I clear my throat. "Not a thing. Unless you mean plotting the battle-ax's demise."

Pen clucks her tongue. "There's been a lot of talk about you lately. You and that Gardener girl." Her dark eyes narrow on me. "Be serious. What are you scheming? She's pretty. Well-bred. Good family…"

"The Luxe," I finish for her.

"You do deserve the best, Stephan. And true happiness. Not matter who that's with," she says, and I know she's talking about CeeCee.

Shit. I don't want to lie to Pen. "I'm thinking of courting her."

Doesn't stop me though.

Instead of being pleased, Penrith's frown gets deeper. "Don't mess with her if you don't mean it. I won't be having that. You can get your thrills with plenty of others, but that girl? She's a forever mate sort."

I need to get the fuck out of Dodge. "Didn't you *want* me to date the girl? When I first got here, you were all about it."

"Yes, but I *know* you."

What the fuck is that supposed to mean? "I'm not saying I'm gonna mark the girl tomorrow or anything, but I like her. We danced at the ball, and you were right. She's a good one."

"You're planning on giving up your career in Emporia for a girl on Sabine?"

"Again, Pen, you're thinking too far ahead. I'm not ruling anything out with Violet is what I'm saying. We'll see where it goes." I swoop down and kiss her cheek. "I've got somewhere to be. Catch you later."

As I leave, my phone rings. Heath. I pick it up.

"What the fuck, dude?" he snaps from the other end.

"That's your greeting?" I say. "And you're single? It's a wonder of the world."

He doesn't laugh. "Real funny. Get here. Now." He hangs up.

So much for friendship.

What crawled up his ass today? Did Violet tell him about our arrangement? Hopefully not, because the less people know of it, the better. Bringing her brother into it will just mess things up. Especially since he doesn't want me near her as it is.

But when I arrive at the Gardener townhouse, I barely have time to knock when the door swings open.

Heath stands there, glaring at me, with the skinny Rue at his side, wearing an identical expression. Only hers sparks with humor and good will. Heath...he looks like he wants to turn my entrails into jewelry or something.

"Have you seen?" Rue holds out that bedazzled phone. "You and Vi are famous. Someone is saying they saw Vi leaving a boathouse by the boardwalk yesterday and you soon after. Is that true? Everyone's talking, not just the QB.

Every. One. Even on the mainland. Stitch has blown apart at the seams."

Ah, shit.

The irate call from Heath makes sense now. This didn't come from Violet. It's worse. It came from the socials.

"Get it?" She pauses, looks from me to her brother. "Seams? Stitches?"

"Go to your room, Rue," Heath says, not lifting his gaze from me.

"Heath!" She rolls her eyes as her brother spins on his heel and stalks off toward his father's office. She bounces along as I follow. "Look, Asher, look. Someone wants to know if you had a romantic tryst at the ball. Did you? I don't know how because Mari and I were with Vi basically the entire time."

That earns a dark expression from Heath as he pulls the study's door open.

"No, I didn't," I direct to Rue, who's hopping up and down on her tiptoes. "As you said, you were at the beach with Violet, and I was at my place all yesterday, fixing it up. I was nowhere close to a boathouse or the boardwalk. They're just rumors." I give her a reassuring smile.

"Ooh! I'm gonna post that. Official quote." She spreads a hand through the air like she's admiring the imaginary post, and my stomach turns to stone.

"Do that, Rue," Heath mutters, "and you're grounded until you're thirty."

"You can't do that."

"Watch me."

"Can I at least have a cat?" she asks.

"No. Go away. I need to talk to Stephan," he says and Rue stomps off.

Heath gestures for me to go inside first. Then he locks the door behind us.

The house is quiet. No intoxicating scent of violets, besides a lingering hint. Not strong enough to suggest she's here.

Is Violet out with another Alpha already? "Where is everyone?"

"Are you planning on ruining her?" Heath snaps, completely ignoring my question.

"She's not—" I stop. I was going to say not my type. "What were they saying online?"

"Look for yourself." Heath sprawls in a large armchair, glaring about.

I pull out my phone. It's pretty bad. There are wild theories from how I'm trying to steal the glory of landing the Luxe to prop up my career, or get back at Felicity, or just because I can. There's even one about Violet having bewitched me with her femme fatale ways or got herself knocked up for fame.

That one is at least more laughable.

But the rumors are painful to read through. There's even a picture of the boathouse the supposed onlooker is claiming he saw us come out of. Luckily, the picture was taken at night, so he didn't catch *us* exactly. But still... We're going to have to be more careful about where and when we meet if we're going to pull this off the right way.

I sit in the chair opposite him and sigh. "I know it's early, but drink?"

He waves a hand, and I get up and pour us both a whiskey.

"Do you have something to tell me?" Heath asks, eyeing me.

"No."

"Is the rumor true, Ashford?" He leans forward. "Were you almost caught *alone* with *my* sister in the boathouse yesterday?"

There's no way in hell I'm telling him the truth. I don't have a death wish. "As I told Rue, I was at my place yesterday getting it ready. There was no reason for me to be by the beach at all."

"Right." But he doesn't look convinced. "You danced with her at the ball."

"I did."

"Why?"

"She's the Luxe." I shrug. "It was just a dance."

"You are supposed to be helping me find Alphas who would be right for her. Not inflate your ego more than it already is."

"I know. I needed to find out more about her—you know, her likes and dislikes, her hobbies, what she wants in a mate. And—"

"And what?"

Oh man, how am I going to say this without getting my head ripped off? "And...I found her interesting."

He blinks. "Excuse me?"

"Violet. She's beautiful. Considerate. Humble. Sharp-witted. Funny..." All true. "And the more I talked with her at the ball, the more I realized I couldn't come up with a single Alpha I knew who would be the best match for her."

"Then talk to the Alphas you don't know."

"That's the thing. I don't think the kind of man exists."

"And you got all this from a single dance with her?" he asks, skeptical. "One dance?"

"You said it yourself, she's special. There's no one else like her, and I see that now."

"Whatever you're trying to say, might as well spit it the fuck out," he says and takes a deep swallow of his drink. "We've known each other for a long time, and I don't appreciate the runaround, so out with it."

Right then is when I consider telling him about the ruse Violet and I agreed to. He is one of my closest friends, after all.

But would he understand? Doubtful. He'll think I'm using Violet to get what I want. That it could ruin her if we're found out.

All true, but I'm not counting on getting caught. That won't be enough to convince Heath it's a good idea, though.

Best not to tell him. Which means I have to act like pursuing Violet is the real deal. Which also means I'm going to get my ass handed to me by her overprotective big brother.

I draw in a deep breath. *Here goes nothing.*

"I...I want to put my hat in the ring of potential suitors for Violet," I say.

He's quiet for a long moment. Too long. Instead of answering, his jaw muscle jumps as he gnashes his teeth together.

"Heath." How do I explain myself? "I know we talked about this before. I know I told you I wasn't interested, and

I wasn't...then. But after talking to her, after...dancing with her—" I almost say *kissing her* and blow it— "I realized she's someone I could really see myself with."

He's still deathly silent, and it irks me.

"After what happened with CeeCee, I haven't thought I could be with anyone else like that again." Mentioning Cecilia makes my mouth dry, but I push on. Bringing my old mate up is the only way I'll be able to convince Heath I'm serious. "So I want to make sure it's okay with you if I take her on a date. Court her, or whatever these old-ass Sabine rules call it. The proper way. She deserves that much."

Heath throws his head back, downing the rest of his whiskey in a single gulp. He slams the empty glass on the side table, and says, as strong and deafening as a gunshot: "No."

"No? What do you mean, no?"

"Exactly that. No. You're not going to court my sister. I won't allow it."

"And what if it's what she wants? Doesn't that mean anything?"

"She's too good for you, Ashford."

Asshat. But I guess I'll take it. It's better than him punching me in the face.

Although that's still very much a possibility.

"So you want me to believe that you've suddenly had a change of heart? As if you own one of those," he says.

"Shit, Gardener. Ouch."

"Does Violet know about your sudden *interest*?"

"Yes."

"And she seems to like you too?"

"I think so. I told her I'd like to come by here and visit her again, if you'd let me, and she didn't turn me down."

He rubs the side of his face, thinking. "And if she does? Turn you down eventually, that is. If she decides you're not the one she wants?"

I hold up my hands. "Then I back off. Simple. I just want a chance."

He studies me. "This isn't a joke, Stephan. This is my sister we're talking about here. Her life. My family's future."

"I know. That's why I want to do this the right way. I—" Suddenly, the study door flies open and I'm smacked in the face by the scent of sweet spring violets.

Heath and I both jump to our feet.

"Rue said an Alpha was here, waiting to see me—" Violet stops, gaze taking in the scene and realizing the said Alpha is me. "Oh! I'm sorry. I didn't mean to interrupt..."

Just her scent, her very presence unleashes something wild within me. It was subtle when we'd first met, but it seems to be growing, taking shape with every interaction we have. I'm not sure what to make of it, or what it means, but all I do know is that the scenes from last night's dreams resurface in my thoughts again, and the desire to defile her, rut with her, speeds through me like a bullet.

Fuck. What's happening to me?

It has to be instincts, my Alpha nature. It sees a pretty, untouched Omega, and wants to claim her as its own. That's all.

I can't let it get hold of me and pervert my common sense. It'll ruin this entire plan.

Their mother appears behind Violet, and any dirty thoughts get cold water splashed on them.

"Mr. St. James," she begins. "You've come to visit us?" She glances at Heath for an explanation, but when he doesn't answer, she looks back to me.

"Please, Mrs. Gardener. Call me Stephan. Stephan Ashford. I left Asher St. James back in Emporia."

She grins at that, and her eyes twinkle with curiosity. "Oh, how intriguing! Are you here for Violet?"

Heath tries to step forward. "Mom—"

"Actually, yes." My gaze captures Violet's, and something passes between us. My pulse cranks up a notch as her breathing increases, making her breasts rise and fall.

"Stephan..." Violet breathes.

"I'd—I'd like to officially court Violet. I was just here to ask Heath his permission," I say, and every eye turns to him.

"That's wonderful! Surely he'll say yes!" Mrs. Gardener says. "How exciting!"

Heath glares daggers at me. I put him in a metaphorical corner, and he knows it.

He can kill me later.

"I'd like to maybe take her out on a proper date soon," I say. "Maybe she can save another dance for me at the next event?"

Mrs. Gardener waves the thick envelope in her hand. "What perfect timing, too. We've just been invited to a garden party at Hargrave House at the end of the week!"

"Well, it's up to Violet too." I lock eyes with her, hoping she can read my mind. If she agrees to this, then there's nothing Heath can say about it. "If she's interested, that is..."

Now everyone turns to Violet.

Startled, her mouth opens, but no sound comes out.

"Vi?" her mother prompts. "What do you think?"

All the color drains from Violet's face. "I... I..."

Then, eyes rolling back, her legs give out, and the princess faints.

Chapter Fifteen

Violet

I'm lying in the warm cozy shade of an oak; the smell soothes, slows my heart down from galloping to an almost steady beat.

"She's ice cold," a deep voice says. "Did she eat today?"

"Oh my goodness, Mr. Ashford, you're a hero," Mom breathes. "A real hero."

Heath grumbles something I can't make out.

"O.M.G.!" Rue's there too. Her flurry of words flies over me. "You missed Vi's crash and burn, Iris and Mari! It was awesome, wasn't it, Dahlia?"

"You moved so fast. You caught her right before she hit the floor." My mom chatters to Stephan almost like she's channeling Rue.

It rushes back to me. I was at the lunch with the other Omegas and their mothers in town. There were snide comments about my dress at the ball, about the Stitch posts suggesting Stephan and I have been sneaking away to private places to do un-Luxe-like things.

And then I...fainted?

No.

I'm home. The lunch isn't why I fainted.

"Ohh."

My eyes open, and I see Stephan first, his honey-brown eyes full of worry. Real worry. He's hovering over me, arm under my head. Next, I see Heath, who's standing nearby, hair a mess from raking his fingers through it too many times. Mom's there, along with every one of my sisters. I'm surrounded.

I try to scramble to my feet, but Stephan's quick to put his other arm under my knees, scoop me up like a child, and carry me over to a chair. Someone presses a glass of iced tea into my hand.

"For your blood sugar," Iris says, then leans in close.

"I fainted," I whisper to her. "I never faint."

"Full-on panic attack, Vi," she whispers back. "Drink."

I attempt a sip, but my stomach is twisted into a tight knot. I'm so embarrassed.

"Feeling better?" my brother asks.

I nod.

"Mom, can you get everyone out?" Heath asks. "If Stephan is going to court Vi, I need to speak to them both. Privately. So close the door."

For a moment I think Mom's going to insist on staying, but then she ushers my sisters out.

When it's just us, worry streaks through me. I don't

know how much Stephan has told Heath, or if he's told him anything at all. But I don't want to ruin our plan.

"Before the Hargrave House party," Heath says, looking a little gray, like the fainting might be contagious, "there are some things we have to get straight. First—Vi, you didn't answer Stephan when he asked if you're interested in him courting you. Are you?"

"I...am," I say, still a little shaky.

Heath shakes his head, as if he's surprised by my answer. "Okay then. So, the rules." He turns to Stephan. "You do this the right way. No dates without a chaperone. Never alone. We don't need any more bad rumors going around than there already are. Hand-holding is allowed. A kiss on the hand or cheek is fucking pushing it."

"Heath!" I gasp.

"Touch her in any way, defile her, and I'll kill you. Do you understand me? I don't care that you're my friend. I'll destroy you."

I know my brother is serious. Dead serious. I know he's protective over all of us, but I've never seen him so aggressive.

"Most important of all, Violet is allowed to be courted by others if she so chooses, and when she's made her decision on a mate, you have to step back, Stephan."

"You say that as if there's no chance she'll pick me," Stephan says.

"Violet's smart. She's not going to put up with your bullshit," he replies. "So let's just say I'll be very, *very* surprised if this—whatever this is—gets past two dates."

"Heath," I start. I don't understand where all this animosity is coming from. "He's your friend."

"You're right. Two dates may be too much, actually."

Scowling, Stephan steps toward him. "Hey, you know me. You know that when it comes to stuff like this, I don't fuck around."

"Yes, I *do* know you. And I know that fucking around is all you've been doing lately. I refuse to let you hurt my sister and mess up her chance at real happiness."

A growl rumbles in Stephan's chest, and suddenly his scent fills the room as his annoyance inflates. "Fuck you, Gardener. If you cared anything about your sister's happiness, you'd let her make her own decisions, live her own life, without the pressures of what society says."

Coming over to me, he takes my hand and places a light kiss on the back of it. My heart flutters. "I'll see you tomorrow night, Princess." Then with one more hard look at my brother, he storms out of the study, leaving me and Heath alone.

"Princess?" Heath asks me in the tense silence. "What the hell is that about?

I wince. What am I getting myself into?

Chapter Sixteen

Stephan

I do another fifteen minutes of weights, and then I hit the treadmill in my apartment. I'm here until I can get my beach house livable, and it's taking longer than expected. At this rate, it'll be finished by the time I'm ready to leave Sabine and go back to Emporia.

Finally, when I decide that's enough, I get off and head to my bathroom for a shower.

I could call Heath to set up the Violet date, but he's a stubborn, cantankerous bastard these days. He's just lucky I hadn't socked him in front of Violet yesterday. He'd been pushing at my patience since I'd showed up at his doorstep.

And here I was trying to be respectable and do the right thing by his sister.

Well, the *fake* right thing, but still. It counts.

Maybe I should have told him the truth.

No. He wouldn't have allowed it, and things would be worse for Violet.

We'll pull this off. I know it.

But first, I need to get the rumors working in our favor. And that means swallowing my pride and meeting with the battle-ax herself.

After getting dressed, I head out to the waiting car and get in.

"The Council Estate," I tell the driver before he steps on the gas.

When we pull up to the massive building with a circle driveway and picturesque fountains, I get out and walk up the marble steps without even a second glance by security.

I find the battle-ax on the very top floor of the mansion, in her quarters above the stupid throne-like room. She's barefoot, her silver hair down, and in the kitchen cooking like she's some domestic goddess.

"Stephan. You came to visit? Or are you here with an ulterior motive?"

I watch as she chops vegetables.

"I need to speak to you about something." The words feel bitter as they fall from my tongue. "I decided to take your advice and look for a mate this Season. I'm going to be courting."

"Ah, ulterior motive then," she says and stops her chopping to look at me fully. "Courting an Omega this time, I hope."

Anger flares in my chest, but I push it down. "Yes. An Omega."

"Alicia?"

"Who?"

"The blonde one you shacked up with on one of your first nights here."

A shock runs through me. How did she know?

"No, not her. Violet."

Her brows lift. "Violet Gardener? My Luxe?"

I hate giving her this, but I nod.

She's still holding the knife, and she points it at me. "What are you up to, Stephan?"

"Up to?" I say. "I came here to tell you I think I found someone. That you were right."

"I saw you dancing with her at the ball. But is it serious?"

"It is for me. And she seems to enjoy my company. I've already talked to her brother."

She studies me. "The Luxe stands above all others. She'll have the pick of the lot this Season. You'll have some serious competition."

"I don't mind a little competition," I reply.

"You can't sully her."

"What do you think I am?" When she opens her mouth to respond, I say, "Don't answer that. But this isn't a joke. I'm doing this the right way. Violet is...well, she's nothing like I've ever expected or knew I wanted."

"Wow, Stephan. You seem really taken by this Omega. She's bewitched you."

"You could say that."

She smiles. "I'm glad you've finally come to your senses and listened to me."

Perfect. She bought it. Relief floods through me.

"Maybe we'll have a mating ceremony before the end of the summer after all," she says with a wide grin. Then she turns and starts chopping her vegetables again.

"Thank you, Monarch."

"Please, Stephan. Call me Sophine. You know you can." She looks at me from over her shoulder. "Lunch?"

But I'm already halfway out the door.

It's a whirlwind week of walks, lunches, and trips to galleries, all with Violet Gardener, all chaperoned by one of her sisters or her mother, of course. But we have to show our faces to make our charade seem real. Although the tagalongs make it hard for me to talk to the princess—really talk to her—besides the normal formalities.

It's annoying, especially since I can't touch her, which I'm finding damn near impossible as days go on. So I settle for what I can get. An accidental brush of our arms, or a quick swipe of her hair behind her ear when her sister isn't looking, and then I take my fill of Violet in my dreams, which have only grown more erotic and realistic. I find myself having to jerk off multiple times a night just to get some relief, but it's never enough.

My body is craving the real thing.

But I can't do that to her. Violet isn't just a quick fuck and dump kind of woman. Even if she wasn't my friend's sister, I don't think I'd be able to do that to her. She's gotten under my skin.

After visiting the battle-ax, news of my courting Violet spread like wildfire through Stitch. As expected, the socials are delighted with what they're calling "a trembling bud" of a romance. Which is exactly what we want.

The garden party is tomorrow, and I decide to risk going out for an early predawn run. There aren't many people about, and with a baseball cap and ear pods, I create a private little world as I pound the path to full-on rock and roll.

When I've run for an hour, I cool down to a walk on one of the lesser used paths. A runner is heading in my direction, and even if I didn't smell her, I'd still know her. The long dancer legs, the graceful way she moves...

But there are violets everywhere.

"Princess."

She stops and almost stumbles, and pulls the pods from her ears, her hoodie still on, big hazel eyes wide. "Stephan. It's a little early to stalk me."

Shit. I like private Violet. A lot. "*You're* stalking *me*."

"No," she says. "That's just your ego talking."

A beat throbs between us in the air, subatomic and everywhere.

"Oh, god. I'm sorry," she rushes to say. "This is the only time I can sneak out to get some exercise, and I think my brain's still half asleep. I didn't mean it."

"But you believe it's true." I step closer to her and lead her off the path to one of the overgrown willow trees.

It's still predawn and in minutes light will start to fill the spaces, but I can see her perfectly. And she's beautiful early in the morning.

She's fresh, untouched by the day and all the worries it brings.

And there's something else, too.

Violet seems free.

"I'm clearly hanging around Heath a little too much," she says. "His bad attitude is starting to rub off."

"It's okay. In my line of work, you need to have a thick skin. Critics can be brutal." I pause. "You know, when we go out or others are around, you're the perfect little pleasing creature. Which could be hot. But you do it to make yourself small, to make sure everyone else is happy with no thought for yourself."

She's silent.

"You hide yourself away."

"No, I don't."

"You do."

"Bullshit."

I snap my fingers. "That. Right there. Real."

Someone runs by and looks over, trying to peek through the branches, but eventually gives up and keeps on going by.

"I'm just me," she says and steps back.

I follow. "But that's the thing. You're you, but only a part of you most of the time," I say. She moves back again, only to be stopped by the trunk of a tree. "With me, alone, you're so much more. You're funny, unexpected. I like that about you."

"Is this where I stumble accidentally into your arms like in some kind of scripted scene?"

Oh, she has a bite.

"Only if you want to." I close the distance between us and slide a hand down her torso. "I like this side of you."

She tries to slap me away. "What are you doing?"

"Seeing if your pants are on fire, Princess."

"They're not!"

But I move closer still, noting the way her breath quickens, how she pushes into me instead of going the other way. "Maybe it's your mouth."

"That doesn't make sense."

"Neither does this."

I know I shouldn't, but fuck it. My head is swimming with violets. And somehow, kissing her is wild, exhilarating, and in this particular place, dangerous.

It's been too long since I've tasted her...

My lips touch hers, and Violet moans. She grabs me, pulling me into her fully. Her mouth opens, her tongue strokes over my lips and...talk about fucking fire.

That touch sets off a bonfire of sensations. She doesn't taste like early morning. She tastes like late nights, like sex, like everything my dreams have conjured, and I slide a leg between hers, pushing her against the tree harder. In her leggings, her pussy's hot and damp on my thigh.

She moans louder, suddenly biting my lip like she can't help it. I can feel the panic flutter in her, but she doesn't pull away as I coax her back into the world of the kiss. Of heat and wetness, of promises and trysts, and she tugs at my hair, demanding more.

Fuck, she makes me see bright flashes of light. She stirs up a wild cacophony of noise and—

"St. James! St. James!"

Oh *fuck*.

The flashes of light? Cameras.

I break the kiss, bury her head in my shoulder, and make sure her hoodie is up.

"Asher St. James!"

More lights flash.

"Are you two in love? Can we expect a mark soon?"

"What about Felicity?"

Shit. Shit. *Shit.*

I tug my cap down, and ignoring the cameras pointed in my face, I grab Violet's hand. "Run!"

Hivemind, my buzzing brood, did anyone order a scandal

With a side dish of guess who?

*If you thought it's about our latest power couple, Violet and Stephan, then you'd be **RIGHT!** Seems they were seen by paparazzi from the mainland who took pics so blurry you'd think they were of a UFO.*

*Of course Miss Violet, our pristine Luxe of this Season, has denied this scandalous **KISS.***

And our sinful dreamboat has made no comment.

But it makes this Queen wonder... Was the rumor about them in the boathouse true?

Some say: He's doing a charity. That this is nothing more than a publicity stunt since he's got all of Emporia waiting for his return. Models and movies stars. Miss V isn't his type...

But come closer, brood.

Closer...

Listen.

No one would blame any Omega for wanting their 15 minutes of fame with a star. But here's the thing...

If the blurry pics were them, then did they simply run into each other OR were they just coming from a night of passion?

Will this force him to put a mark on her neck now?

Or is it just a case of mistaken identities?

I don't know about you, but I'll be watching the upcoming garden party closely, from my ringside seat.

The hot tea is everywhere, and I for one am here for it.

This is going to be the hottest Season in years!

- Queen Bee

CHAPTER SEVENTEEN

Violet

Run.

The word tumbles in my head as my mother rakes me over the coals. It's my first time ever getting in trouble like this. Usually it's Iris or Rue.

"The thing," Mom says as she pours herself a glass of wine, "is you need to be careful. He hasn't proposed. And though you're of age, I really hope you don't ruin things."

She means bring shame on the family.

Mom wouldn't ever say it.

She doesn't have to.

It stings me through the air, and my chest goes tight as the panic starts to unfurl. On top of it all, I feel sick.

"I'm being careful."

"Out so early, Violet. And alone…" she says. "You have

so many other Alphas interested. Maybe it's time to consider one of them."

I may have other Alphas wanting to take me out, but the ones I've dated have been rude, vulgar, or just...not for me. I haven't enjoyed any of their company. Not like I do with Stephan, as scripted as it may be.

I just haven't yet found the one who I want to claim me.

"I went for a run and tripped," I tell her. "It was completely innocent, Mom."

I swallow hard, my throat scraping.

Run.

He took my hand and we ran, people following and cameras clicking. It should've been a terrifying experience, but for once I didn't panic. I didn't fall or faint.

With his hand in mine, I was alive. Free.

We raced into the thick of the wooded area and found a hiding place underneath a leafy bush. He dragged me through the dirt, out of sight, and soon the paparazzi grew bored of searching and left us alone.

When it was safe to crawl out again, we were both covered in filth with leaves in our hair. Then we laughed and laughed, until tears streamed from my eyes and he struggled to catch his breath. He tried to wipe the crud off my cheeks, but when he only made it worse, it started another fit of laughter, and eventually we gave up and went our separate ways.

Stephan could have left me back at the tree. But he didn't.

He could have let my reputation be ruined and went

about his summer as the most eligible Alpha on Sabine. But he didn't.

Mom's still talking. I tune back in.

"These dashing sorts are very nice, Violet, lovely. But you don't stop accepting the invites or dances with other Alphas until you find the right one. The one your heart beats for. True love is out there and you deserve it, too."

True love. I almost want to laugh. It's a fantasy, something in the movies Stephan stars in. I need a practical match.

"Yes, Mom."

"Good. Now go talk your brother down and then get ready. We have that party at Hargrave House tonight."

As expected, Heath's in the study, pulling what looks like a gun from the wall safe behind a painting.

"Heath Edward Gardener, what are you doing?"

"Going to shoot that ex-friend of mine."

I gasp. "Don't you dare!"

"Did you sleep with him?"

"*No!*"

He nods. Grabs a magazine clip for the gun. "But you let him kiss you?"

"I kissed him," I lie, my heart jumping. "Don't tell Mom. Where did you get the gun?"

"It was Dad's."

"Put it back." I cross my arms. "*I* kissed *him*. A peck. And the media has been sent back to the mainland. By order of the Monarch."

"*You* kissed *him*. Sure, Vi."

Am I really so predictable and boring?

"It's true! A peck. It was nothing."

"Do you like him?" he asks, eyes hardening on me.

"Like...him?"

"Yes. Do you like him?"

This feels like a trap.

"Even if Stephan wasn't my friend, he'd be the last Alpha on my list for you. You two are on opposite ends of the spectrum. You're not his type. And he's—"

Annoyance stirs, and my words are sharp. "How do you know what his type is?"

"I *know* what his type is and that's enough," he says.

"You really think so little of me? That I can't make my own decisions?"

His eyes widen in surprise. "You're just so good, Vi. You've always been delicate and compassionate. All Stephan's ever cared about is himself. Well, except—" He stops abruptly and shakes his head. "Never mind. The point is I don't want you wasting your time with him if there's nothing real between you. I won't risk Stephan ruining the Season and your chance at happiness. If you don't care about him, kick him to the curb, and we'll find you an Alpha worth your time."

The moment of anger deflates from me. Heath's just trying to be a good brother. He wants the best for me, no matter how misguided he may be. I have to be more careful with Stephan. I don't know why he keeps kissing me or touching me when he's made his true intentions clear, but I need to be strong enough to tell him no.

Even if my heart and body crave him.

"Heath, please put the gun away," I say. "You can't help me survive this Season if you're in prison."

"I wasn't going to shoot him dead. Just make it hurt. You know, as a reminder."

"What if Stephan wants to mark me? Will you still shoot him?"

"He won't."

"You don't know that." I take a breath. "If he asks to claim me, will you let it happen?"

With a sigh, Heath puts the gun away and locks the safe.

"If he asks and that is what you truly want, then yes. I'll let it happen." Then he looks at his watch. "Don't you need to get ready for tonight?"

Men.

Hargrave House isn't really a house, more like a mansion on steroids in the middle of the richest suburb of Sabine City.

Old brick and older gardens form the huge courtyard. I've seen pictures but I've never been. And it's better than the photos and video tours online.

It's a world of its own, multi-layered, with different areas that provide a different feel or even quasi-privacy. And in the center there are tables, chairs, and a delicate feast of finger foods, and room to stand, mill around, and even dance. Fairy lights twinkle everywhere.

"The QB says the Monarch's making an appearance tonight." Rue's hair is piled up in an Edwardian style for the night. Her phone's in her hand. And she's scrolling.

"Someone's running bets on how long until Stephan gets bored of you," Rue continues. "There's even a poll for how long until you get knocked up."

"Shut it," Iris says, snatching the phone. "No more Stitch for tonight."

"Not Stitch. Over on *TheRealDirt,* it says that Vi—"

"If you get caught looking at any more of that nonsense by Heath or Mom, you'll be grounded. Now, go annoy your little friends."

Rue snatches back her phone and bounds off.

Mari rolls her eyes. She's dressed in a glittery sky-blue dress but no mask, since she's not in her Season yet.

I'm looking around for Stephan, and I hate myself for it, but it's better than giving in to the panic creeping up on me.

I grip my skirts, and a flapper flounces up to me, in gold and white, her blonde hair pinned to look like a bob. It's Alicia. I can tell even with her white mask. She wrinkles her nose at me. "Good lord, what's that you're wearing?

"You look beautiful, Alicia. I love your lace and silk mask." I try to smile.

"I've been trying to work out how you not only got picked as the Monarch's favorite, mousy thing like you," she says, "but landing Asher St. James? It was a complete mystery. But then I saw your dishy brother being all chummy with the movie star and got it. They're friends and this is a favor."

Iris steps between us, poised to attack.

"Those earrings are to die for," she says. "They don't make quality plastic like that anymore—*ow.*"

My elbow meets Iris's ribs and she sends me a look.

I brighten my smile. Heat is starting to crawl up my neck and my chest is tightening. *Don't faint. Don't faint. Don't faint.* "We should have tea one of these days."

"You should—"

"Quiet." An Alpha low command ripples through me at full force and instantly takes hold of the conversation. I glance up just as the scent of earth and oak surrounds me. "Shut your mouth, Alicia, now."

She clamps her mouth shut.

"Go annoy someone else," he says, the command still in his tone. She glares at me but has no choice but to scurry away.

"Do you want us to stay?" Iris whispers, glancing from Stephan to me.

I shake my head. "I'm okay."

Iris takes Mari by the arm and they leave us.

My knees wobble as I gaze up at him.

He did that for me.

"Don't faint, Princess."

Again, the Alpha voice is pitched low, only for my ears. It strokes over all my senses like cool water, bringing me a moment of zen.

The panic leaves me, and all there is, apart from that spa-like calm, is tremors of excitement and anticipation.

It's like being touched.

He's dressed as some dashing buccaneer, with tight pants and billowy black shirt. His mask is simple, like a cat burglar's, and around his waist is a violet cummerbund.

It's like he's walked off the cover of an old-school romance novel.

I lick my dry lips. "I had that under control."

"But I helped," he says, his sparkling brown eyes boring into mine.

I drag my gaze away, past some of the people dancing. I drag it past the glaring, ruffled Alicia whose new friends are trying to soothe her as they show her something on her mini pad, but she's not mollified, she's focused on Stephan and—

"Dance?" I suddenly ask.

"If Bro-zilla is okay with it," he says, a smile in his voice.

"Heath has no choice."

The live music surrounds us as I take his offered hand, and he leads us onto the dance area.

Stephan's hands are warm, and being close to him has an excitement that never fades, even with repeat close encounters with him.

Unlike with the other Alphas I've gone on dates with, the small talk is easy. He tells me some stories about his life in Emporia, all sanitized for my sake probably, and he shows interest in my dancing.

"My agent is excellent. She might be visiting soon," he says as he twirls me around. "I can introduce you. There's choreography, dance companies, all kinds of things you could do. Even a dance school at the National Ballet."

"For who? *Me?* Oh, no, I'm not good enough."

He grazes my ear with his mouth. "Yes, you are."

"You don't know that."

"Actually, I do." He pulls back a little to look at me fully. "Did you know Mikel Petrov records all his dance sessions and posts clips of his most talented students online?"

My next breath freezes in my chest.

"You're on there a lot, you know. Twenty-seven clips, to be exact. And I watched them all."

Oh my god. I didn't know that.

"That's..." *Flattering. Thrilling.* "Creepy."

"It's research. Have to know who I'm fake courting."

I try to think of something clever to say, but nothing comes.

"We get Petrov to be a reference and use those clips, and I'm sure we can get you an audition somewhere. Maybe at Maymont, if you want?"

"M-Maymont?" The most renowned fine arts academy in the entire country? Excitement bubbles up. It's damn near impossible to get an audition, let alone get accepted. If Stephan can somehow get me in, I—

But the hope fades as the truth comes settling in.

"I can't," I say.

"Why?"

"You know why."

The song ends and the band takes a break. I step away. There's a chill in my chest I can't shake.

"Who's Heath talking to?" Stephan asks, looking over my shoulder.

I turn. The man is maybe early thirties, dark curling hair, and very good-looking. From his bearing and clothes, it's clear he's rich.

"I don't know." My brother motions me over with a tilt of his head. "Heath wants me..."

"I'll get us a drink."

As Stephan leaves, I make my way over, ignoring the whispers and the looks that come my way. I think of the calm of oak trees and secret wooded spots where no one can find me.

"Here she is." Heath smiles that smile I hate, the one that's too big, the one that hides things. "This is Violet. Violet, this is Mr. Dominic Stockton. He just got back from Europe."

He holds out his hand, and I go to shake it but he lifts it to his mouth and kisses it. "Call me Dom, please. A pleasure. I was telling your brother I'd love to call on you sometime."

"And I told him how much you'd love that." Heath nods, waiting for me to follow along.

Since I have to be the perfect sister, the perfect Luxe, I say, "I would. Very much."

I have to remember that I might like Stephan, but he doesn't want me. Not really. What's between us is nothing more than an act, something to get us both what we want. And all his talk about Mikel Petrov and Maymont—well, it's a good dream, but it isn't realistic.

Even if by some miracle I could get an audition there, I'd never be good enough to get in. Let alone make tuition. It's too expensive for what we can afford right now.

All the more reason to be pleasant to Dom. Maybe he's the Alpha who'll be best for me.

Heath seems to think so, or he wouldn't have introduced us.

"Violet, I requested a dance on the mini pad," Dom says.

I smile brightly. "I'll accept it right away." To show him I'm serious, I pull out my tablet from my bag and hit the button to confirm the dance.

"Perfect." The Alpha smiles, and my knees should give out. He is gorgeous after all. But he leaves me cold.

"I'll get us all something to drink," my brother says suddenly. He takes off, and I'm left looking at Dom.

"Forgive the forwardness, but now that we're alone, may I ask you something? Something more...personal?"

Uh oh.

"You may ask, but if I find it too prying, I just won't answer. How's that?" I say.

"Very fair." Dom glances at the refreshment table, where both my brother and Stephan are now talking fervently and glancing this way. "It's just... What are your intentions for this Season? I ask because as I'm sure you know, some aren't serious about finding a mate. And I... well, I very much am."

"So am I," I say. "I'm hoping to find my mate by the end of the Season, an Alpha who's a good man, who will do right by me and my family."

"And a pack? Children?"

I nod. "I come from a large family. It's all I know."

"Excellent." He takes my hand and kisses it again. Then there's a soft ringing—his cell phone—which he takes out of his pocket and glances at the screen with a frown. "I'm sorry. I'm going to have to take a rain check on the dance. Work is calling, and they know not to unless it's an emergency."

"Oh. That's okay," I say. "Hopefully it's nothing too serious."

"But I'd love to see you again." His phone continues to ring. "I'll be in touch with your brother to set up something. Maybe dinner at Blackwood Chophouse?"

That's the fanciest, most expensive steakhouse in all of Sabine.

"I look forward to it."

"Until then, Miss Gardener." He finally presses the answer button and walks away.

After he goes, Heath comes over and hands me a drink. "Apple juice."

"I'm not a child."

"Dom left?"

"He got an urgent work call. Or so he said."

"Dom is the CEO of a huge pharmaceutical company," he says. "I don't remember the name, but they make most of the scent blockers on the market. He makes more money than he knows what to do with, travels a lot, but he's looking to slow down. Start a family. Did you like him?"

"He was very polite, but we didn't get to talk much before his phone rang."

"Ah, well, he seems very interested in you. So let's hope it leads somewhere." He takes a gulp of his drink, which, by the sharp, bitter smell of it, definitely isn't apple juice. "But first, we're going to mingle. You and me."

"I'm supposed—"

"Stephan?" He leans in. "I already had a talk with him. Told him to stop keeping you all to himself and let you play the field. Now, you stay with me while we make our rounds. A whirlwind meet and greet."

I don't argue and let him guide me around the courtyard. Some of the men I know, some are older than Dom, some his age. They all seem nice enough with their stiff manners and boring weather conversation. Lawyers, doctors, professors... They all have noteworthy careers and wealth. They would be a fine choice for any Omega looking for a mate.

But they're not Stephan. None of them make my stomach flip like he does.

Heath has an agenda. After each one, he glances at me to gauge my reaction.

"I'm sorry," I say after we excuse ourselves from the last Alpha, a graying man named Fredrick who enjoys playing golf and talking about it even more. "He was too..."

"Chatty?" Heath answers.

I crinkle my nose. "Old."

"Yeah, I figured forty-five was pushing it..."

"He was forty-five?" I gasp. "Heath!"

He laughs, and for a moment, it's a glimpse of the old Heath. "He wasn't actually on my list. I just wanted to see what you'd say."

"I'd say I'm not letting you pick any more Alphas for me this Season."

"Dom wasn't bad," he says.

"You get a D- for the night and that's being generous." I glance around for Stephan, but don't see him anywhere. My stomach sinks.

"Ashford left a while ago, Vi," Heath says.

"Oh." I frown. "I'm just going to go home then."

Heath sighs. "Go with Mom and Rue—"

"She can come with us," Iris says as she and Quinn stride over to us. "We're going to Quinn's."

"I'm really tired, Iris," I say. "I'd rather go home."

She gives me a sharp look. "No, you're going to want to come with us. Believe me."

"You and the little red-headed harpy better not be planning trouble." Heath's gaze hits Quinn.

"Better than being a bore, *Heather*." Quinn sniffs. "You make watching paint dry exciting."

"And you make death by firing squad seem like a good time." Heath looks at Iris. "Behave yourself." Then he stalks off.

"We're going out, Vi," Iris says. "And you're coming."

"No way."

"It'll be good for you," she says. "Believe me. You deserve a break from...from all this."

They take my hands and lead me out to a car that belongs to the Hydes. But as Quinn opens the door and Iris climbs in, I spot Stephan. He's in the shadows, near the edge of the house, partially illuminated by a gas lamp.

My pulse immediately picks up pace. He didn't leave. Maybe he was just waiting for me to finish with Heath's Alpha meet-and-greet.

"Give me a second, okay?" I tell Iris and Quinn and shut the door.

As I hurry over to him, I notice that he's talking to someone—he's not alone—and my next step falters. It's a blonde. A blonde in gold and white.

It's Alicia. And they're a little too close.

"I know you want to," she says. "Using your Alpha voice on me earlier? You can do that again if you want."

"You know why I did that. Because you can't seem to take no as an answer," Stephan whispers angrily.

"Then I'll tell your stupid boring Violet about us." She moves a little more into the lamp's orange glow, and there's something like a mark on her neck. Like a bite mark.

Oh no.

No. No. No. No.

I can't move. Stephan and Alicia?

Since when?

All this time?

A growl vibrates in his throat. "You dare, and I'll do more than use my voice on you. I'll—"

Stephan turns, seeing me frozen in place, and horror flashes on his face. He says something, but the world is in freefall and all I can do is spin around and sprint back to the car.

Chapter Eighteen

Stephan

I take off after the princess, ignoring the viper Alicia's call for me to come back. I don't know how much Violet heard, but from the wounded look on her face, I'm guessing it was enough.

I fucked up big time.

I should have been smarter when I got here. I made a stupid mistake with my dick and now—

Violet reaches a car, gets inside, and slams the door shut before I can reach her. All I can do is knock on the window and pray she can hear me. "Princess! Princess, talk to me." I try the door handle but the lock has been clicked firmly in place. "Violet, please. Let me explain."

Slowly, the glass lowers slightly, revealing Violet's sister Iris and her redhead friend, both staring daggers at me.

"I need to talk to Violet," I say, trying to peer into the darkness of the car. I see a glimpse of Violet's floral dress at the other side of the seat. I can't see her face, but I can sense her pain, her disappointment. A terrible numbness spreads. I don't want her thinking bad about me. "Violet..."

"Give it up, St. James," Iris snaps. "This isn't one of your movies."

Then the window rolls up, cutting off the intoxicating scent of violets, and the car peels off.

Shit. This isn't good.

Why do I even care?

I like her?

She's nice. Sweet. Absolutely beautiful. The pleasing part of her nature both annoys me and turns me on. I want to help her fulfill her dreams and not worry so much about her responsibility to her family. I want her to explore all those secret parts of her that she keeps locked away from everyone, and her innocence makes me want to corrupt her in the best possible way, introduce her to pleasure she couldn't even imagine.

But only with me.

When Heath had told me to leave Violet alone tonight so that she could talk to other Alphas, I didn't want to. But the entire point of our ruse was to find someone worthy of her. And she won't find anyone if I don't let her go. But when I saw her talking to that one rich Alpha, when he kissed her hand... It took everything in me not to storm over and knock him clean on his ass.

I had to leave.

Do I *like* like Violet?

A nondescript limo pulls up next to me, and the window comes down, revealing Sophine in the backseat.

"Get in, Stephan."

I'm too lost in my thoughts to move as fast as she requires, so she pushes open the door with a huff. "Stephan. Now."

I get in the limo and look at the battle-ax. She's dressed in a black suit, her hair back, pinned under a hat. Taking the seat across from her, I open the mini bar between us, grab a bottle of bourbon, and swig from it.

Wincing, she takes out a second bottle and pours herself a glass. "Your time in Emporia has made you uncouth."

"I'm a barbarian."

She sits back. "Tell me, Stephan, did you sleep with that new girl? Miss Dell?"

I open my mouth, but she shakes her head.

"You know what? Don't tell me." Then she fixes me with the kind of stare that makes me rear back. "But do tell me your intentions with my Luxe. The real ones, Stephan. Not that buttery nonsense you spread the other day."

"Why did you choose her, by the way?" I ask. "Everyone knows she doesn't like attention, unlike most Omegas. She doesn't think she's special."

"I know." She smiles, but I can't read it. "Violet's rare. Beneath that martyr layer is a girl who shines in her own way. A diamond waiting to be discovered. She's refreshing, untouched. But she needs a little push. Don't you think?"

She's right. About all of it.

"Bottom line is, Stephan, I like her. And I know you do,

too. So don't fuck this up, or I will bring the Council's fist down on you, family or not."

The car stops, and I hadn't realized we'd been going anywhere. Fuck.

"Get out," Sophine barks. I do, and the moment I step onto the sidewalk, the door closes and the window lowers again. "This is Club Yin. She's in there right now. Go get her."

"Who?"

She grins, as if she knows some deep, dark secret. "Why, your princess, of course."

Then the limo speeds away.

The place is dark, the music moody, and there are bodies dancing close together on the floor. I look for the beautiful flower in the iridescent gauzy dress of greens, blues, gold, purples.

She's there, hair still pinned up, mask pushed up. She's in the same pretty forest or garden ballerina look, the filmy skirt long to mid-calf. She sticks out in a grungy place like this, a shining beacon in the darkness, but I like it. Especially since she's dancing like no one is watching, head tossed back, and finally enjoying herself without strict rules or expectations.

She's so pretty, so lithe, so... It's that intangible something that makes her magic, though.

In that, Sophine is right.

Violet's sister is in black punk-chick clothes that she wasn't wearing at the garden party. The redhead friend's dressed similarly, and I don't remember her wearing anything as hard core, either. They must have changed in the car.

The redhead is dancing with a young Delta, and the little prick's getting a bit too hands-y with the Beta girl. She smacks the guy's wandering hand away, but he grabs her face and brings it close to his and snarls.

Pushing through the crowd, I start toward him, just as Iris shoves the guy a step back. He may not be an Alpha, but he's stronger than an Omega, and from the ugly look on his face, he's not going to let that slide.

The Omegas try to get away by weaving through the crowd and heading toward the stage where the DJ plays, but the Delta follows.

That's when I move.

I hook a hand in the collar of his shirt and yank him back. He whirls on me, eyes wild with fury, but before he can swing, I drag him out of the club and onto the street. A stream of people follow after us, filling the sidewalk with onlookers.

"You think you can fuckin' roughhouse me? Do you know who I am?" the guy slurs as he shrugs out of my grip and stumbles to the ground.

"Do I look like I care?" As he goes to get up, I put a foot on his back and hold him there. "You need to learn how to keep your hands to yourself."

"What's it to you?"

I press harder.

"Let me up!" he growls.

"That's Asher St. James!" someone yells. When I look

up, I see everyone's phones are up, snapping pictures or taking videos, and my stomach sinks.

Shit. Guaranteed this will be all over Stitch for days.

"He helped that girl! I saw it all," another person says. "He's a hero."

"Did he beat him up?"

A young woman steps forward. "Is he bleeding?"

The Delta isn't, but it doesn't matter. This is how rumors get started. The best thing for me to do right now is walk away.

Removing my foot from the asshole's back, I bend down so that he can hear. "I wouldn't do that again if I were you. Consider this a warning."

With one more glance at the crowd, I turn and stroll across the road to a modest park that ends at the long boardwalk. When I'm far enough away, I pick a bench and sit in the dark, watching the water.

It really is the one thing I like about Sabine, the abundance of parks.

My phone buzzes, and with a sigh I pull it out. "Hey, Clea. You're calling fucking late."

She laughs, and the sounds of Emporia in the background make me a little homesick. The pace never stops, and when the noise dims suddenly, I know she has walked into her apartment lobby. That and the echo. "Normally you're out partying at this hour."

Unless I'm on a shoot.

"That dull there?" she asks.

"I keep finding trouble to entertain me."

"I've seen."

Great. "Why the call? Has Felicity broken the deal?"

"No." An elevator dings.

"Is this about a visit?"

"This is about that script you want to make. I read it."

My heart starts to pound. I may be biased but it's brilliant, a project I've work on for years, and poured my heart and soul into after CeeCee died.

"A little rough—"

"Rough? It's perfect."

"No script's perfect. Only those annoying screenwriters think that." She sighs, and I hear liquid hit a glass. "But it could be something. Just not...not for you."

"What is that supposed to mean? I'm good enough." My fingers bite into the phone.

"You're a movie star, a golden darling, a man the girls dream of having. You're single and while that's helped your current roles, it's pigeonholed you. This character you have here is for an actor who isn't the fodder of dreams, who's outgrown sex symbol, poster boy. An Alpha with a mate, maybe kids, like Johann Brigstock. Still sexy, but thinking-man sexy."

"I want to make that film."

"Find a mate the public will like. Something like one of those pretty things for sale on Sabine. A pristine little Omega." In the background the doorbell chimes. "Gotta go. Think about it. Bye."

Fuck. Get mated? I know she's joking, but I want the world opened for me. If I found a mate...

Princess Violet—

No. Heath would kill me.

Probably.

Just thinking about the princess has my mind conjuring

her scent. It surrounds me, those violets. Strong, sweet, and enticing. They paint an image of springtime in my head, of a meadow surrounded by wildlife and cool breezes.

A place where I could disappear to for a while.

"Stephan?"

My entire being lights up, turns electric. Just the breathy sound of my name on her lips has my innocent thoughts of meadows and peace turning into depraved ones, of sinking my teeth into her, getting my fill of her heat, of marking her. The need throbs in me, and I'm glad I'm sitting because my fucking pants are suddenly ten sizes too small.

I don't look up. "Guess I owe you an explanation, Princess."

"Did you mark her?" Her voice is small, wounded, and I hate that I made her feel this way.

"Alicia? No."

She makes a small sound. "I shouldn't care who you... entertain, but then again, this is my reputation and—"

"Some things are complicated. I didn't know she's part of the Season when I met her. And more important, there's nothing between us." *Now.* "It happens."

"What happens?"

I shrug. "Fans, that kind of shit. She's nothing, a troublemaker."

"Stephan, look at me."

I lift my head, and the emotion swimming in her eyes has me in a chokehold. There's pain there, buried down deep. I wouldn't have even noticed it if it wasn't for my career. And on the surface is a thick layer of indifference.

"Did you sleep with her?" she asks and wraps her arms around herself to fight off the chill of the late night.

I don't know if I should answer. But lying... I don't know if I can do that either. Not with Violet.

"There's nothing between us." I repeat that instead, settling for middle ground. "I made a mistake. One I'll never make again."

She is silent while she thinks over my words. Finally, she shakes her head. "It doesn't matter. None of this is real anyway."

And for some reason, those words sear into me and burn. She's right, though. We made a deal to have a fake courtship. That's it.

"Maybe we should just end this now," she says. "Whatever this is."

Wait, what?

I stand. "End it?"

"I don't see any reason to keep the act going. It served its purpose. I've already gone on a few dates, met a couple of Alphas that are...amiable. Any of them would make a fine mate. Or there's Mr. Stockton. He seems very interested in me, and Heath approves."

I laugh. "That walking human sedative? You're joking."

But from the unamused expression on her face, she's clearly not. "He's a CEO. Handsome. Polite. Well-traveled..."

"And makes a tax seminar seem like fun. And let's not forget that he's old as fuck."

"Mid-thirties isn't old."

I ignore that. "The only reason he's even seen as

desirable this Season is because he's loaded. The dude has no personality."

"I can make conversation with anyone," she says.

This is ridiculous. "But he'll bore you to death. You don't love him. You don't—"

"No one ever said anything about love, Stephan. This has always been about finding a *mate* that's good for me and my family."

"Don't you want a love?"

"Every Omega wants to fall in love, but I gave up on that dream a long time ago," she says and glances at the boardwalk in the distance.

Shit. She's starting to sound like me.

"It may be time for us to just...let this go. You can do nothing with Alicia all you want, and I can take my brother's advice and start taking other Alphas more seriously. We don't have to even say two words to each other ever again."

Heath's a fucking bastard.

But I can't blame him entirely. Violet's pulling away, and it's because of me.

"I don't want Alicia," I whisper.

"Well, whoever, then." Irritation makes her voice rise. "Alicia, Jade, Brianna—I don't care! What you do, who you do, is no concern of mine. I'm looking for a mate. Not a fantasy. Something real, not pretend." Her hazel eyes seem to glow as her anger mounts. "I'm done, Stephan."

She spins to leave, but before she can take a step, I snatch her by the wrist to stop her.

There it is again. The strange buzzing underneath my skin that happens whenever I touch her. The images of me sinking my teeth into her, biting her nipples, of her moaning underneath me as I rut away her virginity fills my head.

And her scent is stronger now, more so than it's ever been, stroking over me like fingers on naked skin.

I don't know what's between us, but Violet must be sensing something, too, because she stares at our joined hands, mouth half opened, and breathing picking up.

"Stephan..." she whispers. "Let me go."

I can't. Just the idea of Dominic Stockton or any other Alpha touching her, kissing her, has a possessiveness whipping through me and my hackles rising.

She's fucking *mine*.

"Did...did you growl?"

Her words startle me and make me drop her wrist.

Shit.

Then it hits me.

I know what's happening.

The princess is going to go into heat. Any day now.

Her scent, the overwhelming urge to claim her...

"You need to stop touching me." But she's looking up at me like she wished I hadn't let go.

It's probably dangerous for me to be around her with her heat so close and my instincts in overdrive. But even as I tell myself to leave—take the out she's given me—I'm stepping closer, cupping the side of her face with one hand and pulling her body against mine with the other.

She leans into it. "Stephan..." It's a plea. One I feel and understand.

Dipping my head, I touch her lips with mine. Barely there.

She whimpers.

There's a slam of a car door in the distance, shouts, and when I lift my eyes to look past Violet, I spot Heath stalking over to us. At his side is the battle-ax's Omega, and no one looks happy.

If this truly is the last time I'm tasting Violet's lips, I'm going to make it worth it.

So I close my eyes and I kiss her.

Hard.

Chapter Nineteen

Violet

The first time I was at the Monarch's estate, when I first met the Monarch before becoming her Luxe, feels like years ago. It seemed massive to me then, but now the hall feels too small, too harsh, and the air's way too thin. It's like I can't get enough into my aching lungs.

I sit on a settee while my brother paces. His fury flows off him in waves, his fire-and-smoke scent swirling all around him.

"I should fucking call Mom, Violet," he hisses.

The Monarch's Omega and two of her security detail had taken Stephan and dragged him into a separate limousine, while Heath ushered me into another, and we were whisked from the park in a squeal of tires. I saw him once, when he was marched into the Monarch's estate, but then he was dragged into her interview room and we were left to wait in the hall outside of it.

"Heath—"

"You're young, sheltered, but you're smart, and I thought...fuck me, I thought you'd know better than to fall for lines from an oversexed Alpha."

"I didn't."

My stomach knots, and I'm being crushed. I've brought shame on my family. I already knew I was out of my league. I never should have been named Luxe and now...

"I'm sorry." I look at Heath. "I messed up."

"No, Vi. Don't. I don't really blame you. I blame him. He knows the Season's rules, the etiquette. He was born here. He *knew* what I expected of him if he was serious about courting you, and *still—*" He growls, his shoulders bunching. "Still he risked your reputation."

"Did anyone else see us?"

"No. At least I don't think so. We got there in time."

"How did you even know where we were?" I ask.

"Stitch. Ashford's little fighting stunt was all over the damn app. Rue was practically foaming at the mouth when she showed me," he says sharply. "In one of the videos, I saw Quinn in the crowd and knew you couldn't be far behind."

"And the Monarch?"

Heath stops pacing and comes in close with a hushed tone. "Her Omega was already there. She must have sent him to keep an eye on Stephan."

Or on me.

"Regardless, he took advantage of you. There have been too many close calls as it is, and now this? The Monarch is involved."

I hear the implications loud and clear. If she's now involved, it can't be good. Feeling sick, I close in on myself. Things in me hurt in ways they never have because...I wanted him.

I wanted Stephan.

Even with how furious I was to learn about him and Alicia, I wanted to jump him and rip his cock out of his pants. I almost couldn't control myself. I wanted to do things to him I've only seen glimpses of in porn.

Two minutes of wild things I didn't know how to process when Iris, Mari, and I had looked up naughty sites on the internet when we were younger. Heath caught us, an eighteen-year-old Heath who snapped shut the computer and changed all the passwords to make sure we'd never look at knotting porn again.

But those scenes—of Omegas getting filled and knotted in every hole—filled my mind when Stephan grabbed my wrist so that I wouldn't walk away. And when he kissed me...

Something down inside me, deep between my legs, starts to ache in ways I've never felt. Slick dampens my panties, and all I can do is put a shaking hand to my cheek to try to get myself to settle down. It's burning hot. I'm burning hot. My vision blurs.

"Heath?" Tears burn my eyes. "I don't know what to do."

"Hey. Hey." His fury dissipates as he sits next to me and wraps an arm around my shoulder. "It's okay, Vi. We're going to sort this out. *I'm* going to sort this out. You don't have to worry."

I know he's just trying to make me feel better, but his touch is welcome. Needed. And I lean into him.

"The first thing we're going to do is forget Ashford. He's done for. Stockton's interested," Heath says. "He's good-looking, rich, ready to settle down. I say you go on a few dates, see if you like him, and if you do, there's no doubt in my mind he'll propose to you within the month."

"That fast?"

"He wants a family," Heath says. "You want kids. It works."

As if it's that simple.

The man's everything I'm supposed to want, so I'm not sure why I'm worried about what my brother is suggesting.

"Ashford's a fuckboy. He always has been. There was a time I thought he had grown up, but after—"

"After what?"

He was going to say something, but he changed his mind somewhere along the way. But I want to know.

"Heath?"

"Nothing. I'm saying we find you someone you want. Who will mate with you."

"Mr. Gardener? Miss Gardener?" The man in blue is there, door open. I stand up on shaky legs, and as we step inside, all I can smell is the seductive aroma of rich, earthy oak. The touch of sweetness that turns things on within me.

I grab Heath's arm, both for support and to stop him from rushing Stephan, who's beside the Monarch in the center of the room. She's somehow more intimidating in her black suit than she was when I was first presented to her.

"I have to say, Miss Gardener, you're not the quaint little Omega I thought you were," she says, coming up to me. I dig my fingers harder into Heath's arm. Her gaze flicks to my brother. "Fredrick will escort your brother from the room. He isn't needed for this conversation."

"With all due respect, Monarch. She's my sister and I am her guardian," my brother says with a bow of his head.

Sophine looks him up and down. "You are aware of the importance of an Omega? They are the jewels in our society's crown. With breeding and manners, they are elite. Now add that extra something, that sparkle, and you have the standout."

He frowns. "Violet can find a mate on her own. She doesn't need the Luxe title."

"Oh, but she does. With your family's mishaps with money and your father's untimely passing, you're lucky Mr. Ashford's even sniffing around."

Stephan steps forward. "Sophine, that's not—"

"Shush, Stephan," she snaps, and he freezes. "You've done enough damage with that mouth of yours for today." She turns back to Heath. "Out. Now."

The male Omega, Fredrick, walks over to see Heath out and misery strikes hard. My brother gives me one last sorrowful look before leaving.

When the doors shut, the Monarch waves her hand for Stephan to take the empty space beside me. He does.

"Now, tonight has been...intriguing," she begins, glancing at each of us before resting fully on me. "You know, before tonight, I was considering removing the Luxe status from you, maybe giving it to another Omega, but now..."

Words tumble from my mouth as fear sets in. "Nothing really happened, Monarch. It wasn't much of a kiss. Something innocent and—"

"Not the kiss." She cuts me off. "Stephan informed me of your arrangement."

I look at him as betrayal rips through me. "Wha-what?"

"He's told me everything. About your fake courtship to attract a suitable Alpha and so that he could dodge the Season's expectations of him."

I start to sway on my feet as the room both stretches and shrinks. Prickles dance along my skin, and I'm suddenly feeling too hot, sweaty. But something cool and calm encircles me, and someone's fingers are curling into mine.

"You're okay, Princess," Stephan whispers. Even so low and gentle, his Alpha voice reverberates inside me. "I had to tell her. To save your reputation."

"Interesting," the Monarch says, watching us. "You react to him. Can you smell him? Even now?"

What an odd thing to ask. "Yes. Why?"

"He's wearing scent blockers. Strong ones. As you are. I can't smell either of you, but clearly, you know each other's scents."

Stephan and I both glance at each other and nod.

"They say that means something," she says. "Maybe what Stephan told me is true."

What did he tell her?

I'm about to ask, when she drops the next bomb on me. "Do you like him?"

Oh god.

Humiliation burns. I glance at Stephan.

"Well? Do you?" she presses. "I need to know."

There's no reason to lie at this point.

"Yes, I do," I whisper, "but—"

She nods, as if my answer doesn't surprise her at all.

"But—"

"Unfortunately, there have been too many scandalous moments from you two," she says, raising her voice. "It's almost as if you cannot stay away from each other, even though the courtship is a fake one."

"Wait, no." I let go of Stephan's hand and press it to my chest, where my heart is beating rapidly. "I was trying to end it before...before..."

The Monarch moves to her high-backed chair and sits, one leg perched over the other. "Are you telling me you *want* to end the courtship with my nephew, Miss Gardener?"

Her...what?

Nephew?

When I glance over at Stephan again, he's glaring at her, eyes full of a long-running disdain.

His *aunt*? It makes sense now how he was able to get a meeting with her so easily at the first ball.

What other secrets is this man keeping?

Sophine goes on. "As I see it, you both have two options. I order Stephan back to Emporia, and you, Miss Gardener, will be left to suffer the consequences of these actions, more than likely losing any social standing you and your family now have."

Ruin me, she means. It'll ruin me and any chances I— or my sisters—have of finding a mate.

"*Or...*" Stephan prompts through clenched teeth.

"Or there's a mark."

"What?" Stephan's fist clenches. "Those can't be the only two fucking options!"

"Language, Stephan." A small smile lifts one side of Sophine's mouth. "I'm trying to help you here. If you don't bite her, then word will get out. Violet's only dodged scandal before because of a blurry picture and an unreliable eye witness. Do you think she's going to be able to skate by a third time?"

"No one saw us tonight. We were in the dark. Alone," Stephan argues.

"Can you guarantee that? Will you stake her reputation on it?"

At that, Stephan stops.

Even he doesn't know what to do.

"That's what I figured." Sophine stands again, looking us both over. Then her piercing gaze falls to her nephew and the smile returns, this time stretching across her face. "You're all in now, Stephan. There's no running from it this time."

Hivemind... Can I tell you the Hargrave House party was worth it? Because, brood, it was.

And not just for the views.

Well, maybe the views.

As you all know, this Season is getting hot, getting vibe-y, getting filled with spilled tea.

Before we get to the entrée (or is it the dessert?), I have a few things to tell you...

Miss Felicity Fine is singing songs and dirges about our dreamboat Asher St. James. Yes, Mr. Movie Star is a heartbreaker, as we expected.

Is that why he's here? To escape an ex-lover?

Or are other scandals just waiting in the wings to appear on stage?

One blonde Sabine Omega seems to think so. She's been heard whispering his name, getting cozy in corners, and sporting what people are saying might be an Alpha bite.
And we all know a mark means an Alpha has laid claim, and a mating ceremony is to come!

But others are saying it was all a ruse. Just a bit of lipstick meant to cause a stir.

I wonder what our Luxe thinks about all this?

Miss V was seen leaving the Hargrave House party early and hitting the town for some St.-James-free fun.

GASP!

Is Sabine's power couple no more?

We don't know yet, but the Queen Bee will tell you this:

Our Luxe was seen this morning with a pristine neck. Her throat was unmarked.

But for how long?

- Queen Bee

Chapter Twenty

Stephan

The wait in the Gardeners' sitting room is excruciating, even though Mrs. Gardener serves me tea and offers me cake. My thoughts have been a little preoccupied since the night of the Hargrave party, club Yin, kiss in the dark.

I don't regret much in my life, but kissing Violet purposefully in front of Heath and the Monarch's men? Not my smartest move. But thinking about losing her, thinking that might be the last time I could have her to myself...

There's no excusing it. Now I've fucked this up for the both of us.

Even more so when I had decided to confess to Sophine our plans. To be fair, she was threatening me and Violet with banishment and estrangement, the same thing she did when she'd found out about my relationship with CeeCee. I couldn't care less—I've built my own life away from Sabine and my family's connections. But Violet? Her family is everything to her.

It would devastate her.

So I told the battle-ax everything.

And when she had asked me to tell her the truth about my feelings for Violet...I told her that, too.

Violet perplexes me. I think about her too much. I always catch myself staring, noticing the little things about her—how she worries her lip when she's overthinking or scrunches her nose when she doesn't like something. When she looks at me, really looks at me, I feel...different. Off-balance. And when she's gone, I'm restless.

I don't know what that means, if our act has only confused things more, but I found myself rambling when answering Sophine's question. I like her, I settled on, which is true. And when given the chance to answer the same question, Violet had told Sophine the same about me.

But *like* is a far cry from *wanting a mark*, and that's exactly what she's forcing us to do.

"No, thank you," I say to Mrs. Gardener as she holds out a plate of freshly baked oatmeal cookies. My stomach is doing somersaults. I hadn't slept a wink last night, either.

Heath sits in an armchair reading something on his tablet but makes sure to stop every few seconds to glare at me.

Dick.

Tradition says I'm going to have to ask his permission to claim Violet as my mate, before marking her. I know he's itching to get me alone to either try his hand at beating the shit out of me or find out what happened last night when the Monarch sent him out of the room. Maybe both.

But I need to talk to Violet first. It's why I walked into the lion's den today to take Violet out to dinner for a moment alone with her.

With her heat so close, it's risky, but as long as I don't touch her, I should be able to curb my primal urges.

I've wondered why I seem to be the only Alpha who's being so affected by her heat cues, but my guess is that it has something to do with the fact that I can smell her, even with the blockers on. And, as she confessed to Sophine, she can smell me too.

I've never heard of something like this happening before.

Dahlia plays a somber song on the piano, while Mari doodles in her sketchbook on the couch across from the fireplace. Next to her, Rue scrolls on her phone mindlessly while taking bites of a cookie.

The only ones missing from this family reunion are Iris and Violet.

The doorbell rings, and Rue's up and racing off to answer it before anyone else can. A moment later, she comes in with the biggest bouquet of delicate purple and white flowers—lavender, roses, carnations, snapdragons—and my blood goes cold.

The piano stops as Dahlia turns to look. Even Mari glances up from her sketchbook.

"O.M.G., they're for Violet!" Rue squeals, reading the little note on the wrapping.

"Oh, they're gorgeous, Stephan," Mrs. Gardener says.

Something shrivels within me.

I clear my throat. "They're not from—"

"From someone called Dominic." Rue glances at me. "Who's that?"

Heath's grin is slow and toothy. "It's a very nice Alpha who's interested in Violet. He met her at the Hargrave party and has been hounding me to schedule a date with her."

Fucking asshole.

Stockton's a wet paper bag. And Heath's an asshole.

Rue drops the princess's flowers on top of the piano, much to Dahlia's dismay.

"Oh, and there's this." Iris walks in with Quinn. They're both struggling to hold a basket filled with violets, wine, and assorted crackers and cheeses. "That Dominic fellow sent this too."

Overkill.

Rue pulls out a card and begins to read. "It says, 'Beauty for the b—'"

Iris snatches the card and shoves it back in the basket. "It's Violet's. Not yours."

As Iris and Quinn drop the basket near the piano, Rue whirls on me. "What did you get her?" she asks.

"Dinner with me at the best restaurant in Sabine," I say.

"Mickey's Burger Joint?"

"No, kid, grown-up stuff. Better than flowers."

"It better not be too grown-up," Heath grumbles, but I catch it, and the unspoken threat.

"When is Vi coming down?" Rue groans. "It's taking *forever.*"

"Hush," Mrs. Gardener says.

"I'm here." Violet's there in the doorway, gaze dragging over everyone in the room until finally resting on me.

There's a smile there, but it's forced, masking the stress simmering underneath. The dress she wears is a simple shift of high-necked netting with a lower cut beneath. The green, gold, and violet hues make her skin almost luminous. Her hair is curled and piled up high with curls falling all around her face, where touches of gold glitter are dusted on her cheeks, and I'm struck dumb by how absolutely gorgeous she looks. Less like a sheltered princess and more like a vixen.

"Vi! Look at what Dominic sent you!" Rue points to the bouquet and basket. "Aren't they beautiful!"

She barely looks at them and nods. "Very much so."

"I already volunteered to chaperone tonight," Iris says. "Gonna make sure there's nothing else for Queen Bee to write about these two lovebirds."

Heath pushes to his feet. "Like hell you are. Chaperones aren't supposed to be single or young. I'll do it."

She meets his stare head on and crosses her arms over her chest. "Like you're neither of those things, too? Or is it allowed because, what? Because you're an Alpha? I don't think so. *I'll* be chaperoning."

"Are you sure, Iris?" Violet whispers. "You hate this stuff."

She shrugs. "I got nothing else to do. And besides, I'm starving." She shares a look with Quinn and something secret passes between them. "See you later, Quinn."

The Beta waves, her smile pleasant. "Until next time, Gardeners." She turns to Heath. "*Heather.*" Then she's gone.

Heath grunts. "Betas."

I'll take Iris over Heath chaperoning us any day, so I stand, take Violet by the hand, and walk with her to the door before Heath tries to fight harder against it.

Petit Fleur is one of the best restaurants in Sabine, with a top culinary chef and world-renowned pâtissiers. It's romantic, hard as hell to get a reservation for, and full of the well-to-do. Even the Monarch is known to visit once in a blue moon.

I've never taken any of my flings here—too public for the high-end of society—but that's just the reason I picked it. It's my attempt to put some of the hurtful rumors on Stitch to rest.

Why?

Why do I care what people are whispering behind my back? I don't. Not for myself, anyway. But for Violet? That's a different story. I know she cares, and since I'm partly to blame for the mess she's in, I feel obligated to offer her some peace.

I'm still trying to figure out how to get around the Monarch's mating ultimatum.

One thing at a time.

When we arrive at Petit Fleur, every single eye is on the three of us as the maître d' takes us to the table I requested, nestled in the back corner for privacy. But before we sit, Iris pretends to shiver and makes a show of it.

"Hey, Mr. Fancy-pants," she says. "It's a bit chilly back here under the vent. Do you think you have another spot for me where I won't turn into a solid block of ice?"

"Oh, I'm sorry. Do you want me to find you a different table for the evening?" the maître d' asks, holding the menus to his chest.

"No, no. Not them. Just me. I'm the one with the cold blood."

It's obvious what she's doing—trying to give us the space and privacy we need right now while still following the chaperoning rules. Loosely following them, that is.

"Absolutely." After setting down our two menus, the maître d' gestures for her to follow him, but before she goes, she glances at us.

Violet mouths "thank you" and Iris winks before walking off to a table across the room.

We take our seats.

Eyes and a few heads shift our way, and I notice a tremor that passes through Violet.

"We need to talk," I start in a soft tone. "And thanks to your sister, we can. Make sure you tell her I owe her one."

"She'll hold you to that," Violet says, "but she knows I've been...struggling, so..."

"Did you tell her about—"

"No. She thinks it's just normal Season drama. And I'd like to keep it that way, but she's very perceptive. She knows when things are getting too much for me."

"She *is* your sister," I say.

"Yeah, but I've always been really good at hiding things. Especially about myself." She looks down at the menu in front of her. "I guess I'm not as good at it as I thought. Things are slipping through now. First the near panic attack at the ball, then the fainting. The nights without sleep."

"It's a lot, I know. And now the Monarch is trying to force us to mate."

"Your aunt, you mean."

I nod. "It's an unfortunate truth."

"You don't like her?"

"I know you might disagree with me here, but blood doesn't always mean family," I say. "Sophine has always caused me more grief than anything else. Penrith is my family. That's all I need."

A waiter comes, recites the specials. We both order the duck, and I order an expensive bottle of wine before he shuffles off and we're alone again.

"Why did you kiss me again?" she asks out of nowhere, and I nearly choke on my next breath.

"Kiss you?"

"Yeah, like that. Like you were trying to prove something."

I lick my lips. "I don't know what you mean."

She sighs. "It doesn't matter. Because of it, the Monarch is forcing you to mark me, for us to mate."

The misery on her face is hard to ignore. It tugs at my pride. "Would being my mate be that bad?" I ask. "You told the Monarch you like me."

Her cheeks redden in a slight blush. "I do. You haven't given me any reason not to like you."

I don't know why, but that stings. When she had told Sophine that she liked me, I thought she meant more than... like an acquaintance.

"But to be mated with someone who doesn't want to be mated to me? That's not the life I want for myself."

Ah.

"But you're okay with being mated to someone you don't love."

"You'd rather not be mated at all," she replies with a biting edge.

I look around at the neighboring tables, but everyone seems too engrossed in their meals to be paying us any attention.

"Listen. The Monarch's clearly doing this to get back at me for...for not always bowing to her whim." I almost slip up there and resurrect something I want to keep buried. "I've been thinking of a way to get us out of it."

"Have you come up with anything?" she asks.

"Not yet. But I'll think of something."

She frowns. "I don't know how much longer I can keep this hidden. Especially from Heath. He always shoulders everything. I try but he's carrying the house, all of us."

"He probably would say the same thing about you." Actually, I know he would. He has.

She doesn't answer that. Instead, she circles back to the main conversation. "We don't have much time before the next event. The Monarch's going to want to see a mark..."

"I know."

"And I don't want this ruining anything I may have with Mr. Stockton."

The mention of that man is like a slap to the face. "You're still considering him?"

"Of course I am."

The waiter comes with the wine. He uncorks the bottle and begins to pour us each a generous glass. I chug all of mine before he's done pouring Violet's, and with wide eyes, he refills mine.

When he leaves, Violet continues, "His interest is real. This—" she waves her hand between us "—isn't."

"You know nothing about him," I argue.

"I know nothing about you," she counters.

Well, fuck. She got me there.

I take a sip of the wine, wishing I had ordered myself something stronger. "What do you want to know?"

She rubs her lips together and looks over to where her sister sits eating an assortment of mini quiches. When her gaze comes back to mine, she says, "Did you always want to be an actor?"

Standard interview question. One I've answered thousands of times before. But the question now is do I give her my rehearsed interview answer or the truth?

The truth is more boring, but...

"No. I wanted to be a writer," I say.

"Like writing books?"

I shake my head. "Not specifically books, no. I always liked plays, scripts, that sort of thing. But apparently my face is meant to be in front of the camera. Not behind it. So I took the opportunity and ran with it."

She perks up, sitting up in her chair. "Do you still write?"

"Not as much as I used to," I confess. "It's hard to when shooting days are so long, and then there's rehearsals, and public appearances."

"I would have never guessed a writer. And are these scripts romances like your movies?"

"The complete opposite, actually. Dramas."

"Like...soap operas?" She laughs, trying to conceal it by covering her mouth.

"Hey. Nothing wrong with soap operas. I co-starred in a couple of them." When she continues to laugh, a light-hearted, airy sound, I take her hand away from her mouth and place it on the table between us.

"You really don't watch TV much, do you?"

"Sorry." Her gaze drops to my hand covering hers, and we both pause. A single touch. The one thing I told myself I wouldn't do, and here we are.

And as expected, the simple connection is like a zap right to my cock, my body instantly being able to sense her heat and wanting to rut.

"I hate to break up this little love-fest." Iris is there beside our table suddenly, looking grim. "But the Monarch has just entered the building and is about to sit just a stone's throw away. I suggest we cut this short."

A quick glimpse around Iris to the large round table on the opposite side of the room confirms what she said. Sophine, dressed in a navy pantsuit and matching hair brooch, walks over to it, with Fredrick and two security guards in tow. When she sits, her gaze fixes on me, and she presses two fingers to her neck then taps her wrist.

It's a warning.

I don't have much time to give Violet a mark.

Bitch.

I stand. "Yeah. It's time to go."

CHAPTER TWENTY-ONE

Violet

Iris sneaks into my room later that night.

We're past the age of sneaking about when everyone's asleep, but she's in silly pajamas in bright pink— the only pink I ever really see her wear—holding milk in an old-fashioned white glass bottle and a tray heaped with chocolate chip cookies.

It makes me smile.

There's an ache growing inside me. A restlessness that only seems to calm when I'm around him.

Stephan.

And since I'm not meant to have him, I need to ignore it and push on.

Some sister-girl time will help, so I'm thankful for Iris's impromptu visit.

"If you tell anyone I still own these pajamas, I'll destroy

you." Iris pokes out her tongue. Then she puts the bottle and cookies down on the floor and climbs on the bed.

"I would never."

She studies me. "Maybe if you broke the rules more you wouldn't—"

"Be so boring?"

"So tense."

The scent of chocolate wafts around me, something I normally love, but I'm not sure I can eat it. "Thanks for coming today, by the way. And for giving us space to talk."

She pushes a cookie into my hand. "Eh, Heath being there would've only made things worse. And it's obvious you two have a lot going on." She shrugs. "Eat. At least a bite."

I nibble on one for her, and it's good. "I don't feel poisoned."

"Rue made them for you. And for Stephan, apparently, because she thinks you should hurry up and get a mark."

A shiver races through me. Should I tell Iris about the Monarch's ultimatum?

"Is that what you want?" she asks. "Or is Dominic Stockton the one for you?"

"I don't—"

"It's me, Vi. You can tell me the truth. Hell, if you don't want either, we can come up with a plan B."

"I'm not running off to join the circus or something." A laugh bubbles up at that. But it fades as my stomach starts to roil.

"But seriously, Vi. This is *your* life here. No one else's. You have to do what *you* want. Not Mom. Not Heath. You."

A groan breaks free, and a wave of heat hits. I flap my pajama top to get some air.

"This is a nice night... So..." Iris studies me. "Are you still wearing your blocker?"

I nod.

"Is your stomach feeling like it's being ripped apart?"

"Aftermath of nerves. I nearly had a panic attack at the restaurant once the Monarch showed up."

"Yeah, that was an unwanted surprise," Iris says. "I was really enjoying the food. Were you able to talk to Stephan about what you wanted to talk to him about?"

I nod. "It just...didn't solve anything. Didn't make me feel any better."

"You make it sound like you both are walking to your deaths or something," she says. "Want to tell me what's going on?"

My gaze slips away. "No."

She unscrews the lid to the milk and hands it to me. "Drink."

I splutter at the floral sharp burn of whatever's in there. It's not milk. But the heat burns a path down, and I take another big sip as she motions me to.

Then Iris takes the bottle for herself. "Mother's Milk. Gin, rose blossom, peach nectar, and seltzer."

"Heath's going to kill you."

"Double kill me. I stole it from 'The Dad Room.'"

"Iris." I take the bottle as she hands it to me once more. "You stole booze?"

"Repurposed the mo-fo and then took it to the kitchen, decanted, mixed, and ta-da. I think I have a future in bartending." But her grin fades. "Vi...have you and Stephan...?"

Horror grips me, and she forces me to drink more, making the panic peace out in the burn of the booze. "No. Of course not."

"The kiss?"

I think about the other one when we ran, the good one, the real kiss where I kissed him back. All those others, he mainly kissed me, and they were like training. So that time, in the early hours under the tree, I could feel myself bloom and I did it, really kissed him back as if it was real.

And even though it's Iris, she isn't asking about a kiss; she's asking about something more, something that might make me fall in love.

But love isn't an option for me. I may feel something for Stephan, but he's made it very clear he doesn't want a mate—not really. So if he doesn't find a way out of the Monarch's requirement for him to claim me, then we may be stuck together after all.

And I don't want that either.

"He... I... It was just a peck. It was nothing, really."

"But you like him."

"No, Iris—"

"I know you, and it's not that he's famous or good-looking. You like *him*. And maybe he likes you. He sure seems to. He gets...prowl-y when he sees you, like he's making sure no one's about to go all Alpha on *his* Omega."

"You're seeing things."

"Am I? He might not get it, but I do."

"Iris Anne. You're a closet romantic!"

She takes the bottle from me. "Am not."

"I can't like him," I say, the words spilling free.

"Why not? Because of Dominic? He's old—"

"I think," I say, fiddling with my hands, "he's out of my league."

"Bullshit."

I hug her, and breathe her in, and close my eyes. "I'm not those other girls. They're glamorous, beautiful, sophisticated, and I'm positive there's something with the new girl, Alicia."

"That cow? Rich never means class, Vi. She's rich but no class. New money."

"And you're a closet snob."

She hugs me tight. "Closet? No, I just call it as I see it."

"Thing is I open my mouth and I'm boring. I've never done anything. And…" I squeeze her as I try not to cry. I don't even know why I want to cry. "Why did she choose me? There are plenty of nice, beautiful Omegas out there, one who'll be happy to be his mate, who wants to please. I—"

"Violet." She untangles herself from me. "You are not someone who should settle. And fuck pleasing a man, what about pleasing you?"

"The Season is about finding a mate." I say the words I've already told myself so many times. "It's not going to be Stephan. In the end, he'll want someone more exciting."

"Then he's an idiot."

I take the bottle from where she put it, pick up my cookie, and wash it down with this Mother's Milk concoction. It's growing on me, or maybe it's the fuzzy warmth the booze sends through me that settles and soothes and calms.

Iris gets up and goes to my vanity, picks up my hairbrush, then she comes back and starts brushing my hair. And while I've always liked having my hair brushed, that peculiar massage it gives that's so good at calming, but with the alcohol it's even better.

"If you want Stephan, then tell him. Forget the games. Or if you want Dominic, tell Stephan to fuck off. This is about you. Screw this stupid system."

"Iris!" I gasp at her curse and then laugh. "We're Omegas. We can't. We're built for Alphas. It's in our DNA."

"If you say so." She goes silent as she brushes slowly in a way that makes me want to purr. "If this is what you want, then go for it. If Stephan doesn't bite—literally and figuratively—just find someone else. I'm sure Heath has a list, color-coded and ranked no doubt."

I laugh at that.

"You think all the things that make you *you* are a hindrance, but they show your innocence and that's an aphrodisiac to Alphas. Alphas want a prize mate, innocent, pristine. Untouched. You really are a Luxe."

"I don't feel Luxe-like. I feel...blah."

"Oh, that's just anxiety," she says. "A few more drinks and we can clear that right up."

We settle in, passing the milk and the cookie tray back and forth. I haven't laughed like this in a long time, and it is...freeing.

Rue jumps up and down with way too much energy and glee. "When is the Monarch announcing the next event?"

"There's this regatta today," I say. "And it's pretty. Look at the boats on the big lake. The dresses, the food. Plus we're at the Monarch's estate with the maze."

She rolls her eyes. "I want a ball. Something fancy."

"You can complain when it's your turn for a Season."

I set up the blanket as the rest of my family settle in and Mom starts handing out refreshments.

"I'll be mated before then. I'm finding an Alpha who can't resist me so he'll mark me and whisk me away. And if Asher doesn't have a brother or a friend, then I'll find one of my own."

"You're fourteen." I grab at her, but she dances away.

"Not now, Vi. Later. When I'm of age and all grown up and having heats. I bet they're amazing!"

Speaking of Asher, aka Stephan, he isn't anywhere to be seen. I haven't heard from him or seen him since our date last week. He was supposed to tell me a plan to get out of the Monarch's mark requirement, but he's been missing in action. Even today, he's meant to be here—his aunt Penrith is attending—but he's nowhere to be seen.

I want to cry.

Already there are whispers. They've been circulating about Jade, who's going to beat me to a mating ceremony according to this morning's Stitch and Rue's constant updates. A fresh bite mark shines on her neck today as she struts around the lawn, showing it off and giggling to her friends.

"Vi!" Scooting in, Rue slides on her knees to land next to me and shoves her phone about an inch from my nose.

"Vi! Look! I think it's a surprise ball. There's a lucky dip for masks after sunset. Where's Asher? Or are you dumping him and letting someone else make a play? Dominic? Did you know Heath has a list? I saw it, and—"

"Go get some of those candied apple slices, Rue," Mom says.

My sister sighs and stomps off. I bite my nails.

The whispers are like waves and the sneaky looks are like mosquito bites. They make me itch, want to hide, and still I don't see Stephan.

Rue's right. While I haven't been on dates since the Hargrave party, it's obvious Dominic's still interested in me. Heath says that important phone call had dragged him out of Sabine again for business, but he is returning today for the regatta. He's been sending flowers and gifts every day, and although it's sweet and thoughtful, I can't shake whatever is between me and Stephan.

Unlike Stephan, Dominic is a real possibility. A great choice for a mate. I just have to remember that. And today will be my chance to hopefully make things more official between us.

Since Stephan hasn't come up with a plan to get us out of this entanglement, I have to. If I can secure a mark from Dominic before I see Stephan again, then the Monarch won't have a choice but to let us off the hook.

That's my hope, anyway.

Children chase each other and laugh. It's supposed to be a day of peace without such strict rules of decorum that the balls have, but I can't settle.

Heath's talking to a handsome young man, who's

eyeing me, and then older, good-looking Dominic comes up to him and they shake hands.

Heath gives me that commanding look he has.

This is it. This is my chance.

Holding my breath, I walk over.

"You remember Mr. Stockton?" Heath asks.

"Of course. Thank you for the flowers and all the lovely gifts, Mr. Stockton." I glance at Heath, and to his credit, he smiles at me.

Dominic is staring at me, mouth slightly agape, but then he seems to shake himself out of it and takes my hand. "I'm so sorry. It's just...you are absolutely beautiful, Miss Gardener. It takes me off guard each time I see you."

I blink and my cheeks redden. "Oh. Well...thank you."

"I'm sorry business took me away for so long, but I thought about you every day I was away."

I don't know what to say—his flattery is overwhelming—so I settle for the obvious. "You're back now."

"I am. And I hope you will do me the honor of a walk on this perfect day?" He offers his arm.

I glance again at Heath, who gives me a knowing nod.

"It would be an honor." I slip my hand around his arm and let him lead me away.

The sun is high, drenching the Monarch's estate in gold. The heat presses thick against my skin as I follow Dominic down the winding path. The hedges of the maze rise tall around us, their green leaves rustling in the occasional breeze. It should be beautiful, peaceful even, but my pulse flutters with unease.

"This way," Dominic says over his shoulder, his voice smooth, reassuring. A gentleman's voice.

I hesitate. I shouldn't be here, alone with him, away from the others. A walk around the lawn, in public, is one thing. But we're too secluded over here at the maze for it not to be scandalous.

But he smiles, inviting me to something innocent. "You trust me, don't you?"

I don't, not really. But I want to. I want him to think I'm a true Luxe Omega, a worthy mate for him, so I nod. He's been nothing but a gentleman, offering his arm as he led me away, his voice light with harmless conversation.

We walk deeper into the maze, the sounds of distant conversation and laughter from the lawn fading with each turn. The hedges close in, the path narrowing.

He stops suddenly and turns to face me, removing my hand from his arm and reaching for my other hand. His fingers lightly wrap around mine.

"I wanted a moment alone with you," he says, his voice softer now, intimate. His thumbs brush against my knuckles, a small touch, but it sends a ripple of something uncertain through me.

"We should go back," I say and force a small, uneasy laugh.

His grip tightens—just a fraction. "Not yet."

Then his hands find my waist. Slow, deliberate. His fingers press against the fabric of my dress, a touch that lingers too long.

"Mr. Stockton—" I shift back, but there's nowhere to go. The hedge scratches against my shoulders. "I don't think— My brother—"

He doesn't let go. If anything, he steps closer, crowding the space between us. "Your brother has been pushing us together for some time, Violet." The use of my first name feels wrong coming from his lips. His fingers skim higher, tracing the curve of my ribs. "You're looking for a mate and I'm looking for an Omega who is ready for a pack and children. With your first heat so close..."

My breath catches. I shove his hands away. "How... How did you know that? My blockers—"

He inhales through his nose, trying to draw in my scent. "An Alpha knows. Especially one as old as I am. I also work with the very blockers you wear and know when they're straining to suppress the flood of pheromones you're giving off." His grip returns, firmer now. "I want to own that first heat."

Panic flutters in my chest as he moves closer. I push at his chest but he doesn't budge.

"Mr. Stockton, please." My voice is smaller than I want it to be. "I—I need to go."

His expression shifts, something dark flickering in his eyes. "Violet, I'm claiming you. Isn't that what you want? Your brother has already given me his blessing."

My skin grows cold despite the summer heat. Heath didn't tell me that.

With a swift yank, he spins me so that my back is completely pressed against him. His erection is *there*, hard against my back.

Oh god.

He presses his nose into my hair and draws in another deep breath like he's dying to get a whiff of my scent through the blocker. "I just need to give you the mark and you're mine."

"Stephan—" I don't know why his name comes out of

my mouth, but it does, gaining an angry snort from Dominic.

"That egotistical Emporian fop?" He laughs. My stomach twists.

Then I hear it.

The crunch of footsteps on gravel. Heavy. Purposeful.

Dominic must hear it too because his grip loosens just slightly. But it's too late.

There's a yelp from behind me, and suddenly, he's yanked backward. I am pulled back with him, but his loose footing allows me to break free of his hold and drop to the ground.

I spin just in time to see a fist colliding with Dominic's jaw, and the crack of the impact is sharp in the air.

Stephan stands between us now, his shoulders tense, his usually playful expression carved into something furious. His brown eyes, normally calm, burn with barely restrained violence, reminding me of when he came to Club Yin and defended Quinn from that creep.

"Touch her again," Stephan says, his voice quiet, lethal, "and I'll break your fucking jaw."

"This isn't your business." Dominic barely gets his arms up before the next punch lands, sending him crashing against the hedge. Blood pours from his split lip.

I stand frozen, breath caught in my throat as Stephan grabs Dominic by the collar and shoves him back against the thick greenery. "Everything Violet does is my business. I claimed her."

Dominic coughs. "There's— There's no mark—"

Stephan doesn't wait for him to finish. He slams him back again, then releases him roughly, letting him stumble.

"Don't *ever* put your hands on my Omega again or this Emporian fop won't let you walk away breathing."

For a second, Dominic hesitates. But then he wipes his bleeding lip, flicking his gaze between us before turning on his heel and disappearing back into the maze.

When he's gone, Stephan whirls on me, his shoulders rising and falling with each ragged breath.

I should say something—thank him, maybe—but words stick in my throat. My heart is pounding so hard, I can feel the drum of it everywhere, and all I can focus on is him—how thankful I am that he found me. How close the situation was to getting out of hand, and I—

Eyes flaring, Stephan pulls me to him with a growl, mouth on mine as he kisses me with a savage thoroughness that makes my head spin. Like Dominic, his cock is hard and there against me. But this time, my body reacts with indescribable hunger.

Unless it's the adrenaline coursing through me, Dominic must've been right about my heat being close. I've never felt like this before, aching, and so needy for him to touch me I could cry. I moan into his mouth. Our tongues duel like we can't get enough, and I want to climb into him, on him, let him slide into me deep. I want to do all the things we saw on that knotting porn. Take him in my mouth, have him rut me.

I slip my hand under his shirt and the heat of him sinks into me, his stomach fluttering at my touch, and I go lower, over the belt to the grand prize, his cock.

Feeling him, even through the clothes, is a revelation. He's beautiful, I think, although I can't see his erection. It's thick, hard, long, and twitches when I touch it.

He lets me explore, his mouth now skimming down over my throat, teeth grazing my skin, making me tingle and ache for him to bite.

Stephan pulls my hand from him and raises his head. "Such a good girl, my beautiful girl."

And then his hand goes down my hip, to my thigh, gathering my skirt, and I start to shake, nearly coming apart with anticipation. He shifts, kissing me again, and I'm torn with where I need to concentrate, his mouth on mine or his hand...

Oh, his hand as it slides over my upper thigh, his knee slipping between mine to widen my legs. My pussy throbs deep inside and my thighs start to get wet, like...oh, god...is that slick?

"You're all hot for me. I can smell it, Princess, and it's turning me all the way on." Then he touches the wetness, and I lose my mind. He strokes his fingers along the crotch of my panties and it's pure pleasure, a dull throbbing need for more, and he keeps doing it, making things inside me flutter. Then...oh...god...then he nudges aside the panties and strokes me flesh on flesh.

Electric.

Melting everything.

I shudder, shake, and grip him hard, thrusting my hips forward, wanting more, wanting him *in* me.

He pushes two fingers in, and the stretching invasion is like nothing else. I'm spiraling, climbing, reaching new pinnacles of delicious aching, of tingling goodness.

"Yes, come for me, Princess..."

Stephan starts to rub my clit with his thumb as he thrusts into me, and I lose it. I sob as every atom tears free in a wild euphoric dance as I explode. I spasm as the orgasmic release completely overtakes me.

As I'm at my height, he pulls his hand free, grabs my hair and yanks my head back. It's the sweetest pain.

He growls and starts to suck and lick my throat. I press it hard against his mouth, and I feel it. The shattering of his control.

Stephan sinks his teeth into me, and I twitch as another little orgasm escapes and everything inside me comes alive. It feels so good. Better than anything I've ever imagined, and I'm a whimpering mess, putty in his arms, especially as he sucks on my neck harder.

When he pulls away, I look up at him with blurry vision, lost in ecstasy. He's staring down at me with the same kind of dreamy-eyed gaze.

"Princess... I—"

His lips brush mine, about to kiss me again, when oncoming hurried footsteps steal the blissful moment away.

I turn my head.

That's when Mom, Heath, and all my sisters round the hedge. Every eye widens as they take in the scene.

Mom's shocked silent. Rue's squealing and snapping pictures on her phone. Dahlia's covering her eyes, while Mari is giggling and Iris is smirking like she knows what happened just before they found us.

But it's Heath's furious expression that stills my heart. He's seething. His entire body shakes with the force of it. *"Ashford!"*

Chapter Twenty-Two

Stephan

Shit.

Now I can feel her, the intake of breath, those other vibrations in the air that connect to me and only me. How she's scared, miserable, filled with guilt, and consumed with desire. The princess wants me. Wants to get on her knees and worship my cock. Wants to lie back and spread herself open to welcome me into the depths of her body and take my knot.

I don't just feel this.

I *know*.

Because with my mark, she's my princess now.

What the fuck have I done?

Heath speaks again, and this time it registers. His presence cuts through the haze over me, that connection to her, and she moves into me even as her brother puts hands on me, pulling me away.

And I let him.

"I said what the fuck have you done?" he says, throwing me into the opposite hedges.

"Heath—" Violet's voice trembles.

"Shut up, Vi. Go with Mom, now. I'm going to talk to Ashford."

I look at her, not moving. It isn't for myself, it's for her. She looks like she's going to throw up, and she's avoiding my eyes, like she knows if we connect then things will explode.

"It'll be fine, Princess."

That earns a growl from Heath. But she turns and runs.

Once all the women have disappeared, he rounds on me. "You fucking, pathetic asshole." He makes a fist and draws back, but I launch myself at him, pinning him where I had Dominic.

And the irony isn't lost on me.

The beat in my veins is all for her. *Mine. Mine. Mine.* And Heath's in my way. I could break his neck if I wanted, the way I feel, the way the urge to lay claim surges, and if he's in my way, then ending him will—

Fuck.

Not even with CeeCee did I have this kind of visceral, animalistic response. Where instinct and primal needs obliterate common sense and higher thinking.

I'm blood and flesh and need.

Violet is mine.

Nothing will get in the way.

Nothing. No one.

I swallow hard and force myself to let him go. This is my friend. I shouldn't be fighting him, so I stumble back and wipe a shaking hand over my face. "I'm sorry. I'm sorry. I didn't mean—"

Heath walks up to me, then punches me so hard in the stomach pain blooms as I double over, unable to breathe. Then he shakes his head, as if clearing himself of his own anger.

"Don't you *ever* fucking touch me again or I'll rip you a new asshole. Friend or not," he says.

Threat heard loud and clear.

"I'm sorry. I don't feel like myself." I pace a few steps away and then come back, everything inside me buzzing. "Stockton just... I lost my cool when I saw them together. I..."

"On their walk?" Heath asks.

"He tried to take her. Not just bite. He was forcing himself on her. Touching her." I gnash my teeth as the fury bubbles up again. "The bastard was going to rape her if I hadn't stepped in."

"What?" Heath's anger now mirrors mine. "Are you serious?"

"Dead fucking serious. So if you want to kill someone, kill him. I'll fucking join you."

Heath glances over his shoulder like he's deciding whether to do just that. "He fooled me into thinking he was serious about her."

"The only thing he was serious about was not letting her say no."

"You should have killed him," he says. "Now I'm pissed you didn't."

There's still time.

"So then what?" Heath goes on. "You decided you were going to take his place and bit her instead?"

"I didn't mean to. Violet's so much more than you can possibly even think. She's good, and sweet, and smart, and I needed... I wanted to protect her and I guess..." I look helplessly at her brother. "Man, a part of me thought if she had my mark, she'd be safe. And—"

I stop because there's a cliff drop after that *and*. Something deep and new and wild.

"Shit, Ashford. Do you...do you love my sister?"

I don't answer. How can I when I'm not sure of the answer myself?

Everything is moving too fast. It's like the world has been tilted on its axis and I don't know which way is up.

"You're starting to scare me now. You have that look, one I haven't seen since Cecilia."

I close my eyes. "Please don't say her name."

"But Violet's my sister, Ashford. My *sister*. And it's not like you can give her what she wants."

"Why not? I can be a good mate. I have money, a good paying career. I'll be faithful, and—"

"Vi wants a big family."

Panic swirls up. Oh no, not that. "I can't. You know I can't. I can't have kids."

"It doesn't matter now because you bit her. You can't get out of it. You're going to have to tell Violet the truth," he says. "Talk to her."

I swallow. "I will. When I can."

"As soon as you can. She may not think so, but her

happiness is important, too," he says. "And now, as her mate, that's your responsibility."

Shit.

"I'll talk to her."

Heath nods, seeming satisfied, then turns to leave. I watch him go, letting out a slow breath as the weight of it all settles over me.

I just don't know if Violet's happiness and me being in her life can exist at the same time.

Breaking news, Hivemind!

Some of you may have seen the dashing Dominic Stockton emerging from the Monarch's maze with a bruised cheek and split lip. Everyone's been buzzing about what could have happened to him.

But did you see the Gardeners appear after? With one Asher St. James and a very windswept, dewy-eyed Violet in tow?

And guess who's now sporting a very fresh and swollen...

MARK?

Looks like we may never know what actually went down in that maze, but one thing's for sure, Hivemind...

Mr. Emporia wasn't going to give up his Luxe Omega without a fight.

And now the two are destined for a mating ceremony!

Looks like the Monarch chose right when she made Miss V this Season's Luxe because what an exciting turn of events!

I'll be keeping a sharp eye out. Details to come!

- Queen Bee

CHAPTER TWENTY-THREE

Violet

I don't know what's wrong with me. My head's being pulled in so many directions, and I can't concentrate.

"Vi? Did you see the latest QB? People want to know if you're..." Rue mimes the biggest pregnant belly I've ever seen which earns her a pillow to the face from Iris.

We're upstairs in my bedroom as Mom get things ready here for the party announcing Stephan's claim of me.

Mari looks at me over her sketchbook as Iris tugs the dress tight at my waist. "Did you know your mate's aunt Penrith sent a team of household servants over for us to use from now on?"

"You can't call them that," Dahlia says. "They get paid."

"Workers?" Rue says. "Any good seamstresses?"

"When it's your turn, Rue, I'll make you sacks to wear." Iris glares.

Rue grins. "I can rock a sack. I'll start a trend."

She probably will. "Can you make that less...tight?" I ask.

"Nope." Iris shakes her head. "They're gonna be looking right there." She pokes my belly. "Rue isn't wrong about the rumors."

"But I haven't—"

"We know. Look, you've got a mark. A movie star's mark, too. So everyone's gonna be talking about your ceremony dress and pups next." Iris rolls her eyes.

"She's right," Dahlia says.

So I let my sister poke and prod as she pins the dress. It's beautiful, the material a thick green-black silk, the heaviness giving it a nice drape, and I feel at once grown up in it. And like something is very, very wrong.

I'm beginning to hurt, cramp low in my belly, and I don't know if it's the thick fabric of the dress but I'm sweating.

I really need to talk to Stephan. His marking me has me more confused than ever. He'd promise he'd find a way to not follow the Monarch's mandate, and then he does this, so I need to know why. And why he kissed me like that... touched me like that...

My stomach aches, and I groan.

It's my heat. It has to be.

Before Dominic had turned into a complete monster, he had mentioned being able to sense it, even with the blocker concealing my scent. Stephan could've been wrapped up in his instincts too. It could've taken over and made him—

Regardless, what's done is done. Stephan marked me

and now we're linked together. Destined to be mates. The Monarch got exactly what she wanted.

"What's wrong?" Iris whispers. "Apart from everything."

"Everything. What if…if he doesn't…" I can't say *love*, because for him it was never on the table. "What if he doesn't want me?"

"Then he should have kept his mouth off you." Iris tugs tight on the back of the dress. "Stop ripping yourself in all directions trying to make the world happy. What about *you*?"

Me? I almost laugh. I'm both the least important and most valued player in this. I have the power to make others happy here. It's just that to do it for one side means the other is hurt or trapped.

But I nod, smile, and she carries on.

The doorbell rings and Rue flies out the door.

Downstairs there's a flutter of female voices and then commands are thrown out. I can't make out what, but I know the tone.

"What shoes?" Mari asks, looking over. "Heels in silver or gold? I've got spray paint if you need it. And should we use the diamond tiara?"

Panic starts to bear down. I don't need to play into the princess motif even more. "No, I…no."

Iris accidentally jabs me and I jump. "Sorry."

"O.M.G.!" Rue's back. "The Monarch sent a train of food and desserts. Mom almost fainted when she saw it all! Oh, I can't wait for tonight. Show me your bite again!"

Downstairs, the music's already started and the babble of people fills the air. It doesn't soothe; it weighs me down and not even Stephan's arrival helps. I know when he walks in. I know he's anxious, a little buzzed by this. It permeates me. Scares me, too.

Because it means I'll have to go down soon.

As a fanfare rises, his aunt, the Council Monarch, is announced.

Now I really have to get down there.

Iris knocks as she walks in. For once, she's put on a party dress.

"I got these." She hands me long black gloves. "And something else."

She hands me a small bottle. "Anti-anxiety pills. Quinn got them and gave them to me for you. Contraband from the mainland."

Iris goes to the mirror and starts applying more eyeliner and lipstick.

My hands shake as I open the bottle, and I dry-swallow two.

"They're strong, so be careful." Iris sets down the mascara and sees the lid still off. "How many did you take?"

"Two."

"Should be fine. Let's get you ready, Cinderella." She fixes my hair, pinning it up then pulling strands artfully down. "We leave the bite on display."

I touch it, and it's hot and a wave of desire suddenly passes through me. "Really?"

"Apparently, it shows he owns you." Iris finishes fussing and settles the tiara on, taking her time. "Barf."

Then she fusses with the heavy satin, until it's just right.

"I look...luxe."

"You do." She laughs. "Are the pills kicking in? You feel less tense?"

"Maybe." I don't want to ruin the vibe. The aches and nausea recede, and there's peace and happiness everywhere inside.

Whatever the fallout, we'll deal with it.

Later.

I head downstairs after Iris. And when I enter the great room turned ballroom, the crowd hushes as Stephan walks over.

Everything flip-flops in me. He's the most handsome man, even with that neatly trimmed scruff. But when he smiles, it's stiff. Forced. And something inside me dies.

Something's wrong. No one else seems to notice, but I can sense it.

It's an act.

Before I can read too much into it, he takes my hand and sweeps me into a dance. My focus shifts to the pressure of his palm against my lower back and how good he feels. His nearness. His oak scent.

Then, Stephan leans in. "Are you stoned?"

"No, Iris got me some meds to help with my...nerves."

He eases me closer. "We have good therapists in Emporia. To help manage your panic attacks."

Emporia.

Suddenly the fantasy fades. "We don't have to do this."

"We do, Princess. I marked you."

"But in the maze... You..."

"I know," he whispers. "When I saw that scumbag touching you, I...I don't know. I lost it."

"Why? If Dominic marked me, then we—"

He growls. "Don't even say his name."

I clamp my lips shut as he whirls us around the floor. After a moment, he grits his teeth, like the topic is causing him pain. "You didn't look like you were enjoying him making a claim to you."

"I didn't."

"Then I don't regret anything I did."

"Not even marking me?" I ask.

As the song ends, he hesitates with his answer. Instead, he settles with "We'll talk more about it later," before going over to Rue, bowing, and asking her for the next dance.

My sister's face lights up, and she makes him pose for a selfie before skipping to the dance floor.

"He surprised me." Heath is suddenly at my side. Dressed in a navy suit and his hair swept back from his face, he looks more like Dad than ever before. "I didn't think he had it in him."

I frown. "I'm not sure how to respond to that."

Heath kisses my cheek. "He cares about you, Vi. I should have seen it sooner, but..."

"He's a good actor?" If Stephan convinced my brother he feels anything for me, then he's award-worthy.

"I wasn't ready to let you go."

That takes me aback.

"It wasn't right for me to make you take on this responsibility. It should have been mine," he goes on.

"Heath, you already have so much on your plate. It's—"

"It wasn't fair to you," he insists. "Stephan told me what Stockton did."

My veins ice over. "He did?"

Heath nods. "Let's just say he's lucky he only got an ass beating. If I'd known…"

He'd be dead. I hear the threat loud and clear.

"But I know Stephan will hold up his promises," he says. "He'll be a good mate to you."

And love me?

But the song ends, and Stephan leads Rue back to Mom before heading our way. Heath gives me a slight smile and touches my arm before walking away.

I look at Stephan.

"Can we talk? Alone?"

"Without a chaperone? Is that allowed?"

"You're marked," he says, face and emotions blank—I can't read him. "We're basically mates, so the same rules don't apply anymore."

"Okay." It feels like my insides are quivering, but the medicine Iris gave me is making things float through me instead of weighing me down. I can feel the nerves, the pangs in my stomach, but only simmering under the surface.

I follow him outside to the garden that's ablaze with big, full blooms and beautiful bright colors. The sun is starting to sink below the horizon and fireflies blink around us. We're alone out here and drift farther away from the noise of the party inside.

He turns to me. "Princess. Violet," he corrects, and

then frowns. Uncertainty swims in his gaze. "I want you to know that I...I don't regret marking you."

My breath hitches. "You don't?"

"No. Our relationship may have started out as fake, but there's always been something there drawing me to you."

"Then why do you look like you're about to go to the gallows instead of our mating ceremony?"

He rubs his lips together. "Because I can't give you what you want."

I study him, confused. "What do you mean?"

"Children. I can't give you children. A proper pack."

I'm suddenly struck with a chill.

"I've tried to let you find an Alpha who could give you everything you want," he says, "but I'm also a selfish bastard. Just the thought of you with someone else makes me want to tear out throats."

He closes his eyes briefly, and when he opens them again, they shine with a level of truth I've never seen from him before. "It's selfish for me to ask you to go through with the mating ceremony, for you to give up another dream just to be my mate. You've already given up so much for your family, and I don't want to take anything else from you."

My heart breaks. This is clearly a struggle for him, to confess to me something he's been worried about telling me for some time. But he does care about me. At least enough to give me a choice.

"It won't be pretty, but I had come up with a plan before the maze situation happened. I was going to get so caught up in a scandal that it would leave the Monarch no choice but to give you an out," he says.

"But then what would happen to you?"

"She'd most likely banish me."

I gasp. "Banishment? But your career—"

"I would figure something out. Now that I've marked you, it makes things a little more complicated, but maybe if—"

"I don't want an out," I say. "I don't."

He stares at me and his brow wrinkles. "Did you hear me? I can't ever give you kids."

"I heard you. And there are other ways to become a mother or have a pack." I shrug, pretending as if it doesn't bother me like it does. But I can't have him sacrifice himself because of me. "We can adopt or foster. My sisters are bound to have a handful of kids. I'm sure our house will be full every weekend with nieces and nephews."

"You're...okay with this?"

I offer him a small smile. "We started this fake relationship together, and we're going to see it through."

He gently touches the edge of my bite mark. "As something real."

My heartbeat races and excitement floods me. "Only if that's what you want," I say.

Laughing, he wraps his arms around my waist, hoists me into the air, and spins. "Who wouldn't want a princess of their very own?"

And in that moment, with my feet off the ground and fireflies twinkling like earthly stars all around us, I think I can do this.

Because...because I'm pretty sure I'm falling for him.

Chapter Twenty-Four

Stephan

My princess.

She'll always be that to me, even when we're mated. Even when she's mine in every way that matters.

I know I promised Heath I'd tell her the truth tonight, but I can't. Not yet. I'm not ready to tear open old wounds, not when things between us are finally falling into place.

Is that selfish of me? Probably. But I haven't felt anything even close to this since CeeCee.

It just took seeing Dominic's hands on Violet to make things clear. It's been something I've been avoiding since first seeing her jog across the street in her dance outfit.

I care about her.

It's why I stayed away from her before the regatta. Not because I didn't want her, but because I couldn't give her what she wanted—a pack, a future built on something whole—and if I went through with the battle-ax's plan, I wouldn't be able to give Violet those things.

But I also couldn't go through with the alternative. Sleeping with someone else, making it public to create a scandal? It would break her heart. I thought I could do it. Thought it was the right thing.

But when it came down to it, I just couldn't do it.

Would it be so bad to have a mate again?

As I look at her tonight and take in her smile, her beauty, I believe it's time.

And now that I know she's okay with us not having children, that makes the guilt a little less. I hate to make her give that dream up, but I'm not reliving—

Not after last time.

As I said, old wounds.

Even outside, surrounded with all the floral scents of the garden, her smell's intoxicating, more than usual. It's like she isn't wearing a blocker at all. If I were a betting man, I'd bet by tomorrow she's going to be dragging all the Alphas in town down around her, and she's going to be in agony.

It's impossible not to touch her in any way I can. The urge to push her up against one of the trees or press her back in the garden's dirt courses through me like a constant stream. I know we're supposed to wait until after the mating ceremony to officially consummate the union, but god... With her on the verge of her heat, I'm about to throw all that out the window.

Fortunately—and unfortunately—Mrs. Gardener

walks outside at that very moment, sees us together, and her grin instantly falters.

"I think we need to end tonight a little early," she says, glancing at me.

Violet scrambles away from me. "What? Why, Mom? Nothing happened. We thought—"

"It's not that, dear," she interrupts. "You're going into heat." Then she looks at me. "Isn't that right, Mr. Ashford?"

I nod. "Yes."

"But I feel fine. Just a little cramping, but that's it," Violet says, eyes widening.

"For now. It'll be in full swing by tomorrow," her mother explains. "It's not safe for you to be out and about anymore. Too many unmated Alphas here."

"But—"

"I'll say your goodbyes and usher everyone out. Stay out here."

"I'll stay with her," I say.

She nods. "Thank you." And with that, she heads back inside.

When we're alone again, Violet turns to me. "I don't understand. You both are making it sound dangerous—me going into heat."

Her naïveté is charming but a little startling. I reach out and run a finger under her arm. "Wow, they really don't tell you anything about being an Omega, do they?"

"They do. We learn about knots and heat and all that."

"But not the details of it all," I say. "Did they teach you in school about how painful heats are? Or that any unmated Alphas will be unable to control themselves if they get too close to you during one?"

Her expression turns scared. "What do you mean by not control themselves?"

"Remember what happened in the maze?"

She shivers. "With Mr. Stockton?"

"Yes." A growl rises from the pit of my chest. "And me."

This time a tremor runs through her for a different reason. I breathe in and instantly regret it. Her scent increases with her arousal. She's extra sweet, and my vision clouds.

Fuck.

I have to shake my head to clear it. "Try not to think naughty thoughts, Princess. It makes things worse."

"I'm sorry," she mutters. "Why isn't it affecting you, though?"

"Oh, it is. It has been for a while. It's why I've had such a hard time keeping my fucking hands to myself. Your scent is everywhere."

"But I'm wearing blocker. I've always worn it."

"As I told the Monarch, for some reason I can still smell you."

"And I can smell you."

"Yeah, I'm not sure why, but I'm not sure I'll be able to keep myself from rutting if we were together tomorrow, when you're in full heat."

She presses her thighs together—I *see* her do it—and I know I'm in trouble. We both are.

Mrs. Gardener pokes her head out the door again and waves us inside. "Okay, everyone's gone. We have to get you up to your bedroom, Violet. There's a lot of work to be done."

Through the door, I hear Violet moan, and it's like a call to a deep part of me that has nothing above the base needs, no reasoning, nothing. Her moan slices deep, pulls me to her. I'm having issues controlling myself, but I hang on to whatever threads of decency I have.

I've been in the hallway of the Gardeners' house since the dinner last night. I helped gather the fluffiest blankets the family owned and grabbed every pillow I could find to help build Violet a nest in the center of her childhood bedroom. Her sisters brought in some of her favorite books, three heating pads, an entire case of water, and candles. I even helped Rue hang fairy lights after the light-blocking curtains were pulled shut, and once the room was dark, warm, and up to Mrs. Gardener's standards, I was ushered out, along with every sister besides Iris.

While Heath, Mari, Dahlia, and Rue eventually went to bed or found other things to occupy their time, I've remained rooted to the spot, unable to leave.

And then, around two in the morning, the moans began, her agony vibrating through every fiber of my being.

It is my job to protect her.

The instinct overwhelms to the point I want to wreck this place, barricade us in her room, do anything and everything I can to ease the pain for Violet. If she didn't smell so damn divine, I'd be able to concentrate. As it is, I want—*need*—to protect her, and I want—*need*—to devour her.

All I can think about is if I'd bitten her earlier, then we could've had the mating ceremony already, and her first heat would be at my home with me.

But no matter what my instincts urge, I can't rut her. Especially during her heat.

I don't know how I'm going to survive this. We can't go our entire life without having sex.

"Changing your mind isn't that much of a crime if you do it now."

I turn and look at my aunt Pen climbing up the stairs slowly and with shaky legs. In one hand is a bottle of bourbon and in the other is two glasses. Her cane is tucked under her arm.

My savior.

I go over and help her up the last few steps before taking the bottle and glasses so she can steady herself. "What are you doing here? And so early in the morning?"

"It seems your friend is worried about you," she says and taps her cane on the floor twice. "He called me. Thinks I can talk some sense into you and make you go home."

"Who? Heath?" I grunt. "Why didn't he come up and tell me himself?"

"Because he knows you're stubborn as hell and won't listen to him."

"The pot calling the kettle black there," I say and begin to pour the bourbon into the glasses for us. "He probably doesn't trust that I won't break down this door and fuck his sister."

When Pen winces, I try to apologize but she waves her hand. "It's not even the worst I've heard you say."

"It is true, though." I hand her one of the glasses.

"Mr. Gardener has reason to worry. You don't want to ruin Violet before the mating ceremony," she says.

"Yeah..." *That's the least of my concerns.*

"Stephan," she says, crossing her arms. "I wiped your butt when you were a baby. I know you. So when I ask you this, I want you to be honest with me."

I take a huge swallow of my drink. I hope she's not going to ask if I love Violet, because that's complicated. *Like* her, sure. I like Violet very much, but love is different. That notion died with Cecilia.

Her stare hardens on me. "Why?"

I frown. "Why what?"

"Why did you bite her?"

"Because Sophine made me. She gave us an ultimatum."

Her gaze searches my face, and I know she doesn't believe me. "You've never been one to follow her rules or play her games," she says.

"This time she threatened Violet."

"Did Sophine make you beat up that Stockton fellow, too?"

Damn. She got me there. "Not exactly. But he deserved it. Actually, he got off easy if you ask me."

"Right."

"That also could've been because of her heat," I explain. "But none of that matters now. I marked her, I claimed her. She's mine now, my responsibility."

"Not because you love her?"

Truth is a twisty, complicated beast, and I think... Fuck, I'm looking forward to learning all the princess's secrets.

"Well?" she presses.

"I don't know what I feel."

Before she can continue, Mrs. Gardener opens Violet's door just enough for her to squeeze through, and my body jolts to attention. Even through the crack, the air beats with the desire and sexual explosion that's coming from Violet. I can almost see her scent, and that need pouring off her wraps fingers around my cock.

She's so fucking potent.

The need to get into that room beats through me, and my sights zero in on the small opening.

"It hurts..." Violet's moan is loud, and I go for the door.

It's quickly slammed in my face, making me drop my glass of bourbon. The glass shattering is like a gunshot to my senses, and I blink.

Shit.

I have to remember that no matter what, I can't go into that room.

The lock clicks in place again.

This is going to be harder than I thought.

My own temperature's high. I don't know how long it's been. My mind feels like it's fracturing with panic and worry. And fuck everyone. How the fuck can I protect my princess if I'm not with her?

How can I rut and knot and ease her pain if I'm on this side of the door?

She's in full-on heat now. It permeates everywhere, and me stuck on this side is a fucking joke. I get up and start pacing.

What time it is, what day, I have no fucking idea, but the princess in heat has been calling to my darker, feral side, her pain and my need to protect.

Through the door I can hear her sister trying to soothe her. My job. Mine. My Omega's in there.

I go for the handle.

It's still locked.

"Go away, Stephan!" Iris yells.

Behind me I note footsteps, but I really don't care. When a cry of pain breaks into my heart, I howl and step back, then throw myself at the door, the lock giving way. I rush in. My princess is curled and wrapped and the scent in the room is so fucking sweet. So fucking potent I almost fall to my knees.

But I rush to her, only to have a dark-haired warrior tackle me. Behind me, Pen's voice rises, sharp.

"Stephan!"

I stop.

My hands are on Iris, who's shoving at me, and I stumble back. The need to rut and knot my princess hasn't gone, but that feral need beyond sense has lessened enough for cool thought to step in.

"Get out, idiot!" Iris shoves me again. "You won't ruin this for her. Out!"

"*Stephan.*"

My aunt's using her fucking Alpha voice on me.

I leave, the door slamming shut in my face again, and I

hear the sound of heavy furniture scraping the floor. They made a fucking barricade.

I almost laugh, or cry. I don't know. The need for Violet is clawing at me.

Pen holds out a glass. "You're losing it. Drink."

I snatch it from her. "I don't give a shit. I want to look after her."

"Or do you just want to get off?"

"Shove it, Pen."

I'm shaking.

She just motions to a seat in the hall. I don't want to move from where I am, but I go. I can still see the door. The one with the broken lock.

"You could go in, I know," she says. "Overwhelm the sister and have your fill. But it'll ruin her."

"Would it matter? She's already mine. I've already claimed her like...like..."

"Cecilia? You're at a crossroads, Stephan. But if you truly want things not to end up like that, don't go in. There's time enough later."

I shake my head. "I don't want her to die."

"Oh Stephan, not that. I didn't mean that. Sophine's stupid game and Cecilia's death aren't the same. And for what it's worth, do this the right way and it doesn't have to be something that earns Council sanctions."

"So that's all that matters?"

"To the Gardeners with all those Omegas? Yes. But for you? It *should* matter. A good start to this, an honest one, is a great starting place." She pauses. "As for the rest? It doesn't have to have the same ending. You need to know that. What happened to Cecilia isn't Violet's fate. You deserve happiness, too."

I don't say a word, just take the bottle of bourbon and go and sit outside the door.

Pen's wrong. But what's done is done, and it's up to me to protect Violet in all ways, even from me. Because...shit... because what I told Pen earlier is true. I don't know what I feel for Violet.

But...whatever it is, it's starting to consume me.

What has this Omega done to me?

CHAPTER TWENTY-FIVE

Violet

From somewhere in the sea of haze and a deep, insane lust that rocks my very foundation, makes me fever-hot and slick between the thighs, the scent of oak anchors me.

I want him. It's a desperation that makes my clit throb and swell, my pussy lips ache for a tongue, and my insides long for invasion, a swelling, a cure to the pain that gouges in.

But his scent. It's there.

In me.

His voice is a low, cool stream of words that lick against the heat I can't control myself.

And where's Iris and Mom? She's been here, too, a rock to cling to when my mind was gone, when the pain flared.

Thoughts fracture, and I press into him, his shirt damp

with perspiration, and together our scents mingle into something so much more.

But there's no flesh, just softness of sheets, and the voice is in my head.

"Here, Vi..." Iris presses something cold against my forehead, and I take her hand, and drift once more.

I catch pieces of Stephan's voice. Iris's cool disdain threaded with humor, and I think the worst has passed.

But I keep drifting.

The world is dark and warm and quiet when I wake next. Things shift in and out of focus and my body is hot, restless, needing.

This is home, and oak's in the air and smells so good. He's embedded in a blanket I cling to, and then he's there. Stephan. My Stephan.

We're naked, and he's doing things to me, so much but not enough, like it's nothing but air.

In that world, he's now just there. And then we're dressed. He slides under the covers, kissing my face, biting once more on the mark, and I push into him.

More.

I try to capture that sweet relief.

It feels good when you do that.

I don't say these things out loud, but he hears. And he doesn't say a word, just kisses me deep, then trails tiny licking kisses to my throat, and this time he bites hard, sucking and licking his mark and I moan.

Yes...

The pain flattens, stretches into pleasure, and I rub against him.

And then there's nothing at all, and I go from dream to dreamless.

Stephan's there again. Really there. I'm still feverish, but not like before, and coherent thoughts drift.

One thing hasn't changed.

I still need him to give me some kind of relief. Or maybe I just want him to touch me. I shift against him and his arms tighten. Real. Solid. Not a dream.

"I'm only allowed in because your heat's done, and I promised everyone I could control myself. So don't tempt me," he mutters.

"It's not quite done."

"We can't have sex before the ceremony," he whispers. "It would ruin you."

"I don't care."

"Fuck…"

"It still hurts."

"You're going to get me killed." Stephan slips his hand into my pajama bottoms, and I shudder as everything in me lights up. The ache deepens, and I rotate my hips for him.

"Holy fuck, Princess. You're so hard to resist. Almost impossible."

"Then don't."

"These promises are important." He sucks in a sharp breath, and I feel his fight against himself, the shake of his resolve even as he strives to strengthen it.

But he touches me. Fingers gliding through the slick, leaving pleasure in his wake, and he doesn't penetrate like he did when he claimed me, but he teases, and brings his thumb to my clit, rubbing and stroking until that pleasure builds, crescendos, and shatters into an orgasm that leaves me floating, depleted, in nothingness.

Except there's an itch of need that remains. I need more of him. I need him to knot in me, to rut, and shatter me in a completely different way to satiate me.

I try to get his fingers in me, at least, rocking up against them.

All he does is remove his hand and fix my clothes, holding me tight.

"I can't, Princess. I'm not sure I'll be able to stop, and these things are important... To your family, to you. I want...I want to be the mate you deserve."

"Stephan..."

He hushes me, and then uses his Alpha voice in an equally low yet commanding tone. "Now go to sleep. You need to rest. And anything you need, it's yours. I'm yours."

"My mate." And I pass out.

The next time I'm aware of things, properly aware, the room's full of a soft green-hued light and I blink, looking around.

Next to me, Stephan's on his side, his scruff on the wild side, the sexy muss of hair tousled like worried fingers moved through it, and he smiles, smoothing a strand of hair from my hot face.

"You're a little cooler to the touch now. How are you, Princess?"

Oh, god, we're not even in a bed. They set up something on the floor so comfortable I could burrow in and hibernate for years. A nest.

I shiver, aware something momentous happened...is happening? Aware of the incredible intimacy of the moment.

I lick dry lips, and he hands me a bottle of water.

"Not sure. Embarrassed?" I shrug, getting a little fuzzy again. "Am I meant to feel different?"

"I don't know, do you?"

I try to sit up, but my head spins. "Maybe. Where's Iris?"

"Napping. My aunt Pen adores her. Iris has been your fierce defender," he says.

I try and get up again. Slower this time. "I should go to her."

"Stay there. You were in heat for four days," he says. "Let her rest. Are you hungry?"

"Yes, but I can't eat." A restlessness comes over me. "What day is it?"

"Day five, and you're not in danger of me taking your innocence like you were days one through three. Do you remember anything?"

I don't know when my sex dream was, but it sounds like he brought me to orgasm yesterday. Am I going to be this messy every time? This much trouble?

"Last thing I remember was calling you my mate. I'm sorry." I bury my head in my hands, but his soft chuckle offsets the tendrils of panic and mortification.

"That was yesterday," he says. "The earlier days were bad. You were in and out, and Iris and Pen had to stop me coming in. I would have... I would have fucked things up."

I swallow, throat dry even though I just took a sip of water. He puffs up the pillows so I have some height, and then, when I say I need the bathroom, he leads me to the little en suite.

The en suite's kept in the dark, but tiny fairy lights give me enough light to see, and the flickering candle emits the scent of soft spice.

My gaze catches my reflection in the mirror. My curls from the dinner party have all spilled free from their pins and fall in a frizzy mess around my face. There are dark spots under my eyes and my skin is ghostly pale.

Dear god, Violet. You look a fright.

When I go back in, embarrassment creeps in that Stephan's seen me like this—a mess.

"Iris is still sleeping, but I have fruit and crackers if you change your mind about eating."

He leads me back to the nest, my legs wobbling. "I can do this myself."

"Yeah?" Stephan says. "But you have me to help."

Once I'm settled, he slides in next to me, on top of the covers, and of everything, his heat, his presence, his scent, those are the most important things in the room. My stomach still hurts and my skin shivers with flashes of heat, but Stephan makes it better.

There's something I should say to him. Something I can't. That I think I'm falling in love with him. He makes me feel breathless, boneless, and safe. He calms and excites in equal measure.

But there's a deeper level, and I'm sinking down into it.

Maybe I'm naïve. I know I'd given up on the idea of mating for love a long time ago, but fate's supposed to be a fickle mistress.

Is it possible she decided to drop love into my lap anyway?

Chapter Twenty-Six

Stephan

"Stephan, can I ask you a question?"

I watch Violet closely. She just sits, perfectly still, drinking her water, and I pour myself some bourbon, put on some music, and run a hand through my hair as I sip. "Of course."

"If you can't have children, does that mean you won't be able to...you know, help me with my heat next time?"

Help is a loaded word there. She's asking if I can still have sex.

I almost laugh, but when I see how bright red her cheeks are turning, I stifle it. "Yes, I will, Princess. I'll be able to rut and knot inside you. Is that what you're asking?"

She shifts, her face burning. "Yes."

I rub a thumb over the blush. "Don't worry. Next time, I'll be with you through the entire thing."

She's going to think I'm shooting blanks or something, but that's okay. Better that than the real reason.

I'm going to have to call Clea and figure out how I can fuck Violet without getting her pregnant, even in heat. She'll have an idea.

I finish my drink.

"Stephan, it's okay," Violet says. "I've been thinking about it, and I'm glad you told me. It'll be fine. We have time to work out alternatives."

I nod slowly and study her profile. I can't tell what she's feeling. I'm connected to her. That's a result of the bite, but the effects were intensified from her being so close to heat. Now that she's coming out of it, we only have the connection of the claiming. But when she looks at me, it's with a calm, tired face, and I tell myself she truly is fine with it.

Like the princess says.

"You've gone from a man who doesn't want...this..." She spreads her hands. "To one who bit me in a fit of...of lust? And now is saddled with me?"

She's having doubts.

"I'm not saddled," I say. "Minds change, things change."

"Like feelings?"

"Yes."

She nods. "We come from different worlds. You're Emporia, a famous actor, and I'm...this."

That's where this is coming from. She's afraid she isn't good enough for me.

"Oh, Princess... You're anything you want to be. You've just been putting everyone else in your life first. It's time for you to think about you and your happiness. And we don't come from different places. I'm from here." I go to take her hand, but change my mind and exchange her water for a glass of liquor instead, topping it off. "You know that."

"Stephan, I... Out of everyone, you make me feel special, out of all the Alphas in the Season, out of anyone I've met. I wanted to be a dancer. I thought I could be somebody with that, but I wasn't good enough, and..." She breaks my heart when she laughs. "It doesn't matter. This isn't a sob story, it just *is*. Thing is, you left Sabine, and I just toe the line."

This time I do touch her. I take her chin and gently turn her face to me. And I try not to think of her reaction in the maze to my praise, how the need to please is bone deep, sexual.

No...she wants the praise, which is why she aims to please in that way. And I think it's why the spotlight makes her panic. It's too much for her and her little kink that's unexplored. One we've barely scratched the surface of.

"You don't toe the line with me. You might panic about doing the right thing with me, but I've seen the real you here and there. Do you know how many people fall all over themselves to do my bidding on a daily basis? Way too many. But not you. From insisting you didn't know me—"

"I didn't."

"Maybe, but you kept it up, Princess. And I bit you because..." *Instinct, nature, jealousy.* "I wanted to. Couldn't stop myself."

"I just thought..."

I breathe out and let go of her face, and after a

moment's hesitation, I pour a tiny finger of bourbon for myself.

"You think a lot. Too much. It gets you into trouble." I chuckle, even though it touches nothing inside. "As for living arrangements, I'm here for the summer. I have a career I'm not giving up, but I want to move into better roles, maybe do some directing, other stuff. We can work out logistics. Spend time in both places. You could stay here, and I would fly in for work. But I won't live here full time."

I have to tell her. At least some of it.

"When I was young and stupid, Princess, I met a girl, the wrong girl. Pretty, sweet, a whole lot of sass. She didn't come from money. She wasn't—" My princess puts her hand on my arm. And I cover her fingers with mine, drawing in her excess heat. "My father didn't approve, and the battle-ax was emphatically against the match. When the Monarch says no, then that's it. So we ran off. Heath knew, and some others, and my aunt Penrith helped. But the thing is, because of all this, Cecilia—that was her name—Cecilia didn't get the care she needed until it was too late."

"Stephan?"

I swallow. "With you, I'm doing all the right things, everything, from here on out. From not sleeping with you before the mating ceremony, to obeying all the fucking rules. I'm doing it so history doesn't repeat. I'm doing it for the approval Cecilia and I never had."

She's silent a long time. "What happened?"

I down the drink.

"Cecilia died."

Long time, Hivemind, or maybe it feels that way.

*Our latest glamorous party seems to be the party of the Season.
The event of the year.*

*And to quote some of my little honey-gathering brood who
were there, it was "divine."*

*A dinner party that "sparkled with wealth and the
glitterati."*

A dinner party that "dripped with charm and class."

What?

*You **KNOW** this?*

Of course you do. The claiming was announced here and

Everywhere.

Emporian heart-crusher Asher St. James

and the Luxe of the Season Miss Violet Gardener

Can we talk about that dress she had on?

Hot. Classy. Perfect.

She's ready for the Emporian red carpet.

But now it's over, and...

chirp chirp chirp

crickets

*For **FIVE** days.*

What is going on?

Told you the tale would get a little twisty.

Stay tuned.

- Queen Bee

CHAPTER TWENTY-SEVEN

Violet

"O.M.G., Vi, you don't look different," Rue says, circling me the moment I come out of my room and make my way downstairs. Stephan left last night to freshen up at his place, since he'd refused to leave while I was in heat. "Do you feel different? You've been gone six days." She shimmies like some stripper on a TV show. "Do you feel like a woman?"

"Leave her be. She needed to rest up away from little ghouls." Iris smacks Rue playfully on the head, making her shriek, which brings everyone else rushing in.

"Hey, Sunshine," Mari says to Iris, who's most definitely not sunshine, "you've had her for five days now. We want to catch up with Vi and hear her dish."

"My..." I trail off as heat burns my face. "Marigold," I hiss. "Nothing happened."

"No, a lot happened," Mari says, "and we want to know what it's like."

Dahlia appears with an armful of books. "She means the heat, not the sex."

"No one," Heath thunders, "is having sex."

"You know what I think? If Heath isn't getting any, he doesn't want us to have any S-E-X." Rue sings the letters out.

Heath stalks up to her. "You shouldn't even be using the word. Hell, you shouldn't even know about what it is. Now go and...do some chores. As penance."

As Rue scampers off, laughing hysterically, he looks at something on his tablet. I'm exhausted and I want to sleep. I want to wrap myself in dream Stephan until I can do the same with the real one.

Maybe he told the truth about wanting me, and I think he did, just like I know there's a world of difference between want and love.

For someone who never wanted a mate, I heard how he spoke of Cecilia. With love and—

"Vi, study," Heath says.

With a sigh, I follow him in and close the door.

"Did he touch you?"

I lift my chin. In my head I can hear an alternative-Violet challenging him on if he really wants to know, but I'm never that. Heath might want to half murder his friend most of the time, but he's anxious too. For me and my virtue, for the family, our reputation, our chances of Stephan's—

Oh, crap. Stephan's loaded and, beyond the Emporia

stain, comes with a stellar pedigree, and it must crush a part of Heath that he now has to rely on his friend to help us.

"No. He was good." He *did* touch me, but not in the way my brother's asking. The dream stuff doesn't count, and neither does him getting me off by just stroking my clit. My virginity is still useless and intact. "Stephan took care of me...well, Iris and Mom did. Stephan had to stay away through most of it."

I don't want this conversation. At all.

All these rules...

"Nothing happened."

He nods and sits, rubbing his chin. "Are you okay?"

"It's life for an Omega."

"Christ, Vi." He slumps a little.

I want to ask about Cecilia, but I don't. I'm not ready for that. I'm not jealous. She's gone, but Stephan loved her, I heard it, and— "He told me he can't have kids."

His brow rises. "He did? You're okay with that?"

"We could adopt. There are options..."

Heath frowns. "Maybe. I don't know if they're on his agenda." Then he looks at me. "Vi, you'll work it out. You always do. And people change their minds. Fuck, I just wish there wasn't our whole world riding on this."

He tosses a cream-colored letter at me. "Arrived this morning. Mom's waiting in the drawing room for you."

I look at the letter. "This is an invitation to an exclusive masked black tie, black dress persons-of-mystery party, thrown by the Monarch. Tomorrow night."

"Go catch up with Mom. I guess you'll be seeing Stephan again sooner rather than later."

"Are you sure?"

It's the next day and Rue hasn't shut up about me being a changed Omega. From girl to woman to full-blown sex goddess is her idea of it all. And it both makes me want to groan and laugh.

"I'm not now, nor will I ever be, a sex goddess."

She waves her phone in front of me. "Eyes on me. The QB is throwing out so many theories. I could just die. If I knew how to contact her...them...him?" She sighs. "I would."

"You can." The moment the words are out I regret them, but Rue doesn't notice as she eyes the boxes on my bed.

"No, I'm not posting on her site. If I'm to give her dirt, then I'd want an exclusive Stitch of my own." She cuts her eyes to me. "Do you have dirt for me?"

"No."

She pulls at the white ribbon on the glossy box. "Can we open them? The tiny violet spray is adorbs, and I think Asher could work on his card writing skills—"

"His aunt probably wrote it."

"Oh." She bites her lip. "Maybe he got his people to send them to you? You know movie stars...they have people for everything."

She says this like she knows.

But I can't deny the thrill. Even if Stephan didn't buy it himself or pick it out, he still thought of me and—

He can't have children.

I blink, go still. A big family has always been part of my future. And this will take getting used to. But we can adopt, and it's not like I wanted a child immediately. I push it all out, and Rue's still talking but her words aren't registering. I pull the ribbon, lift the lid, and part the tissue paper.

Oh. My.

"I *so* want to be you." Rue starts touching the dress.

I let her take it out and hang it because it makes her happy.

"What do you think of the dress, Vi?"

The violet-black asymmetrical number is long at the back and on the left side, with enough leg on display on the right to border the line of comfort for me.

"It's pretty and it shimmers."

Rue sighs. "Gorgeous. Breathtaking. It's the very latest, too. It's your size! How'd he know? Put it on! Look at that low back and the strapless bodice! And he got you shoes! The latest purse! Oooh, a mask! Mari!" Rue cries out. "*Very* latest, Vi. As in hot off the latest runway. As in *couture*. No trends here—this is timeless."

She does a swoon as Mari comes in, who nods. "Very nice."

"Stephan sent it to her, with the shoes and the mask and the cutest little bag. To die for, right? She won't tell me how he knows her size, and I'm trying to get her to model it for us before the party. Why do you think he didn't send me one? I need a new dress. Something sophisticated..." Then she stops, sucks in air, and rushes out the door. "Iris, Quinn, wait. Let's get Heath to buy me a dress!"

Mari and I stare at the dress. It's utterly gorgeous. I haven't tried it on yet, but I suspect it's my size. He might have guessed, and Iris might have told him. I don't care. I've never owned something this expensive, this up-to-the-minute.

It's frivolous, and guilt hits me.

"You'll look good, Vi. You always do," she says with a laugh. "But try to be more relaxed. Now, go put it on."

With a sigh, I figure I'd better start getting ready. I shower, and then when I get out, I notice something else in the box, under another layer. Lingerie.

Not underwear, *lingerie*. Violet-tinted to wear beneath the violet-black shimmer of the dress, violet scraps of lace. I pull everything on and pin up my hair, right as the doorbell rings again and Rue lets out a wild squeal.

I don't even want to know.

There's a knock, and Iris stomps in.

"Where's Quinn?"

"Annoying Heath. We're going to the event with the family, so... Stephan is downstairs waiting for you, and I'm not into him but oh, boy, does he look *fine*." She fans herself then starts to fuss, redoing my hair and putting my mask on for me.

I slide my feet into the shoes and put my mini pad into the bag, unsure if I need to have it, and then I head to the door.

"Stop."

"What is it? Have I done the dress up wrong?"

"No, but..." She holds out the blocker which I forgot. I apply it. "Now, go down and wow him."

Stephan's eyes light up when he sees me, and the dread that came over me each step down vanishes, replaces by a deep warmth that radiates out. In that moment, I could walk in the sky, conquer my fears.

It's a fantasy, a fallacy, but one I indulge in for a few precious seconds.

"You look beautiful."

"So do you," I breathe.

Heath crosses his arms. "You two are going ahead of us. The Monarch wants a private word, apparently. Behave, Ashford. I'll know otherwise."

"Really? Are you spying? That's disgusting." Quinn sidles up to him and pinches his cheek but he swats her away. "What's the matter, *Heather*? Jealous?"

He glares at her. "And all the men are knocking at *your* door, Beta?"

"Heath," Iris says.

"You two make such a beautiful couple. I'm just sure you'll make the most perfect babies," Mom says, and Stephan and I both instantly stiffen.

"Er—thanks, Mrs. Gardener," he replies. "We should go."

Rue bounces over. "Asher got us dresses, too. I could just die! It's almost as good as the Trixi loot he sent."

"Wait, what?" Mari rushes over. "Us too?"

"No way." Dahlia's getting up from the piano.

As pandemonium breaks out, I drag Stephan out the door.

The limo is impressive, and I'd be impressed if I wasn't suddenly overwhelmed with a rush of nerves. Stephan sits opposite, and he opens a bottle of champagne and pours me a glass.

I study him as I take it. "You look different. More...Emporia."

He's in a slender black suit to match my dress, which I'm assuming is also wildly expensive. I can catch glimpses of his socks that match the color of my lingerie. And heat pours through me.

Heat at the thought that I'm wearing something so sexy. At the thought that maybe he picked it out himself. And color coordinated with it.

The mask he's wearing doesn't stop me seeing the glint in those dark brown eyes, and his scruff is trimmed, along with his hair. There's a ring in onyx on his pinkie and one on his other thumb, and while I've never thought about jewelry on men, I like it on him.

There's something wildly dashing and sophisticated. Hot.

Or maybe that's just him.

I gulp the champagne and glance out the darkened window, right as he presses a button that rolls up the privacy screen between us and the driver. "This isn't the way to the party. At least, I don't think it is..."

"Fuck Sophine. She can wait." He tosses back his own drink, and his eyes glitter as he slides over to me, his hand slipping up along my thigh.

Everything goes into freefall. My heart beats wildly, and I can't think.

This is basic instinct.

This is feral need and desire.

It's intoxicating, freeing, and it scares me to death.

My whole chest throbs. "W-What are you doing?"

"I couldn't have you while you were in heat."

I swallow. "You're not meant to have me now."

Stephan smiles and then closes the gap, his fingers a light dance of sparking desire over my skin, so light it's almost not there and yet I feel it to my very last atom.

"Thing is," he murmurs, lips traveling along my throat, his mouth not touching mine where I want it, his fingers not going where I want them, "you get all tense and then a panic attack comes on. Seems like I have to relax you."

Now he nibbles a path from my throat to my ear, and he sucks on my lobe. Everything is wet between my thighs, and I swear I'm a furnace that keeps combusting and melting over and over again.

He touches my inner thighs, parting them. Shock waves of need roll through me.

"What are you doing?" I ask again.

"Relieving stress." He eases me back until I'm sprawled on the seat and he hovers over me.

"You said we couldn't."

"When you were in heat, all I did was touch. Now I need to taste. But you'll still be a virgin. I'd be remiss if I didn't show you one other way of pleasure, Princess."

He kisses me then, a deep, slow kiss that undoes me from deep inside. And then he goes down on his knees, pushes the skirt up to my hips. "My mouth, Princess, on your sweet, wet pussy."

"Wait, what? What are you—"

Panic flutters as he peels my panties to one side, and then his tongue and mouth close over my lower lips.

And I lose my mind. Completely.

CHAPTER TWENTY-EIGHT

Stephan

Fuck, she comes a little, not much, but the act of me putting my mouth on her is enough. And I'm so fucking hard, I'm going to almost regret this.

Almost. But now her taste is in my mouth, on my tongue. And there's no way I can fucking regret it.

I lick her, up to her clit. It's not slick, but she's so fucking sweet, so divine, I know if I'd done more than touch her as she came down from her heat, if I'd been allowed near her while she was in the throes, no one could have stopped me. Not one person. I'd have killed everyone just to get her taste.

And then I'd have spent a week rutting her, knotting her. I'd have done it, prolonged it as much as I could, and then repeated the act until neither of us could move.

I can barely keep my dick in my pants as it is, and she is

beyond anything. This sacred gift belongs to me and only me, and if anyone, ever, tries to touch her, I'll rip them apart limb from fucking limb.

Slowly, torturing us both, I lick her, dipping my tongue into the tight heat of her canal, and the tiny little throbs of her cunt on my tongue almost set me off.

She tastes the way I think violets should. Sweet and addictive, like honey. She's summer. Spring.

She's all the decadent things I've ever had, and she's mine.

I suck on her clit, and she cries out. I want to just get her off with my tongue, and as she starts to writhe against me, pulling at me, shoving that fucking hot little pussy into my face, grinding it, I know she wants more, so I add my fingers.

I'm going to add eating her out for hours to my list of things to do to her after we're officially mated. Just her naked and me buried between her legs, praising her, feeling her shudder and squirm and come on my tongue.

I push two fingers into her, curling them to stroke against that spongy knot of nerve endings in her, and she cries out.

Lifting my mouth, I look at her, thrusting in a slow, deliberate rhythm with my fingers. "Open your eyes, Princess."

She does.

"Good girl, sweet girl." I watch her as I dip down, licking her and lapping at her stiff little clit. "Mmm, fuck, Princess. You're delicious."

She whimpers like speech is out of her reach, and I return to my dessert because that's what she is, sumptuous, special, something wonderfully sinful I could indulge in daily.

Her movements start to get frantic, her fingers tugging at my hair and her thighs squeezing at my head as I push her higher and higher.

She starts to stiffen and fight and then she comes, her pussy clenching my fingers, her juices so fucking delicious. I keep going, right until I get one more extra set of spasms from her, and she cries out.

Then my princess shudders and lies back, boneless. I slowly pull my fingers out, sucking them clean, and then lick her pussy one more time, all along her inner and outer lips, sucking on them until I'm sure I have all her juices. I lap her clit but she twists from me.

Grinning, I put her lace panties back in place, the ones I picked out yesterday. Violet is dreamy, her eyes dilated, slightly unfocused, but I help her up, putting her back together. Then I sit back and wait for my raging boner to go down. I'll have to deal with the ache until I can get home to relieve it, but that's fine. It's something I sort of want. A reminder of this with every twinge of discomfort, every ache in my balls tonight.

I wipe my face with a hand towel.

She sits up, unsteady, and blinks, like a whole new world's been opened to her. Like all this time, I was the key.

I lean forward.

"That, Princess Violet, is called eating you out."

The battle-ax is in full commander mode. A dress today, a simple drape, no latest style for her, but it's encrusted with jewels. All, I assume, are real.

"Something has changed."

Violet, bless her, blushes bright red and twists her hands in front of her. I don't need to read her mind to know what she's thinking.

Us in the car. Pussy-licking.

"He didn't... We didn't..."

Sophine sighs. "This..." She waves a hand in the air like the room we're in is the party. "This is just a normal event. But it's one where I'll be announcing the date of the mating ceremony."

"Want to let *us* know when? Since we can't do that our fucking selves apparently?" I snap.

"Stephan. You're my sister's son. I didn't like your father and I never let him speak to me that way, and that goes for you too. So watch your tongue."

"Glad the dead can defend themselves, here."

It doesn't matter that I share her sentiments of my fucking father. But she sided with him in the whole thing with Cecilia. So fuck them both.

"Even Penrith doesn't have the guts." She looks at Violet like she's studying a hothouse flower for bugs. "I'm the Monarch and you are my Luxe. I get to decide."

When Violet doesn't reply, Sophine raises a brow and smiles. "There's no point in waiting, in my opinion. You both were so eager to get into this *situation* that I think sooner is better."

Is she punishing us for faking a relationship and

manipulating things in our favor? I wouldn't put it past her. The woman can carry a grudge.

It must run in the blood, because so can I.

"Out with it already." I glare at her.

"This coming weekend."

Violet's panic spikes. It rolls off her in waves.

"Calm," I say, using my Alpha voice. I touch her hand, and the Monarch's eyes lock on the subtle connection. "Don't you think that's going to set tongues wagging?" I ask her.

"It's more to pin you down now, Stephan," she says, lifting her nose in the air. "You have seven days."

Shit.

"It was a nice party, don't you think?"

She looks at me, then leans on the balcony railing of the second floor. The door's open and the balcony's a good size. Little lights twinkle and the chatter and music from below drift up. There's even a gentlemen's room across the hall from this modern event hall Sophine chose for this evening's event.

So fucking old-fashioned...

"We have seven days." The princess pauses, looking out. Not at me.

I can still taste her. I'm thinking of asking her to move in with me, but when I'm about to say those words, she turns, looks up at me.

"Are you okay with that, Stephan? Do you need to do anything, see anyone? If you do, this week's a good time."

"Do what, exactly? I dated. I won't deny I have a past, but I wasn't seeing anyone when I came here."

She nods. "Your co-star... Rue told me about her."

"That's...complicated." Violet's too honest, so in case someone here asks her, I'll keep it like that til I can explain. "But there's nothing to worry about, nothing unfinished."

"Okay. Well, this is your week."

Someone comes in. I look over, mentally measuring the space between us.

Heath, and he glowers, gruff at his edges. "You two shouldn't be here."

"Neither should you, Gardener."

Violet moves away. "There's too much Alpha energy here. I'm going to find Mom and see about going home. Don't kill each other."

When she goes, I think about what she said. There's Cecilia's parents, if they're still here on Sabine. Last time I saw them, they made it clear what was already in my head. My fault.

Which is why Violet's never—

"You told her?" Heath asks, leaning his hip on the balcony railing next to me. "About Cecilia?"

I sigh. "Yes and no."

"And that means...?"

"I told her we were together, and that I lost her, but I didn't say how."

"She mentioned to me about you not being able to have kids."

"I never said I wasn't able," I say. "I told her I couldn't."

"Ashford," he growls. "They sound pretty damn similar to me."

"What the fuck do you want me to do? I'm not ready to remember that part of my life yet."

"It's not fair to Violet," he says. "She wants kids. You know this. It's not that you can't have kids. It's that you choose not to because of what happened years ago. It was tragic, yeah. But that doesn't mean it'll happen again."

I cross my arms and peer out onto the street below where cars pass and couples stroll along the sidewalks. "It's better not to risk it."

"Stephan—" He rests his hand on my shoulder, but I jerk away, anger biting.

Why doesn't anyone understand? The pain, the absolute torment I went through when I lost them...

But then, like usual, the rage deflates into a heavy, heavy sorrow.

How could they understand? There's no way to put that kind of loss into words.

I don't know what this is, what I feel inside for Violet, but it's big and there and fierce. I could spend forever trying to satiate myself on her sweetness. I'd kill for her. Maybe that's enough, so I squeeze my eyes shut for a moment and draw in a deep breath. "I-I won't lose her too."

When his hand returns to my shoulder, I let it stay.

"Gardener," I begin after a beat or two, "I have some stuff I need to do before the ceremony. Do you think you could come tag along? We can make it like old times."

"Without the girls?"

"For me, yeah, but you're still available."

His brotherly touch turns into a fist, which he hits me on the arm with. "Not interested."

"Okay, not like old times then."

"What did you have in mind?" he asks.

"I don't know. I figure we'd say fuck it to the traditional bachelor party bullshit. Maybe take some days, go somewhere, away from here."

He shakes his head. "I'm not going anywhere. I can't. There's a lot to do. I don't shop for fucking dresses, but Violet—"

"I'll pay. Or I will through Pen or Clea," I say. "As for arrangements, something tells me the Monarch will deal with that. She seems very fucking invested in this for some reason. But I like to think we're both overdue for a vacation."

"I don't know."

"It'll only be for a day or so. Three tops."

"Three's pushing it."

I smirk. "So is that a yes?"

"Fuck no."

My lips split into a full-on grin. "I'll take that as a yes."

The drones are working overtime, getting ready for a royal affair...or as near to one as we're going to have here on Sabine.

Call it Emporian Royal.

But there's more buzz than just the drones at work.

GOSSIP

From everywhere.

One Fine gal who twinkles like a star is having a field day chewing through the scenery that this mating ceremony's littered her film set with. It should be her moment, she's saying. Cue a shiny award for Felicity. Maybe she should have invented a baby.

Speaking of...

Come closer, my brood, and get that Hivemind spinning. We

knew the ceremony was coming and in time for it to be a Season highlight.

But this soon?

Right after the claiming announcement?

Could there be a honey bun cooking away? Is that why everything is rushed?

Or...

Let's face it, maybe our tired old Monarch is wanting to rest her wings and her wannabe crown. She's perhaps looking to inject some fire and sparkle into this Season. And this mating ceremony would be the way to do it. Create gossip.

*I can tell you if there is a bun, it's one that doesn't show. Miss V usually wears loose or skimming, but lately the outfits are tight and **TIGHT**. So no reason to rush if that's true.*

Do you think there's been some messing about, or will the perennial Miss V walk down that aisle as pristine as a dewy violet?

My money is on the latter. Where's yours, Hivemind?

- Queen Bee

Chapter Twenty-Nine

Violet

I whisper the words: "Today's the day."

It's my mating ceremony today.

No matter how many times I say it, the whole thing still doesn't feel real.

Mom hasn't stopped fussing with all the RSVPs that have poured in. I don't even know who half the people are. I would have just liked something small, my family, Stephan and his family...

But he's famous, and he's the nephew of the Monarch, something I try not to think about. *Secret* nephew, because as far as I know, other than his aunt Pen and Heath no one else knows.

"O.M.G.! It's your mating ceremony. Why aren't you dancing or throwing up, or—"

"Rue!" My mom admonishes her. Then she looks at me

with a smile as she steps into the room. "I've been so busy working with Penrith to get everything just right that I fear I've neglected you."

She hovers, and Rue suddenly looks as horrified as I feel.

"Mom, I don't need the Alpha–Omega talk."

Her cheeks start to turn pink. "I just wanted to check on you."

There's shouting and laughter from downstairs. The doorbell rings.

"I'm good, Mom."

It's a lie. I'm falling apart. Nerves leap, and I think I'm going to faint every five seconds. But I smile brightly for her.

"Your brother and Mr. Ashford should be back by now..." She gets up as the door rings yet again. "Is anyone going to get the door?" She hurries downstairs.

"It's, like, seven a.m. Do you think they gambled and went to Emporia and found some high class—"

"Stop watching old films, Rue."

I'm worried Stephan's decided he can't mate with me. Or Heath's gone and murdered him.

Both are equally possible.

"Did you see today's Stitch from the QB? She's running a poll to see if people think Asher's run off and is going to leave you disgraced, jilted at the altar."

"Give me that phone." Iris stomps in and snatches the phone from Rue.

Rue tries to grab it, but Iris holds it above her head. "Iris!"

"No. Go do something. Go help Mom, or set out

everyone's outfits, including Mom's. It's going to come down to a screaming fight at the last second, so stay off your phone and help out." Iris pins our little sister with a dark glare.

"But Mari and Dahlia are already at the cathedral." Rue looks to me for help, but I'm a mess and I can't spare the strength to intervene.

"Doing their part. Dahlia's organizing the music, and Mari's setting things up." Iris motions to the door. "Phone later."

When Rue goes, Iris chucks the phone onto the bed and grabs my hands. "Icy. Try not to be so nervous."

"Do you have any idea when Heath will be back? He hasn't even been answering Mom's calls," I ask softly. "What if everyone on social media is right?"

"About Stephan?" She laughs. "I was there when he almost broke through the door to get to you when you were in heat. And when he wouldn't leave your side after you were done and resting. That last part means something to me more than the first. But they're both important, Vi. Are you happy?"

Why does everyone keep asking me that?

"Yes." I look at Iris. All the things I haven't said press at me, but I keep them locked in. "Terrified."

"He paid for the dress."

"They're going to judge me. It's cream-colored."

"Just a shade of white, Vi. And it's satin and simple and so *you*. I'm not girly, but that was a fun shop."

The dress was made for me, and Penrith had the best designers and seamstresses flown in to meet us at a local dress shop.

Iris laughs again and squeezes my hands. "We went on that shopping trip, and the looks on those other Omegas faces... Delish. I could eat off that memory, especially that little witch Alicia. She wore a sour expression all day."

"I think..." I swallow. "I think Stephan knows her, somehow."

Her lips press together. "In the past, right?"

I nod.

"Then my words stand."

The front door slams, and Rue shrieks. "Heath!"

My sister turns to me. "Time to start getting ready."

The day has a whimsical quality. Or maybe it's just me, hyperaware of everything and unable to concentrate on anything.

I almost start hyperventilating when I peek out the window of the limo. There are so many people heading into the cathedral.

"The lookie-loos," Iris says, squeezing my hand. "They want a glimpse of your dress."

Heath leans forward. "You're doing fine, Vi."

"I might throw up."

"Save it," he says. "Throw up on Stephan."

"Heath!" Iris glares.

My brother grins. "It'd make my day."

"No one is throwing up."

The limo pulls up and my other sisters are there waiting, Rue with my bouquet of wildflowers. Mom wanted roses, but the wildflowers were something I stood firm on.

Hothouse roses, fresh roses clipped from a gorgeous rose garden, it doesn't matter where—not for me. I wanted something softer, less lofty. So Iris, Penrith, Mom, and I ended up with flowers that included the namesakes of my sisters and Mom.

Heath gets out of the car first, and then Iris, and finally me. The sun's too warm as it hits me, and my toes are like ice in my shoes. But Iris smiles, adjusts the beyond-pretty veil she made for me, and then Rue runs up with my flowers.

The music starts, and the girls go in, my beautiful sisters.

How perfect this day would be if Stephan loved me, was falling for me the way I'm falling for him.

"Vi..."

I turn and look at my brother, who's frowning thoughtfully.

"I know Dad should be the one walking you down the aisle, and really, you shouldn't be in this position—"

"No—"

"Hush, Vi, my turn. You always want to put others first and do the right thing for us. But for what it's worth, for my...skepticism on this union, Ashford cares. He'll look after you."

"And the family."

Heath glances away. "Not what I meant."

"I know he's good," I say. "But—"

"I love you, Vi. You deserve happiness. I hope...I hope you both find it."

"I love you, too. And..." I suck in a breath. I want to say *I love Stephan,* but I can't. "It's going to be a good match."

A good match.

He doesn't say *Stephan told me he's madly in love with you.* He doesn't say *Vi, Stephan's falling for you.* He just looks at me in that Heath way, like he's reorganizing a list, like he's trying to make room for me if I stumble and break my own heart.

But I won't.

I need to put him at ease.

"I'm going into this with open eyes."

I expect him to breathe out in relief, to offer me platitudes or even warnings.

He doesn't.

All Heath does is smile and hold out his arm.

One foot in front of the other. I grip my brother's arm so tight, and I almost crush the wrapped stems in the bouquet.

The cathedral is huge. I feel swallowed by it, and yet in a way it also feels so small that I can't escape.

I don't look up until Heath transfers me to Stephan to take his place at his side.

The sight of Stephan lifts me high in the sky and then slams me back to earth. My stomach flips, and my vision hazes over. I'm overcome by something so enormous that I step back.

I'm going to run.

Chapter Thirty

Stephan

"Princess, breathe," I whisper.

I know she's going to try and run. I lock eyes with her and then, pitching my Alpha voice low to her, I command, "Stay. Please."

I don't know where the *please* comes from. It isn't necessary, but there's something so fucking heartbreaking about her that I'm compelled.

She's gorgeous. A dream.

I know she would rather us be doing this in a tiny chapel with just family. She doesn't like this fanfare the Monarch insisted on. But the dress, though, the dress is perfect.

"You're beautiful. Stay. Be my mate."

Her eyes shimmer and a small smile breaks free. "Okay."

One of the Council members, someone under Sophine, is dressed in robes and heavy gold jewelry and officiates the ceremony. Sophine is in the front row, staring directly at me, with all the other Council members. But Penrith is with the Gardeners and there's something about that which makes me happy.

The officiant begins the vows, offering us the platitudes about the importance of the mark, how she must now mark me after we're mated to complete the unbreakable bond, the bond that means she's mine to protect, to breed, to love forever more. And she's there to bear my children, remain loyal, and to honor me.

It's archaic bullshit and yet...the words resound through me.

"You may mark your mate, Violet."

I lift her veil, dotted with tiny violets, and I can see her pulse throb and leap near my mark. I reach out, pushing into the reddened flesh there.

Her eyes flare at my touch, her cheeks turn a pretty pink. I take a step closer, and at the officiant's nod, I offer her my throat.

For a moment there's panic, but the lust my touch and small bite set off crushes that, and she puts one hand on my waist and the other on my cleanly shaven cheek, and then...

Oh, fuck me.

Violet bites me, her teeth setting off a fire, scratching an itch as she then sucks. It's like she's sucking my cock, taking it all the way down to the back of her throat, on her knees and naked in front of me, everything mine for the taking.

The bite, her soft licks and sucking motions,

reverberate through every cell and go on seemingly forever yet only for an instant.

When she stops, I think I look as dazed as she does.

"Now you may kiss."

When I kiss her, she's even sweeter, and that circle of connection from the fresh bites is strong. Her desire is mine. It beats in me even as it flows in her.

"Ashford," Heath hisses, and I dutifully break the kiss.

But the fresh memory of her tongue in my mouth licks at my cock, and though I'm managing not to have a scandalous erection in the cathedral, I can feel her temperature rise, her slick juices flow, and honestly, I'm not sure how I'm going to get through the reception without ripping off her dress.

But the ceremony is done, and we head down the aisle together as mates.

I can't stop touching her. My princess is a vision, and I'm dying to get at whatever she's wearing under her dress.

Of course, I'm going to have to work out sex. I can control coming, I know that, but with her...

Clea's here, and I'm hoping she brought the thing I asked her for late last night when Heath had finally gone to his room and passed out. There are some things you never want your friend to know about, especially when he's the overprotective brother of your mate.

Mate... The word washes through me, in all its meanings.

"How are your first hours of being my mate?" I whisper in her ear. Thank fuck for some traditions, like dancing at the reception; it means I can touch her all I want. Within reason.

"Surreal."

I frown, turning her as we dance, and I then bring her in close. "Surreal? Happy surreal?"

There's a moment where she's about to slide into her people-pleasing mode, but I hold her gaze and her fingers tighten on my shoulders. "It's... We don't know each other. Not really."

"We have time to find things out." I go closer to her, brush her ear with my mouth, and breathe in her personal perfume, that heady sweet floral burst of violets that's *her* and has me hooked. Because it does. She does.

I care.

I really fucking like her, and I didn't ever expect to. "I know you like it when I go down on you, and I bet you want that again. Be my personal good girl."

"Stephan..." My name's a soft moan, and it slides against my skin.

"I know you like it when I finger you, taste you, kiss you."

She grips my hair and pulls me closer to her, and we touch intimately far more than is decent, even for a mating ceremony in Sabine. There should be a tiny smidge of space between us, and I fucking love that the good princess doesn't care when she's lost in me.

And all we're doing is dancing.

What's it going to be like when I get her naked—

"You can't speak like that, Stephan."

"Why not?"

"If someone should hear..." She grips me harder, and my mind heads all the way south, gutter-bound.

"Good. Let them. You're mine now."

With that, she turns her face and kisses me, tongue and all. It's a wild ride of a kiss. It's naked and new and a little all over the place, but it's also the most exciting kiss I've ever had.

Because it's from the real Violet, the brave girl who when she gives herself a chance doesn't care what others think. It's the most perfect kiss, and I want to sink down into the magic of it.

But she breaks it seconds after she starts it and pulls back as the music ends. "I like you clean shaven, but I think I like your scruff more. It's the real you."

Then she surprises me even more by walking off to her sisters who are sitting at the family table. And I...I stare after her.

In fact, I'd probably still be standing there in the middle of the room if Clea didn't come up and hand me a drink. With it, though, she had palmed me the very thing I'd asked for.

I transfer the pills to my pocket and take a sip of the bourbon before anyone can see.

"Are you sure about those?" she asks.

"Not yet, no."

"You know what I think—"

"Now isn't the time to repeat the lecture, Clea." The pills are insurance, a way to do things. I don't want children. I don't want to risk Violet. And I...I'm not lying to Clea. I don't know if I'll use them. That's a tricky situation.

"Buying something like that here is impossible for me." I have another sip. Clea knows. Then I look at Violet and nod. "She told me she prefers the scruff. That it's the real me..."

I smile.

"She seems sweet, and she's very pretty. I see why you're doing the besotted act..." She stops, takes me in, and slowly smiles. "Stephan... It isn't an act."

"She's...nice."

"Nice." Her smile gets wider. "I'm so glad I pushed the mating plan. With a girl like her for a partner, you can step back, create mystery. It'll allow you to shift your career trajectory. Hell, maybe you can get that script made, if we clean it up."

"It's fine as it is."

"Stop talking like you wrote it. You like it, I know. And the part's perfect for an actor who's risen above rom coms. Felicity, you should know, is having a field day with the mating ceremony. Back-to-back interviews. I think I'll take her on as a client."

"Turncoat."

"Her agent sucks, and Felicity needs to back off with the interviews soon or she'll over-saturate and self-sabotage. Now, be a good friend and introduce me to your mate's brother. He's delicious."

I should correct her on the mating plan. That went out the window for me as a catalyst because I got to know Violet. Like her. Want her with a ferocity I sometimes don't know what to do with. I think... Shit. I think I still would have marked her as mine even if that bite meant the end of my career.

I'd find something else.

The princess chats with her sisters. Pen is beaming, and the battle-ax has shifted to the shadows to observe. Violet's relaxing a little.

And me? I want to get the fuck out of here. She's mine, and I've waited long enough already. I want to go. Get started on the honeymoon I made Heath help me plan. It's short, three days, more symbolic than anything. Mainly because I don't trust the battle-ax to demand a weekly appearance from us or threaten shunning Violet and her family from society.

Call me a paranoid Alpha, but I don't trust that woman. At all.

"Heath," I say when I catch up to him. "This is Clea, my agent. Clea, this is Heath. Have fun. I'm taking my mate."

"That's my sister." Heath narrows his eyes.

"My mate now, dude." I slap his back and walk off before he can say something else.

Not that he'd do a thing to disturb Violet's perfect day, but it's also Heath and he's protective. He knows me. But not the me with Violet. No one knows *that* me.

Except perhaps the princess.

Clea's dragging him off. She'll probably get him to bed, too, but it isn't my concern.

Getting out of here is.

Sneaking out is impossible, I realize when I reach Violet. No one's about to let the Luxe of the Season go quietly. A group of Omegas follows us, and Violet throws the bouquet, right to her sister Iris.

I open the front door of the Gardener townhouse, and picking up my princess, I carry her to the waiting limo and we get inside.

"Ready to start a new life, Princess?"

She smiles at me. "Yes."

The mating ceremony was spectacular,

and our movie star pulled out all the stops we'd expect from Emporian royalty.

Her dress, his tux—all stunning.

And what more perfect backdrop than

THE CATHEDRAL, HIVEMIND! THE CATHEDRAL!

Gossip fodder for other Stitchers, social media hounds, and press from the mainland who did NOT get even a day ticket to Sabine.

Oh, and...

The Monarch?

*Dressed in a slate-gray gown and matching cape lined in
royal blue.*

ROYAL, HIVEMIND

*I'm not a fan of the over-the-hill Councilwoman but she
makes a splash,*

keeps things interesting, and her outfit reflected that.

*But no one's here to read yet another description of outfits, are
they?*

You want the juice, the deets, the tea.

*According to sources, Heath Gardener whisked Mr. St. James
away to some old and boring country hideaway for things like
reading, fishing, and keeping the movie star from dipping
into the wrong honey pot.*

No last wild dance for our movie star.

*Of course, the Luxe had a party with all the Omegas of the
Season in attendance.*

*I say party, but more like a boring dinner or something. Who
cares?*

*Everyone in the Gardener house was tucked away before the
sun truly set.*

Here's the dish you've been waiting impatiently for...

The couple couldn't seem to keep their eyes off each other.

*So maybe it's **true love** after all.*

But while they left the party early for some much-anticipated alone time,

there is another tidbit...

Sources say his agent was in town, and St. James and the agent discussed a mating plan.

Felicity Fine, sources say, is now represented by his agent, too.

What plan?

What is going on?

And where are they going for the honeymoon?

More importantly, will this arrangement work,

or will St. James reject Violet when he's done with her

and throw the whole Gardener family into ruin?

PSSST

IRIS GARDENER CAUGHT THE BOUQUET

AND WE ALL KNOW WHAT THAT MEANS!

Stay tuned, Hivemind.

- Queen Bee

Chapter Thirty-One

Violet

"Whose place is this?" I look around. It's a stupid question. It smells of oak.

But I'm nervous.

I eye the suitcase sitting there, handle up, ready to be rolled. It's mine. I recognize it, and the thought of someone going through my stuff and packing is...

Intrusive.

I'm not sure why. My sisters and I pack for each other all the time. When we're going to spend long periods in the country estate, or back to the townhouse. The odd occasion we head over to the other side of Sabine, past the countryside, for the beach, where it's mostly large vacation homes.

Maybe it's because I'm feeling suddenly adrift, not belonging to the family anymore. At least not like I was.

I'm mated. Owned. His.

"Mine. I live on the top two floors when I'm in town, which usually isn't often, but...I own the whole beach house. Your brother helped me set it up properly. Not all the rooms, but some. He and I also spent some time in the country, just us, hanging out. But this was a project I wanted to do."

"You don't have to explain where you were." And I know Heath wouldn't let him do anything out of line. But I keep that to myself.

"I'm not. I figured..." He shrugs as he smiles. "This would be ours. Yours and mine."

A large empty house made for a family. But I put on a bright smile. "I'd love a tour."

"How about I show you the basics? A lot of the second floor is untouched, and the bottom floor we did up so you —so *we* could welcome guests. You have free rein to do whatever you want with the rest of it."

For some reason his words hit me wrong.

I get to do whatever I want? Where will he be?

But he's a movie star. With a career. He's not giving it up and...

And he hasn't asked me to come with him.

I could, I guess, do everything to please him, go with the flow, be the good girl, the right girl, the easy to deal with girl. And I am. God, he must think I'm boring. "I think I'm a little overwhelmed."

I want to go home. I want—

"Hey." Stephan pulls me to him and kisses me. "This is new for me, too. Right now, I'd really just love to strip you naked."

My eyes widen. He's so forthright with his sexy talk. Like at the mating ceremony while we danced.

"I thought about taking you to some exotic destination, but I figured you'd like this better. Something more low key, private, and away from everyone else."

"Like a love nest?"

"Don't say nest, but..." He takes my hand and leads me upstairs, to where the bedrooms are. He pushes open another door and leads me up more stairs.

It's the attic, but where a servant room was once upon a time is now a nesting room. Painted in cool, comforting greens and rich golds and browns. There are fairy lights and candles ready to go. And I can smell him in the air, or more specifically, our mingled scents from the blankets.

"I told you how you reminded me of a secret place in the forest, or something similar, and..." I turn, vision blurring. "Stephan, you did this? For me?"

"You need it. You can spend time here, rearrange it, do whatever you like to make it yours. I just wanted this here now, so you'd know."

A small sob of a laugh escapes me. "It's...everything."

He pulls me to him, his mouth trailing over mine like he's savoring me. They're slow, nibbling kisses, as if he's got all the time in the world, and they're so soft my eyes flutter shut and I float on the heat he sends rolling through me. It's a heat that doesn't burn. It just sets off sparks of delight that whisper inside.

Exploratory kisses, meandering, and I'm lost in them, sinking but not drowning. I sigh, and he laughs against my lips.

"I could do this forever. Your mouth is so fucking soft,

so sweet, and then when you let me in…" He kisses a trail up to my ear. "It's like tasting heaven."

He kisses me deep, and my head spins, and that heat between my thighs flares. I'm wet. I want him to put his mouth there again. I want his fingers. I want to fly in his touch. And most of all, I want to experience sex. All of it. Rutting, knotting, every single thing I know he can give me.

Stephan lifts his head and trails fingers over the neckline of my dress, and then down over my breasts, circling where my nipples push against the thick satin. "God, Princess, I can't wait to see you naked. You're already a work of art, but I want it all."

He sighs.

"But?" I ask.

"But I should take it slow for your first time, make it special." He gives me a dark, smoky look, and in the light in my nest, his hair is deep burnished gold, the dark part of the blond turned into something holy.

"Oh."

"There's time for down and dirty, Princess. The first time I get your body is going to be where I teach you, where we learn together, explore. And…Violet?"

"Yes?"

"I saw your face earlier when I mentioned you can do what you want with this place. I said that because while I'm not giving up my career, I'll be taking you with me only when and if you want to go. But this should be your domain. I want you to explore your tastes. Have something of your own. With me."

I take off my veil and look around, then lay it over a fat sofa in the room for, I guess, when I start going into heat or coming out of it. And when I am, now he doesn't need to be kept away. It's going to be months away, the next one, and I'm both glad and regretful at having my first one before we mate.

I don't think I want our first time to be while I'm out of my mind in heat, but I would have liked to be crazed and attacking him. Next time.

"I think I'd like this in here," I say, running a hand over the veil. "Iris made it for me, but it's from our mating ceremony."

He nods then undoes his bowtie and pulls it off. He tosses it. "You can have that, too. Anything. Now come on, I have drinks and some snacks for us, and we can have them in the bedroom. You can model the lingerie I got you..."

My pulse won't stop jumping, and my hand shakes as he hands me a drink. It's that strong, sweet alcohol smell of the drink he likes. Bourbon. I don't mind it, but I'm not really used to booze, and softer drinks might be more my style.

Yet this feels...right.

A grownup drink on a very grownup night. He kisses me, the taste of the bourbon on his lips enhancing the rich, dark tone of him, and my stomach flutters with winged thrills.

The bedroom is masculine. Both light and dark wood, and a four-poster bed that I'd love to hang gauzy material from. Earthy tones to go with the room. But romantic for me.

No, for *us*.

The bed is huge, and I gulp and turn, taking in all the space. There's even a sofa, an armchair, and a coffee table in here. I almost giggle. The master bedroom with the master himself.

But it's not funny. I'm just drenched in nerves and—

Stephan runs his knuckles down my back. "I think you need to take this dress off. You're getting all damp."

I quiver, and try and reach for the zipper, but he kisses my shoulder now, and the zip hisses as he undoes it. Then he steps back, taking my drink as the dress falls.

Exposed. This is the most of me a man's ever seen. The lace balconette bra covers barely anything, and his gaze drops like lightning to my nipples that pucker and ache as they push at the lace, starting to peek over the top.

Then his gaze shifts down to the cream lace covering my pussy, and he lingers, making me throb within.

I can feel myself getting wet, and I'm sure he can see it. From his smile that slowly blooms, I'm positive.

"Here." He hands me back my drink, pulls out his phone, and presses a button. Slow, seductive music plays. Then he throws off his coat, kicks off his shoes, and unbuttons his shirt, flashing me an expanse of that golden, famous flesh.

There's a bowl of berries, all kinds, on the coffee table, and the bottle of bourbon picking up a deep amber glow from the warm light of the room.

"That class you went to when I first saw you run across traffic, can you show me what you learned?"

I freeze. "Is... Is this what we do?"

"We're mated. We can do anything, and as I told you, I'm taking my time, but..." He puts his hand on his pants, and runs his fingers along his covered dick, showing me how big, stiff, and thick it is.

My mouth waters and my throat closes, all at the same time. This is a lot, too much. And I step closer, fascinated above all else.

"Are you hard?"

"Like you can't even imagine."

"Did I do that?"

"Oh, Princess, you've been doing that to me since early on. Most of the time I try to control it, but now?" His brown eyes lock on mine. "Now I don't have to. I'm fucking aching, but I want to see you dance."

Putting down my drink, I take off my shoes and close my eyes. I turn my back and move awkwardly to the music and slowly start the dance Mikel Petrov taught.

As a teacher he was all about certain movements and then taking those as the basis to create a dance that would never be the same twice, but could be something I could make recognizably mine. I lock onto that in my mind.

On an idea of a man I want to impress, seduce. He's just an idea, a way in, but somewhere the self-consciousness vanishes. The idea solidifies.

The imaginary man shifts and morphs into Stephan, and then I let the music in, let it take over, and start to really dance.

It's a wild sensual beat in me that this dance takes me on, and I'm lost in it, bending, twisting, moving to the music, the steps flowing from me, and I'm free.

I lose myself in it, so deep that I'm part of Stephan and apart. I'm the dream, the fantasy I can never be in real life, but the freedom has wings and—

"Come here, Princess."

The soft purring growl is an Alpha's command.

I stop, and as heat streaks through me, the brush of humiliation, I do as he demands.

It's not until I look up that I almost stumble.

He's got his cock in his hand—it's huge, with a long, veined shaft and pink head—and he's slowly, lazily pulling it.

"Stephan..."

"Kiss me, Princess."

Not his Alpha voice, but it's such a command I can't help but fold down into it. To give him what he wants.

I get down on my knees and go to kiss his cock, but he stops me. "I meant—"

But I want to. It's an overwhelming urge to see what it's all about to touch, lick, and taste a man, and I put my hands on his thighs and take him into my mouth. He shudders.

He's salty, slightly sweet, and totally *him*, a rich taste I can't get enough of. The scent of him is everywhere, invading me. And when I swirl my tongue around the tip, he winds his hand in my hair and thrusts up, his cock hitting my lips.

"Up. Be a good, sweet girl, Princess."

"But—"

"You're such a pleaser, Violet, so please me by doing what I say."

His words are a lightning bolt through me. "I thought—"

"Later," he says, tightening his hand in my hair, a

pleasing pull against my scalp as he urges me up. "I can wait for that. Up here. On my lap."

He guides me so my legs are on either side of him, and he loosens his hold a little on my hair as he rubs his cock against my pussy.

When he brings me in for a deep, hot kiss, I can't think. I don't want to think. Not when feeling is so good. Every single part of me is alive.

Stephan kisses a trail to my ear. "You dance like a fucking dream. An erotic dream elevated by your pristine, princess-like aura."

Then he takes my mouth again and picks me up, carrying me to the bed. He lays me down and slowly pulls off the balconette bra and my panties until I'm naked before him.

"So fucking stunning."

With his fingers and mouth, he starts to explore me, and even though I want to watch him, drink him in, I'm so overwhelmed my eyes flutter shut. I float on a sea of sensations he releases in waves.

His touch is pure delicate fire. Everywhere his mouth and tongue touch me it flares, from my throat, over the bite mark that he sucks on, then down.

Down. From nipple to nipple, he spends time sucking, nibbling, devouring until I'm writhing.

Then down over my stomach, down along my pubic bone. He reaches the top of my pubis, and parts my thighs, his mouth avoiding my clit and pussy, his fingers too. Even though that's where I want him, *need* him.

Instead, he starts to kiss and nip my inner thighs, tiny

pinpricks of pleasure, and I'm so lost, so needing, that I don't know what to do but clutch at him.

He licks up the slick that's making me so wet, along with my juices, then his fingers touch my pussy, and I nearly leap off the bed, everything jumping.

But Stephan goes with it, pushing his fingers into me. Then his thumb pushes into my ass, making me cry out, unsure how to feel. Weird, good. I don't know. All I know is that thumb makes everything else feel like it veered up a thousand levels of awareness and pleasure.

I want to speak, but I can't find the words as his tongue makes short work of my clit, like he has a mission. With his fingers and his mouth, working a rhythm, the pressure builds and explodes in me in fast order, and I shudder and shake, the roll of the orgasm rocketing through me.

Stephan pulls out and then he's back. The whack of material hitting the floor registers and then is obliterated as he comes up over me.

"This might hurt at first..."

I nod, drawing in a deep breath and bracing myself.

He thrusts in.

Deep.

My eyes fly open as the invasion of him in me is complete. My pussy throbs hard around his shaft and grips him. "Stephan..."

"You're so fucking tight, so good, oh, god..."

He begins to thrust into me, slow deep thrusts, and I'm swept along. He's hitting that spot inside that makes me tighten, tingle, and this time when I shatter, it's like the whole world comes with me, breaking into tiny glittering pieces.

Is he going to knot?

But he pulls out and says, "I'm not done. Turn over."

CHAPTER THIRTY-TWO

Stephan

I'm the king of assholes.

She's orgasmic like she should be with her mate, but even as I withdraw from her sweet, tight body, I can feel that beat in her, the hunger for more.

Right now, she probably doesn't understand what that craving's for, beyond the initial orgasm and pleasure I can give her. But she will.

It's in her nature. Like it's in mine.

The urge to rut, for me to knot, that thing that'll give her untold pleasure, and just maybe end in pregnancy.

And death.

I lost one love.

I'm not losing another.

But Violet, the eternal good girl who can dance more seductively than an angel who's fallen, is obedient and I fucking love that. She's quivering as she turns. I stroke a hand over her ass. So tight and sweet, I can't resist biting her, and she moans.

I go lower, and flip underneath her, so she's essentially sitting on my face, and the view's stunning. Christ, this cunt is a work of art.

I try to calm the urge to rut her. It's why I'm beneath her, why I pulled out. I *can't* rut her. If I do, I'll fucking knot.

But I know how to please my little pristine princess with the slight praise kink.

I breathe.

Slowly, I draw her down so I can run my tongue over her sweet, hot flesh. She's a mix of slick and juices, and she's beyond delicious. I suck on her inner lips, her outer ones. Then I thrust my tongue into her, and she moans low and starts to move.

Violet sighs as I move up to the prize of her clit, and I start to lick and toy with it, loving how she pushes into me, how she's teetering on pure instinct. I push my fingers into her; the flutters of her pussy are a delight, and I slowly ease my thumb back into her ass.

It's tight, too. That stretch that makes my cock twitch. Almost as good as the stretch of her pussy. But her ass is an option. All those nerve endings...and I can knot and release there if I can't control myself.

But with her so new at this, that will take time.

Then there's her mouth...

I start to thrust into her, licking, sucking, trying to get my fill, and she cries out as she comes hard, grinding down on me, trying to pull away the moment it gets to be too much.

And I softly bite her clit. That makes her scream, makes her dig into my scalp as she rubs on my face. I pull back, letting her think the ebb's the end.

It isn't.

I need more of her. So much more.

I'm going to have to come, I know that.

My balls ache, my cock is aching, too, and the pressure to release is building toward explosion.

But I hold it, because there's something in that denial, something that I know will increase my pleasure when I give in, but I need her to come more.

I need to try and milk her dry of pleasure until she's boneless, mine, nothing more than a vessel for me to bend and mold to my will.

I can't fucking wait to fuck her mouth.

I keep thrusting my fingers into her, and I start to push her through the orgasm, shifting the pressure to her ass, more thrust, deeper, until she starts to grind again, her clit throbbing on my tongue.

I lick, suck, and as I do, I keep thrusting into both holes, keep building her until she screams once more, and everything in her spasms. Clit, ass, cunt.

Easing out, I roll her to her back and kiss her deeply, taking my time to touch and stroke her, to calm and build her back. And then I look at her. "We're not done."

"I want...I want...I want your knot."

Those are dangerous words, and I hold them at bay.

This time, she's how I want her, stripped back of everything but her innate honesty, her eagerness to please, and I coil my hand in her hair and pull her head up to me. "I'm going to teach you how to give head. And then I'm going to fuck your mouth and come."

"Yes."

"Look at you..." I sit up and pull her around my cock, heavy, hard. She's clumsy, boneless as she slides on the bed. I help her off it, pushing her down to kneel on the floor between my legs, and Violet looks up at me, utter perfection. "Such a good girl."

A shiver runs through her. I can almost see it dance over her skin.

I'm so on the verge that her sucking me is going to take a Herculean effort not to fucking come immediately.

So I toy with her, tweaking her nipples, watching those shivers of need dance.

"You know," I say, pulling her up as I lean over to kiss and nibble at her lips, "for someone who can't stand being the center of attention, you're lapping it up right now."

I sit back, loosening my hand a little, and with my other one I start to slowly stroke myself.

"N-No."

"Yes, Princess. You're lapping it up, aren't you? The star in my world, in my fucking fantasies, that's you right now."

"I just want to make you happy."

I sigh and take one of her hands, and I wrap it around my cock in lieu of my own hand. Little shivers of hot and cold dance over me at that light grip. "Then make me happy, learn how to please me. There's no formula, just do it."

I want to push her out into the unknown, see what happens.

"What do I do?"

"Put your mouth on me."

She doesn't move, just jerks my dick in delicate strokes that drive me crazy. Then she moves in and starts to lick at me, and I nearly lose my fucking mind.

Her tongue is pleasure, torture, and the promise of something more. It takes everything I have not to direct or instruct as she explores, her other hand coming to my balls to touch and squeeze.

She could go harder, but there's something in her princess-delicate ways that drives an Alpha out of his head and into rut space.

But I don't go there. Can't. I somehow manage to stay away from that madness, just outside it, and I sink down into her ministrations.

The lapping, soothing, torturous tongue, her fingers as they squeeze and glide, and then...

Oh. *Fuck.*

She opens up her mouth and wraps her lips around my head, her tongue sliding under the edge, along that highly sensitive spot, and she jumps as my cock twitches.

I let go of her and bend over to fist my hands into the sheets as she starts to lick and suck. I'm big so she has to stretch, and I'm cataloguing all the differences with her mouth to her cunt.

Here she's soft and hard, the dichotomy making me ache more. Her teeth are a scrape against me, and she starts to drool as she takes me so far that I hit the back of her throat.

Soft heat and wetness. Smooth, hard roughness.

The two go together in ways I never thought about, ways I don't think I'll now stop obsessing over.

She lurches, coming up and sucking in a deep breath before she goes down again. Up and down, no rhyme to it, no rhythm. And because she doesn't have an agenda, I'm being fucking tortured.

Violet gets me to a place where the pleasure starts to build and build, and then she abruptly changes, and it dissipates.

If I could bottle her learning technique as a device for sadism, I'd be richer still.

Then something snaps in me. The way she's drooling, half choking, makes everything so fucking slick I can glide, and I need to be deeper. I need that control.

"Good girl. What a fucking great job, Princess."

She makes a sobbing sound, and I thrust up, choking it off. I ease her head off me.

"I don't know what to do." Her hazel eyes are so big and pleading. Her dark hair is a mess still coiled in my hand, and I fucking love it.

"I'm going to fuck your throat, Princess. I don't think I can be gentle with it, though. Ready?"

"Yes. I can handle it."

"Let's see just how well you please me."

And I meet her gaze as I guide her mouth back to my cock. This time, I'm in the driver's seat. I have many reasons. I don't want her to think she's doing it wrong; I don't want to get lost in this and lose the edge.

I need to fucking come. In her. Any way I can.

So I start to thrust, guiding her with my hand on the

back of her head, and she picks up where she was, not so delicate this time.

Violet is learning to read the smallest things so she can please me, make me happy. And she's sucking harder as I get rougher. The power surges through me, the aching need. The push to come.

I start to lose control. I'm panting, grunting. My cock in her throat is exquisite, a thing I could live on for life. And I want to destroy that goodness, tear it down and rebuild it just for me.

I want to master her, rule her, make me her reason for being. Make her the perfect fucking Omega. My Omega. My mate, my creature for pleasure.

I want to watch her beg and crawl to me. I want to watch her come so hard from me knotting that—

Fuck. *Fuck.* I start hammering into her now. I don't care in that moment that she's struggling, making choking noises. I make her take me so fucking deep I'm marking her everywhere, and my spine and skin are sparking now.

My balls are so high, tight, the ache almost unbearable, bordering on pain, and then I come. The pleasure floods me as my cock jerks and empties into her throat.

And then with one last twitch, I pull her off me, and she comes up with a heaving intake of breath, her face wet with drool and tears. And incredibly, she comes back, licking me, sucking at the tip that's so sensitive I almost shriek.

She cleans me, the perfect Omega, the perfect girl, my mate, and her long licks soothe the beast that still prowls within my skin, the one that wants the ultimate release.

I pull her into my arms and I kiss her, licking up her

tears, taking her mouth in deep, slow kisses that drown me in her. And then I pick her up and carry her to the bathroom.

I turn on the shower and wash her clean of her blockers, of our mixed sex scents, of the sweat and the fluids that cling still between her thighs. I turn this into a ritual for her, to show her she's important, special, a high goddess, *my* goddess.

I'm a mess, a total wreck. My thoughts are scattered except for one thing.

Now I've had her, I'm never going to let her go.

CHAPTER THIRTY-THREE

Violet

I never knew things could be like this. Of course, this is, by definition, the honeymoon phase.

Sex is eye-opening, wonderful, and yet there's a nagging thought that there should be a higher peak.

I look over at my mate—*my mate*—still sleeping, the sheets tangled and all that naked flesh showing.

I start getting hot, so I turn. My phone lights up on the nightstand, and I grab it as I head down to the kitchen on the floor below. The other floors are going to be my works in progress, but I love living in his space, what he had as his two-floor apartment.

It's intimate. I look at the text from Rue, of course. She's all emojis and runaway sentences about the ceremony, what we're doing, and Queen Bee's latest Stitches. It's a little reminder of home that I need right now.

Shouldn't you be asleep?

Rue's right on top of it.

RUE

Got lots 2 do, Vi. A LOT 2 catch up on. Heath says ur in the Caribbean, but I don't believe him. The QB just announced the latest ball. There r others y'know, still wanting a mate. The unmated Omegas, the poor things. They can't all b luxe. Can u believe Mom said we might not b going? But u will so we will.

It's like talking to her directly, only in text form.

Before I can send off a response, my phone shows she's still typing, so I pull out things from the fridge and search for a pan to cook in.

Eggs. Spinach. Feta.

Also berries, and a thick plain yogurt that's so creamy and decadent I could eat it by the spoonful. Then in the pantry I pull out the nut and seed granola. Perfect.

I look at my phone. New message is through.

RUE

Tell Mom we r going. U r. W Asher. Ur the envy of so many. If he doesn't have a bro, does he have a friend who'll wait 4 me?

I text back, and I slice the berries and heat the pan.

> No brother, and I'm not sure Heath's
> going to allow you to be with an older
> Emporia man.

RUE

> He'll b a star!!! No. I meant here. I might
> want 2 move, but not sure.

She says this like she's twenty-one and about to have her first Season. I bite down on my smile as I whisk the eggs and chop the spinach. It probably needs tomatoes but there aren't any. I find some parmesan and grate it, adding it to the feta. I wilt the spinach in the pan, quickly adding some twists of pepper, then I toss that on the cheeses.

RUE

> No, I want 1 of his friends from here.

> Heath will kill you and the guy.

RUE

> Heath's so stuffy.

Oh, Heath will love being called stuffy. But he can barely tolerate me with one of his friends. I don't think he'd let another sibling run off and mate with one of Stephan's.

RUE

Heath's spending time with Asher's agent! Anyway, Vi. The BALL. Monarch announced it and the QB. I luv her. I want 2 go as her. Mask wise. The ball is honey and nectar. I could just DIE, Vi. Anyway, how's the S-E-X? As good as all the books I read? The Stitch graphic novels? It looks really raunchy. Esp 4 Omega/Alpha. Knotting iz hawt

She breaks off. And there's nothing.
I'm about to text her when I get another message.

RUE

Don't encourage her. As far as she knows, you and Stephan hold hands.

It's definitely from Heath. It reeks of stuffiness. I shake my head and text Heath back.

Give Rue her phone. Or maybe I will share every sordid detail.

HEATH

Fine. But first, fair warning. Everyone's coming to visit soon. Mari got it out of me where you are. Then she and Iris are in the middle of an argument with the red-headed hanger-on about the virtues of an at-home honeymoon and if it can be called that. Shit. Now Rue's involved. Dahlia's playing Beethoven's fifth. And Mom just joined in and said he'll take you somewhere nice soon. I better go deal. Love you, Vi.

Love you too. All of you.

I smile.

We *do* hold hands.

I lower the heat and put a chunk of butter in the pan, then pour in the eggs to make the omelet. When they're almost done, I add the filling, fold it, and the toast pops up right on time.

The scent of oak envelops me, warm and slightly spicy with a hint of sweetness, as Stephan wraps an arm around me.

He pulls me in to him. He's not wearing a shirt. And my body instantly heats and melts. "Mmm, Princess, fucking hot in bed, ready to please, can dance and cook, too. My god, is this my life?"

I turn and rub my face against his chest.

I don't even know how real he's been, or if it's just kindness, or the newness of this, but I'm overcome. "Domestic, that's me. The living stereotype of an Omega."

He spins me to drop a kiss on my lips.

"No, never. You? Princess, you've got deep, untapped treasure, and I'm a greedy man who will mine all your jewels."

He kisses me slowly, until I'm slick between my legs and his erection is pushing into me. I want to test out my new skills on giving him head, but I remember what Heath said, and while I'm wearing Stephan's T-shirt and nothing else, I don't want my family turning up when he's balls to the wall in me.

"Sit, I'll serve."

But he just smiles as he pinches a slice of strawberry and eats it. He pours the juice and the coffee, and flips the toast to a plate.

"You take the food, and I'll bring the drinks. We can eat on the back balcony off the living room. It overlooks the water and is private because I own that slice of beach too.

"Sounds nice."

I take the tray he loads and make my way upstairs.

The street he lives on is more exclusive than ours and our townhouse is pretty much up there. There aren't many houses along the beach, and in the distance, I can see people strolling on the sand. I think about the snippets of bad boy Asher St. James I've read about, all the endless women, the drinking, the fast cars.

The lazy smile of a charmer who breaks hearts.

Asher might be Stephan, but Stephan is so much more. Private and public, and this is private.

Or maybe he had trysts here.

Not, not here. This place is too personal.

At least that's what I tell myself.

Because there's nothing to base any of those drifting thoughts on.

"Here's your juice," he says, handing it to me. "Drink it all up. Got a feeling about this weekend..."

"I'm up for sex."

"I've created a monster." He drops a kiss on my head. "And I'm happy about that."

We eat breakfast, making small talk. It's so nice, I could get used to this. I *am* getting used to this, I realize.

He's attentive, charming, and he likes being with me. And even I know the chemistry's through the roof; neither of us can get enough of the other.

Early days...very early days, I tell my rapidly swooping

and soaring heart, the one that's falling hard for him. Early days.

"After we finish, we should definitely take advantage of —" He swears as his phone lights up, annoyed at the interruption. And then his face takes on a grim expression as he reads the message.

"What is it?" I ask.

"What do you think? My fucking aunt has demanded we turn up at the Council. I guess this honeymoon's over."

My heart starts to go crazy for all the wrong reasons.

"Just Sophine being Sophine. Nosy as shit and with something up her sleeve, no doubt. Fuck, I hate this place."

That makes it go crazy again.

"Not because of you, Princess. It's the battle-ax. Once we step out there in public again, everyone's gonna know we're here. Our little home is now just a haven to come to. Come on, I guess we'd better get this shit over with."

The Monarch isn't in her throne room, and I think it's the first time I've seen the buzz of the inner workings of the Council as we pass people working.

She is, however, in a resplendent office, and when we arrive, she sits at her desk, silvery hair up, slate-gray suit on, tapping something on her phone.

After a few moments, Stephan sighs. Loudly. "If this is a power play, then get over it."

She raises a perfect brow at him and doesn't respond.

Stephan might be able to speak to her like that, but Sophine is above everyone, and I'm shaking inside, my stomach twisting because her displeasure is obvious. It stings the air, but Stephan seems unmoved. He just goes over to the bar and starts opening and sniffing the booze. Then when he finds something he likes the smell of, he picks it up.

"I think I'll take this for our troubles and go—"

"Arrogant behavior didn't work on me when you were a child. Why do you think it'll work now? Might I remind you the Season isn't over, and you need to behave. Or it won't reflect well on the Gardeners in future Seasons, and that will sit on your shoulders."

He stalks over to her and sets the bottle down roughly, leaning on the desk and glaring at her. She glares right back.

They're both being childish, but obviously I hold my tongue. I've been mated for mere days now, and even got mated to avoid scandal. Her threat is very real.

The realization slams me back from the small cloud I've been on and into reality once more.

Maybe Stephan and I have something, and I hope we do. It feels like we do, and I'll do everything to make it a happy life for him. But I'm aware of how it started, when he bit me, marked me.

"I know you and your nephew have your differences," I say, voice shaking, "but I'm sure he's just upset our honeymoon was interrupted."

"I'm sure he was," she says, sending him a long side-eye.

"Clearly I'm fucking pissed about that, but whatever beef we have is with each other, so leave Violet and her family out of this."

A flicker of a smile appears on her mouth.

"Now, Violet." Her gaze swings to me. "Do you have any idea who this nasty little so-called Queen Bee is?"

I stare at her. What a weird direction this has gone. "No idea. It could be anyone. It could be a group... I... I don't have much of a social life."

"And we're meant to be on our honeymoon," Stephan says again to emphasize that point. "You know, following the societal rules."

Sophine smacks a hand on the table. "You're still part of the Season, which is why you stayed here." A small smirk plays across her face. "I ask because I'm going to find this person and destroy her. Whoever she is."

"Maybe it's a man," Stephan says. "Fredrick looks untrustworthy to me."

"The Queen Bee is female. I'm aware of that much. She can create a persona and disguise herself but only a female would be able to observe like this. You're a male, Stephan, you wouldn't understand. You'll both be at the ball. This weekend. Honey and Nectar. You, Violet, will be my eyes and ears. Anything you find out, report back."

Chapter Thirty-Four

Stephan

My princess is panicking, bursting at the seams with anxiety.

We're still in the building, the actual Council building in Sabine. Not the estate where Sophine holds court, but where the workers come and run the world, or so it seems.

I take Violet's hand and squeeze. "This way." There's a supply closet we just passed and right now there's no one in the corridor.

I drag her in and lock the door.

"Why are we in here, Stephan?"

I back her into a shelving unit, and put a hand on the shelves either side of her head, boxing her in. Her scent weaves enticing paths around me, all of them leading to her throat, her lips, those lovely tits, and lower still. At least, those are the places I want to go.

"To calm you down, Princess. You're a little high-strung."

"And locking me in here where we could be caught is a way to calm me?"

I smile and bend my head, running my lips along her sweet throat. "Maybe I'm training you to channel your anxiety into more useful arenas."

"N-No, I think you're making it worse."

"I think you're not being the good girl you usually are. Not...obeying me. Your mate."

I can almost feel her turn molten as she stands there. The heat of her radiates, and I stroke my tongue slow over her pulse, its leap like a jolt of need to my cock. I close my mouth around that part of her neck and suck.

She moans and the shelves shake as she grabs for support.

Then I bite. Slowly.

It's not hard, that bite, but it's a lesson in deliberation and drawing out a moment. The tension in her heightens and twists into something new as she waits for me to bite harder.

I release her, and the air is so tight around us it holds us still. I look at her, and those hazel eyes with the golds and greens are liquid jewels, and desire beats in the air.

"Turn."

I step back and she does.

"Hold on to the shelves." She goes to grab the ones near her breasts, but I have an idea. "No, lower. Lower. Stick out your ass so you're bent at a right angle. Perfect."

She's a morsel, a meal, a breath of fresh air, hot trysts in the dark, long slow sessions. She's all of that. More.

But I think what I want is fast food done right.

I want to make her learn to turn her anxiety on its ass. "Hold, don't move."

Of course she does as ordered. My fucking pristine princess.

She's tense, the same energy as her anxiety, high but focused, not fractured, not pulling her apart. That's what I want from her.

I look around. My meal's cooking, and I'm getting ready to devour when it's done. There's a bunch of rulers on the shelf opposite me and I pick one up. Metal and heavy, it would be a tool to inflict pain and punishment. Perfect for my purposes.

I don't say a word to her, just lift her floral dress, pleased at the yellow lace panties she's got on. Not the color. I don't give a shit about that, but the way it cuts up, showing me most of her cheeks.

Fuck yeah.

I slide a finger along the edges over her ass and she sighs out a small moan. I can smell her sweeter than heaven violet scent. It's almost as good as the sweetness her heat brought on, but her sex scent's more than sweet enough. Dangerously intoxicating.

But I have plans too for me coming, plans that involve her on her knees, mouth open.

I slip my fingers lower, then down along the seam of her cunt, so hot, so wet, it makes my cock rock-hard and my knees weak.

"Oooh..."

I smile, then lower her panties to just the tops of her thighs, and I trail the ruler over her ass.

"What's that?"

"A metal ruler."

Even though all I'm doing is holding it there, she jerks. I want her to imagine what I could do to her with it.

"Don't hit me," she whispers, her voice twisted with want, sexual need, and a kind of fear that raises the hairs on the back of my head. Anticipation.

"No? Don't you want to know?"

Her breath comes fast and a trickle of juices runs down her thigh and soaks into her panties. I want that juice. I want her desire. Her arousal. I want—need—her to pulsate on my dick.

"You won't hurt me, Stephan."

I raise the ruler high and bring it down, so it makes a sound in the air, stopping just before touching her with it. Then I put it back on her ass, placing it gently. "No?"

"No."

"But you're not obeying me. And usually you do, Princess. You're usually utterly perfect, so good."

It's like I shot a volt of electrical current into her.

"Please don't."

"I have to." I unzip, free myself, pumping for a few seconds, then I let my junk go. "Don't tense. It'll hurt more."

A squeak escapes Violet, and I bring the ruler fast through the air and stop well short of it meeting her flesh, and instead I bring my hand down in a smack that leaves a light little pink patch.

Violet lets out a tiny scream. "Oh, God."

With that, I drop the ruler and it hits the floor with a

clang. I fist my cock, part her folds and plunge in, stretching her and slamming to the hilt.

Oh. Fuck. It's like coming home. She's tight and wet and so primed that little spasms milk me. Then I start to move.

One hand on her hip to hold her, the other on the shelf to stop me slamming her into it.

My Violet might have a little praise kink; she hates it and craves it at the same time, and it seems to get her wetter when I make her squirm with praise.

But putting a little twisted fear in her is almost as good as praise.

Her slickness from arousal allows me to slide in and out hard and fast, lets me get so fucking balls to the wall deep in her that slamming her is borderline close to rutting. And I want to.

Fuck, do I want to.

To let go and just own her in all the ways pushes at me, but I'm not going to. I know how this meal ends.

I move my hand from her hip, around to her clit and start to stroke and toy with it, all the while aiming to hit that spot in her that feels good to me and makes her insane.

She's pushing back, moaning and panting, and the urge to let go gets stronger, my hold on myself thinner. I'm aching and flying high. Aching because I need that knotting, flying because there's nothing like Violet.

Then she comes, a gasping cry as she shudders on me, her cunt spasming hard.

My knot starts to swell, and I pull out.

"Drop to your knees and open your mouth."

She does and swallows me down, bobbing up and down on me, taking me so deep I'm hammering her throat.

And then I'm coming.

Papers and supplies fall and clatter. I almost bring the shelf down on us. The orgasm seems to last forever, with me grunting and jerking as she drains me.

When the tremors finally end, Violet stares at me, her eyes glazed, and I drag her up and crush her to me, kissing her deep and long, the kiss the last bite of my fast meal.

She tastes so sweet as always, that Violet taste, and she tastes like me.

I break the kiss because I know we need to straighten up and get out of here. I let her go, tuck my dick away, and do up my pants. Then pull up her panties and smooth down her dress.

"I just meant for you to open so I could come in your mouth."

"I wanted to," she says, a little laugh escaping. "I thought you were going to hit me with that ruler."

"And maim that gorgeous ass?" I kiss her hard. "Never. We should get out of here."

"How do I look?"

"Like you just got fucked by a movie star."

"Your ego..."

I unlock the door, grab her hand, and pull her into the hall, bumping into someone. "Oops, that's not the exit," I say.

I don't stick around long enough to see who it is. Instead, I make her run with me for the exit. Her head's back, laughter rolling from her, her cheeks pink.

She's a different woman when she's like this.

No, not different.

She's the woman she's always been. The one she's hidden away so long.

One I could fall in love with.

If I were a different man.

There's a group of people waiting at the unlocked gate to our beach house.

I help Violet out of the car, sliding my phone away. I need to text Clea before she returns to Emporia in a few days. But first, I need to help the princess deal with her family's visit.

When I spy Pen among them, I adjust that to *our* families.

When we're all inside, Rue takes a break from taking selfies in Asher St. James's home to ask Violet, "Are you pregnant yet?"

The comment gets a side-eye from Pen to me, a growl from Heath who stomps off into the fenced-in yard to make a call, and a sigh from Violet's mother.

"Rue, that's not how it works," Iris mutters.

Rue frowns. "I know."

"I'm not sure she does," Mari says then smiles at her mom.

"Do you have a piano?" Dahlia asks.

I shake my head, so she just goes into the sitting room to read the book she pulls from her bag.

Violet throws me a helpless look. I know she's worried

she looks like she just had sex, but she doesn't now. "I'll give you all a tour," she offers.

"And I'll help Stephan get refreshments," Penrith says.

When they all leave, we go into the kitchen. As Pen fills a pitcher with juice and makes a pot of tea and coffee, she presses her lips together. She's clearly got something on her mind, so I sit at the table and wait.

"Stephan, get the cups and saucers, and I'm sure you have cookies. I know I sent over a lot of supplies like that."

"Yes, ma'am."

I get some from the pantry, and almost jump when I turn and find her just standing there, blocking my path.

"You've told her, of course."

I note it isn't a question. "Told her what?"

"About Cecilia."

"Some."

"Stephan—"

"We're not having children."

A sigh comes from her like a balloon deflating. "Oh, Stephan."

"Not your concern. And not up for debate."

"As your constant supporter, even when you do truly stupid things, I'd like to think it *is* my concern. And you told her something. A girl like your Violet is made for babies, for a family."

"No."

"And if it happens?"

"It can't." I meet her gaze. "I took care of it."

One thing about Pen is that for all her outward manners and adhering to the ways of society, she doesn't really give a shit. She doesn't balk. "She's okay with all this?"

"I said I'm taking care of it."

"How?" she asks.

"I don't want to lose her."

Pen crosses her arms. "I asked *how*."

Now I move closer to her, annoyance sparking. "As I said, not up for debate."

From upstairs comes laughter and it gets louder as everyone starts to head back down here.

Pen meets my glare head on. "This isn't over."

But it is, at least for me.

Because the contraceptives I got from Clea should already be working. But I'll have to up the dosage soon before I can knot her safely.

While crushing up Omega contraceptives and putting them into my new mate's drinks might not be exactly ethical, it's better than the alternative.

I can't lose her.

Ooh la la, my faithful brood. Do you think they went to the City of Love for the honeymoon?

You know who I mean, Hivemind!

The prince and princess of the Season, that's who!

*Some **rumors** claim they might have gone off to some fast-rolling city of sleaze instead, so our Asher could show the wallviolet an education.*

Some claim he left her here and went off on his own.

Others state they went to Emporia.

But you know what?

Not a single photo on any

app

social media

gossip mag

or *feed*

Nothing at all. Not even a blip from my faithful brood.

So, Hivemind, if you didn't catch them anywhere, where do
YOU think they've been?

COME CLOSER...

I got it from a good source they might have just stayed right
here in Sabine.

What do you think?

In other news...

One of the blonde beauties on the Omega Season circuit was
seen doing **untoward** things with one scarred, drop dead
gorgeous older man. Some might say he's a bit of a lady Kill-
er.

And his to-die-for, melt your ovaries and set you in heat pal
had his hand up the dress of one recently nearly marked
dark-haired Omega and his tongue down her throat—
helping her through tough times or just talking REALLY
close?

Ladies, I urge you to keep away from rum and reputation-ruining bars like some of the ones in the Lower Side. Their names are left out for obvious reasons. Those obvious reasons being that the Monarch is a fan of the Bee, or so I hear.

Speaking of the Monarch...

With one mated pair under this Season's belt, things might be getting a little competitive with who's making it next to the altar.

But luckily the Monarch

being a total fan

is having another masked ball.

Honey and Nectar themed.

Told ya she's a fan.

It's this Friday.

Bring your bee themed masks.

I for one can't wait to see if there's not just a twist but a sting...

- Queen Bee

CHAPTER THIRTY-FIVE

Violet

The rumor at the ball, which I know is true, is that Sophine is displeased with whoever Queen Bee is.

More so after the last Stitch they posted.

And to be honest, I'm not exactly overly pleased with whoever it is, either. All that stuff about me and Stephan is a lot. And then what she says about Sophine? Dangerous. To be fair, she's mostly nice enough about me, but...

"Look at me, Vi," Rue says, dancing up to me. "I am the Queen."

And she dances away.

But whoever it is, the real queen, should be careful.

"That child's going to be the death of me," Heath moans, as Rue in her Queen Bee mask dances on the sidelines of the ball. "And wearing that fucking thing, is she crazy?"

"It could be her," Quinn says, appearing out of nowhere. "What if Rue is the Queen Bee? And don't swear, Heather. It doesn't make you cool."

"I said that." Iris adjusts her black mask with little antennae. "The part about Rue. Though I agree you're not cool, Heath."

"I'm going to go help your idiotic mate, Vi. That's how annoyed I am with you lot." He kisses my cheek. "Not you. Don't look so stricken."

He takes off to where Stephan's been waylaid by some of the other Alphas and a few Omegas I don't know that well, but they seem nice. Rue told me they're just big Asher fans.

Now that's something I'm going to have to try to get my head around.

People in our world might be huge fans, but for the most part they hardly ever let it show. I think those girls held it in as long as they could and now that he's off the market...

"Are you jealous?" Quinn asks, nodding.

It takes me a moment to realize she aimed that at me.

"No." I try to smile because it flusters me on certain levels.

It is true. I'm not jealous. Maybe I should be? I guess it's the newness, the fact he's never done anything to make me think he's looking elsewhere.

Okay, there was the conversation he labeled as "complicated" with Alicia, but if anything happened, it wasn't like he got turned down by her and I'm the consolation prize.

Someone turning him down is laughable.

"Oh, Lord," Quinn says. "You are totally in love."

"I'm mated."

"Yes, but..."

"Leave Vi alone, Quinn. She doesn't need to start hyperventilating." Iris looks at me. "Do *you* think it's Rue?"

"The Queen Bee?" I half laugh. "Maybe if she wasn't so nice. Also, I'm not sure she can keep a secret. Everyone would know if she was. I know the Monarch would love to know who, though."

"Wouldn't we all," Quinn says. "The Monarch must be angry. She's not here."

"She'll be watching, I bet," Iris mutters. "Not that I care. God. You'd think I'd be out of this patriarchal mess since you're an old mated lady now."

"Thanks," I say, taking a sip of the punch. "You didn't have to come."

"I did. You need support." Then she looks me up and down in the gold dress I have on. It has a black underside to the long skirt. "I love how you're still not doing the latest fashion stuff. This look suits you, Vi. It's your look. As Rue would say, it's up to the minute *and* timeless, not trendy."

She waits for my response. When I don't have one, Iris squeezes my arm, like a mini hug. "It's strange to see you not panicking."

"I'm not the center of attention."

It's not exactly true. I mated with Stephan and the center of attention seems to be him. But then again, even if I get the fallout from him, he wore me out so much before we came here that I barely had the energy to get on my feet at all. All that sex, all those orgasms before getting dressed. I'm not sure my panic button works right now. The anxiety one, either. And if I feel a little anxious, like I did when we walked in, he'll say something full of praise or nice in that particular way that sends shivers right down my spine.

"No, there's a little change, but...this isn't the place." Iris spots Mom. "Damn, forgot to get her a drink and she's stuck talking to Alicia's pompous mother."

She takes off with Quinn, and I make my way to the powder room, but it's occupied.

"Madam, there is one on the second floor, to the right on the landing," one of the servers says, pointing to the stairs.

I nod and take my time.

There are things you can never whisper about in balls, especially when a Season's member's parents host it.

Like Alicia's parents.

This isn't a townhouse like ours. It's in one of the outer park-studded areas of Sabine. Still city perimeters, but the estate's classed as a townhouse, even though it's huge. Probably because they're new and couldn't get a country estate like most of those belonging to the established Sabine families.

I head to the upstairs powder room, which is free.

After taking care of business, I look at myself in the gold-rimmed mirror. Behind my honey-gold mask, my eyes look big, but the color brings out the softer, lighter tones in the brown of my eyes, making them look like how Stephan describes.

My stomach flips, and my heart squeezes at the thought of him. I know Quinn's right. I have fallen.

Utterly, irreversibly in love.

Someone knocks on the door, and I call out, "One moment."

I fix my hair, which is pinned up, tendrils falling artfully down, and I reach in my bag for my lipstick, but realize forgot it. I bite my lips to bring a little more color and then head to the door.

A girl goes in, muttering, "The mated don't need that long."

I shake my head and start for the stairs when I overhear my name.

"Violet? Oh, come on." Alicia laughs. "Do you think Violet and Stephan are actually doing it? She's such a bore."

I'm on the wrong side of the door, and a wave of panic comes over me. I have to step past the open door to reach the stairs and—

"Anyone tell you it's rude to eavesdrop?" Alicia says, suddenly there and looking utterly angelic and beautiful in white-gold dress and mask. She grabs my hand and pulls me into the room, where about six girls sit with a bottle of liquor on the table. I know their names, I do, but they spin, jumbled, in my head and my chest starts to tighten. "Look who I found."

"We were talking about your honeymoon," the redhead —Jade? yes, Jade—says. "Drink?"

"She doesn't drink," someone else says with a laugh.

Another girl leans forward, eyes excited. "Where did Asher St. James take you for your honeymoon? Somewhere exotic?"

I try to speak, but I can't, and my vision blurs. It's only Stephan's scent as his warm breath touches my skin, whispering *perfect girl, so fucking good* in my ear, that keeps me on my feet and not unconscious on the floor.

But he's wrong. I'm not that at all. I've crumbled, retreated back to what I truly am, an anxious mess.

"Don't be stupid," Alicia says with a laugh. "He didn't take her anywhere. Look at her... I don't know what dirt your family has or what they paid the Monarch to get him." She presses in and her blocker hurts my nose, makes breathing harder. "I fucked him and he was good. Did he tell you that? Did he knot you, too? Because that's so fucking good."

She steps back and laughs. "Look at her face. Stephan hasn't knotted her, so their mating isn't valid."

I've got to get out of here.

"Come on," Jade says. "She's just jealous. Tell us what it's like being knotted, Violet."

Another girl sighs. "Heath is hot. I wish he'd take part, now Violet's taken the catch of the Season off the menu."

"I bet he's still on it," Alicia says. "She can't hold him. He'll be sniffing around the Lower Side—"

"Problem?" Oak swirls around me. I know he's got a blocker on, too. But I can always smell Stephan. And the moment I smell him, hear him, the panic, the anxiety recedes.

"No," I say. "No problem. Are you ready to go?"

He slides an arm around me. "With you? Anywhere."

Stephan draws me in and kisses me so thoroughly my legs are wobbling when he's done. My lips tingle, and I'm hot, bothered, so turned-on I actually forget we have an audience.

But Stephan lifts his head. "Ladies."

And then we're gone.

Down the stairs, and instead of into the ballroom, he makes a right, dragging me into a darkened room where he shoves me against the wall, trailing a hand up my thigh, under my dress.

He nibbles my throat, making me explode with bursts of light, and I'm ready to drown in him.

"You shouldn't fucking lie to protect people when they don't need it. Alicia and those like her will resent you for it, Princess."

"I want to go."

He sighs, feathers a kiss on my lips. "As soon as we can, we're out of here."

"I'll hold you to it."

After the run-in with Alicia and her gathering of Omegas, Stephan sticks to me like glue. Which unravels me.

Thoughts ping off each other, my needs growing, and he seems to know it because he gets us out of the ball as soon as he can. I don't know what he says to Fredrick or my mother or the hosts, but soon we're in the limo heading back to his—*our* place.

The air's throbbing with scent and desire, and I'm so overcome with a need to have him, to pounce, devour, demand his knot, that we barely make it in the door before he has me against the wall.

His mouth is hungry, an answer to my own needs, and it feeds my fire with bites and licks, his tongue a masterful manipulation of the emotions that sing in me with every brush and tease, every parry and withdrawal. I drop down, clawing at his belt, freeing his magnificent cock.

I don't know where this burst of confidence comes from, but suddenly I want to show him what he's taught me, what I've learned. I stroke him, running my thumb over the precum, and then I lick up along the underside of his shaft to play with that area under the head that sometimes makes him howl in a way that hooks into me, makes me his submissive creature.

He sucks in a sharp breath, a growl of sound uttered from the depths of him, and his fingers sink into my hair.

"Fucking little goddess," he mutters. "Your mouth is decadence personified."

Stephan thrusts at me as he grabs my face, my jaw, forcing it open with gentle pressure, and he slams back into my throat, almost choking me.

It's a choking I crave, the hammer of his cock, just like I crave the control, I crave the taking of it from me, like he's doing now. I've pushed him over an edge, and he's getting bigger in my mouth, stretching me so I can't do anything but suck and be that passageway to his pleasure.

My pussy contracts like he's in there, and a wave of pleasure so intense it almost hurts passes through me as my clit throbs.

He pulls free before he comes and drags me up into his arms and then into the kitchen. There he leans me over the table, my feet touching the floor, and he throws up my dress, ripping at my panties. He sinks into me, hard and fast, and I cry out.

Stephan grabs my hair, pulling my head up. "Are you trying to make me lose control?"

"Yes," I breathe. "Yes, I am."

"Naughty minx."

Those words feel just as good, just as strip-me-down-to-the-bone dangerous as his praise, making me his center of attention. And I throb and contract around him. Not quite orgasm, but something close.

"Fuck." He pulls out, and then he fingers me and withdraws, only to push a finger, then another into my asshole. He works it, pleasurable, strange, so good.

He's touched me there before, played with me, but this feels like intent. And there seem to be a million more nerve endings springing into life as he pulls his fingers free. Something wet and silky slides between my cheeks.

"What are you—" I look over my shoulder to see him holding a bottle of opaque liquid. Then the smell hits me—coconut. He's poured coconut oil on me. "Stephan—"

But I'm silenced by something much bigger than his fingers pushing against my tight hole this time.

"I'm going to fuck your ass now, Princess. Finally own all of you. Your pretty, perfect ass. Hold still."

I do. Every single part of me is focused on him, on what he's doing, and he stretches me so wide that I want to reject him. I try to stay relaxed, try to allow him entry even as my clit starts to throb harder than before. Which makes me want to grind down into the edge of the table.

It's impossible, how deep he's going, how much I seem to stretch, and then he sighs, his hips touching my ass and I know he's in. All. The. Way.

Then he starts to move and the slide in and out is odd, but he's stroking something with each push and pull, and soon my whole body is focused on that, and his movements stop being slow and deliberate and hit harder, more forceful, more erratic.

"Oh, fuck, Princess. *Fuck*."

He starts to hammer me, and I push back into him, and soon he's slamming me so hard the table moves, and a deep throbbing pleasure, different from the one in my clit, begins. It sings so loud through me, that pleasure, and I come so hard I think I black out for a second.

I'm still throbbing, still coming, and his movements are hard and fast. I don't think I've felt him so big, so *there*, but with a cry, he pulls out and his hot cum hits my ass and my back, on and on. Finally, grunting, he collapses on me, breathing heavily.

He kisses my cheek, my throat, my shoulder. "We should get cleaned up."

Stephan gets up and starts to help me.

And that's when something snaps inside, and I turn, looking at him as he's putting himself away.

"Stephan?"

"Yes, Princess?"

I swallow. "Tonight, the girls, they were talking about knotting."

He goes still, but I continue, the words rushing free.

"I don't have any reference for it, but they said you haven't, and can...can they tell? I mean if someone's been knotted or not? Can they? I don't have any reference. I don't know. But sometimes it feels like something's missing with sex. It's fun and all, and I've never experienced the pleasure you bring. But...but beyond that, it's like something isn't there..." I swallow again. "Have you knotted me?"

Chapter Thirty-Six

Stephan

I'm ashamed to admit it, but I walk away. How the fuck am I meant to answer that?

With a *no*, obviously.

Her blow jobs are mind-destroying. Her pussy a marvel designed to make a man rut and knot even when she's not in heat and not careful.

Do I fucking tell her I'm scared of accidentally knocking her up? That I'm waiting until the contraceptives take hold, the higher dose I've leveled it up to, so we can do that, and I can avoid something happening?

I'm *craving* the rut, and I want to give in to the need to knot. My reaction to her heat means I need to dose her. Again.

I turn on the shower and strip, getting under the water spray.

My princess doesn't join me, but I know she hovers. I feel her, smell her. She's a constant prick against my resolve, which is why I need to make sure she's safe.

When I get out and dressed, she's no longer in the bedroom, where she followed me to.

Violet's on the balcony, where she sits on the love seat, her hair damp from the downstairs' shower, and she wears one of her simple sundresses. Not one of my T-shirts, not pajamas, a dress.

"Princess?"

She doesn't look at me and it does something to me deep inside, like it creates an empty hollow that I'm suddenly desperate to fill. But the thing is she'd never understand the why, unless...

Unless I manipulate it to the right place.

There's a bottle of bourbon on the small table, and she has a glass in her hand, with a healthy measure poured, but she makes no attempt to lift it to her mouth.

So I pick up the bottle and take a swallow. The backyard with its high privacy walls creates an oasis of quiet, but I imagine I can hear the city live and breathe. The whoosh of cars, muted voices. It's the right time for the end of the ball, for theaters and cinemas to empty, for the late-nighters to head home after a drink or lingering at a restaurant.

It's liked the dialed-down-to-under-one version of Emporia.

I sigh as I take another sip.

We should be fucking like rabbits, exploring the insane highs of knotting pleasure, and instead all I feel is cold inside, and the gulf that vindictive little creature Alicia caused.

"Violet, look, I—"

"I don't think you have, Stephan," she says, "knotted, I mean."

And in the low light her cheeks take on a luminous pink hue.

"You said you don't know."

She lifts the glass, then drops it back to where she just cradles it. "Alicia—"

"She's nothing."

"You...she said you knotted when you fucked her. She wanted to know if you'd knotted with me. Am I too boring? Not enough? I know I shouldn't be saying this because I'm here to make your life better, but if I don't, I—"

"Stop. You're not here to make my life better. We're here to explore and build a life together. And as for her...I told you it's complicated, but it's not." This I can do, even though I don't want to. "Before I met you, when I arrived, I met a girl and we'd had enough to drink that I had a one night stand. I wasn't into her. Not beyond the need I had to have sex with someone."

Her face is a mask, but I'm close enough I can feel her withdraw, the distaste...not judgment, exactly, but distaste at my actions. And it makes me feel about as sleazy as what happened was.

"Once. I had no urge to knot. So no. It didn't happen. I didn't know she'd be part of the Season, and I honestly didn't care because I wasn't planning on taking part, no matter what the battle-ax wanted. Then I met you."

She's silent for a while. This time, she takes a drink, her nose wrinkling. "You met me?"

"Yes. I didn't know you. I knew you were an Omega, were probably part of the Season, so I kept visiting that boathouse, hoping I'd see you again."

Her eyes dart to me. "And yet you don't want to knot me?"

"I *want* to, but...with Cecilia..." I take another swallow.

"You still miss her." She glances away, and my heart dies a little. How do I say this without making her feel unwanted?

"To be honest, yes. A part of me will always miss her, I think. She was my first love. But you're my future, Violet. I'm here with you now, and that's exactly where I want to be."

She finishes her drink. "Was she an Omega?"

I sidestep that because I can feel where she's going. She needs to understand, just like Pen, that now I'm bonded to her, bound by our mating bites to protect her, keep her safe. And I fucking will.

No matter what.

"I haven't knotted yet, but it's not because I haven't been tempted—I have. Many times."

"Then why haven't you?"

It cuts right through, unleashes feelings I have no name for.

"Because it scares me..."

Her brow furrows with confusion. "Does it hurt you?"

Man, they really don't teach Omegas anything about this in Sabine. "No, no. It scares me because it brings up memories I'm not ready to touch yet."

"About babies."

I pause, my heart pounding. Wait—does she know?

"How you're not able to have them?"

I let out a held breath. Shit. For a second, I thought she'd known my secret all along.

"Yes. But that's not a reflection on you, Violet. It's me."

"So you'll *never* knot me, then? Even when I'm in heat?" she asks. "I told you I can put my idea of a big family aside for you. We can explore other ways to have children when the time comes."

"I know. I know. I will knot eventually. I just...I just need some time." I rub a hand over my face, get up, and pace, taking a long swallow from the bottle before bringing it to rest on the ledge of the balcony. I look out at the darkness of the ocean, then up at the warm glow of the full moon.

"You're right," I say. "I need to let the past go completely. It's time. And if you're ready, then so am I. Next time, I won't hold back. But knotting doesn't happen every time. That just isn't how things work."

Another twist on the truth. With her, I could rut and knot in her until the end of days. In others, no. But my innocent, pristine princess doesn't know this.

"Are you sure?" she asks, big eyes watching my every move. "I can wait."

I put on a smile and turn. "Don't you worry. I'll show you how sure I am soon enough."

CHAPTER THIRTY-SEVEN

Violet

My dreams take an erotic turn.

Warm lips are gliding over my flesh, making me throb inside and ache, making my nipples peak.

Hands slide up over my bare skin, flaring sparks where they touch, making me wet, and all I can smell is the erotic secret edge to oak.

He captures a nipple between his teeth and sucks hard, and I cry out, feeling it everywhere. He releases it, biting and licking a path up my throat, to my ear where he bites down, making me gasp and clench and sigh.

The touch is magic, like lights coming on within, like I'm a network of pressure points, receptors for the pure ecstasy he brings.

The beard is both soft and a delight of roughness that surges arousal higher.

"Princess..."

I moan low. This isn't a dream; the hair between my fingers, thick and soft, is Stephan's. I'd know the power of his touch anywhere, but I hover between dream and awake, liking the way it expands horizons. Not pleasure, but it blurs edges, and like this I don't need to think, I can just *be*.

Pulling him closer, I urge his mouth to mine, kissing him deeply, sliding my tongue into his mouth and taunting his. I kiss him first. I tease the way he teases me, I find all the hidden depths and pleasures in the heat and wetness, the taste of him.

He's hard.

So hard. His cock is pressing at my thigh. I push up, flowing over him and then I straddle, reaching down to squeeze, tease his turgid flesh.

I rub him against my opening before I sink down, rising and falling, loving the stretch, the way he opens me, fills me, makes me complete in a way I don't understand.

He drags me down, kissing me hard, our tongues a duel of madness. My hips undulate on him and then he flips us, thrusting up into me, so deep he hits a part of me that aches each time he slams in. The kiss grows deeper, more lush, more filled with desire and all delicious things.

Is he going to knot?

He begins to slam, movements slipping into wildness, and my breath catches as he kisses down to my throat to bite me like he's claiming me all over again. I wrap my legs around him and—

Stephan lifts his head, stills, deep inside me, and then he kisses me again.

"I fucking love the taste of you."

"Keep going." I move under him to start that wild ride again.

Stephan groans, pushes my hands away as I reach for him, and pulls out of me.

"No!"

"Yes..." He kisses his way down my body, finally coming to a heated rest right between my legs. "This fucking view," he mutters, sucking on my clit, making the flames inside lick so high I just might combust.

And yet I need more. I need him. All of him, I need the heights he can take me to, the wild depths. All of it.

Stephan doesn't need to ask. He knows me now. I lift my hips to him as he buries his face between my legs and he starts to suck and lick and nibble, making the ache in me flare into wild need. I don't know if it's just arousal or slick, but his fingers slide into me so easily, even as he widens them to make me stretch, something that shakes me down to my soul.

How he can wring out these deep moments from me, make me want more, is the kind of mystery I'll happily spend my life exploring.

Stephan starts to thrust with his finger as he sucks around my clit. I whimper, shifting, trying to get his mouth exactly where I want it, exactly where he doesn't want to go.

He's a monster, building and building the pressure, his fingers sliding in and out, turning me into a ball of excited, needful energy. If I could just get him to close his mouth around my clit, offer me the heat and soft stroke of his tongue, I'd be happy. I'd be there, almost there.

But he dangles the orgasm out of reach.

Oh my God, now he pushes his thumb into my ass, the

place he invaded and brought me to a wild and pagan pleasure last night, before—

I block out the talk, going to bed, being in his arms, my lonely tangled thoughts, I block it all out and latch onto the renewed tendrils of pleasure.

And then he does it, while thrusting into me, pistoning in gentle pumps. His mouth finally takes my clit, and I'm consumed by that burst of warm wetness, the gentle suck that won't stop.

"Stephan..." He's built me up and up and now...now it's almost too much. Because that suck stops being gentle. It has force behind it, and tongue now, tongue that pushes and stimulates beyond what I can take. I shudder, trying to twist free.

He won't let me.

His arm pins one of mine, his free hand grips my other hip, and I'm caught, at his mercy. The pressure changes again; it's aggressive now, a scrape of teeth added to the suck and lick and thrust of fingers.

I'm gone, I'm fevered, my clit's too sensitive, I'm too sensitive, I need him to stop, I need...

"Oh, *God*."

I need more.

He doesn't stop.

Stephan doesn't stop.

He keeps licking, sucking, nibbling my clit, and his fingers keep working me, keep working that spot.

I thrash, trying to get away, the throbbing spasms of my orgasm still ricocheting through me.

"No, no, it's too much, please."

Stephan has turned into a sadist, and he keeps going,

not letting up, not even to speak to me. And I can't escape him. I sob, everything fluttering to get free, to find a moment to breathe. And then...and then it changes again, into something deeper, like I have to pee, a pressure starting up inside me and the throbbing beats of the orgasm don't dissipate. They start to build in a different way.

Like it's coming, this time, from *beyond* my clit, and not like how it was when he fucked my ass. This is different. It's a clanging throb. The beat is from inside my soul, and as the orgasm blooms once more it takes all of me on that journey, and I come so hard I think I pee.

I'm sobbing, a mess, on the verge of blacking out, as I'm hit by wave after wave of chaotic pleasure.

"That's it, Princess. You're doing perfectly for me. I knew you could take it." Rising up over me, he starts to fuck me again. It's so hard and deep, it makes the bed shake and creak loudly.

"Stephan..." His words light an inferno in me, and my back arches as every part of me catches fire.

This time, when he comes I can feel him. His cock twitching as spurt after spurt hits inside.

He kisses me again, this time tiny kisses, butterfly wings over my lips. When he pulls out, I'm exhausted, happy, and he tucks me into his side and whispers, "Sleep."

Next time I wake, I'm aching, sticky, and alone. I touch the other side of the bed, but Stephan's not there and the pillow is cold.

I lie there, the mid-morning sun streaming in through

the curtains. I know he didn't knot again last night. The need for it is still there in me.

Was he close?

Frustration swamps me as I drag myself up and shower. The thing is I don't know. I'm not experienced.

I'm not his first love, or even love at all. I can't hate a dead girl. I can't be jealous of her having him before I ever met him.

The heaviness settles on me, in me, and it's hollow, too. A strange feeling and one I'm not used to, the hollowness.

I miss my sisters.

When I get dressed, there's a message from Mari on my phone. And my heart leaps.

MARI

> There's some kind of Omega thing today. You're exempt, like that Jade girl who's marked and Tamborine. Want to go gloat? You would enjoy that. I'll draw them for posterity, and then we can go check out all the hot men on the Lower Side. With you as chaperone, of course.

Who's Tamborine?

It's Mari so I never expect her to pay attention to people that don't interest her. It's either a noisy girl or a musical one or someone with a name that sounds like...tambourine?

I call Iris. "Who's Tamborine?"

"I know what one is but not anyone with that name, Vi. Shouldn't you be naked and hanging from the ceiling—"

"Iris!" I head down to the kitchen, wanting coffee. There's a glass of juice sitting there, condensation on the glass and cold to the touch, with a little handwritten note stating *drink me*.

I don't know where Stephan is. He's not here. I can't smell him, and the place feels empty.

I drink the juice as I set up the coffee machine.

"Sorry," she says, not sounding sorry in the least. "Who's tambourine?"

"Mari said there's some thing for the singles, and we should go and gloat and someone named Tamborine got marked—"

"Oh! Tamara. She's one of the quiet Omegas. I'm shocked you aren't friends."

I finish my juice. It's a little too pulpy today, making it slightly gritty. But I don't want to complain. "You make being quiet sound boring."

"I don't know her. She seems nice, which is why..." Iris stops. "Are you okay?"

"I just miss you guys."

"Well, we'll collect Quinn and we can all go gloat."

"Mari wants to then ogle boys."

"I can do that. Ogle. But beyond that—nope."

I laugh. "Fine, we'll meet you there."

"You. No mated Alphas allowed."

There's a moment of hesitation, but then I say, "Okay. Let me know what time and I'll see you."

I text Mari:

> Coordinate with Iris, and I'll be there.

MARI
Excellent. Mom says we need to bring
Rue. She's hosting a mothers' lunch and
is in a tizz.

Probably, I think, because a lot of the other mothers are competitive. I know for Mom the Season might be deemed a success for me, and other parents would rest on their laurels, but she has four other daughters, and one son who's using our father's death to escape a lot of the scandal he caused by not participating before Dad's death. Not really. Never with intent. Before, he was having too much fun. Now, he's full of burden.

I sigh and take my coffee, drinking it as voices fill the downstairs.

My heart skips a beat at the sound of them. And I smile. Heath and Stephan.

"Oh, good, you're up, and you had your juice. Heath's here."

"She can see, Ashford."

"I'm going to meet my sisters."

Heath straightens. "Duty calls. Raincheck, Ashford?"

"Not you," I say. "My sisters and I, just the girls. It's fine. Mom knows."

If my brother's here, it's good for me to go out, let them bond properly. I know there's still some feelings on Heath's side about this union with his friend.

I go to leave, and Stephan slides an arm around me and kisses me.

"Okay, okay, Jesus, dude. That's my sister."

"Deal with it, Gardener."

"Not a chance." Heath mutters something crass under his breath.

"I'm going," I say.

"We'll talk when you get back," Stephan says.

Hivemind...

Rumors swirled as to my identity at the

Honey and Nectar Ball...

Or so I hear.

Were they close?

Who knows?

I'm not going to tell. Are you?

*The ball was held at Miss Alicia's palatial abode. She looked beautiful and many Alphas were drawn by the honeyed nectar look of her. But a **WATCH OUT** is in order because she's more like a wasp than a bee, with a sting to match. Just ask our mated Luxe herself, who seemed to be fodder for Alicia's fire and stinging tongue.*

I hear she asked some very

KNOTTY

questions.

Any truth to the rumor?

*I'm not one to stick my nose into mated people's affairs,
especially ones sealed with a bite, but.... Mr. St. James and his
mate left soon after.*

There were

ACCUSATIONS

of a

DIRTY

DEAL

with our

Monarch.

Truth? Rumor? Or all lies?

*Who knows...but it all comes out eventually, doesn't it, and
with the gathering of unmated, unmarked Seasonal Omegas,
I'm all eyes and ears for scandal.*

And with rumbles from other shores, maybe we'll get another twist in this tale from the movie star himself...

Stay tuned, brood.

This Season ain't over until the Monarch herself sings.

Or at least cuts someone down to size.

- Queen Bee

Chapter Thirty-Eight

Stephan

I stare at Heath, a little sweaty from the work we just finished and probably a little exasperated. "C'mon man, I could use your help."

I figured now, with him feeling good about a little manual labor, I could bring up the scripts, but no.

Heath's got his ducks in a row in his head and probably all with lists. Even down to Rue. Pros and cons and the kind of mates she might attract once she's of age.

I know fucking Heath, I know he's now getting things ready for the rest of them, checking out Alphas who aren't even close to the next Season.

The scripts should be a good distraction, one in particular, to anyone but him.

"And it's the kind of thing you want to do," I add.

"I looked them over, and I know which one you wanted me to focus on. I took time out of trying to keep my sisters from exploding into a sea of scandal, one of which you facilitated—"

"And got out of."

"Not cool, dickwad." Heath frowns and crosses his arms, leaning against the wall in the living room. "Besides, I handed you my notes. I'm not about to pack up and leave my family in the lurch to gallivant on some fucking movie adventure for months. Or years. Or however long it takes to tell this tale. I know you—"

"It's a good opportunity. It's one you wanted."

"Want*ed*, past tense. Responsibilities exist. Something you need to keep under your hat. You know my sister wants a big family, and I don't know what the fuck your plan is there, but you have to man up. She's not an Emporia girl. Those people will eat her alive and you know it."

"Violet and I have talked. And it's between us so don't go sticking your nose in."

"I don't want to know about your sex life with my sister." He shudders like he bit into something incredibly bitter. "It's a violation on every level. Just...if you hurt her, I will kill you, understand? Vi is special. They all are, but Vi's..."

He flounders, and I get it. The three eldest have a special bond. Especial him and Violet. But he sees her as delicate and breakable, and I think she's a lot stronger than that.

Just like her quietness hides a lot of depth, and her willingness and drive to please houses not just a slight kink, but shadows over her keen observation and bluntness and humor.

She's the full package, and she's more than he's willing to see.

Fuck, I sound like I have it bad.

"We talked, that's it. Pages aligned." That's true, now. And if I had to twist the truth a little, take some matters into my hands then...

"And Emporia?"

I sigh. We haven't discussed that yet. Heath and I have spent half the day chatting and finishing some of the fixes I wanted on the ground floor. It's still her playground, but it should be solid before she plays.

Instead of answering him immediately, I pour us each a drink. He snatches it, and eyes me with dislike that can only come from a place of brotherly love. A violent place that has resentment and all kinds of other things in there.

Anyone but Violet and this would be an open, honest, normal conversation.

Now I have to spend time stepping around landmines.

"This isn't my home, Heath."

"But it's hers."

"I live in Emporia." I take a sip and rub the back of my neck. "Look, I could spend time between both places, and yeah, okay, I'm doing that, as you know I'm fixing this up as a home for us."

"We. *We* are doing that. And a holiday home? A visit for a week each year home? A stop by when you might feel like it home? Or a dump Vi here while you do fuck knows elsewhere home?"

He's dangerously close to meeting my fist.

"I'm not cheating on Violet, and I'm not about to. So if you even put those ideas in her head, I'll..."

"What? Hit me? Bring it the fuck on." He downs his drink.

I thrust the bottle at him. "I like my mate. I don't want her upset if I kill her stupid brother."

"So what are you gonna do? You can't take her away from her family."

The words *why not* play at the edges, but I keep them tucked inside. "I'm not planning to, but do you want her to just be like all the other Omegas here?"

"I'm not—"

"You don't have a say in our lives, Heath. I'm a successful actor. I'm trying to shift to a more serious career which means more selective roles, behind the scenes shit, things that I *want* to do rather than just go with the money-making flow." I look at him. "Don't you think Violet deserves to find herself?"

He studies me for a long time then pours a large drink, shaking his head. "You're heading out of here, aren't you?"

"Clea called early this morning."

Heath finds the bottle label suddenly interesting, and I say, "Maybe she's why you don't want us to go? Are you scared?"

He scoffs. "We had sex. She didn't threaten me. And is she my type, yeah, to a point. But she's definitely a woman who doesn't want anything serious. I don't have room for that. The 'to a point,' before you say it, comes into play over the fact I'm here and she's there. I can't go there. Family."

"Well." That's...a lot of information. And Clea was just as cagey. Maybe—

But they can sort their own shit out. I don't have the bandwidth, not with my princess there because he's fucking right. I'm not sure Violet wants to handle Emporia fulltime.

Personally, I know she can. Violet's so much stronger than she gives herself credit for.

And now I have my own anxiety-control methodology with her...

"Stop grinning. I don't like where your thoughts might be."

I pick up a cushion and throw it at him. "Jesus, I can smile. Not all of it's about sex."

He grabs the cushion, tosses it to the sofa, and then flops down. "I think Violet might love you. And she shines like she used to before her anxiety started to eat at her. Mostly before Dad died."

"You noticed?"

"I'm her brother, asshole. Of course I know she suffers from panic and anxiety."

"I'd like her to get therapy, and maybe in Emporia..."

"Don't tell Mom." He shrugs. "She's not against it, but the pressure on Violet over all this has added to it, the Season I mean. And Mom probably feels like it's her fault, too. She just wants the best for us all. Mom already asks why Vi quit dance."

"Because she doesn't think she's good enough. I first saw her running to a dance class, y'know."

He holds up a hand. "Keep your meet-cute shit to

yourself." But he winces. "Money. She quit because the lessons cost money, and she thinks Dahlia needs the money spent on her. Vi's a beautiful dancer. You should see her, really see her dance, on the stage. She's excellent."

I don't say a word because I get the feeling anything I say will be taken wrong. Shit, it *will* be wrong. My private dances are not things anyone else should know about.

So I change the subject.

"I'm going to take Violet to Emporia for a few days. I have some meetings. I was meant to stay away the whole summer but being mated changes things."

"And a little press opportunity no doubt. How you've changed now you have your good girl Omega, and no more women, booze, drugs."

Anger flares. "I'm not—"

"I'm just repeating rumors. I've never known you to be out of control. Not since—"

"Where are your sisters?" I don't need him to finish the sentence about Cecilia and the baby. Saying it just makes the terror of it happening again too real. "Whatever Omega thing they're at has to be over by now."

He frowns. Texts. Then texts again. Finally, he texts a few more times. "Rue's not texting back. Or Vi."

I try Violet. "Maybe they're not near their phones."

"Or Mari or Iris took them."

I nod at him. "Don't you have some tracker on Rue?"

"Oh, fuck." He opens an app. "Son of a..." He looks at me. "She's in the Lower fucking Side."

"Heath, wanna go get a drink downtown?"

He tosses down his dregs and stands. "Try and stop me.

Come on. We've got some bad Omega sisters and one idiotic Beta girl to wrangle."

I wince. "Do not say that to them if you want to live."

"You are drunk."

I try to sound stern, but I fail.

Violet grabs at my face, stroking my beard, her cheeks pink, lips inviting, and so fucking pretty it almost makes my knees give way.

"Nooo," she says, "I'm not." Then Violet goes up on her tiptoes and whispers, "Just a little tipsy. Quinn brought some vodka. Dahlia and Rue didn't have any."

It seems there was some kind of outdoor jazz concert here in the gritty little park near the water in the Lower Side.

A lot of the Sabine college students were here and enough well-heeled society so the girls were fine. When we arrived, it was clear they'd sat away and kept in a group, not that that stopped Heath.

I knew he wasn't going to drink when he got here. His sisters and their wellbeing, not to mention reputations, were on his mind, so they were grabbed and hauled into the limo we'd taken.

Violet and I are walking back.

"Let's go to our special place," she says.

Our...? I don't know what that means, but I'm bemused enough to go with it, and we take off arm in arm along the oceanfront, the neighborhood changing as we walk.

It hits me where we're going and I just let her lead me, past other couples, until they thin out and we finally reach the boardwalk with the old abandoned boathouse.

She pulls me inside and kisses me.

This is dangerous, thrilling, how she rubs on me, her hands all over, undoing my pants and—

"Violet."

"I don't want to be me for the evening." She puts her hand on my dick and grabs me, motioning with her head to the darker, sheltered back of the place.

"Princess."

"Tell me I'm your good girl."

"Are you?" I ask, trailing a hand down her spine to her ass. She starts to slide down me, and I let her.

She frees me and my back hits the wall as her cool fingers slide over my hot cock. And then she sucks me into her mouth, going down on me as she does so. Damn, has she come a long way in a short time.

My princess chokes herself on me, all on her own, bobbing in shallow bursts that keep me buried against the back of her throat; her swallowing as she does so is almost too much.

I grab her, pulling her off me.

"You're a good girl, Princess. My good girl. Such technique, such sexy little noises. Fuck."

Christ...that shiver running through her sets the fever in my blood to boiling.

My control is slipping fast. I lift her and turn, and she hits the wall, and I claw between her thighs, pulling at her panties. Something rips, and the panties are loose in my hands. Fuck it, I'll buy her more. A whole fucking shop of them just so I can rip them from her.

I start to shake as I devour her mouth; her taste is sweet, addictive like a drug.

I'm lost to it, and I can't get enough. The scent of her is so strong that I move from her mouth to her throat, and as I do so I thrust into her.

She's tight, welcoming and so fucking slick, the fever in me boils over. I start to pound into her, not caring where we are, who might see. All I care about is this, being inside her, marking her in every way I can.

I can't stop.

I don't want to stop.

She's in my blood, in me.

This is rough, harsh, fast, and she grips me tight, so tight, all the while sucking me deeper into her, and she comes alive like never before. She's clawing at me, her nails digging into the back of my neck, her mouth on me as she starts to come.

Hard cock-breaking spasms, the type I have to clench my teeth to stop the howl of *yes* that's inside me.

And then I feel it, the surge of the knot coming up and filling, my cock growing, going deeper. She screams as she starts to buck and shudder on me as we're locked in place and my knot swells inside her.

Her little frantic movements set off my orgasm and I come so fucking hard, I almost collapse. I have to catch her and myself from slamming to the floor.

"Fuck! Princess!"

She's whimpering, crying out. Her entire body is

shaking as she soars right along with me. "Oh, God, Oh, God. I love you, Stephan!"

Incredibly, her words make me come harder, longer, and I don't know how long the pleasure washes through us, wave after wave. It's a wild ride, and I don't want to be anywhere else.

As it finally starts to ebb, I stay knotted as I rock her on me. Her tremors of what seems to be a never-ending orgasm ripple over my dick, until finally I start to deflate, and as I ease out of her, she crumples into me. I hold her close.

Just hold her.

When she said those words to me, something stirred, something big, and I think... Oh shit.

What if I love her, too?

Slowly, I rearrange her clothes, then mine. I try not to think about how I ended up knotting and what that might mean. She's been on the contraceptives for a while now, and they should prevent anything from happening, but...

Now what I'm doing secretly feels more real. More cruel.

When we can both walk, I lead her out, tucking the ripped panties away.

"Stephan...that...that was knotting?" she asks, still bleary-eyed.

"Uh, yeah." I'm not usually one to be lost for words, but I sure as fuck am now.

We walk, heading slowly to where I can call for one of Pen's cars. I pull Violet against me and search for something to say.

She just told me she loves me.

"I have to go to Emporia. *We.* We're going, for a few days," I say.

My princess just nods.

What if I love her, too?

Because that's what it feels like inside.

Shit.

What the actual fuck do I do now?

CHAPTER THIRTY-NINE

Violet

I'm filled with both excitement and trepidation.

The trip to Emporia seems so last-minute. Even though he had to let his aunt Sophine know he had business.

I know he doesn't trust her, but... She's not about to interfere with business that he has, and no matter how they antagonize each other, I highly doubt she'll do half the things she threatens him with.

Funny how I'm not as frightened of her as I first was. I'm still in awe. She's a powerful woman. But then again so is Mom. In her way. Not every powerful job's the same, and raising such a big family, keeping us all together...it takes power of self, lots of strength.

I keep that to myself. And of course, Mom cried when I told everyone we were going away for a few days.

Rue asked a million questions, and I stayed the night before we left, giggling and talking with my sisters. And refusing to answer any sex questions Rue threw my way.

As for Iris... It's something we never discussed, I know she's snuck off with boys but we've always had a *don't ask so they can't get the other into trouble* policy.

I look out the window at the sea between the island and the mainland. I honestly can't stop staring, watching how our little green island disappears, and then blue and now more blue, and the approaching city, glittering in the dusk.

Stephan's been reading scripts and sending texts in the luxury helicopter, but I think soon we'll be over land and then...

My first trip outside of Sabine.

He glances at me, down at my bunched hands on my jeans, and then at my face again. "It's okay, Princess. You're with me."

"But you're not Stephan, you're Asher now." It's a really stupid thing to say, but his clothes are more the flash and cool of Emporia where the rich and famous live, play, and make entertainment. He's shaved, too, which makes me sad in a way it didn't when he'd shaved for our mating ceremony.

It's part of his persona, so those cheekbones can cut glass, so his million dollar smile isn't detracted from. The guy with the scruff is my mate. And I get it, he makes movies, but it's like a gulf suddenly appears the closer we get. The buildings seem to gain height as we fly over them. There are over-manicured suburbs with modern houses and then cliffs and white sand beaches.

We come up to a mansion on the top of a small cliff,

with the beach just below, and the helicopter lands, touching down on a helipad.

"No, Princess, I'm me. Always me. Asher's nothing more than the persona I am when I give interviews. When I'm out in public to be seen. You get the real me, for what it's worth. Your brother will tell you." Then he frowns as the door slides open and a man stands there, offering me his hand.

"Don't ask him, on second thought. Who the fuck knows what he'll say," Stephan mutters behind me.

But when he's out, he takes my hand, leading me up a winding path to a huge patio, complete with an outdoor kitchen, an enormous pool, and deck chairs everywhere. He leads me past tables and chairs under a cover, and then through two square pillars to an outdoor covered seating area, with arm chairs and a coffee table and sofas. Beyond that is a big fireplace, and huge glass sliding doors, which are open. Beyond that another seating area.

I gulp. "This is yours?"

"Yeah, but I only use this shit for entertaining. I'm one person. There're only so many places I can be bothered to hang out in. Although..."

He eyes a sofa and a wicked glint shines, but he shakes his head and leads me up a sweeping staircase. There's a smaller seating area, beyond that a kitchen, and then, I assume, bathrooms and bedrooms. "This is where I spend a lot of time."

"This is ridiculous, Stephan," I say. "So much space."

"Have you seen where my aunt lives?"'

"But—"

"Nothing." He takes my face in his hands and tips it to

him. "This is nothing compared to some places. But..." He drops kisses on my lips, my eyes, my cheeks. The phone in his pocket buzzes, and he sighs, his forehead touching mine. "But princess, as much as I want to hang in here all evening and indulge in my fantasies, we have a party to attend."

"A party?" My heart sinks. "I didn't pack a dress."

"Had some delivered today. I'll show you the bedroom and..." He leads me through the living area and down a hall, into a huge master bedroom that overlooks the beach. "Later, I'm going to fuck you all over the place, brand it ours."

"An Emporian party? Can I just stay here?"

He laughs and maneuvers me to the bed when he takes me down onto it with him. "Hell no. I want to show off my hot mate. Besides, Clea would kill me. You have to be there. Think of it as payback for the Season ball shit."

Stephan bites my wrist. Sliding his hand down my top, he flicks open the little buttons on it so my bra's exposed. He toys with my nipples, making me moan.

"The shower is huge," he whispers. "Maybe get in there."

I roll onto my side. "What am I wearing for this thing? I don't—"

"Hang on." He gets up and goes to a walk-in closet I didn't see. It's more like a room to the side, and he flicks through shimmery, glittery material. "This."

He comes out holding up a sequined dress that to me is scandalously short, and in a soft lavender gray. It's gorgeous.

"Lingerie and shoes to match. Get in the shower. I need to make some calls."

The bathroom's marble, and the shower is huge, just

like he said. I shuck off my clothes and turn on the water, and two showerheads come to life. I don't mind using his soaps. It's all him.

I'm washing my hair when air brushes me.

Then a body. And he's hard. Erect.

My temperature shoots high. He takes over washing my hair, massaging my scalp as he goes. His touch is so gentle, so caring, so...*loving* I think I want to cry. Then he rinses, applies conditioner, and takes the sponge, using the body wash to slowly clean me in almost erotic moves. He takes care of my breasts, spending time on my nipples, then down over my stomach and between my legs.

At some point, the sponge is gone and it's his fingers gliding over me. He walks me backward in the spray, his mouth capturing mine in a long, slow kiss that unravels me.

Stephan goes down to his knees and starts to lick me, toying with my clit, and I mewl. I can't help it. The sensations race through me in waves. I tug at him because I need more. It's almost frightening how the need for him barrels over me. Almost but not quite, because I know what's going to happen.

Parting my pussy lips, he sucks and licks, darting his tongue into me until I'm a mess. Then he comes up, picking me up so that my back is pressed against the marble, and slams his cock into me. "So delicious, Princess. Each time you taste even better than the last. I should just wear our sex scent on me tonight."

"Oh, God."

He thrusts into me, hard, fast. It's a down and dirty ride, one that has no room for mercy, one that makes me ache and beg for more.

"Harder, please, harder!"

"Anything for my princess," he growls and bites me, his hips pistoning into me. And when I start to go off, spasming, it sets him off and his cock grows, swells, and I cry out.

"Oh, yes, yes. *Yes!*"

He knots hard in me and then he moves even faster until I'm screaming, biting him, the pleasure immense and it fills every cell. It's pure heaven.

He comes and comes as I shake from my orgasm that doesn't seem to end.

When it's over, I don't even think I can speak. He holds me, the two of us joined as the water needles down on us.

He says something, a mutter lost where his mouth's buried against my skin, but my silly, romantic mind morphs it into words of love.

One day, I think. *Maybe one day.*

When we step from the sleek limo, screams and shouts erupt. Our names are shouted and flashes blind my eyes. I just let Stephan take my hand and help me out, into the building we've pulled up in front of, where two beefy security men usher us inside.

I'm still dazed, still depleted from the sex in the shower. I think I'd let him lead me into a war zone.

"Smile, Princess."

I look up at him, doing just that, and a flash bursts just inside.

"Official photog. Clea likes to handle things."

He takes me upstairs in a gold, mirrored elevator, up to the penthouse suite.

I recognize a few faces, and I know half the people are famous. I recognize Felicity Fine from all the Stitch posts Rue has shown me, and she swans up, air kissing Stephan.

"Asher," she says, as if all the drama she created never happened. "How are you? And O.M.G.!"

She looks at me as I try to control the urge to laugh at how much she sounds like Rue with her O.M.G.

"Asher, she's beautiful! And she bagged our perpetual bachelor." She leans closer to me. "If anyone asks, just say—"

"Violet has no interest in getting involved."

"And," I say, putting my hand on Stephan's arm, "no intentions of talking to anyone. Can I take your photo for my little sister? With me and Steph—Asher? She'll love it."

"Sure! Gimme your phone. I'll take the selfie. I know the best angle for myself," Felicity says, yanking Stephan into the photo. Then she hands back my phone. "We'll have lunch!"

The moment she flits off to someone else, Stephan leans in. "Rue loves the blue-and-orange-haired singer over there. If you can get Trixie to take a photo with you, you'll be her hero forever."

"You mean *you're* not her favorite superstar?" I tease.

He snorts. "She has no taste."

I half go to kiss his cheek but stop myself. "I'm sorry, I—"

"You're allowed to kiss me. I kiss you all the fucking time." He pulls me into his arms and kisses me outrageously. Then he sets me straight. "Tomorrow I have some meetings, but I'll take you to a fabulous dinner. And I have a surprise: a dance class with the Emporian Ballet. A very small one with the esteemed—I forget his name, whoever the choreographer is."

But I know. I just stare at him. "But how?"

"I'm famous. I know people." He takes my hand. "Come on, I'll introduce you to some others, and Clea said she'll pick you up after the dance class and take you to lunch."

My gaze slides to Rue's favorite singer. "Do you think we can see her?"

He sighs. "Sure."

We weave through people to the singer. She grins. "Asher! And you must be Violet. I'm a little bit of a Stitcher myself, so I read Queen Bee. You're too pretty for him." Trixie's gaze slips to him. "Did that girl, Rue, get all the merch?"

"That's my sister." Oh, Rue's going to love this story, about how nice the star is. "And she loves Queen Bee. Could I get a selfie?"

"Of course, and tell your sis that she can come to any gig or meet-up when she comes to visit. I'll put her name on the VIP list."

She chatters to me for ages, and somehow, along with Stephan's presence, it makes the evening pass quickly.

It's not until we get back to Stephan's that I realize I didn't panic once.

The dance class was a dream, and when I get changed, I go to where Stephan dropped me off to find Clea. She gives me a hug. "Where do you want to go? I told Stephan I'd take you anywhere you want."

"I don't know. I'm not fussed. Wherever you like to go, I'm happy."

"You're both like your brother and not at all," she says, opening the door to the car so I can get in. She follows and tells her driver to take us to Rinaldo. "You'll like it."

I do. The place is untrendy, a hole in the wall, but it smells good and feels cozy when we step inside.

They clearly know her, and we're taken to a table in the back. She orders wine and the tasting menu for two.

"I take it you come here often?"

"As much as I can. I bring my most trusted clients here, and clients who need to be out of the spotlight. It's half shark, half babysitter, half whipping boy, this job." She laughs. "Make those thirds."

We sip wine, and I relax. I like her. I know why my brother slept with her—at least, I'm assuming he did. She's gorgeous, and not interested in clinging to anyone. She's a world away from girls on Sabine.

From girls like me.

I don't want to cling.

"You know, I'd have said you're not Stephan's type," she says, "yet I think you are. And you're as besotted as he is."

I look down. "I worry I'm too ordinary."

"No. You're different. You're sweet and real and open. He doesn't have that, especially here." Then she tops off our glasses. "Oh, I meant to ask, how are the pills going? Are they working?"

I frown. Does she mean the anxiety meds Iris gave me at the dinner party? That was ages ago.

I'm trying to find something to say when she adds, "No side effects?"

This is an odd conversation. "No."

"Good, they're not meant to have any, but you never know. Omega contraceptives can be seen as bad form, but it's your body. Let me know if you need more. Sabine can be a little behind the times."

I almost spit out my wine.

Did she say *contraceptives*?

"I'm not on contraceptives."

Her brows pinch. "You know, the ones Stephan asked me to get for you, since Sabine's rules are so strict. I wasn't sure if he'd given them to you yet but...I left him another pack. You should have had them in your luggage when you arrived."

"Stephan..." I swallow, start to shake. "I–I didn't know about any—I'm not on any—"

The look of horror that hits her face tells me everything.

I jump to my feet, and everything feels wavy. Spinning. "I need to go."

Chapter Forty

Stephan

The meeting is long and boring, the kind I hate attending. But they're important to attend when I want more creative control, or like now, a shift in focus.

I want that shift in focus. Not just for my career, to get onto the path I want, but I think I want less time in the limelight. To be pickier, make better films in all the ways I want to do it.

And to spend way more time with Violet.

Who the hell ever thought I'd want to make career changes because of a woman?

Clea will come in later this week to close a deal if I want it, but first I have to want it.

Violet dances sublimely.

My princess is an angel. Sexy and earthy when she wants to be, ethereal and fluid like something that stepped from a fairy tale, too. I stayed too long in the watching room behind the mirrors in the small class, but how could I not?

My fucking mate dances like movement was made for her.

Christ, she even had fucking Felicity posing for a selfie at the party, which she hates. But she did it and smiled about it. Earlier I met her briefly. That campaign of her endless press junket about me has stopped, now that Clea's taken her on.

We'll still make those movies, but as friends, people who reconciled.

What did Clea say to me last night?

Everyone loves a redemption story, and everyone loves to see two ex-lovers act as lovers on the screen. Even if that whole side of the story isn't true. The public doesn't know. But we'll both make other films, new films, better films, and I understand Felicity wanting to make a switch from starlet to serious actress before she gets too old.

It's different for men, she told me.

She said one other thing earlier: "Treat Violet right. You hit the jackpot."

I know that. I'd be blind not to know that.

But Felicity knowing it? And telling me, adding how much she likes Violet? That's one for the books.

I shouldn't be surprised.

That's my princess. Winning people wherever she goes.

No wonder Alicia's so jealous.

I drag my mind back to the meeting.

"Things like that," I say, "work better down the track, like a reunion."

The Alpha studio exec leans forward. "Would you be

interested in that, with us, down the track, as a first dibs option?"

"Clea would need to discuss with Ms. Fine," I say, "but I don't see why not."

The meeting continues with renewed interest.

When I'm done, I shake hands, have the requisite drink, and speak utter bullshit. And then I'm free. I can head home, maybe have a snack of the princess before we go for dinner.

Finally, I head for the car, and get in. There are a ton of missed calls from Clea, probably wanting to tell me how much she adores Violet. I knew Violet would turn heads.

My phone starts to ring again. I answer. "Hey, Clea—"

"You better get your ass back here, or your life's going to unravel."

She hangs up.

What the fuck?

I call her back, but she doesn't pick up.

Instead, I go to text Violet but stop.

What am I doing? Why would she know? Clea's a professional and it's probably something small, an article with a scandal she wants stomped out.

Clea can take care of it. I pay her team for that.

So I delete the message before sending. Violet's still new to this world. She doesn't need any of the micro bullshit drama that happens on a daily basis. I need to ease her in.

The driver doesn't need to be told where to go since my next stop was always home. It's a long drive, so I grab my bag from the floor where I left it, and pull out my script. Mine. Not one of the other ones.

I haven't opened my copy for a while. I keep meaning to. I don't want to mess with perfection, but maybe I'll—

Someone's been fucking putting notes in it.

I frown.

Is that... "Oh my fucking god, Princess."

I start reading her notes, the little changes, and at first there's the burn of displeasure. It's searing hot because she's messed with things she knows nothing about. But that fizzles out in a pool of shame as I realize not only are her notes insightful and smart, she's mostly right with her cuts. Her little suggestions for changes make it better.

"Well, fuck." I shake my head. "Looks like I might have mated a goddamned script editor in the making."

I settle back and read.

I'm so engrossed that I almost don't realize we've pulled up, but I'm full of energy, a renewed determination to get this movie done and about how special my mate is. How much I—

I stop. Clea's town car is there, and her driver is reading his phone while he waits. But I don't see her. Normally this wouldn't bug me, but combined with her call and the plethora of missed calls, it does.

Maybe there was a zombie invasion, and I missed it. I can joke, but it doesn't stop the wrongness that's heavy in the air.

That's when I see it.

The helicopter.

It's not booked until the day after tomorrow. So why the fuck is it here?

Pushing the front door open, I'm about to go upstairs when I happen to look across the foyer through to the great room, at Clea charging toward me. But my gaze is caught on what's behind her. A stiff-backed girl sitting, not moving. It crushes a part of me.

"You." Clea's lip curls. "You'd better fucking sort this out. If you don't, if you fuck it up, then you deserve it. And don't ever get me to do your dirty work again."

With that, she storms out.

Silence falls with the slamming of the door. No one, nothing, moves. Not even a breeze through the open glass doors to the right of Violet.

"Princess?" I aim for casual. "Do you know what that's about?"

She doesn't speak.

Beyond her, I hear the helicopter blades start to whir.

"Violet?"

She remains silent.

"C'mon, Princess, talk to me."

I go to her and she flinches when I touch her, so I drop my hand from her shoulder and walk around to her front. She's staring ahead, not at me. She's so pale that I don't know what to do.

She doesn't look like she's been crying.

I swallow.

No. She looks way worse than mere tears.

She looks like someone ripped her heart and soul from her.

"Please?" I whisper. "Please tell—"

"You didn't just lie to me, Stephan." Violet takes a breath, and somehow her words are coming out calm, almost emotionless, which feels worse than anger.

"Lie?"

"*Lie.* You didn't just do that. You betrayed me in the most invasive, horrible way you could." On her lap her hands clench tight around a glint of silver. A small rectangular package.

"I haven't touched anyone but you." I lick my lips, go down in front of her so we're at eye level. "Not one other person. Fuck, I haven't even thought about being with another woman since I met you. You're it."

She looks right through me.

"It's not just about sex," Violet says. "I never asked or expected you to love me. Just *like* me. *Respect* me."

I frown, chest going tight. "What are you talking about?" But as I glance at the package in her fist again, I know. The pills. She's figured it out.

Now she looks at me. Right at me, and it fucking kills me.

"You told me you couldn't have kids."

"Violet—"

She laughs a little, a soft sound that scrapes me down to the bone. "You told me you couldn't. And I...I felt bad for you. I tried to be accepting, change my dreams, all for *you*. All for a lie."

"Princess," I say, aching to touch her, but everything about her stiff demeanor says don't. "You have to let me explain. You matter more to me than anything—"

"But I don't, Stephan. If I did, you would have never done this to me."

I run a hand through my hair, stomach roiling sickeningly. "Let me explain."

"I'm tired of your explanations, Stephan. I'm tired of... well, of all of this."

"I gave us a way to safely have sex—"

"Safely? Safely? For who? You?"

"For us."

"No." One word and it's emphatic. "You didn't care enough about me to let me choose my own future, to entrust my own body to me. That's not a mating, it's not a relationship. It's manipulation, betrayal."

"That's not true. There are reasons I can't have children."

"*Won't have*. There's a difference between can't and won't." She laughs again. "It's why you tried not to knot, isn't it? You probably thought someone as stupid and naïve as me wouldn't even know the difference, but you never counted on others talking. On my own body telling me. You didn't care about anyone except yourself and your wants." She stops.

"She died, Violet." My heart is breaking, and my voice cracks. "Along with the baby. I lost them both during childbirth. I don't want you to die." Tears sting my eyes. "It was the pills or—I can't...I can't lose you, too."

"You manipulated the truth, and you lied to me," she says. "Our relationship has been a ruse since day one. And it seems it never stopped being that. As much as I wished..." She squeezes her eyes shut as if the words pain her.

"You have to understand..." I move closer, spread my hands. The panic in me is beating hard in my throat, ripping shreds from my insides. "I did it for us, to protect you. I want you safe. You need to understand, Violet."

She rises to her feet. "I understand everything now. Goodbye, Stephan."

Then Violet takes her wheeled luggage bag and heads out to the helicopter without looking back.

CHAPTER FORTY-ONE

Violet

It's humiliating. Even through the bone-numbing pain, it's humiliating.

But Penrith greets me when I land, just hugging me tight.

"It's okay, sweet girl. It's okay."

"No," I whisper, "it's not."

But she just takes me into her country estate where the helicopter landed, and in her cozy small drawing room, one designed for intimate conversations, for coddling and calming and comforting, she seats me and pours me a healthy drink.

Mercifully, it's not bourbon. I don't think I ever want to see or taste bourbon again.

"Gin with tonic," she says. "Not very creative, but I

have port which isn't strong enough, and some of Stephan's favorite, which I'm assuming you don't want."

"I shouldn't be here."

She sets her mouth in a thin line. "I'm this close to breaking a five-year silence with my sister to tell her about our nephew. But Sophine is hardline on many things, and I don't want you or your family to get hurt by shrapnel from their beef. If that woman would learn to just soften…"

I take a gulp of the perfumed drink, not sure where to go. If I go home, then everyone will know about it, *everyone*. I know Mom and the family are at the townhouse right now, waiting for our return, to show solidarity or whatever you call it for a sham mating to a coward who drugs you behind your back because…

A sob breaks free. "I'm sorry. I know I shouldn't be here." I finish the drink and stand. "Clea said you'd fly me back, so thank you, Ms….uh—"

"Ashford. Neither my sister nor I mated. Not officially. Which is why seeing her as a draconian head of the Council annoys me so much. It doesn't matter." She smiles. "You were saying?"

"Thank you for helping me. But I need to go. I just…" I look at her helplessly. "I can't go home…not to the family townhouse or Stephan's beach house. And I can't stay here."

"You can. You can do whatever you want."

"It'll bring scandal down. The Season isn't done. I just…I can't bear being at his place. It smells like him. And… and I can't."

"Like here?" she says, gently. "You can still smell him here?"

"Stephan smells like oak, and it's soaked into this place. It was his family home, right?"

She looks at me and shakes her head. "Amazing. And yes, it is the family home. His scent will become part of the background, eventually."

I don't know how true that is. Stephan's scent is powerful to me. I can pick it up here, at his home in Emporia, at the beach house he owns. Part of it is the bond we share from mating. But part of it is just...him. Me and him.

It used to bring me peace, happiness, a special place to be.

But now it's a constant reminder of all my shortcomings, of the wreck of my heart. Of his past. Of his betrayal.

"I don't think it will," I whisper.

"Maybe not," she says. "And the Gardener family townhouse?"

"If I go there then whoever Queen Bee is will find out. She'll bring scandal down on us because...because of me. I will have failed everyone."

She touches my cheek. "Violet, no, you won't. Stephan, now that's a different story. I should have known that boy—" She breathes out. "He told you about Cecilia?"

I nod. I spill the things he told me, and I shrug. "He just doesn't want children with me. I don't even want to start a family immediately, but...there's a difference between a man stating he can't have them and a man not wanting them."

"It's his story, but I can tell you Cecilia wasn't from society. That shouldn't matter, of course, but...well, to certain people it did. And Stephan is so pigheaded, so determined to take care of matters himself that when Sophine and his father refused the mating of him and Cecilia, they took off. She was a Beta, pregnant, and there were...complications."

She keeps her hand on my cheek, and it's comforting. "He told me. But..."

"But he lied, he manipulated. Granted he thinks it justified, coming from what he believes is a good place, but you're right to be upset, to feel betrayed. You're right to do whatever it is you need. You're not at fault. Any scandal is his to bear, not yours."

"I don't..."

There's a knock at the door.

"That'll be your sister and brother. Just know Stephan really does care. And he's absolutely and perhaps irrationally terrified of the same thing happening again. To you."

But it doesn't matter. I can't.

Right now, I can't. I'm in such overload, I'm in danger of shutting down.

"I'll be here if you need me. A call or text away."

There's a commotion, and Heath bursts in, wild-eyed, furious as he takes me in. "What did that fucker do?"

"Language," Penrith says. "And don't upset your sister any more than she already is."

Heath straightens. "Where is he?"

"In Emporia, I assume," Penrith says as Iris rushes to my side and pulls me into a hug. My limbs are heavy, and I slump into her so close to crying it's a wonder I haven't burst like a dam.

"Iris, take her," Heath barks. "I'm going to see if I can get a ride to Emporia—"

"Take care of your sister," Penrith says. "We'll talk tomorrow, Heath."

He sets his jaw, and I know I should calm him, but I don't have it in me. I nod goodbye to Penrith, who must have called them before I arrived, who knew where I'd be happiest. I want to thank her, but I can't find the words.

Everything is numb. Heat crawls up my neck, and my vision darkens.

We get to the car. Heath is driving. I catch sight of him in the rearview mirror, frowning, expression savage. I hear Iris from what seems a vast distance telling him now isn't the time.

Then...everything goes black.

I wake up to my sister's face close to mine, sunlight streaming into our country home. I almost scream.

"What happened?"

"Oh good," Iris says, "you're alive. You passed out in the car. Now don't worry. Only Heath and I know you're back. The socials and Stitch are talking about Felicity and Asher reconciling as friends and how she liked his mate... you, but that's it. Both he and you have disappeared. General rumor online is that you're both having a second honey—"

I bury my head in my hands, and she touches me lightly.

"I'm sorry, Vi. I just thought you'd want to know there isn't any scandal."

"Yet," I say. "Yet." I lift my head. "He told me he couldn't have kids. He can, but he doesn't want them with me. And..." I swallow. "And...oh, Iris. Am I wrong?"

The whole story tumbles out of me, and she listens to the entire thing in silence.

When I'm done, she stalks to my bedroom window and stares out. "I don't think we should tell Heath. He might kill him. I mean, I want to kill Stephan myself, but Heath actually might."

I jump up, my clothes rumpled and I don't care. I don't even care I slept in them. But I need to shower, to change, to burn these things since I can still smell Stephan and I want to be done with him. Entirely. "Where is Heath?"

"He drove back to the townhome to see Mom and the others, to pretend it's all fine. This is a mess."

"I know." My voice is strangled. "And it's my fault."

"How is that, exactly?" She's as savage as Heath. "You are innocent. He took your rights from you. I don't care if that man thinks he's doing the right thing..."

Iris trails off, then she turns and smiles.

"Go shower, and I'll make breakfast."

I do just that, mainly because I need it rather than I trust her motives. Oh, they're not against me, but I think she's up to something. And when I dress and step into the hall, the lack of cooking smells alerts me. As does the absolute silence in here.

I peek out the window and almost collapse.

There, out in the front gardens, in the big patch of

grass, is a sleek black helicopter. And Iris is screaming at someone.

I grip the sill.

At Stephan. She's screaming at Stephan.

For a moment, I think of hiding, but anger overtakes me, and I fly out, taking the stairs two at a time. I burst out the front door.

"Violet," he cries, moving Iris out of the way. He strides toward me. "Please listen."

"Go away!" I say, turning and going back into the house.

But voices follow. Stephan, Iris, and someone else.

Things thump, and I get to the library, ducking inside.

Stephan appears, as does Iris, and he has a huge bunch of wildflowers. Like my bouquet.

The thought makes a sob climb up my throat.

"I told you to get out. You're not welcome here," Iris says. "Don't make me call Heath."

"And he'll do what? Fight me? It's been done," he snarls.

My traitorous heart lurches and leaps, and the scent of him starts trying to seduce me. But I harden my defenses.

"Touch my brother, and I'll kill you," I tell him.

Iris adds, "And I'll help. Give me those."

She snatches the flowers.

"Five minutes," he asks quietly. "Please."

"And then you'll go?" Iris stares at him as he stares at me.

"Yes."

"Vi?" She glances at me for approval.

I think it over. I want to say no. The word forms in my mouth, but when my lips move, "Yes" comes out.

"Five minutes," Iris warns. "Clock running. Door open."

The moment Iris is gone, Stephan closes in on me, and I'm melting, I hate myself for it, but I melt. "Step back."

"You don't want that."

I close my eyes, harden everything I can. Then I open them and look right up at him. "I do."

For a moment I don't think he's going to, but he does, and then he sags against a bookshelf.

"I'm sorry. I'm so fucking sorry. I got you flowers. I've brought gifts. Tell me what you want me to do to make up for this. I'll do it. I'll—"

"I want you to turn the clock back and undo what you did. Can you do that?"

"You know I can't. Look, Princess—"

"Violet."

"Violet." He sucks in a breath. "I don't—*can't* lose you. You want a big family, so yes, I took matters into my own hands so you'd be okay. I should have talked—"

"You should have," I say. "I didn't want kids right away."

"An Omega? Conditioned to be the perfect mate? What else should I think?"

"Nothing. You should have spoken to me, asked." Fury moves like a gale through the shattered landscape of me. "If I wasn't even worth the conversation to you, then I don't want you."

"You don't mean that."

"I do." I say this quietly, but it's the truth.

Gifts? Flowers? That's not him admitting wrongdoing. It's not love and it's not an apology. It's excuses and laziness.

He's not sorry for what he did. He's sorry he got caught, sorry I don't see his reasons for doing it as valid.

Stephan doesn't see me as anything other than a poor substitute for the dead.

And that hurts.

"You don't need the full five minutes. Take your gifts, your flowers, and go. It's over."

And with that, I turn and leave the room. I want him to come after me, I do.

But he doesn't.

This relationship, this mate bond, has been exposed as nothing more than lies. So I just keep walking.

CHAPTER FORTY-TWO

Stephan

Screw her.

For the past week, Violet's returned everything I've sent her. Or at least had them sent to Pen's place.

My so-called aunt's even chastising me. She seems to take great delight in letting me know Violet's been rejecting my apologies.

And me?

I think *bender* is the word. Drinking, gambling...

Shit. Tonight, I'm going to go out, paint the fucking town of Emporia red with a nice little starlet I met and befriended on my last film. She wants the exposure, and I want to show Violet I'm just fine without her.

I'm not, but I'll pretend to be. I just can't think of how to get through to her.

"Can you stop pacing, Stephan," Pen says on the phone screen where I've sent the video call.

I eye her with the dislike I save for the battle-ax. "Why'd you call?"

"Darling, you called me. I just texted about the failure of your latest attempt to win your mate back. Who knew diamonds don't work for some."

"What the fuck does she want, then? I've tried everything."

"Maybe the unfettered truth and a real apology. Maybe for you to do something actually meaningful."

"I'm *trying*."

"You fucked up."

I grab the bottle of bourbon and take a deep swallow. I'm fucking aware. And it hurts like I never imagined.

"She wants this bond gone," I say.

"Do you blame her? Sophine and your father screwed up by not helping you with Cecilia, but things happen. Things out of our control. And Cecilia—"

"That was me. I killed her. I killed the baby."

"Oh, my love, that's bullshit and you know it. You're simply not that powerful. Life happened. And maybe part of that's my fault. I should have stopped you when I saw you with her that first time. It was early enough."

I frown, take another swallow. "You couldn't."

"I knew what she was. If you're that powerful then I should have seen it."

"Don't be stupid."

She offers a sad smile. "Some things are just not meant to be. You know that."

I've had enough. "Violet doesn't want me anymore.

She's rejected me. And I deserve it because I...I never deserved her. Talk to you later."

"Stephan—"

I hang up and slump down on my sofa.

I know what happened, and I know I fucked up, and I know that I should have laid it out, bare bones, to Violet from the start.

But I didn't. And I can't take that back.

My doorbell rings.

I wipe a hand over my face and get up, traipsing through the monster mansion to the front door. I do have staff. I just sent them on vacation because, in the mood I'm in, I'd probably fire them all otherwise.

I jerk open the door and sudden pain explodes in my face. The bottle of bourbon in my hand falls and smashes as I reel back.

Another punch, this one to the stomach.

"Fuck!"

"You fucking cunt." Heath hits me again.

I hit the floor.

"Stop."

This time he kicks, his boot landing in my ribs, and pain blooms in ricocheting waves. He's fucking bruised them, maybe even cracked a few. *Fuck*. I scramble away as he goes to kick me again, and I get up and launch myself at him.

We roll, fists flying wildly, but luckily his anger is making him clumsy, and I manage to pin him. "I said *stop*."

But Heath isn't having that. He flips me and hits me again but I block it from connecting with my face.

I throw him off me. "I mean it. Fuck."

"You're a piece of shit." He wipes his mouth, breathing hard.

"I know."

He just snorts. "My sister has a tender, sweet heart. And you...you fucked it up."

"I know."

He blinks, surprised by my admission. "You know?"

I nod. "I fucked up, and I don't know what to do."

Heath stares at me for a long time. Then all the fury seems to wash away and he shakes his head. "What have you got to drink in this place?"

With a sigh, I lead him upstairs to the bar. I select another bottle of bourbon and crack it open, pouring generous shots for us both.

He takes a glass from me then sits opposite. "A fine fucking mess, asshole," he says.

"I take it you know everything."

"Oh, yes. Your aunt told me what you did, and honestly, I should bury you."

I should just let him. "The contraceptives won't hurt her."

"Contra—" He holds up a hand, eyes narrowing. "What? No one told me that. Oh, let me fucking guess. You either made her take them or gave them to her without her knowing."

"Something like that." I take a long pull from my drink.

"Harm comes in all shapes, Ashford. I get why you'd want to do it, but you know you had nothing at all to do with Cecilia, right? It was a freak thing."

"I got her pregnant."

"You fucking ass. If you were leading her into a life of

crime with high stakes, yeah, your fault. But that?" Heath shakes his head. "It's like me saying if I'd stopped Dad the day of his accident he'd be alive, and therefore it's my fault he's dead."

He looks down.

"It's the hardest part, knowing shit happens we have no control over. It'd be better if we did. But that's false thinking, and you...you fucked up with Violet by trying to control that."

"She'll never forgive me."

"She shouldn't," Heath says bluntly. "As of now, the scandal's been held under wraps, but man...it's not gonna be for long. There's a dinner with the Monarch. You need to be there."

"Fuck that."

We drink, and he keeps checking his phone. It dawns on me he's trying to keep an eye on things at home, and I'm guessing Violet's still at the country estate. Still hiding. Still doing the right thing as much as she can for her family.

"I'll shoulder the scandal."

"Or you could, y'know, fix shit."

"Don't you think I fucking tried? Violet wants nothing from me. All my gifts and apologies are thrown back at me. I'm just..." I take a deep breath. "I'm just lost. For the first time in my life, I don't know what to do." I breathe out. "I did this not to lose her and I ended up losing her anyway."

"You're right."

"I think...I'm in love with her."

Heath doesn't say anything for a while. Then he has a sip and says, "I know. That's the only reason why you're still alive."

"So what do I do? What grand gesture is grand enough to win her back?"

"There isn't one. Time? Or maybe you simply missed out."

"Fuck."

He stands and sets the glass down. "Did you tell her, Stephan?"

"Tell her what?"

"That you love her."

"No."

Because I didn't believe in it anymore until the princess upended my life.

"Then," he says, "you're a fucking fool."

"Why are you standing?"

"Because, asshole, I didn't come here to drink with you all evening. I came to bring you back—by the Monarch's decree."

"Oh, fuck that."

Heath grabs me and hauls me up. "This isn't about you and your beef with the Monarch. It's about Violet and her reputation. So get ready. We're leaving in ten."

The Queen fucking Bee has been busy, buzzing about the lack of me or Violet being seen either on Sabine or in Emporia. But as I read all the Stitches from the Bee and others, it seems my aunt has put out a public announcement about a dinner.

As we land at Pen's, I'm aware that it's not just about me. It's Violet who's meant to turn up.

"This is as far as I go," Heath says. "This is supposedly a private dinner with you and Vi and the Monarch."

"That all of Sabine knows about."

He sighs and gives me a shove. "Move. I don't know if my sister will show. The rest is up to you. And if she does, tell her. You at least owe her that."

The moment I exit, the helicopter takes off, presumably to drop Heath at home.

I make my way in.

Pen is there, not looking happy. "Tried to tell you, but you hung up."

"You're working with her?"

"I'm not doing anything. The Monarch insisted. *Decreed.* She's in the dining room."

My princess? I can smell her faintly, but I don't know if it's in my head or from the last time she was here or if...

I don't think. I run into the dining room, only to have hope crash down.

Sophine stands, drink in hand. "You're late."

"Where's Violet?"

"Not here. Just know that if she doesn't show, I'll be forced to make an announcement by the end of the week than your mate bond is null and void. You foolish, stupid boy."

"Man."

"*Boy.*" She flicks a hand at me. "First you run off with someone beneath you, someone who isn't even an Omega. At all. If you'd waited, held off, I'd have told you."

"You shouldn't have the right to play with people's lives."

"That's interesting coming from you, isn't it?" The

battle-ax looks at me. "You then get yourself a reputation even some alley cats would be shamed by."

"Like you even care."

"And then you sink so low with your mate. Drugging her?"

"Contraceptives."

"Even worse. I don't allow them unless applied for and with specific reasons."

"Because you like being draconian?"

"I need to keep track of lines, of people, of pregnancies and lack thereof. You don't understand."

"Stop being such a—"

"*Shut your mouth.*" The Alpha voice washes over me, making me want to do just that, but at the same time I fight it. I'm as strong as she is. But...I let her think she wins. I don't finish the insult.

Because it'll only make things worse.

Finally, Pen joins us and it's just horrible. A clock that isn't there ticks and no one speaks. Food is brought and taken away untouched until it's blindingly obvious that Violet isn't turning up.

The humiliation is crushing.

I fix the battle-ax with a glare. I'm sure she's loving this.

She stands. "Thank you, Pen," she says.

Pen just mutters something and raises a glass mockingly.

"One week, Stephan. Or it's null and void, and you'll have to face the consequences, as will Violet."

With that, she sweeps out.

"Fuck this." I pull out my phone and go into my

banking app. I make a huge transfer to Heath, sending him a note.

> Half's for your family, the rest is for Violet. I'll make monthly payments.

He texts back.

> Idiot

Five minutes later, I get one more text. My heart skips a beat then stutters and turns to stone.

> I don't want your money. Heath will return it.

"Fuck me."

Pen sighs, pushes a drink across the table. "Not going well?"

"She won't accept a thing from me. Not one fucking thing."

"Have you thought," Pen says, "that you're doing it wrong?"

I pick up the drink and frown. "How am I doing it wrong?"

"Grand gestures are nice, but the small ones, those matter." She shrugs.

"Like what?"

Pen only smiles. "That's the thing about the small ones. They come from the heart or not at all."

Hivemind.

Remember when our Luxe and her movie star took off and made an Emporian splash?

Yes, me too.

WHERE ARE THEY?

Or

Where is our LUXE?

We all know trouble in Emporia is broadcast in dark, black, blank silence.

Troubling, I know.

Mrs. St. James isn't a boat-rocker. She isn't even a boat-roller. So there's no tea to spill. No hot topic gossip about her.

So, it must be

HIM.

Asher.

But what? They were the darlings there same as here without any effort and her real Luxe quality shone.

(Seriously, that dress! Anyone? The short sequined number? Who knew she hid such fantastic billion-dollar legs?)

The Monarch has decreed a penultimate ball of the Season and they're meant to star. At least that's the rumor I hear from those in the know. He's back on the island, so we must assume she is too.

Together or apart, we won't know, and until there's an official announcement about whether the Luxe and her mate are attending, we won't get closer to the truth.

Scandal? Or just mated life?

I don't know...

BUT

A birdie whispered there might be the scandal of not just the Season but the decade coming!

Stick around and be sure to return tomorrow for the scandal tally, the marked, the singles, and who's tipped to end the Season with a mate...

Don't know about you, brood, but I can't wait until this new ball.

Let's see if it's a curve.

- Queen Bee

CHAPTER FORTY-THREE

Violet

My mother actually squeals when the doorbell rings the Sunday after the ball. We didn't go.

I didn't go.

It was hinted at that as Luxe I needed to be there, but I'm not going to be seen with Stephan. My heart's too wrecked. And he...

He's stopped trying to win me with meaningless gifts and guilty pay-offs.

He's stopped completely.

Iris looks at me as we stand at the top of the stairs. My heart's going a mile a minute, only because the Monarch's here.

"Monarch," Mom says, dangerously close to borderline simpering. "Come in, please."

Shit. Why is she here? Did Mom...?

I told Mom and the others when they arrived yesterday at the countryside estate that Stephan was busy. When I lied and said I wasn't going to the ball because I didn't feel well, she just stared.

And hadn't said a word.

"Why is she here?" I whisper as Iris comes up to my side.

"You know Mom doesn't believe you," Iris hisses. "She's worried about you and Stephan."

Me and Stephan, like that's all I am now, part of a unit, a mate to an Alpha.

"You don't think...?" I stop and swallow.

"That Mom contacted the Monarch? God, no. She wouldn't. Even if she wanted to, she wouldn't. It's our Mom, not one of the other ones. Like Quinn's." And Iris takes my hand, linking our fingers.

"O.M.G., it's the Monarch," Rue says, and Dahlia starts to play something regal on the piano.

"Rue. Go to your room."

"Maybe you're right," I say. "She has all of you to mate off."

"Not me," Iris says. "We need to hear what's happening. She might be here to announce the dissolving of your mate bond."

That sends a knell of pain through me, even though I want it.

No, *want* is the wrong word.

"Where's Heath? Iris, you and Rue make sure everyone's on their best behavior."

"What are you going to do?"

"I don't know..."

"Phone." Iris holds hers up, nabs Rue as she barges up the stairs. "I'll text."

I nod.

When Iris has dragged Rue down the stairs, I put on a dress, then change and change again. Then I stop.

It's the Monarch, so simple and classy.

So I pull out one of the outfits Iris made and put it on, a simple silk dress in the palest of lavender, and I find a pair of low heels and slide them on. I leave my hair down.

I'll go down, pretend, say I made a mistake. Beg for my family to be left out of any scandal. As I rise, my phone buzzes.

> IRIS
>
> No idea where Heath went. Monarch is being waited on. Mom's about to birth litters of kittens. I think she wants blood.

Then:

> IRIS
>
> Monarch bloodthirsty, not Mom.

It buzzes once more.

> IRIS
>
> She hinted that Mom isn't a good Mom.

I can fix this.

Inside, my anxiety is rising, the panic growing, but I raise my chin, fix a smile, and head down.

Every eye turns to me when I enter the living room.

"There you are at last," says the Monarch in a chiding tone.

"Oh, Violet," Mom says, "I knew something happened. Are you okay?"

"Is *she* okay?" The Monarch shoots up from her seat. "I'm being ridiculed. All because you can't contain your children."

Something in me snaps.

"My mother has done a magnificent job," I say. "With all of us. And I know that because you chose me as your Luxe."

"Maybe," she says to me after a long moment, "I was bored."

"Violet..."

I ignore Mom.

"Maybe. But Stephan did choose me."

"And yet you can't seem to make it work. He might have screwed up, but as his Omega, you're meant to endure. To overcome and forgive. No matter what it is."

I narrow my eyes. I'm sick of being as perfect as I can be. I'm sick of bending over to please everyone, while ignoring myself and my needs. I'm tired of being taken advantage of, used as a pawn. I'm not the same naïve Omega I was at the start of the Season.

"Omega or not, I'm a human being, and I'll not let anyone hurt me the way your nephew did," I say. "My mate bond, my *life*, has nothing to do with you. I stand by that."

Sophine comes right up to me. "Be very careful."

She uses her Alpha voice, but I fight it. That command that's hidden in her words. She isn't telling me to be careful, she's ordering me to shut up.

Silence rules in the house and even Dahlia's stopped

playing the piano. On my periphery are all my sisters and Mom, all not moving. Even Rue.

Meeting her glare, I take a step forward, so I'm in her space. "That's all I ever am. Careful. Everyone else comes first. You, Stephan, my family. And only my family gives back. But I think I understand why Stephan did what he did."

Mom moves then, her hands on me. "Sweet Violet, what did he do?"

I shoot her a look of misery, but I can't focus on anyone but the Monarch. Her command still stings. But my ire, my love for Stephan and my family is stronger.

I refocus on Sophine. "What he did is also your fault. He was young. Younger than me, only around Iris or Mari's age, when you just...turned your back on him. Abandoned him. Maybe if you'd supported him—"

"Then he would've sullied our family's name and reputation."

"Fuck your reputation," I snap, and there's an audible gasp around the room. Letting the curse go makes me feel more powerful. "If you'd taken an interest, been there, maybe he wouldn't be as scarred and she'd be alive."

Sophine stares down at me "But then there would be no movie star Alpha for you, and you and your family would sink under your father's debts."

My fury whips into an inferno. "Stephan is more than a star. He's real. He screwed up, yes, and I'm so furious at him I can't see straight. He's an idiot, a moron, but I know in my heart of hearts he crossed those lines because his family failed him. *You* failed him. You're his aunt, one of his only family members left. He did what he did because he didn't want to lose me like he did Cecilia."

"The girl," the Monarch sneers, "was a Beta."

"So? How could you let your social standing come before your family? That is weakness."

Her eyes widen. "How *dare* you. There are risks with Beta/Alpha pairings. Risks Stephan didn't want to listen to. That's why—"

My hands ball into fists. "If they loved each other, you could have...you could have done so much more. Most importantly, you could have been there to help pick up the pieces."

The silence is almost oppressive. And I can feel my family gawp at me. I don't even have to look to know.

"Are you done?" the Monarch asks suddenly.

"Yes."

To my surprise, she pulls back, the hard lines of her face softening some. "I like you, Violet. I always have. It's why I chose you to be my Luxe. So much potential. You just needed a little *push*."

I stare, a bit dumbfounded by her words.

"You're perfect for him. I know you'll sort it out." She starts to sweep out then stops. "Stephan is in Sabine. He's at my sister's. So if you decide to see him..."

"Be kind?" I shake my head. "I won't—"

"Hell no. Show no mercy. I own my part in this. I failed him back then. But Stephan crossed lines with you. Even I know that. So do make him prove himself worthy. He is, by the way, worthy. He just needs..."

"A little push?"

"Exactly." Smiling, she leaves.

When the door shuts, I almost collapse.

"I think..." I raise my head, trying to finish the sentence, but apart from Mom's worry and confusion, my sisters all smile.

Heath strolls into the house. "Was that the Monarch? What did I miss?"

"It was wild," Mari says. "Totally wild. Vi was magnificent."

"Heath, what is going on?" Mom demands.

"Go, Vi!" Rue shouts. "You rule!" Then she pauses. "No, I mean *go*. Find Stephan. I want a movie ending."

I look at my brother. "I need to get to Penrith's. Can you call a car?"

He nods, and I head to the door.

I guess I should end this once and for all.

Chapter Forty-Four

Stephan

"You look horrible."

I'm in the ivy-covered gazebo in the back garden. The only fucking place that doesn't smell like her, and now she's spreading her scent out here.

"I'm surprised you're here." I don't turn and look at her.

"This has to end, Stephan. It's..." She pauses. Because it's Violet, the girl who hates to disappoint, to hurt. "I think—"

"I did something to hurt you," I say, cutting her off because I'm not yet ready for goodbye, not until we have to. "I lied and justified and twisted it so it made sense. But the core was real and honest, Princess. The core of it."

"I know. You didn't want history repeating."

This time I turn and look at her. Fuck, she's beautiful.

My heart, that shouldn't be able to break any more than it has, breaks some more.

"Princess—Violet, I was so fucking terrified of losing you. I didn't even realize why at the time, but I was terrified of losing the girl I'd fallen head over heels in love with. I couldn't risk it. If the same thing happened, then..." I suck in a breath and scratch my bearded cheek, trying to find the right words I need to say.

The truth.

The lame, bare, makes-no-sense truth. I drop my hand. "I fucking fell so hard in love, and I was just so hell-bent on making sure you were safe, packed up in cotton wool, that I took matters into my own hands. It wasn't that I didn't trust you. Never that. I didn't trust myself. I wanted you so desperately, loved you so much that I couldn't admit it, and I..."

Shit.

"You break down every fucking barrier there is. I can smell you through blockers, you invade my dreams. I crave your touch, your scent. You make me want to see you smile, live your dreams as a dancer. I want to give you every happiness you've denied yourself for the sake of others."

I stand.

"And... And I want you to carry my child. I want to try again, even if it terrifies me."

"Stephan..."

"But not as much as never having you, never knowing you, never growing old with you. Losing time with you is a nightmare. I can't function without you. The thought of any other Alpha even thinking of touching you, Princess..."

I take a step toward her and make myself stop. "I can't handle it."

"Stephan, I'm an Omega. I'm made for an Alpha. And yes, things could go wrong, but we can't predict tomorrow. I could have an accident. Or—"

"Stop."

She just looks at me.

"I fucking love you, and I should have told you. I'm *in love* with you. If I could take it back, just talk to you honestly, I would. But Violet, being with you for a minute, an hour...I'll take that over a lifetime with anyone else."

I start to shake. Violet...she's my chance to leave the pain in the past and start anew. She isn't Cecilia, and I'm not the Alpha I was back then.

I love her as a man, not as a boy.

She humbles me.

I go down on one knee in front of her and take her hand gently in mine. "I love you, Violet, with everything I am. For always. Can you find it in yourself to forgive me, to give me a chance?"

She's crying. A tear hits my hand.

"You, Violet, are the love of my life. You saw the real me when everyone else saw Asher St. James."

Violet looks at me for a long moment. I start to get up, but she puts her hand over mine and comes down to her knees too. Then she takes my face in her hands.

She sighs and rests her forehead against mine. "You hurt me. Betrayed me."

"I know. And I have nothing to say but I'm sorry and I promise to never do that again. Never lie, never hurt you, and never ever betray you."

"As wrong as it was, I think I understand. You did it out of fear and love. I do forgive you because I love you. But...I want that new start, Stephan. You and me. And I want to have children with you. One day."

Everything feels different now, like we've crossed some invisible line from broken to whole. I'd come too close to losing her because of old fears and my own stupidity, and that's something I'll never risk again.

My princess...

This time I don't need to think. I kiss her then, slowly, softly. It's a promise, a new start, and full of love. When I come up for air, hope beats inside my chest.

"Me too."

Oh, my brood, it's time to say goodbye to the Season.

We just had our last ball. Summer is done and the scandals, too.

Our Luxe and her star announced they'd be splitting time between Emporia and Sabine, so buckle up in case any other movie stars come here.

As for our marked Omegas?

NINE!

Is that a record?

But who's on deck for next Season? Can't wait to find out! But the most scandalous of all is that our newest blonde bombshell is on the shelf until next Season. Maybe she'll be Luxe material?

I can't wait!

*Hope you've got some honey in reserve. I think next Season will
be even sweeter than this one!*

- Queen Bee

EPILOGUE

Violet

A Few Months Later

"I was fixing all your errors, Stephan," I say, squealing as he rips the script out of my hands and starts to tickle me.

I wiggle away in our beach house's master bed, but he catches me, kissing me. I sigh into him, and slide my tongue against his, deepening the kiss. He pulls me in closer.

"Thank you," he whispers. "For this."

I know exactly what he means. For forgiving him, for giving him another chance. But the thing is, he's done everything to keep proving himself, winning my trust over and over, and I'm... I love him. So much.

Tugging at his scruff, I grin. "You mean picking apart

your plot holes and the long speeches you give the character that's clearly you?"

"Please, Princess. If I gave this script to Rue, she'd love it."

"Rue's fourteen and addicted to terrible movies. There's this Alpha starring in them. Asher St. James? He's awful."

"And yet you have posters of him in your bedroom." He bites my neck, nipping hard at the skin.

My gaze goes to the mating ceremony photo of us, our second one where it was just us and family. No fuss, no Queen Bee.

It was just perfect.

"But I'm already taken. I have this guy. A little scruffy and arrogant. I feel bad for him because he worships me."

"The ground you walk on, Princess. Every fucking spot. And he's a jealous fucker, too."

"I love him, though. He grows on me."

"Does he?"

I laugh and burrow into his neck, breathing in that oak scent that riles excitement and calms nerves. That scent is also one of coming home, always and forever.

Stephan gets to see the side of me that only my family's seen, the one who existed before the responsibilities of the Season. Before Dad's death.

Stephan takes my hand, kissing my palm. "Tell me again how you put the battle-ax in her place. It really gets me going."

I laugh. "I've already told you a hundred times."

"Yeah, but Rue tells me you were like 'O.M.G.,

Monarch. You need to leave me and my mate alone and mind your own business'."

"That is scarily good."

"I know."

I lean up on him, half across his chest. "I blame you if the script isn't ready for the meeting next month. I really don't know what I'm doing."

"I know," Stephan says. "You're harsh about it. But a natural. Do you know how pleased people are with that trash one you fixed in days?" He shakes his head. "I think we'll be fine. Besides, I've got some things on my mind right now."

"Like?"

"This," he says. And then he begins to kiss his way along my body. Stephan pushes up my T-shirt—well, his T-shirt really—and starts to suck and lick at my nipples. I moan. "My princess..."

Another moan breaks free as he doesn't stop, as the pull of his mouth on my flesh sends darts of desire south, and I start getting wet, real fast.

Deep between my thighs I'm beginning to throb with need.

My heart squeezes as he kisses lower, one hand stroking over my pussy. He slides his hand in, fingers brushing down over my clit and then through the wetness, along my slit, working me, parting me. I lift my hips to him, happy to have my blow job that morning returned in such enthusiastic and measured ways.

He does that, balances the two, and it makes it all the more thrilling when he loses his control and knots in me. That pleasure...that's something else yet again. But when his mouth comes down on my clit and pussy, I lose my mind.

He kisses down lower then pulls my panties off and starts to lick and suck me. "So fucking hot, Princess. So good of you to keep your pussy wet just for me. Wet and delicious."

He laps at me and then slides his fingers in, stretching me.

I know his game. He likes to start out gentle, and then tease me to the ends of sanity with slow, soft, meandering thrusts, until he bites down on my clit and makes me come, screaming.

Or he builds it up too hard and fast and pushes me into orgasm after orgasm, making me squirt.

Sometimes he just plain stops—sometimes in the middle of me coming—and fucks me. Ass, pussy, mouth, the flavor of choice I mostly leave up to him.

But I know his game.

The end of which is almost insanity followed by mind-blowing pleasure.

Tonight, he fucks me slowly with his fingers, this time building me up, my heart pounding, body tense, only to lead me off that cliff. Then he takes me back just before I can come.

Time after time, he does this until I'm sobbing, begging, pleading for sweet release.

And then when I can't take any more, he comes up and slams into me, taking me hard and fast, his cock stretching me, going so deep I start to come in violent, pleasure-gouging spasms.

It doesn't seem to end. And I'm lost, gone, mind wild.

And when he knots, I scream. I can't help it. He's bigger, deeper, hitting all the special pleasure spots in me, like he's made for that, made to fit. And together we fly over another edge and the waves pound us over and over again.

When we come back, I can't move. I can barely get enough oxygen. His scent permeates me, and I just moan.

"Good, Princess. Such a good, sweet girl. For me. Just. The. Way. I. Like. It."

Another spasm hits me at his words, and as he pulls out, I try to roll over. But he stops me, holding me there in place, those brown eyes warm, full of love. His dark, dirty-blond hair is a mess. "You're a beast."

He grins. "One who loves you."

"Let me up so I can get to that script. I know you'll punish me later." But I'm smiling, too.

"Once. I threatened to spank you with a ruler once."

A thrill ripples through me. "So you did…"

"Princess, you naughty girl. Fantasize about it all you want, but you wouldn't like it. I wouldn't like it. No welts for your perfect ass. If you want, I'll spank you."

"No!" Then I eye him with suspicion. "Are you distracting me because we both know your script needs work and you don't like criticism?"

"Take that back. We both know it's perfect."

"It's not perfect," I say. "But it's good."

He laughs. "I know. But not as good as you. I do love you. So fucking much, Violet."

"I love you, too." But there's more. Something I've been holding onto. A truth I've carried with me for days.

Even after all we've been through, after everything we've fought to hold onto, a part of me is terrified. Terrified that this will bring back memories of what he lost. That the pain and fear of it will swallow him whole.

But I can't keep it from him. I don't want to.

"I have... something to show you."

He shifts slightly, propping himself on one elbow to look at me. The concern in his eyes is immediate and his brows draw together. "What is it?"

I reach for the nightstand and open the small drawer. The test is right where I left it, the little white stick that had brought me both excitement and anxiety when those two pink lines appeared.

Now, I hold it between us.

His gaze drops to the test, and for a heartbeat, he doesn't move. Doesn't breathe.

"I'm pregnant," I whisper, the words trembling as they leave me. "Stephan... We're going to have a baby."

Stephan blinks. His face is an unreadable mask, and for a moment, I wonder if he's really moved on from his past after all. I brace myself, waiting for whatever comes next.

But then something breaks through.

"Violet..." His voice cracks and his eyes shine.

But it isn't fear I see. It isn't sorrow. It's joy. Pure, unrestrained joy.

He cups my face, his lips crashing against mine. Laughter spills between the kisses. His hands are trembling as they cradle me, and when he pulls back, there's no mistaking the happiness etched across his face.

"We're having a baby," he repeats, like he needs to hear it again just to believe it.

I nod, a tear slipping down my cheek. My insides are buzzing with nerves. "We are. Is-Is that okay?"

"Fuck, Princess. It's more than okay. It's..." He smiles. "It's everything I have ever wanted. Am I scared? Hell yeah. But—"

"You're not going to lose me," I whisper, my fingers brushing through his hair. "You're not going to lose *us*. I promise."

That's all it takes. His arms tighten around me, holding me like he never intends to let go. And in that moment, I know we'll be okay.

We're going to have our own pack. Our own family.

Our own movie-worthy happy ending.

THE END

Thank You

for reading *Violet: Omegas in Bloom*

Start reading the next book in the series

FALLEN OMEGA

All my life, my dad and I lived as outcasts in Starlight City. We dodged the council's oppressive laws. But when a sudden accident takes his life, I'm left alone, undocumented, and ultimately screwed.

With my heat coming and no drugs to help me through it, desperation drives me into the hands of the Unholy Trinity. Dante, Knight, and Reaper are three deadly Alphas ruling the city's criminal underworld, and they offer me temporary protection—but only *if* I follow their rules:

1. Sing in their club

2. Obey them without question

And, most importantly…

3. Don't sleep with any of them, no matter what our primal urges say.

Easier said than done.

They might call me Angel, but these dark gods are determined to corrupt me.

And now, with an old enemy and the council after me, I don't have much of a choice.

To save myself, I'm going to have to let myself fall.

Fallen Omega is a contemporary Omegaverse standalone with dark themes and multiple love interests.

More Books by Brooke Harper

Mafia Rose

Wilt

Thorn

Bloom

Wild: A Mafia Rose Novella

Root: A Mafia Rose Novel

Thieves' Honor

Pretty Little Things

Wicked Little Lies

Cruel Empire

All That Glitters

Fool's Gold

Omegas in Bloom

Violet

Iris

Marigold

Dahlia

Rue

Heath

STANDALONES

A Mafia Mistress for Christmas

Fallen Omega: A Dark Omegaverse

All Eyes on Me: A Short Story

About the Author

Brooke Harper creates dark and sexy worlds for her characters to play. A lover of strong coffee and old tombstones, she spins dark tales of sex and sin, pain and passion, and misery and madness that'll have you flipping the pages and begging for more.
AuthorBrookeHarper.com

Join Brooke's Reader Group